MURDERER OF THE YEAR

A True Story

by Bill Bowman

PJB Creatives, Inc.

www.pjbcreatives.com

Bowman, Bill
Murderer of the Year, A True Story/Bill Bowman
ISBN 978-0-615-34117-0

www.pjbcreatives.com
Printed in the United States of America

To PJ, with whom all things begin and end.

*In memory of Carmella Estelle Caliendo Bowman,
whose spirit will never end.*

Acknowledgments

This being my first reportorial-based book, I feel obliged to thank not only those who have helped me in my research for this volume, but also those who have served as guides and inspirations in my journey to this point. It seems the most logical way to go about it is chronologically.

My thanks, then, to my parents, William Sr. and Carmella Bowman, for having the good sense to add to the family and for pushing me in the right direction educationally; to reporter extraodinaire Jack Germain, whose "war stories" inspired me to pursue a career in journalism; to Emily Van Ness and Warren Sloate, who gave me the tools I needed to pursue that dream; to Jean L. Whiston, for teaching me the rest, and for giving a green reporter the opportunity to cover the story of his young career; to Wesley Brown, who reacquainted me with the art of creative writing, to Roger Cohen, for keeping me out of P.R.; to Sensei Gary Alexander, for showing me that a person, while he may be strong of body, is truly weak if he is not also strong of character, and, most of all, to my wife, PJ Parker, without whose love, understanding and support this book would probably not have been written.

Regarding this book, I would like to thank all those friends of the victim and defendant — named and unnamed within these pages — who opened their homes and their sometimes painful recollections to me. A special thanks must be extended to former Middlesex County Second Assistant Prosecutor Thomas Kapsak and former Middlesex County Deputy Public Defender (and now Superior Court Judge) Bradley Ferencz for their immeasurable help in laying the groundwork of my research. My thanks also goes to Joseph Zimmerman, Dennis Watson and John Haley of the Middlesex County Prosecutor's Office for their assistance in my research.

Methodology

The information used to write this book was gathered through a variety of sources, including voluminous reports filed by municipal police, county investigators and defense investigators, witnesses' statements and testimony, the author's interviews with the story's principals and the author's own notes and recollections from the trial.

Although many of the original witnesses were interviewed by the author, the heaviest reliance was placed on information supplied to county and defense detectives at the time of the original 1983 investigation and on testimony from the 1984 trial. In most cases where someone's recollection had been altered by time, I have used their statements as originally made in 1983. I have also omitted the names of some individuals, changed the names of others, at their request, and substituted initials for others.

Conversations are either presented verbatim (as in the case of witness statements and trial testimony), inspired or enhanced by individuals' recollections, or extrapolated from the summary form in which they appeared in police and defense investigators' reports. In all cases, however, the original subject matter remains intact.

Also included in this narrative are a series of oral histories, labelled

"Voices", provided by friends of Cathy Warner and Gene Berta. These selections, intended to illuminate the chapters after which they appear, were culled from hours of tape recorded interviews conducted with the subjects by the author.

Bill Bowman
Somerset, New Jersey
November, 2009

Catherine Neal Warner

In 1983, she was only 29 years old and already a divorcée and a widow, her second husband having died in 1980 of Hodgkin's Disease. At 5'6" and 125 pounds, with curly nut-brown hair framing an angular face and soft brown eyes sometimes magnified by large glasses, Cathy's wasn't a classic beauty, but she had a gentle, innocent look that men found appealing.

Saturday, July 16, 1983

THE CALL came to the South Plainfield, New Jersey home of Richard and Gloria Neal early that afternoon.

Richard Neal answered the call; a female voice asked for his wife.

"Hello, Mrs. Neal?" the voice said to Gloria Neal. "I'm calling from Middlesex General Hospital in New Brunswick. I don't want to alarm you, but we can't reach your daughter Cathy."

The nurse's intentions notwithstanding, Gloria Neal felt the first traces of worry setting in.

"Why are you trying to get her? Is something wrong?" she asked, hoping her voice would not convey the panic she was beginning to feel.

"Well, we think something might be wrong. She was supposed to be at work yesterday and she didn't show up, and that's just not like Cathy. And we just thought that since she was supposed to be on holiday, that she might have been delayed in getting back, or forgotten when she was supposed to return to work, or something like that. We didn't call yesterday, but when she didn't show up again this morning, we thought we'd better; some of the girls on the floor are getting upset, they think something might be wrong. I'm calling you because you're listed as the person to call in an emergency."

"Well, we haven't heard from Cathy for a couple of weeks, but we'll run over to her house and see if she's all right."

As she shakily replaced the phone in its cradle, Mrs. Neal instinctively knew she had reason to be frightened. She knew her very responsible daughter, and it was very unlike Cathy to not call in if she was due to be at work and for some reason wouldn't be. Cathy, 29, had been a registered nurse at Middlesex General since February and at John F. Kennedy Medical Center in nearby Edison Township for eight years before that; she loved being a nurse and she had made some close friends at the hospital. As far as "forgetting" was concerned, her daughter just didn't do that.

Gloria Neal quickly picked up the phone and dialed Cathy's number. She impatiently listened as the phone rang on and on, but there was no answer. Unable to conceal her worry, Gloria called out for her husband, Richard.

"That was the hospital where Cathy works," she told him, pointing to the phone. "They said she was on vacation for a week, and that she was supposed to be at work yesterday, but she wasn't, and now they can't get a hold of her. I just called her house, but she didn't answer. I think something terrible has happened."

"Now just calm down," Richard Neal told his wife. "You stay here and try to call her again, I'll drive over to her house. I'm sure she's fine."

But Gloria Neal did not want her husband to go alone, so she awakened their son, Gary, who worked nights and was asleep at the time, and told him to get ready to accompany his father to his sister's house. As soon as her husband and son left, Gloria dialed Cathy's number several more times. She never got an answer.

The Central New Jersey boroughs of Metuchen and South Plainfield are near one another; Richard and Gary Neal did not have to travel long before reaching Cathy's Durham Avenue, Metuchen home.

When they first arrived, the Neal's thought Cathy simply wasn't in because they didn't see her car. But they soon dismissed that notion when they pulled into the driveway and saw the car parked near the back of her home, on the grass. Thinking this odd since Cathy was a creature of habit and always parked in the front part of the driveway, Richard and Gary Neal got out of their car and walked over to Cathy's black Ford Mustang. Odder still was what they saw on the ground: strewn about the driveway and in the bushes near the car they found unopened packages of hamburger and frankfurter rolls, as well as loose hot dogs and some packages wrapped in what looked like butcher's paper. Richard Neal picked up one of the wrapped packages and opened it; inside was about a pound of ground beef, looking like it had recently come out of the grinder.

After repeated knocks on all the doors and the calling out of Cathy's name elicited no response, father and son decided they would just enter the house. Richard Neal tried to open the front, side and back doors but all three were double locked with dead bolts (Cathy had never furnished her parents with a spare set of her house keys). At the same time, while walking around his sister's home looking for another way in, Gary Neal was struck by something else that wasn't quite right: every one of the shades on the first floor windows was, untypically for his sister, drawn, blocking any view into the house, heightening his mounting sense of panic. But, as he drew closer, he noticed the shades could not obstruct a sight that could make one's skin crawl. At first he thought the screens of his sister's house had come alive, writhing and waving, taunting him from behind the security of the locked windows. He realized in one horrible instant that the screens were caked with hundreds and hundreds of buzzing flies, swarming in layer upon frenetic, coal-black layer.

Gary rushed to the front of the house and told his father what he had seen. Richard Neal was now convinced that his wife's suspicions had been accurate. "Something's not right, Gary," he told his son, "call the police." Wordlessly, Gary ran across the street to the Durham Cafe, a small neighborhood bar and restaurant, to carry out his father's instruction.

Metuchen Police Officer Pasquale Sardone arrived about ten minutes later.

The elder Neal led Officer Sardone to his daughter's car, showed him the sealed packages of meat and rolls and told him of the phone call from the hospital. Sardone rechecked all the doors and windows — noting to himself the implications of the flies' presence — and, after he had satisfied himself that entry to the house could not be gained in a conventional manner, the men decided to break in through a window. Richard Neal was about to walk over to a neighbor's house and borrow a ladder to help them do the job when Edward Jones, an elderly, bearded man who rented a bungalow at the rear of Cathy Warner's property, ambled toward them. Jones had just returned home from visiting a friend and was attracted by all the commotion he saw on the side of the house.

"She's not home; she went on vacation, I was talking to her Thursday," Jones volunteered to the policeman and now very worried father.

Despite Jones' assertion, the Neals and Sardone were convinced that they had better investigate. It appeared as though the most convenient way in the house was through a basement window under the back porch; Gary, being the most nimble, was elected to break into his sister's house. Richard Neal heard Jones say, "He's going to need a sledgehammer", but ignored the remark. After smashing the glass with his foot, the younger Neal crawled through the window into the house's dark, clammy basement, then crept up the wooden and cement steps into the kitchen, unlocked the back door and let the others in.

Edward Jones was the last one in; Richard Neal was about to tell the old man to leave the house, but changed his mind when he saw Jones was determined to remain and find out what was happening. Jones, looking up into a window, noticed that it was caked with flies. "She must have left some meat out," he thought.

Upon entering Cathy's small kitchen, the men were immediately enveloped by a blanket of hot, stale air. Contributing to the oven-like condition were the facts that Metuchen, like the rest of Central New Jersey, had been suffering under a record-setting heat wave for more than a week and that the house was locked up tight, as if its occupant hadn't planned on being home for awhile. A cursory inspection of the kitchen and living room, which, with a hallway leading to the front door, comprised the first floor, revealed nothing irregular; both appeared to be in order. There were dishes in the sink, assorted papers on the kitchen table and the room looked as though it could use a coat of paint, but nothing seemed extraordinary. Officer Sardone did notice a closed door off the kitchen, but for some reason at that moment decided to not open it.

"Mr. Neal, I'd like you and Mr. Jones to stay down here," Sardone said, as he and Gary Neal climbed the stairs to investigate the second floor.

Ignoring Sardone's instruction to stay in the kitchen, Richard Neal was about to begin his ascent to the house's top floor when Edward Jones yanked open the door that Sardone had bypassed, that of the first-floor bathroom. The two were blasted by a nauseating stench, an odor unlike anything either man had ever before encountered, nor would ever be able to forget.

"Got to get the flies off the meat," Jones mumbled as Richard Neal, his heartbeat thundering in his ears, stepped into the bathroom, over to the tub and, with a trembling hand, pushed aside the semi-closed shower curtain. What assaulted his senses was a parent's most gruesome nightmare: the discovery of the nude, rotting body of his first-born child, Catherine Neal Warner.

Cathy Warner was lying on her back in several inches of water, a legion of maggots infesting her face and upper torso, nearly obliterating her facial features; indeed, the body looked as though a sculptor, suffering a spell of creative frustration, might have pushed in the side of his clay figure's head. Her knees were bent so that the body would fit in its porcelain coffin; her arms, crossed at the wrists and loosely bound with what looked like several plastic strips, dangled over the edge of the tub. Her watch and a gold ring still decorated her left hand.

Richard Neal found it difficult to speak under normal circumstances; his larynx had been surgically removed, and so was only able to talk in a hoarse, raspy tone. On that hot July day, gazing down at what remained of his daughter's dead body, all Neal could do to summon Officer Sardone was pound on the wall.

Sardone raced down the stairs when he heard the banging and met Richard Neal, sobbing and stumbling into the kitchen. Neal's face was ghostly pale as he pointed with great effort to the half open door. Sardone could immediately smell an odor he had thankfully experienced only a few times before. For all his years on the force, Sardone still wasn't prepared for what he saw in that tub. Opening the shower curtain fully, Sardone jumped back as the curtain rod fell, clanging against the top of the tub. His stomach roiling, the policeman quickly left to call his findings in to headquarters.

Gary Neal, meanwhile, had raced down the stairs after the officer.

"Dad, what is it? What happened to Cathy?" he asked, as he tried to brush past his father and enter the bathroom, the source of the foul odor on which he was beginning to gag.

The elder Neal would not let his son pass, summoning all his strength to keep him from entering the bathroom.

It was nearly 3 p.m., some 20 minutes after Gary Neal had originally placed the call requesting help. Standing in the kitchen, Sardone used his walkie-talkie to call in his report to headquarters and requested a detective with a camera be sent to the scene and, as is common in cases of unattended deaths, asked that the Middlesex County Prosecutor's Office Major Crime Unit and County Medical Examiner be notified.

"Come on, I think you two had better wait outside," Sardone said to the Neals.

Before he could usher them out, the phone rang. The men looked at each other, then stared at the phone until Gary reached over and answered it.

"Hello?"

"Oh Gary!" He heard his mother's voice. "You're there! Is Cathy there? Is she all right?"

"No Ma," Gary said. "Cathy's not here. She's dead."

Stricken, Gloria Neal found her way to a nearby chair, falling into it and nearly dropping the phone.

She put the receiver to her ear when she heard Gary calling her.

"Ma, we've got to stay here for awhile, until the police come," he told her. "We'll be home as soon as we can."

Gloria Neal couldn't answer, she let the phone drop back into her lap as she rested her head in her hands, her body shaking with every wracking sob.

In their grief, the father and son were easily led; the officer gently took the phone from Gary, hung it up, then guided them to the front porch, leaving them alone to console each other. Remembering Edward Jones, Sardone reentered the house, finally spotting the man standing in the backyard, surrounded by an audience of curious neighbors drawn by the commotion. Jones was engrossed in a detailed narration of his gruesome discovery when Sardone asked the onlookers to return to their homes. Curious as they were, the neighbors eventually complied with the policeman's request.

Metuchen Police Sgt. Ralph Salamone was next on the scene.

"We got a bad one, Sarge," Sardone said as his superior officer walked into the house.

"Homicide?"

"I'm not sure, but there's something you should take a look at." Although the doors and windows had been opened to air out the house, the officers' senses were still brutally assaulted by the stench. The sergeant followed Sardone into the bathroom; "*I'll never get used to this*," he thought as he looked down at Cathy Warner's body.

"I don't know, Sarge, this just doesn't sit right with me," Sardone said, as he pointed to the plastic strip that appeared to bind Cathy Warner's lifeless wrists.

"You call the County?" Sardone asked.

"Yeah, right after I called headquarters."

"Okay, let's just leave everything and wait 'til they get here."

The officers walked into the kitchen, where a small monthly desk calendar was neatly displayed on the table, open to the current month.

"Look at this, Sarge," Sardone said as he picked up the calendar. "She's got every day crossed off, up until the seventh." Flipping back through the year, Sardone noticed that each day's box was crossed off with a similar diagonal slash.

Sardone and Salamone also found on the table a letter from Cathy Warner to Edward Jones, dated January 11, 1983, informing him that his monthly rent was going to be increased from $50 to $100. Several more letters were found in the outside mailbox, postmarked July 6 and July 7, 1983. Sardone also showed his sergeant a business card he found stuck inside the front screen door. The card was from Jerry Celentano of South Plainfield, and on the back was written, "Let me know if I can help."

Middlesex County Detective Dennis Watson was trying to escape the summer heat with his family at the Metuchen Borough pool when his beeper went off. Being called away on weekends and in the dead of night was something to which his wife Patty had grown accustomed, so it came as no surprise to her when he returned from the pay phone and told her he had to answer a call.

"We've got a mysterious death on the other side of town," he told her. "I don't know how long I'm going to be."

Driving to the address he was given, 125 Durham Avenue, Watson remembered that his supervisor, Lt. Joseph Zimmerman, was spending the weekend in Point Pleasant, N.J., a popular Shore resort near Seaside Heights, more than an hour's drive from Metuchen. *"Well, I may not have to call him at all,"* Watson thought. *"He's not gonna want to fight that traffic."*

Unlike most of his colleagues, Watson had virtually no police experience when he was hired as a county detective. In 1970, armed with a college degree in sociology, and perhaps in homage to his literary namesake, Watson set his sights on the Federal Bureau of Investigation, to which he was accepted. After two years in the FBI training program, Watson realized that his future did not lie with J. Edgar Hoover's brainchild. He was brought into the Middlesex County detective bureau under an experimental program instituted by then-Prosecutor John Kuhlthau in 1972. Kuhlthau purposely hired college graduates, like Watson, who had an interest in criminal justice, desiring to teach them the rudiments of detective work while they were on the job. Watson spent five years on the gambling, narcotics and organized crime task force, and was also assigned to the department's white collar crime unit. He was assigned to the Major Crimes Unit on May 1, 1981.

At 31, Watson looked younger than his years. His 5'10" frame hinted at an athletic background. With his sandy blond hair, parted in the middle and framing a roundish face, Watson's easy smile and outgoing manner contributed to his good looks.

Dennis Watson pulled up to the front of Cathy Warner's house shortly before 4:30 p.m. By that time, several more Metuchen police officers had arrived and were busy securing the scene. The morgue keeper from the office of Dr. Marvin Shuster, the county medical examiner, had yet to arrive.

Although he had been a member of the Major Crimes Unit for just shy of two years, Dennis Watson was well acquainted with the smell of death. He could tell by the odor that stung his nostrils even before he reached the front steps that what awaited him in the house was going to be very unpleasant.

Sardone caught up with Watson as he was about to climb the first porch step. With a jerk of his head, Sardone motioned the young detective over to the side of the house, out of the earshot of Richard and Gary Neal.

"It's a nasty one, Dennis," Sardone said. "She looks like she's been dead for a while. The two on the porch are her father and brother. "

"Any idea how she died?"

"I don't know; my gut says it wasn't natural, but the way the body's decomposed, it's hard to tell anything."

Watson sucked in a deep breath of fresh air and exhaled slowly, "Let's go take a look."

The stench worsened as Watson climbed the steps; he knew what he was about to see was going to be bad. "*Man,*" he thought as he glanced at Richard and Gary Neal, "*I hope they don't know what's in there.*"

The first thing Watson noticed when he walked into the house were the flies. Thousands of them, he thought, plastered on the window panes. The Metuchen officers had already opened all the windows, but that had relieved neither the infestation nor the odor.

Once inside the bathroom, Watson winced when he saw the decaying body in the bathtub.

"Nobody should have to go through this," the detective said, to no one in particular.

"It looks like her hands were tied," Salamone offered as he walked into the bathroom.

"Yeah," Watson agreed, getting down on one knee to get a closer look at the plastic strip. "It looks like one of those zip-lock strips you use to tie a garbage bag." Then, looking closer, he said, "her hands may have been bound at one time, but they aren't now; the ends aren't connected."

Watson's attention was diverted by the sound of the phone ringing. Straightening up, he walked into the kitchen and picked up the receiver.

"Hello?"

There was a silence of several seconds, then, "Can I speak to Cathy, please?"

"Who is this?"

"This is Merelyn Daniel, I'm one of Cathy's friends from the hospital. Cathy didn't come back to work when she was supposed to, so I just called to see if she was okay. Can I speak with her?"

Watson had to come up with a quick lie; they didn't know with what they were dealing yet and he didn't want to divulge information to an unknown voice on the phone. "Well, her parents are here, and a lot of other people are too," he said, adding, "we've got everything under control. Why don't you give me your number and I'll have her get back to you."

Watson realized what he said was ridiculous, but he could think of nothing else on the spur of the moment.

Daniel warily recited her number, then hung up the phone. Worried because Cathy had not reported to work in two days and was seemingly unreachable, she and her friend, Rosemary Cascella, had gone to Cascella's house after their shift at Middlesex General was completed to look at a map of Metuchen and try to pinpoint where Cathy's house was. Rosemary had been there once and vaguely remembered it; Daniel had never been near the home. Their plan was to locate Cathy's home on the map, then go over to her house to see if she was all right. They had resolved that if her car was in the driveway and she did not answer the door, they would break into her house and see if she had hurt herself. But now, after the strange conversation with the man who answered Cathy's phone, Daniel couldn't hide the worry in her voice as she turned to her friend.

"Something's happened to Cathy."

Watson decided it was time to call Lt. Zimmerman. Using the phone that hung on a kitchen wall, he dialed the county dispatcher and asked him to beep the supervising detective.

Joe Zimmerman and his wife, Claire, had a system worked out for when they went to a beach or a pool: they would go into the water in shifts, with one staying behind to monitor his beeper. The beeper had become something of a chaperone, intruding into their lives at will. But it was an intrusion they both accepted.

Zimmerman was enjoying his turn in the cooling surf when he looked toward shore and saw Claire alternately waving at him with one hand and pointing to the small, black box she held in the other. The same box that, for the 17 years he had been a county detective, had indiscriminately torn him away from dinners, picnics and sound sleep. And other things.

"Shit," he muttered, as he began to swim in.

It could be said that Joe Zimmerman bled policeman blue. Born and raised in New Brunswick, he had joined the city police department after high school, serving with that force for six years. Deciding that police work wasn't the career he wanted, Zimmerman opted to follow in his father's footsteps as a tavern owner. He purchased a bar in Seaside Heights and moved his family there, but, missing law enforcement, returned to his native Hub City after three years. Zimmerman had no desire to return to the municipal force, so he instead joined the county detectives. Like Dennis Watson, he was assigned to several different divisions before the Major Crimes Unit. He had worked his way through the ranks before winning a supervisory role.

Zimmerman exuded a presence that made him seem even more intimidating than his six-foot frame would imply; one knew one was with The Law when with this detective. His strong, chiseled face was highlighted by piercing blue eyes. At the same time, hearty smiles were not foreign to his features; he was generally an easy-going, affable man, but, like all good detectives, could become a cool, calculating inquisitor when the need arose.

The Middlesex County Detectives Bureau Major Crimes Unit, like other Bureau teams, was led by an assistant county prosecutor. In July of 1983, the head of this unit was Second Assistant Prosecutor Thomas J. Kapsak. Kapsak and his team were involved in all investigations of mysterious deaths. (Even though an autopsy had not yet been performed, it seemed likely to the officers that Cathy Warner had not died of natural causes). In 1983, at age 43, Kapsak had been with the prosecutor's office for 13 years, devoting his courtroom talents exclusively to murder trials since 1980.

Kapsak brings only one or two cases to court each year, usually those which are totally circumstantial. In the year of 1983, one of those cases would be the murder of Catherine Neal Warner.

A soft-spoken, reflective man, Kapsak reminds one more of a college professor than a man whose greatest pride – aside from his family– is sending murderers to prison.

Thomas Kapsak didn't consider what he did for a living a job; he believed it to be his personal mission in life to convict murderers and give them a reserved seat on Death Row, or at the least a life sentence in state prison. He had a reputation within the department as one of the most tenacious attorneys in the county. He wouldn't talk about his record, but others did: to that point, Thomas Kapsak had not lost a murder trial. As one detective put it, "if Tom Kapsak is prosecuting you, you've got a problem."

The Second Assistant Prosecutor was, ironically, born and raised in South Plainfield, although he had never known the Neals. It was perhaps because neither of his parents, Rose and Thomas, Sr., had the opportunity to enjoy much formal schooling that Kapsak had been a driven student, excelling both academically and athletically at South Plainfield High School.

After receiving a degree in history from Rutgers University – it was the only college he thought his family could afford – Kapsak attended the University of Pennsylvania Law School, graduating in 1966. It was while he attended law school that he was reunited with his high school sweetheart, Rosemary. The two were married before Kapsak's final year.

He has no recollection of it, but Rosemary Kapsak swears all her husband talked about during law school was becoming a prosecutor.

"When I decided I wanted to be a prosecutor, it was because I believe in the system," Kapsak remembered. "I think criminals get away with too much, and I think people need to fight for what is right. That battle appealed to me and I wanted to be a part of it. If I can relieve the family's suffering a little bit by at least letting them know that the person who caused all that grief is going to be punished for what he did, then it's a worthwhile effort for me."

It wasn't long before Edward Jones' meddlesome curiosity began to try the patience of the investigating officers as they searched through Catherine Warner's home July 16; although he was repeatedly asked to stay out of the house, Jones insisted on watching the police at work and adding his own commentary. At approximately 3:30 p.m., Sgt. Salamone called in to headquarters, requesting that Jones be taken in to keep him from disturbing the crime scene. An officer brought him in and seated him in a booking room to await questioning. Shortly thereafter, Metuchen Police Lieutenant Edward Studnicki introduced himself to Jones and told him that he was sending him home, but warned him to stay away from the crime scene.

"Some officers will be by to speak to you later," Studnicki told Jones.

Studnicki's phone rang again at about 4:15 p.m., it was Salamone.

"Lieutenant, I think you'd better come down here and have a look at what we've got."

"All right," Studnicki, "Stud," to his friends, told the policeman. "I'll be there in a few minutes."

Studnicki didn't really want to go, but he knew he had to. He knew Cathy Warner casually, as a neighbor; his house was situated next door to hers.

Studnicki looked down at the lifeless body of his neighbor and shook his head. "She was such a pretty girl," he said.

Walking out to the porch, the lieutenant introduced himself to Richard and Gary Neal, both still reeling from the shock, and offered his condolences.

"I knew your daughter since she moved in," Studnicki solemnly told Richard Neal. "She was a very nice girl.

"I think it would be best if you stayed out here, so the police can do what they have to," he continued. "A detective will be out here to speak with you shortly, then you can go home."

The lieutenant found Salamone and Sardone in the kitchen.

"I'm about done here," he told the officers, "I'm going to head back to headquarters. Keep me posted."

At 4:25 p.m., Middlesex County Medical Examiner Dr. Marvin Shuster informed Sgt. Salamone that he would not be able to get to the crime scene that day, and asked the policeman to call in another local doctor to make the official pronouncement of death.

Studnicki hadn't been back in his office long when he received yet another call from Salamone.

"Lieutenant, we need someone to come pick up Edward Jones and keep him at headquarters. He's just won't stay out of our way."

"What's he doing now?" Studnicki asked.

"Well, that's the other thing," Salamone answered, while looking out at the subject of his frustration through the kitchen window. "He's out in the backyard right now, boozing it up. He's getting out of control. I'd like to keep him sober until he's questioned."

"All right, I'll send someone down there."

Jones was returned to headquarters, where he was told to sit in the foyer. Several minutes later, Studnicki saw him wander past his office, apparently on his way out the door. The lieutenant quickly intercepted Jones before he went very far.

"Mr. Jones," Studnicki said, steering the drunken man back into the foyer, "I told you you can't go back to the house. You have to wait here for a detective to ask you a few questions."

"Okay," Jones told the officer.

Satisfied that Jones got the message, Studnicki again sat him down in the foyer and returned to his office.

At about 5:30 p.m., Studnicki saw Jones pass his office, once more stopping him as he was again walking out of headquarters. Realizing that he could not trust the elderly man to remain still by himself, Studnicki placed Jones in a jail cell, where he would await a detective's arrival. Studnicki also told Jones that he was being charged by the officer at the scene with interfering with a police officer in the performance of his duties during a police investigation.

Det. Watson, Lt. Zimmerman and Sgt. Salamone finally did interview Jones later that day. Jones confirmed that the house he lived in was owned by his landlady, Catherine Warner. He said the last time he saw her was on July 12, when she appeared at his door late in the afternoon to tell him that she would be going away for a while and ask him to watch her house. He remembered the date, he said, because his son and daughter-in-law were visiting that day.

The message Joe Zimmerman received on the afternoon of the 16th, when he called the county dispatcher, was to contact Detective Watson at the scene of a mysterious death. Watson gave Zimmerman a thumbnail description of what he had found, after which Zimmerman told him to preserve everything as it was until he could get up there.

Hot Saturday afternoons are no time to be driving on any arterial roadway even remotely close to the New Jersey Shore, as Joe Zimmerman found out that day. He didn't arrive at 125 Durham Avenue until later that evening, after the body had been taken away and Richard and Gary Neal had returned to their home. Cathy Warner's remains would be stored overnight at Perth Amboy General Hospital morgue, where Dr. Marvin Shuster, the Middlesex County medical examiner, would perform an autopsy the following day.

Watson filled Zimmerman in on the details of what had transpired that day, including his conversation with the Neals before they left the Warner residence and the call from Merelyn Daniel. As far as either the father or brother knew, they said, Catherine Neal Warner was not suffering from any disease that would have caused her death.

"Besides," Watson added, "those plastic ties around her wrists tell me this was definitely not an accident."

After inspecting the downstairs bathroom, Watson left Zimmerman upstairs, to Cathy Warner's bedroom. There, resting on the floor at the foot of her bed, were two fully packed suitcases: the first an overstuffed brown vinyl suitcase, the second, a small, multi-colored plastic case.

"Looks like she either came back from a trip, or was planning on taking one and didn't go," Zimmerman said.

"She was definitely going somewhere," Watson told him. Handing him the list found on her kitchen table, he added, "looks like she was going to be gone a while."

Zimmerman perused the list; on it were such reminders as "call post office", "hold mail", "garbage", "photo bag", "pillow", "blanket", "suitcases" and "Call to reconfirm flight!"

Zimmerman spent the next several minutes poking through the contents of Cathy Warner's purse – a two-toned bag with burgundy sides and a dark brown leather strip along the edges – which he had found and dumped onto the bed.

"Look at this," he said to Watson, as he picked up an empty U.S. Air ticket folder. Opening it up, Zimmerman saw that the folder had once held two tickets, issued in the names of C. Warner and G. Berta, for a round-trip flight between Newark International Airport and Minneapolis, Minnesota.

The U.S. Air flight on which C. Warner and G. Berta were booked was scheduled to leave Newark Airport at 4:45 p.m. on July 8, arriving in Pittsburgh at 5:52 p.m. The flight then was scheduled to leave Pittsburgh at 6:55 p.m. and arrive at 7:25 p.m. in Minneapolis.

The July 11 return trip was scheduled to leave Minneapolis at 5:15 p.m. and arrive in Newark at 8:32 p.m. The itinerary indicated the trip had been scheduled through the Menlo Park Travel Agency in the Menlo Park Mall, Edison, New Jersey.

"I wonder who this G. Berta is," mused Watson.

The answer was discovered in Cathy Warner's checkbook. In it, Zimmerman found a voided check, in the amount of $5,000, made out to Eugene Berta. Based on the voided check, he and Watson concluded that the "G. Berta" on the airline itinerary could be the "Eugene Berta" who was supposed to have received the $5,000.

Even more interesting was what Zimmerman found in her check register: the crossed off entries for $5,000 and $350, and then the duplicate entries right below them.

"I guess she changed her mind," Watson observed.

"Yeah," Zimmerman said. It was probably the last time she did."

"Well, looks like she was a train traveler, too," Zimmerman said, picking up an Amtrak schedule. The schedule was for service between Boston, Mass. and Washington, D.C.

The first parts of what would evolve into a complicated puzzle were becoming clearer to the detectives: First, Catherine Warner and Eugene Berta had some sort of relationship; second, the relationship was strong enough for Cathy Warner to have written a check for $5,000 to Gene Berta; third, something had happened to change Warner's mind twice about giving Berta the check; fourth, Catherine Warner and Eugene Berta had been scheduled to go together to Minnesota; and finally, that someone, or two someones, may indeed have made the journey.

The name "Berta" was familiar to the Metuchen police; the Berta family members were long-time, well-known residents of the area. In fact, Sardone had had Gene Berta over to his house three times in as many years to do electrical work. The police would still have to definitely determine that G. Berta and Eugene Berta were one and the same, and also the exact location of G. Berta's residence, as well as have to question this "G. Berta" about this trip. But at least they had a name, and one that could possibly be directly linked to the victim – a crucial factor in the early stages of an investigation into a mysterious death.

"So what do you think?" Studnicki asked Zimmerman when he, Watson, Sardone and Salamone had returned to Metuchen police headquarters later the evening of the 16th.

"I don't know yet, Stud, but there's a guy we need to talk to, his name is Eugene Berta. You know him?"

"Gene? Yeah, I know him. He works on a Rescue Squad in Edison. Lived here a long time. Why do you want to talk to him?"

"Well, we found an airline itinerary and a voided check for $5,000 with his name on it. He may be able to tell us a little bit about Cathy Warner. Do you think you could ask him to come down here tonight?"

"Sure, I'll give him a call."

Studnicki reached Berta at the Edison Rescue Squad No. 2 headquarters. Berta agreed to talk to the detectives, but he asked if Studnicki could pick him up.

"My van's still out of commission," he explained.

By 8:30 p.m., Berta had been introduced to detectives Zimmerman and Watson.

At age 34, Eugene Thomas Berta was an intimidating man. He stood 5'10" and weighed close to 200 pounds, most of which was a significant beer belly. He sported shoulder-length black hair and a bushy beard of the same color.

Berta lived with his then-wife Gail and four children: twin daughters – Heather and Joella, 10 (his wife's by his first marriage and adopted by Berta after he and Gail wed), and two other daughters – Winter, 3 and Amber, 2 – borne of their marriage. Berta also had a son, 12-year-old Eugene Jr., his by a previous marriage, but who lived with his mother, Berta's first wife, Kathleen. The first Mrs. Berta divorced Eugene Sr. in 1973 after several years of marriage, charging him, according to court documents, with cruelty.

Although his list of vocations varied from electrician to truck driver, Berta seldom found work; instead, both he and his current wife found it necessary at times to add their names to the state's welfare and unemployment rolls. Berta's last requiring of the public dole was necessitated by his convalescence from a serious auto accident in May of 1983, during which he had sustained several broken bones and which had killed the driver of the other car. Fault for the accident was laid on the other driver; Berta was issued a summons for driving without an insurance card.

Berta spent the majority of his time at the Edison Rescue Squad, which was headquartered in the Menlo Park section of Edison Township, and of which he was captain in that summer of 1983. His 18 years of achievements on the squad had earned him an honorable reputation as a saver of lives throughout Metuchen and neighboring Edison; in May, the Edison Township Kiwanis Club had named him a "Man of the Year" for 1983 for his numerous contributions to the community. A number of Metuchen residents would later have cause to recall the times that Eugene Berta had helped them, or saved the life of a loved one.

Joe Zimmerman first interviewed Berta at approximately 8:45 p.m. on July 16 — five hours after Cathy Warner's body was discovered — in an interrogation room at Metuchen police headquarters. Also in attendance were Detective Dennis Watson and Metuchen officers Salamone, Sardone and Studnicki. It was the first of four interviews Zimmerman would conduct with Berta in the ensuing four weeks.

Gene Berta did not strike Watson or Zimmerman as Man of the Year material that evening. Standing before them was an overweight, balding man with long, greasy hair and a straggly beard, who behaved as though he were granting the police an immense favor by showing up at all.

Handing him the airline ticket folder, Zimmerman asked Berta if that was his name that appeared on the itinerary.

"Yeah, that's me," he said, nonchalantly flipping the folder back on the table, around which the men had seated themselves.

"Can you tell me why you and Cathy Warner were going to Minnesota?" Zimmerman asked.

"First off, I went to Minnesota to look at some farm land. I never planned for Cathy to go."

"But that's her name on the itinerary, isn't it?"

"Yeah, that's her name. Look, we talked about me buying a farm out in the Midwest. She bought the tickets and made all the reservations, but I never intended to take her."

"How long have you known Cathy Warner, Mr. Berta?"

"Well, I've known her for a few years," he told the officer. "I did some electrical work at her home. I was friendly with her, but I got the feeling that she felt there was more to the relationship than I did."

"Did you ever borrow any money from Mrs. Warner?" Zimmerman asked, without telling Berta about the voided $5,000 check found in the dead woman's checkbook.

Berta admitted he had. "I borrowed $10,000 from her, but it was a personal loan," he explained. "She gave it to me in two $5,000 checks."

By now, about 15 minutes had passed. "Why are you asking me these questions?" Berta finally wanted to know.

"Cathy Warner has expired," Zimmerman told him.

Berta was silent for several seconds. "What do you mean by expired?" he asked.

"I mean, Cathy Warner was found dead in her home this afternoon."

Berta's face remained impassive. He didn't even blink.

Just then identical bells went off in Watson's and Zimmerman's heads; this guy, they both thought, is one cold son of a bitch.

Making a mental note of Berta's blank response to the news, Zimmerman pressed on with the questioning.

"Mr. Berta, can you tell me when was the last time you saw her?"

"Yeah, it was last Friday. I picked her up from work early that day."

"And did you have any conversation?"

"She continued an argument we had the day before about me not taking her to Minnesota with me, " Berta replied.

"I just don't understand why the reservations were made out in both your names, and you decided against taking her," Zimmerman said.

"I told you, I never had any intentions of taking her," Berta said, with more than a trace of irritation in his voice. "I don't know what was in her head when she made the reservations. I told her I was going with my wife."

"Okay, so you took these tickets and these reservations that had been made and paid for by Cathy Warner, when she though she was going, and you went to Minnesota with your wife?" Zimmerman asked.

"No, I went with a friend."

Zimmerman shot Watson a glance as the two digested what they were being told.

"*The pile is getting higher and higher,*" Watson thought.

"Can you tell us your friend's name, Mr. Berta?"

"I'd rather not," he said, for the first time showing a little discomfort.

"Mr. Berta, I'm afraid you're going to have to," Zimmerman said. "Now, once again, what is the name of the friend you took to Minnesota?"

After several minutes, Berta told them.

"Her name is Patricia Bauer. She lives in Edison. I didn't want to tell you because she's married to an Edison policeman, and I don't want her to get into any trouble."

"Okay, Gene," Zimmerman said, as he leaned back in his chair and shot another glance to Watson. "Can I call you Gene? Okay. This is quite a story you're telling us. I'm still unclear about a couple of things. You said you last saw Mrs. Warner last Friday, that would be July 8, when you picked her up early from work and then the two of you argued about her not going to Minnesota, right?" Berta nodded his head. "Okay; can you be a little more specific about that day? Anything at all that you can tell us would be a help."

Berta let out an audible sigh, as though he found dealing with fools very tiresome. It was at about that time that Watson decided he didn't like this man.

"I drove her to the Metro Park railroad station in Iselin in her car so she could catch a train to Alexandria, Virginia to visit her sister," Berta began.

"Okay," Zimmerman interjected, "and when was this?"

"This was at about 10 p.m. on July 8," Berta sighed.

"And then what happened?"

"After I left her, I parked her car and called Pat to come and pick me up at the station. By that time, we missed the flight to Minnesota and had to make a new reservation for the next day."

"Did you see Mrs. Warner after you returned from Minnesota?" the detective asked.

"No," Berta replied. "When we got back to New Jersey on the night of the eleventh, I went down to Seaside Heights with my wife; I was there until the fourteenth."

"And after you got back from Seaside Heights, that was on the fourteenth? Did you try to get in touch with Mrs. Warner then?"

"Nope."

"Okay Gene, I guess that's it for now. Can you tell me where we can find Patricia Bauer?"

"Yeah, she should be still at the rescue squad."

Berta gave Zimmerman the phone number, after which the detective went to Studnicki's office to make the call. He waited several minutes after asking for Bauer before her voice came on the line.

"Mrs. Bauer? My name is Joe Zimmerman, I'm with the Prosecutor's Office in New Brunswick and I'd like to talk to you."

"What do you want to talk about?"

"There are some things I have to talk to you about, can I come down now?"

"Well, I guess so."

"Okay, we'll be over there in about five minutes," Zimmerman told her. "I just need you to promise me one thing."

"What's that?"

"I don't want you to talk to Gene Berta."

"When?"

"Within the next five minutes."

"Well, why not?"

"I'm just asking you to do me this favor. Will you?"

"Sure . . . okay."

"Great," Zimmerman said. "We'll be there in about five minutes."

"We're going to go speak with Pat Bauer now," Zimmerman told Berta, after the detective had returned to the interrogation room. "Would you mind waiting here a while so we can get over there?"

"No, I don't mind at all, " Berta said, as Zimmerman and Watson took their leave.

"What an arrogant bastard," Watson said, when the two detectives were in Zimmerman's car. "I don't see how a guy who looks like that could be hot with the ladies, but here he is stringing along three of them!"

"Something just doesn't sound right, Denny," Zimmerman told

him. "Here we have Cathy Warner paying for this trip, making all the reservations and everything, and then Gene Berta tells her she's not going and she decides to visit her sister. Something just doesn't sit right."

"His reaction when you told him she was dead was all wrong," Watson added. "You'd think, the guy knew her, you know? He'd show some kind of emotion. At least ask how it happened. Say what a shame it was. Something!"

"Yeah; can you believe he asked me what I meant when I said she expired? He's been on the rescue squad long enough, he knows what it means. And then he just sits there, cold as ice."

Zimmerman and Watson rode the rest of the way in thoughtful silence.

Merelyn Daniel and her husband, Kenny, were returning to their Somerset home at about that time. After Merelyn had left Rosemary's house earlier that afternoon, she had driven home and suggested to her husband that they go to a movie. It would have to be an early one, she reminded him, because she had to be at work at 7 a.m. the next day.

When they walked in the house, Merelyn noticed that the message light was blinking on her answering machine. Playing the tape back, Merelyn felt a chill go through her spine as she listened to the voice.

"Mrs. Daniel, my name is Joe Zimmerman. I'm a policeman, and I'd like to talk to you about Cathy Warner. Please call me as soon as you get in, no matter what time it is." Zimmerman left the number of the Metuchen Police Department.

"Oh God, Kenny," she gasped, cupping both hands over the front of her mouth, "something's happened to Cathy."

"Now stop being such a pessimist," he told his wife. "Cathy's all right. Just call the man back and see what he wants."

Merelyn Daniel called the number she was given, but when she asked for Zimmerman, she was told that he was not there. But she was put on hold as soon as she mentioned her name. Zimmerman had left word that he expected calls from Daniel and Cascella, and asked Studnicki to take them in his absence.

"Hello Mrs. Daniel, this is Lieutenant Studnicki of the Metuchen Police

Department, Lieutenant Zimmerman isn't here now, but if you have a few minutes, I'd like to speak with you."

"Sure, what's this all about?"

"Can you tell me the last time you saw Cathy Warner?"

"Yeah, it was about 1:30 or 2 o'clock last Friday afternoon. She had left early, and she gave me the report on her patients. What's this all about?"

"Ad you didn't speak to her or see her after that?"

"No, she was supposed to come back to work yesterday, but she didn't. And then my friend Rosemary and I called her house this afternoon, and a man answered and said he'd have her get back to us. Where's Cathy, is she all right?"

But Studnicki was not answering any questions.

"Mrs. Daniel, Lieutenant Zimmerman will probably want to speak with you tomorrow, will you be at home?"

"No, I'll be working tomorrow until 3:30. Why can't you tell me what this is all about?"

"Okay Mrs. Daniel, thanks very much for getting back to us. Good night."

Merelyn Daniel stared at the receiver for several minutes, listening to the dial tone. Then, turning to her husband with a scared look in her eyes, she said, "Kenny, something's the matter; I think Cathy is dead!"

"Get out of here," he replied, putting one arm around her as he took the phone from her hand ad replaced it in its cradle.

"I'm telling you, Cathy is dead! Why would that policeman be calling me back?"

"Now, you're just over-reacting. Let's go to sleep, ad tomorrow you'll find out that everything is okay."

But sleep would not come to Merelyn Daniel that night.

Pat Bauer was panic-stricken. "I know those two guys were sent here by my husband," she told her friend, George Taylor, as they sat around a card table in the basement of the rescue squad headquarters. "He's just trying to find out where I went last weekend."

Bauer and Taylor were sitting by themselves in the rescue squad's basement/rec room. Pat had had an uneasy feeling since learning shortly after she had come on duty that night that representatives from the county prosecutor's office had called for Gene, and that he was in Metuchen talking with them

The entire preceding week had been unnerving for Pat. She had spent most of it arguing with her estranged husband, John. They had been fighting since Pat returned from Minnesota on Monday and found John laying on the downstairs couch, after he had moved out six months before. Pat had told him to leave the house twice since that night, the second time accentuated by her tossing his clothes into the front shrubbery. "You haven't lived here for six months, and you think you can just walk right in and act like nothing's happened?" she had yelled at him. The hostility had reached its zenith the day before, when she had to spend the day in Edison municipal court answering a complaint filed against her by John after she had disposed of his clothes.

John had promised her that he would take their son away from her; Pat was convinced that he had talked some of his police friends into finding out where she went the weekend before. But she had resolved that she wasn't going to tell them anything.

The two Middlesex County detectives were given a chilly greeting by Pat Bauer when they arrived at the Edison Rescue Squad at approximately 10 p.m.

"You can't park here," Bauer told Zimmerman before he had a chance to turn off his car. "You have to move your car."

"What do you mean?" he asked.

"You're parked on the garage apron, your car will be in the way if an ambulance has to get out, so you can't park here."

Zimmerman stared at her a few moments, then wordlessly moved the auto into the street.

"One for me," Bauer thought to herself.

Pat Bauer's alarm heightened when she saw four men climb out of the car.

"What's the matter?" she asked, her voice rising in pitch. "What do you want to talk about?"

"We're from the prosecutor's office," Zimmerman said. "We just want to talk to you."

"About what?"

"About an accident you had with the squad's rig," Zimmerman lied.

"I didn't have any accident with the rig," Bauer told them, folding her arms in front of her. "I'm not talking with anybody."

"Well, we want to talk to you," Zimmerman repeated.

Pat Bauer walked over to her friend, George Taylor, who was standing off to the side, observing. "George," she began, poking her thumb toward the two detectives behind her, "these guys are from the prosecutor's office and they say they're here to investigate an accident I had with the rig. George, I didn't have any accident with the rig!"

"Wait here," he said, "I'll straighten this out."

Taylor walked over to Zimmerman and Watson and, after several minutes of hushed conversation, turned on his heel and walked back toward Bauer.

"Patty, talk to them," he said, as he passed her and re-entered the rescue squad headquarters.

"But I didn't have an accident with the rig," she protested.

"Pat, look," Zimmerman said, softening his voice. "We just said that to you because we need some information, we need to talk in private. Is there some place we could go?"

"All right," she said hesitantly. "Follow me."

Bauer led the detectives down the stairs to the rec room, which also served as the squad's dormitory. The group pulled up chairs around a card table.

Watson's amazement of Gene Berta deepened as he looked at Pat Bauer. He couldn't figure out how this attractive woman – mid-30s, 5'9", blonde hair worn up, blue eyes and trim figure accentuated by the tailored pants and tight-fitting blouse she was wearing – could go for a slovenly-looking guy like Berta.

Before he started with his questions, Zimmerman held the airline itinerary in his hand, nonchalantly slapping it against the edge of the card table. Bauer noticed the front of the itinerary emblazoned with the Menlo Park Travel agency logo.

"*Oh my God*," she thought. "*They found out where I was! John must have told them!*"

"So, Pat, where'd you go last weekend?" Zimmerman asked, still casually slapping the itinerary against the table.

"That's none of your business," was her icy reply. She tried to keep her eyes off the ticket folder Zimmerman held.

"Look, we're from the prosecutor's office," he reminded her, "I'm afraid you'll have to tell us."

"I don't care where you're from," she snapped, losing her patience. Bauer was nervous, but she wasn't going to let herself be pushed around. "You're friends with my husband. What I do is my business and what he does is his business. We're separated, he is living with someone else, this is my business. I don't care if you are detectives, I'm not telling you anything."

"Mrs. Bauer, we're not associated with your husband," Zimmerman told her, trying to calm her down.

"Oh, you're all brothers," she said with a mocking laugh. "You guys all stick together."

Changing direction, Zimmerman said, "Pat, I understand you know Eugene Berta?"

"Yes, I do. He's the captain here."

It was late, and Zimmerman was in no mood to play games.

"Look, Pat, we know you and Gene were together last weekend," he told her. "Gene told us that he was with you. Can you prove that you were with him?"

"Yeah, I can."

"Okay," Zimmerman said. He was finally getting somewhere. "Can you tell us where you and Gene went last weekend?"

"We went to Minnesota."

"And when did you leave?"

"We left Friday.

"*This is like pulling teeth,*" Zimmerman thought.

"And what time did you leave?" he asked her.

"Well, I picked Gene up at about 10 p.m. at the MetroPark railroad station in Edison," Bauer recalled. "Then we drove to the Howard Johnson hotel near Newark Airport, where we stayed the night. Why do you need to know this?"

"Can you tell us why you and Mr. Berta went to Minnesota, Mrs.

Bauer," Zimmerman asked, again ignoring her question.

"Gene wanted to look at some property in Moose Lake. He had long-range plans to move there. He said he might like me to come along with him."

"Okay. When did you return to Metuchen?"

"On the eleventh."

And what time was that?"

"We got back here at about 10:30 p.m.," Bauer said. "I dropped Gene off at the train station, and then I went home." Sheepishly, she added, "Then my husband and I had a fight."

"You went away with Mr. Berta while your husband stayed home?" Zimmerman asked, trying to keep the surprise out of his voice.

"Well, we're estranged," she explained. "He moved out a while ago and I guess he moved back in over the weekend."

"And how long ago did you and Mr. Berta plan this trip, Mrs. Bauer?" Zimmerman asked.

Pat Bauer hesitated a few minutes before she answered: "Oh, about two weeks. I don't understand all this, what's going on?"

"We're investigating a murder," Zimmerman told her.

Bauer felt a strange sense of relief. "Oh! I thought you were friends of my husband's and that you were trying to be detectives for a divorce hearing."

"No, Mrs. Bauer," Zimmerman assured her. "This has nothing to do with your husband.

"Pat, would you be willing to come down to Metuchen police headquarters next week and talk to us there?"

"Sure," she answered, shrugging her shoulders. "When?"

"How about Tuesday at 7 o'clock?"

"Okay."

Their interview concluded, Zimmerman and Watson left.

Bauer stayed downstairs after the detectives departed. She was soon joined by George Taylor.

"What was that all about?" he asked.

"I'm not sure," Bauer answered. "They wanted to know where Gene and I went last weekend, and then they said they were investigating a murder! I don't know what's going on."

About 20 minutes later, Bauer received another phone call, this one from Gene Berta.

"Patty, did some men come to talk to you?"

"Yeah, who were they?"

"They're from the prosecutor's office, "he told her.

"What do they want me for?"

"I don't know. But just tell the truth, Patty, just tell the truth. Listen, I'll be down in a few minutes, and then we'll talk."

When he arrived, Berta ushered Bauer back down to the rec room. The two sat close together on a cot, out of earshot of anyone else.

"Now Patty," Berta said, looking into her eyes, "I want you to tell me everything you told them."

Bauer related the entire conversation, including how Zimmerman slapped the brochure against the card table. "That made me think they were working for my husband, because the other night he kept yelling, "I know where you went, I went down to Menlo Park Travel'," she told him. "I thought that was just his way of letting me know that my husband told him everything.

"And I told him that we left on Friday."

"Well, we did," Berta said. "What's wrong with that?"

"They didn't actually ask me when we left for Minnesota, they just asked me when we left."

"You just have to tell the truth, Pat," he reassured her. "You have nothing to worry about if you just tell the truth."

"What do you think, is she handing us a line?" Watson asked Zimmerman, as they drove back to Metuchen police headquarters.

"No, I think she's telling the truth, but she's not telling it all," Zimmerman replied. "We didn't get the whole truth from either one of them tonight, but we will, Denny, we will. I get the feeling that Mr. Berta likes to hear himself talk. And you better believe I'll be there listening."

Once back at Metuchen headquarters, Zimmerman presided over a meeting of himself, Watson, Metuchen Chief Studnicki, and officers Sardone and Salamone. The group thus assembled, the county detective outlined what they had all found out that day.

"We've got a dead body with a plastic tie around its wrists," he began. "We've got an empty airline ticket folder, and a voided $5,000 check, from Cathy Warner to Gene Berta. We've got Gene Berta telling us that he knew Cathy Warner a little, and that Cathy Warner, on her own, made and paid for all the reservations for a weekend in Minnesota for two, and that she 'loaned' him $10,000. And then we've got her going to Virginia when Gene tells her he's going to Minnesota with his wife. Then he really goes with Pat Bauer, who comes home to have a fight with her estranged husband."

"We've got a mess," Watson added.

"Well, the autopsy is tomorrow. We'll know more then, so I think we should call it a night," Zimmerman suggested. No one disagreed.

Zimmerman and Watson walked together to their cars, each absorbed in his own thoughts. Suddenly, Joe Zimmerman stopped and grabbed his younger colleague's arm.

"Jesus, Denny, I just thought of something! Do you know the first thing these rescue squad people do when they're about to transport a dead body?"

Watson shrugged. "No, what?"

"They bind the wrists together so the arms don't flop around."

Voices— Merelyn Daniel

"Cathy and I worked on 'Four Tower', which is internal medicine, at Middlesex General Hospital. We had a little bit of everything; geriatrics, no surgeries, but some cardiacs, a mixture of patients. I had been there about six months and Cathy started orientation. What you usually do in orientation is they usually buddy you up with another nurse. Because we were both RNs, sometimes we buddied up. And I liked her, we became friends. She had a nice personality, she was an excellent nurse, she was very serious about nursing.

"We talked a little bit, everybody always talks a little bit about their families, but Cathy never was one to really discuss her family life. She had been married twice, her second husband died of Hodgkin's Disease, but she didn't elaborate on the amount of money left to her, we just didn't discuss it. She came to my house, she had dinner with us, she met my daughter and my husband and all in all, she was just a really nice person.

"I found out that Cathy started out as a home health aide and put herself through school, she became an LPN and then an RN. I respected her for that, that she decided what she wanted and went to school for it and got it. We were talking about family one day and I was saying that my parents paid for me to go to school, and she told me I was lucky because her parents didn't do nothing for her and anything she got she got herself, on her own. From our conversations, she made me believe that she had been on her own for a long time, like since she was 17 or 18. She never said anything about her home life; she never talked about her parents. She didn't talk about her first husband; she was really young, in her teens, when she got married for the first time. Then she married this other fella, then she told me that he had died and she had taken care of him throughout his illness. That was really about it; she didn't tell me if he had property or how old he was, but from what I gathered from Cathy in passing, he was young and he was sick for a long time before he passed away.

"About a couple of months after she started working there — you always talk about your boyfriend — and that's all she talked about was this fella. And then I asked her about him, and she said, well, sometimes I see him and sometimes I don't. And I asked her why, is he married? And she said yes. And I said you don't need to be in that kind of relationship! Because there was a surgeon who used to come up on the floor who wanted to date Cathy; he kept coming up and asking questions about her. Cathy had low self-esteem; she didn't feel that she was worthy of dating someone with those kinds of credentials. She was a good person and a good nurse, she had all the qualifications, she just felt that she wasn't good enough.

"Anyway, she started talking about this fella she was seeing who she met when she was on the rescue squad. And he told her that he had a bad marriage and the only reason he was staying with his wife was because of the kids and he had talked Cathy into buying this house that needed a lot of work. He said as soon as they got the house all together, he was going to leave his wife and take the kids and he and the kids were going to come and live with Cathy. Rosemary and I was saying to her that this was not going to be. At the time, I'm married, Rosemary's engaged, and we're saying to her, it's not going to be that way, he's not going to leave his wife. I didn't know she had been giving him money or anything like that."

"She told me about this guy, that he was big, her Teddy Bear, or Huggy Bear, and you look at Cathy and you picture in your mind what her fella would look like, and then you meet him, it was such a letdown. It was like, okay, Cathy, maybe he is a real nice guy.

"She said he talked her into buying that house because when they got married, they were going to have to have someplace to go. It was a fixer-upper in Metuchen.

"All she talked about was Gene. Gene this, Gene that. Gene said we're gonna do this, Gene said we're gonna do that; he's gonna come and help me fix up the house, he was over, he did some wiring; you know, things like that. In conversation, she'd talk about Gene a lot and what they were going to do and how his wife was terrible and she didn't take care of the kids and how, eventually, they were going to get married and the kids were going to come live with them. Cathy wanted kids real bad, she wanted a family, she wanted some kind of stability.

"Sometimes he was supposed to come over and he didn't and she'd come into work the next day and she'd be a little down. Sometimes he would not come and not call, and she would have gone home and fixed dinner, expecting him to come and he didn't. But we knew when he came because she was up that day. They talked about what they were going to do with the house; remodeling stuff, and wiring, they were going to put in a new porch, and they were going to add more rooms to the back of the house. From what I gathered, it wasn't a big house. Rosemary was telling me that it wasn't in the nicest area of Metuchen anyway. We were kind of worried about her being there. She could have bought a condominium with the money.

"Once I found out he was married, I didn't have too much to say because I thought that Cathy could do a lot better. And then when I met him, I knew she could do a lot better. He looked like a trucker. When he came to the floor, he never had too much to say to any of us, never made any eye contact with us, just, 'hi, how you doin'. Come on Cathy, let's go'. Not a lot of conversation at all with us.

"Sometimes, after a weekend we were off, she'd come back and say that she went on the road with Gene. She never said where she went. Once she knew how Rosemary and I felt about this relationship, she didn't go into great detail because we told her she could do better. I felt he was a married man giving her the standard line, 'my wife doesn't understand me,' and just kind of using a young, vulnerable girl. I didn't know she had so much money, we didn't discuss money. She was a young girl who he was taking advantage of. You could look at him and tell that he was much older than we were, and I just thought that he was giving her a line. I didn't see the great big deal about him when I met him.

"Cathy said they were going to go away because they were thinking about relocating, and they were going wherever they were going to look at homes. And then from there, they were going somewhere it was warm. But the main purpose of going away was for relocation, Gene wanted to relocate. They figured it would be better for them and the kids if they relocated. Gene told Cathy that Gail wasn't a fit mother and that he could probably get custody of the kids. She truly believed that he was going to at least be able to get his kids. From what I gathered, he said that his wife didn't really want the kids, so it was just a matter of getting a divorce and getting custody.

"She went over Rosemary's house a couple of times to help her plan her wedding. I know there was a couple of other young married couples and they would go over to Rosemary's after work. But she didn't socialize with us a lot because Gene didn't want to be around us so much. Which was typical, because most married men don't want to be around a lot of other people. So we would go out after work, or have lunch together.

"One day in May, she came into work and she was so upset, that after work we went to a bar in Highland Park, on the main street. Anyway, we went in there and we started talking; she told us about how Gene had an accident and ended up in the hospital and that's when Cathy found out he was still living at home with his wife, he had no intentions of leaving his wife. I think that's when his wife found out about Cathy. He had told her that he had moved out, but that she couldn't call him because where he was staying didn't have a phone, so he would have to call her. And then when she went to the hospital, she found out that he was still living at home; and not only living at home, but living a married life! So Cathy went home and got all of his clothes and left them on his porch.

"She told us that she didn't want to see him anymore. And I said fine, good riddance, you don't need that. Date other people, go out with other people! And Rosemary and I were both looking around for fellas for her to date so that she wouldn't get back in that environment.

"Everything was fine for about two months, and then she said to me that after he got out of the hospital he was calling her. She said that they had gone out, and they had had a talk and they understood one another and that he was coming back under her rules. That he was going to come back on her terms and that she gave him a deadline, she didn't tell me how long she had given him, but that he had a deadline and that if he didn't make a move to leave his wife within that deadline, she was going to leave him. She didn't go into depth about what the ground rules were. He gave her a ring; it wasn't like an engagement ring, it was more like a friendship kind of ring. He gave that to her, and we were standing in the medicine room and I was saying, 'Cathy, are you sure you want to do this? Are you sure you want to get back in this kind of relationship? You're out of it, why don't you just stay out of it and go find somebody who's single, who you can build a relationship with and not this creep who's married and who's not going to leave his wife, who's handing you a bill of goods?' She said, 'well, he came over and we talked and he knows how I feel. I gave him a ultimatum and we're going to be going away soon.' We didn't discuss it after that.

"They broke up before Rosemary got married, and that's when he came back into the picture and he came to the wedding. At that point, I had had it with him because I knew that he was living at home and we knew that everything we had said was true about him and she still brought him to the wedding. And it was at the wedding that she told me they were going away. I asked her where she was going; Rosemary got married on a Saturday, Cathy told me she was leaving the following Friday for the weekend. I was really mad, because Cathy and Rosemary were going away and leaving me and I was going to be stuck by myself.

"Rosemary's wedding reception was at a catering hall on Route 9. My husband Kenny and I got lost, of course. I didn't know where the place was. We hadn't been in Jersey that long. We met her at the reception because we missed the wedding, and so did Cathy. We were there, and then Cathy and Gene got there. And what struck me so odd about Gene's dress; this was the summertime, he had on cowboy boots, corduroy pants, a shirt and a plaid jacket, like a herringbone jacket. And I said to Kenny, 'that ain't no way to dress for no wedding. Here Cathy's looking all cute in that little dress of hers and he's looking like a leftover from the Salvation Army'. Kenny kept telling me, shut up, because you don't like him and anything he does is wrong.

"But Kenny sat there, and he was very sociable. He talked and laughed, and they were talking about their watches. And he told me that the watch he had on was a gift from Cathy, and it was an expensive watch. And I'm looking at Cathy and I'm glaring at her, and she's looking at me sheepishly because he knows that I'm pissed at her because she's buying this cretin gifts. I had just bought Kenny a watch for Christmas, and he had his on, and they were comparing watches. I was furious with her for buying this watch. It was the kind that you had to open up, a metal band. It was a real good watch.

"Kenny was saying, 'see the one I got, how come you didn't get me one like that?'

"Kenny and Gene talked about trucks and cars and about Jersey. My husband's very sociable. If I don't like you, I don't like you and you know it. But Kenny will be sociable to you, but I won't. Gene knew I didn't like him, but he knew that I tolerated him because of Cathy. I didn't go out of my way to be nice. If he asked me a question I answered it. Rosemary didn't like him either."

Voices — Joy Niemiera

"We met at JFK. We worked on the same floor, 3 East. They were urology cases. This was February of 1977. I graduated from nursing school in summer of 1976 and then in February I was up at Edison in '77. Cathy was there first. She got married in February and Greg and I got married in May, so we were close as couples. She was getting married and I was getting married, that sort of thing. She had a very small wedding with John, and I had a very small wedding myself.

"We probably talked about husbands when we first started getting to know each other. She had a really rough time with John being sick. I was helping her cope with that. It was really hard, a young woman with a husband with cancer. In '77, he was sick, he had Hodgkins, so he had surgery. It wasn't until the end that he got real bad. Shortly after they were married he had the lymph glands done. He had gotten a good report from the beginning, but you marry for love, and they say that love is blind and marriage is an eye-opener.

"She talked about her first marriage. She was a young girl, inexperienced. She got married to get out of the house. Her parents, from what I know of them from meeting them myself, they're nice people; I didn't get that perspective from Cathy.

"I can remember she would always be late leaving work; patients came first and the paperwork came after. Invariably, she would be there 4:30, 5 o'clock and she would get in trouble for that. Supervisors would literally yell at her and say that she couldn't stay anymore to do her paperwork; that she needed to get the paperwork done along with the patient care. And obviously, you have to cut back on your patient care to get your paperwork done. And I can remember Cathy being in tears about that. That happened often. Cathy was just a very caring, softhearted individual.

"We socialized a lot. With John having a gas station, it kind of made our scheduling difficult. I worked nights some of the time; Cathy worked 3 to 11, so the relationship was more Cathy and myself. We would go over there when they had their apartment and whatnot. We rarely worked the same shift. Toward the end of my being there, we worked probably the same shifts. We talked just about every day, either on the phone or at work.

"She was a great source of comfort for me. I have a son, Greg, who's a quadriplegic and blind and retarded, because of a mistake a doctor made when he was a baby. As my son was in a coma, Cathy would often come to the hospital in Philadelphia and sit with me. She was a real true friend to do that, to drive to Philadelphia from Edison to sit. There aren't too many people who would do that. Greg was in a coma for four months. Cathy would often come and take over for me, give me a break. Even at home, she would come. It's quite frightening to people who have to deal with a child who has nothing but seizures all day. It's not a pretty sight. Cathy just had a terrific sense of compassion, a sixth sense about how to comfort somebody.

"Cathy didn't care about my son's seizures. She made like he was the best thing ever. There are some people I have to explain Greg to, but I never had to do that with Cathy. By the time he was two, he had pneumonia 27 times. He has 100 seizures a day. He had an oxygen tent; every hour, I had to replace a five-pound block of ice. I would get exhausted. Cathy would come over and let me take a nap or let me go out to get away. For a while, my daughter had juvenile arthritis, so I had a baby in a coma and a 2-year-old who couldn't walk. Cathy would just come over with McDonald's, or she would just call and say, 'I'm taking you out to dinner.' I don't think any other of my friends has done that since.

"She had a New Year's Eve party the January that John died, it was just a weird feeling; Greg and I both felt that that would be the last time we would see John; although we did see him again in the hospital, he really did not know that we were there. Things started going downhill for John about six months before he died. He went fairly quickly when things started to go. He was buried Valentine's Day. That was tough for her. She held up very well. She held up as well as any human being in a tremendously stressful situation.

"After I left JFK, Greg and I moved to Trenton. Cathy and I got closer when I was in Trenton. There were a lot of late night talks.

"The first time Cathy mentioned Gene Berta was the summer of 1980. I don't remember the context. She told me she re-met him at the rescue squad. She didn't rejoin. I remember her getting a teddy bear necklace from him and a teddy bear for Christmas, and I remember thinking, that's just great. She called him a teddy bear.

"The first time I actually met him was at her house. I had spoken with him over the phone, but never met him until Greg and I went to help her in that home on New Durham Avenue. It was a painting party. She built him up, but he didn't live up to my expectations. First of all, I didn't hold him in high esteem anyway because of all the things that he had said he was going to do and did not do, stringing her along. No matter what we said to try to point out discrepancies, it didn't matter, she really cared for him. He would say things like, 'If you give me the $6,000 to do my siding, I'll leave my wife and we'll get married.' The $6,000 went, the siding never got done, he never left his wife. Or, 'If you go to trucking school with me and buy me this truck, we'll truck the country and it'll just be you and I.' She kept her end of the bargain, he did not. I just remember the 18-wheeler came in, and it was thousands of dollars and he wants one and she loves him desperately. Oh please. I was not happy with her with the decision to buy him a truck, I was angry with her, as friends can get angry. I really cared for Cathy and I just felt that this guy had gotten everything he wanted from Cathy and when he was done with her that he was going to be done with her and she again would be in pieces and the friends were going to have to come again and put them back together. She just didn't deserve that.

"She desperately wanted a child; he kept promising her, next month, next month. As it worked out, she was much better off. His wife was pregnant with twins at the time, and I remember thinking, okay, this guy is cute: he's got his wife pregnant with twins and this other woman on the side. That's wonderful. This was all before I had met him.

"They had been seeing each other for a couple years before I ever met him, but she would always talk to me about him. I was the safe person, I didn't live in the area. She could talk to me and I didn't know him. She used his name, his initials — G.B. — 'my Teddy Bear'.

"We went to help her paint her house, and in he walks with his twins! I thought, this is cute, you bring your kids to your girlfriend's house, that's exciting. He had lots of hair and a beard. And Cathy said, 'this is Gene.' My husband and I looked at one another; this is it? I just remember thinking that he was such a smooth talker and such a manipulator and kept telling her what she wanted to hear. He kept saying they were going to get married. It's always, we're going to get married, but it's next month. I gotta do this, and I gotta do this. Bail him out of this and bail him out of that. The day we met him, he didn't do anything while we were there. Gene just kind of popped in and just took off. She might have asked me what I thought and I probably lied. At that point I was pretty much ... I had just told myself that I wasn't going to down him anymore because the more we downed him, the more she clung to him.

"I can't recall a single thing he gave her, other than this Teddy Bear necklace. And I remember thinking it looks like a piece of shit.

"I knew when things had gone bad the day before because she would come in the next day with a long face. She was madly in love with him. In the beginning she talked about it with me, but then I just kept pointing out these discrepancies in his stories, and then after a while she just stopped. She didn't want to hear it. I caught on to him early on. Then again, I was not in love with him. I don't hold anybody in high esteem who leaves a pregnant wife to go bar hopping or whatever it was he was doing. Obviously the man is ill.

"Shortly after we met him, she came to visit me and she was very, very upset. It took me hours to get her calm. I don't remember the details exactly, it had something to do with he wasn't going to marry her, or they had had a fight or something, and she had finally come to the conclusion that this guy was a jerk. She had pretty much decided that she was going to leave and be with her sister and start a new life. I never saw her after the fact, but I remember her telling me the night she was extremely upset and spent the night with me, that this was another reason that she felt she needed to get away — they would have these fights and there would be physical fighting.

"She said she realized that he wasn't going to leave his wife. And I said, oh, about time! We had talked about her going down to (her sister) Mary Beth, that she really had no reason to stay here and I felt that it would be better for her to go and leave it behind and start anew. She could take the money, what she had, and go. And by the time she left, I was really quite sure that that's what she was going to do. I don't know what happened in between.

"About a month later, in June, I got a phone call from Cath. She wasn't happy; it was basically, 'Joy, I'm going to meet with Gene and I'm going to really try and get my money back, the $40,000, and I just want to ask him why.' And I said, 'Cathy please, don't do it. Don't meet with him because you'll never get that money.' A couple weeks before she's at my home crying, he's no good and on and on; and now we're going to meet with him and get our money back! I was just, come on, you're not. And I remember saying, 'Cathy, please, chalk it up to experience; I know it's a lot of money and it's difficult to walk away from it, but please, just walk away.' I had an uneasy feeling during this conversation. So we just went back and forth, it wasn't a long conversation. We had words and that was the last I heard from her.

"He gave her a ring when they got back together. It was probably with her money."

Voices — Donna Tokar

"I met her at lunch or dinner at Kennedy Hospital, through some people that knew her. Then we used to eat together at work. It must have been 1981. I really got friendly with her in 1982. I had her in my wedding in 1983. We got friendly real quick. She was a nice person.

"She used to stand there forever with her patients. She had such patience with them. She never got out of work on time. Only if she really tried. She would always stay and make sure everybody was comfortable one more time. I make sure my patients are comfortable an hour before I leave so I could do my notes and get out of there.

"Everybody used to sit together at lunch. She used to work on the floor that I was working on, and the people who worked with her sat with us; that's how I got to know her. She was working part time, she didn't have a steady floor, she just worked part-time.

"When I first met her — I can't remember how we started hanging around together — we started going out, she would go out with me every once in a while. The first thing I really remember her talking about was Gene Berta. She never called him Gene Berta, she always called him G.B., because he was married and she knew it.

"When I met him, I couldn't believe it was him after she went on about him; how wonderful he was and what a nice guy he was. She had been going out with him, I think that's what she said. She had gone out with him before and she always liked him, and then she had married her husband, and then they went their separate ways. That's what she said happened, but that's not what really happened. He chose his present wife, but she never said that. I found that out later, from her, though. And then she doesn't remember saying that, the other way. It was just blind love. She just absolutely adored him. Nobody could say anything bad against him. She didn't even care when he shaved his head. It didn't bother her, she didn't think it was odd, even though he looked horrible, he looked frightening. I said to her, why does he do that? She gave me some lame excuse about it just being for the summer. I said well, why doesn't he shave his face, too? That (beard) must be hot! He's ugly. He wasn't a nice person, so it made him look worse.

"I can't remember anything specific she said about him. She just talked about him, she had been meeting him, or seeing him. She went back to the first aid squad again, after her husband died. I guess that's how the whole thing started back up again. She went looking for him.

"When I met him the first time, I thought, 'I know this guy!' I knew that I knew him from somewhere. One of the first things I asked her was, does he shave his head? (He had hair then). I just knew him from squad things; I was on a different squad. His eyes looked evil to me. When I first met him, about five months after I met her, we were at a diner. Me and Cathy went to the diner, and he was supposed to meet us there, and he did. It was the Greenwood Manor in Woodbridge. Cathy and I used to go other places. Every once in a while we went out to a club; the Captain's Wheel. She was always very quiet when we went out. She wasn't like me. I was more apt to talk to everybody, but she didn't do that.

"I thought he was going to be this handsome, intelligent, ideal person. I remember thinking, before I met him, I'm really glad he treats her so well. Well, he practically ignored her, he didn't hardly talk to her; he was more interested at the time in talking to me. He was saying stuff like where do you work, what do you do, are you married? He was more interested in finding out about me. He didn't even sit next to her! We were sitting on opposite sides of the table, and then she got up and sat on my side and he sat across from us, which I thought was odd. She got up when she saw him come in. He just kind of motioned to me to slide in, and then she slid in next to me. He was asking me how did we know each other, what shift did I work, how old am I? He was specifically asking me stuff. Then I said, 'I know you, you know my father.' He said, 'who's your father?' I said, 'Don Rolley.' He said, 'oh yeah, I know him.'

"So I said to my father, 'Dad, isn't Gene Berta ... what do you think of him, don't you think he's strange?' He said, 'Yeah, why, you're not going to go out with him, you know he's married.' I said, 'Yeah, I know. I just saw him the other day.' Then it kind of all fit in; that's why she never told anybody his name, because he was married. That's why she would go by his initials.

"So I said to her, Cathy, I mentioned Gene to my father and he said he's married. Is that true? She said, he's separated. I said no, he's married, he's living with his wife. She goes, well, you know, they don't get along ... So I would say things like, did he leave yet? Did he leave yet? And she would get very defensive, she didn't want me thinking anything bad about him at all. So, I didn't say he was wonderful, but I didn't say anything bad about him, either. I didn't want to get her mad because she was very nice and she was happy.

"They used to fight often. But she was so defensive of him, but she never used to discuss their fights. She would be mad, and I would say, what's the matter. And she would say, you know. And then I would say, you know, I don't know about him. And then she would make excuses for him! She would always make excuses for him. She would make excuses for him if he cut her arm off. She would say it was an accident. I was afraid of him. He was scary.

"I don't know what he did to her, I never pressed her on that. But they used to really fight. She must have caught him or something, he was a real flirt. She would just think that that shouldn't be allowed. He was probably going out with a lot of girls. He really wasn't specific to any type; anybody who would have him, he would have. He was just strange. To bring your 12-year-old son to somebody's apartment and have sex with your girlfriend and leave your son in the living room, I think that's pretty odd. Or they used to take a shower together; the son was out there, he knew what they were doing. That kid idolized him, too. Everybody idolized him.

"She used to do everything for him. She used to have Playboy magazines delivered to her house for him. She'd always be at his beck and call. She probably believed he loved her.

"She didn't get along with her family. For some reason, she started talking to her sister. Then she went to see her, she hadn't before that. She didn't get along with her parents, they were alcoholics she said. She didn't have a good life. She always said I had a good life, my parents were good to me. She was always good to other people. I don't remember anybody saying anything negative about her."

Voices — Dennis Malinowsky

"Cathy was a very tender, caring person, very sweet. Her one problem was she couldn't keep her legs shut. She was everybody's girlfriend. She lost a lot of respect that way. I remember Gene telling me that he had asked her why she was so loose. She said, 'It was worth it just to be held for a little while.' That's sad.

"If you look at Cathy and Gene's relationship; when he wanted her, he wanted her, but if he wanted to go someplace else, he went. It's a basic story for any addictive type relationship. That's the story.

"She was clean, always had her stuff together, but she was very lonely and needed a lot of love. And she really wanted to share her life with somebody that she could call hers. And Gene picked up on it and just ... I mean, I think he cared for her, but not enough to do anything about the situation. I mean, he knew, why buy the cow when the milk's free? But with him, if the milk dried up, or if he didn't like that flavor that day, he'd just go to another cow.

"I dated her a couple times. Everybody did. Everybody who was on the first aid squad who was of legal age did. She never told me anything about her home life. Dawn Farnell told me stories about her mother. Cathy's mother telling Dawn's mother — they were, what, 12, 13 years old, 15 maybe — they were wearing mini skirts to school. 'Oh, your daughter's going to get in trouble wearing clothes like that ...' "

"I told Cathy one night, we were sitting at a diner, I said, 'Cathy, look; I don't want people to associate you and I together, get that through your head. I don't want your name and my name put together in any fashion, even in a sentence.' But that didn't deter her from pursuing me."

"I liked her, I thought she was a nice girl, she'd do anything for you. But I didn't have to respect her. But it wound up that she did have a problem, and she was taking care of it."

Eugene Thomas Berta

EUGENIA BERTA GAVE BIRTH to her fifth and final child, Eugene Thomas, on March 18, 1949. Baby Gene soon joined his father, Alexander, two older brothers and two older sisters on the family farm on Grove Avenue in then-rural Edison Township.

The Bertas were described by a friend as a family of farmers and hunters. Alexandria worked at the local Metuchen Library as a librarian. Gene's affection for weapons was probably spawned by his father, who was employed by the nearby Raritan Arsenal. Gene learned to shoot at an early age, practicing his art on squirrels and rabbits, which he would then skin. "Plinking" was the word he used to describe his past time.

Eugene Berta developed a need to be involved at an early age. At 8 years old, he, like many other American boys, became a Cub Scout, joining Pack 17 of Metuchen. At 10, he started a paper route with the help of his father — he was still one year too young to handle the route on his own. A year later he became a member of Boy Scout Troop 24 of Oak Tree, New Jersey, and was also made an altar boy and junior usher at his local church.

Gene Berta's involvement in safety-related organizations started when he was 12, when he joined the Iselin Safety Club.

During his junior high and high school years, young Berta joined a number of school and outside organizations and also started his own lawn mowing business; but it wasn't until he was 15 that he discovered the group that would prove so important a role in his later life, the Edison First Aid Squad.

At 15, Berta was still too young to officially join the organization, but that did not deter him from attending meetings and spending time at the squad headquarters. Upon turning 16, Berta became a member of the squad's Cadet Corps, putting all of his energies into learning life saving techniques. By the time he was 17, Gene was the first member of his Masons-sponsored group, the Order of De Molay, to win the "First-Aid Bar" of merit.

On a somewhat paradoxical note, it was also during that year that Gene Berta founded the Order's rifle team, which was later sanctioned by the National Rifle Association. Berta built the team's rifle range and, with the help of several other members, even wired it for electricity. Later in his 17th year, Berta was awarded a certificate of accomplishment by the N.R.A. for completing its safety and training course in small arms.

By the time he graduated high school, Gene Berta was considered a marksman, having been acknowledged as such by the Order of De Molay.

In 1968, at the age of 19, Berta married Kathleen Cook; the couple had their first and only child, Gene Jr., on August 5, 1969. Berta, at the time, was still maintaining the lawn and landscaping business that he had started six years earlier. Berta thought he could do better for his family by joining an armed service, so he applied to the United States Navy. His application was later denied for medical reasons.

By the time he was 20, Berta was thrust into positions of authority on several fronts; at home, he had a new family; he was by this time Scoutmaster of Troop 17 — the youngest scoutmaster ever at that time — ran his own business, became a senior usher at his church, and was elected a 3rd Lieutenant in the Rescue Squad Cadet Corps. The next year, 1970, those responsibilities increased — he became a member of the Order of De Molay Advisory Board, joined Mt. Zion Lodge #135, Free and Accepted Masons of Metuchen and, perhaps most important to him, was granted senior membership in the Edison Rescue Squad.

It was in 1973 that Berta received his first official public recognition: The Edison Township Kiwanis Club named him their Man of the Year for his work with the rescue squad. As tokens of the group's appreciation, Berta received a certificate and a toy ambulance.

At the same time his public life was reaching its zenith, a part of Berta's home life was falling apart: Troubles with his wife Kathleen finally resulted in divorce; she had sued Gene on charges of cruelty and was awarded custody of their son, Gene Jr.

In July of 1973, Berta expanded on his entrepreneurial instincts and founded Berta Electric, performing small jobs for local residents and business owners.

Some men meet women in bars, others in health clubs, still others prowl supermarket aisles. Gene Berta met his women on first aid calls.

It was while he and his rescue squad team were wheeling a patient into the John F. Kennedy Hospital emergency room that Berta first noticed the short, curly-haired E.R. secretary, Catherine Neal Tingley. The two became friendlier over a period of time; among the things Berta learned through their long and frequent conversations was that Tingley was separated from her husband, William Tingley, after he discovered she was having an affair with a hospital orderly. Catherine Tingley joined the rescue squad shortly after she met Berta.

About a year after meeting and beginning a relationship with Mrs. Tingley, Berta was responding to another call when he struck up a conversation with one of the patient's neighbors, Gail Holley Amaniera. A casual conversation revealed that Gene Berta used to deliver papers to Gail's family home in Edison. Never one to waste time, Berta asked her out that night, an offer which she quickly accepted. Like Catherine Tingley, Gail Amaniera was estranged from her husband and waiting for a divorce. But unlike Catherine, Gail had twin daughters to show for her union.

The remainder of Berta's life up until May of 1983 — and the relationship he had with two of the main women in it — is best described by the man himself, in his own words. Following are excerpts from an autobiographical outline authored by Gene Berta:

"III. Adult Years

Was dating Cathy Tingley and several (10-12) other women at this time. Was having a sexual, casual, caring, friendly and open relationship with all women involved during the time frame of 1972 through 1974.

Gradually stopped seeing, dating and sleeping (sex) with all but two women, these being Gail Amaniera and Cathy Tingley.

Set-up (sic) an apartment in Edison and lived with Gail and the twins as a family. At this time, Mr. Amaniera would occasionally visit his daughters at the apartment, which was confusing for the twins as they knew me as their "Daddy." The day before the twins' second birthday, September 8, 1975, was the last time Michael (Amaniera) saw the twins until approximately the fall of 1977. Legal custody and adoption was filed for, granted, and signed in the summer of 1978, just before the twins entered Kindergarten at Menlo Park School. Their records were all changed to read — Last Name — Berta.

Cathy Tingley, who was sure she would marry me, was devastated when she learned from Gail that we were living together. Furthermore, when several Squad members would get together and have a party, Cathy would invite friends (nurses, secretaries, clerks, etc.) from J.F.K. Hospital to come and during the course of the evening, have sex with most of the guests in attendance. About this time, M.K. also joined the squad for a brief period of time. M. had become engaged to a nurse at J.F.K., but during the engagement, his fiance learned of his affair with Cathy and broke the engagement. This nurse worked with Cathy Tingley's mother-in-law, Mrs. Tingley (Sr.), who subsequently learned of the affair from the nurse and passed the info onto Cathy's husband, who eventually divorced Cathy as a result of this affair. The parties occurred from time to time and sex with Cathy at these parties was common knowledge to both male and female members of the Squad, as Cathy would boast of her sex life.

When Gail and I had a brief separation in 1975 (early summer) I again stayed, and spent much time, at the Squad and saw Cathy quite a lot, while maintaining contact with Gail. When I was temporarily blinded in an accident at the Squad, I returned to Gail's apartment and stayed with her and the twins. Upon learning of all this, Cathy appeared at the door of Gail's apartment and demanded to see me. Gail rudely explained that I was in bed, resting and asleep, and that she, Cathy, could not come in nor see me and closed the door in her face. This infuriated Cathy. During my convalescence, Gail and I worked out the details of an open relationship and marriage and began making plans for same. Again, Cathy was devastated when Gail told her of our plans to marry in the near future.

On December 18, 1975, Gail and Gene were married in Perth Amboy, NJ in a private, civil ceremony. Witnesses were Mr. Bart J. Ruis and Mr. James Sumka.

IV. Adult Years - Married to Gail A. Berta

Gene, Gail and twins moved from garden apartment to rented house in November, 1975, in Edison, NJ.

We moved to larger house in Metuchen, NJ. (1976) At approximately this time, Gene was having an affair with M.S. of Edison, NJ. During this time, Gail was pregnant and we had another couple over for the night, for partner swapping and group sex. During Fall of 1976, Gail miscarried a son at end of first trimester (3 months of term). (M. and Gail both pregnant at same time).

(In 1977) M.S., who was also seeing two (2) other men sexually, became pregnant and delivered a son at J.F.K. Hospital. She stayed with Gail and I for awhile during her pregnancy, and subsequently put baby up for adoption immediately after birth. She informed me that she thought the baby to be mine, and in turn informed Gail of this. Gail suggested that we try to adopt the baby. The baby, unfortunately, was already adopted thru agency in Woodbridge, NJ.

Gail Berta and R. had an affair. Gail checked-in (sic) by phone each duty night at Squad, prior to going to R.'s apartment for remainder of evening.

(1977)

John Warner married Catherine Tingley at St. Luke's in Metuchen, NJ. (1977)

Berta Electric building up into lucrative business venture. (1977)

We moved to a two-family house in Metuchen, NJ. I continued holding various executive and line officers positions in Squad. (1978)

Began doing work at John Warner's Exxon station. (Electrical repairs).

Adopted twins Aug. 1978 before Kindergarten.

Late summer, we had K. and E.V. over for a weekend of partner swapping (Friday through Monday).

We bought house at 7 East Walnut St., Metuchen, NJ and began repairs immediately in October, 1979.

Gail became pregnant with Winter - Aug. 1979.

Gail and I attended the wake of John Warner - Feb. 1980.

Daughter born - Winter Marie Berta, on April 30, 1980.

Cathy Warner was visiting Connie Baran on semi-weekly basis and on one such visit to Squad, she said hello to me and chatted for quite awhile. She then saw Connie coming and they left together.

After several brief conversations at Squad over period of several weeks, Cathy and I went to diner for coffee and conversation. We discussed getting together on occasion for talk and whatever else happened.

After many months of occasional visits, our relationship grew closer, our visits together more often, and Cathy was saying she loved me on a regular basis.

Marriage with Gail was shakey (sic).

Affair with Cathy continued and progressed in closeness and caring. (1981).

Daughter born - Amber Alexis Berta - October 16, 1981. Gail had tubal ligation at this time.

Cathy was once again devastated when I told her of Gail's pregnancy and soon delivery date during Gail's last trimester. Cathy was so upset, she called and spoke to most of her friends about this knowledge. She also contacted J.F.K. Mental Health to set up counselling (sic) sessions.

When I informed Cathy of Amber's birth, she literally fell apart. She broke down crying and stated the baby should be hers, not Gail's. How could I punish her like this? This emotional state continued for several weeks, and eventually faded with time.

On June 23, 1981, while returning from California to New Jersey with a 42,000 lb. load of Honey Dew Melons, my co-driver lost control of the tractor-trailer truck we were in, drove over a low embankment and overturned the entire rig. After being taken to a satellite hospital in Casa Grande, Arizona, we were both transported by ambulance to Phoenix International Airport and subsequently flown to J.F.K. International Airport by our employer, Paul's Trucking Corp. of Woodbridge, NJ. We were both transferred and transported by the Squad ambulance to our own municipalities for follow-up medical care. I was admitted to John F. Kennedy Medical Center with an A-C separation of my left shoulder, which required surgical repair.

The shoulder was repaired thru open-reduction surgery by Dr. Jesus Medina of Edison, NJ. After the incision was made and all bones were realigned to the socket, Dr. Medina inserted two (2) stainless-steel pins for support, immobility and healing. These were later removed by Dr. Medina and I was released from his care for the injury and repair. My convalescence was then taken over by Dr. Caroline McCagg at the Robert Wood Johnson Rehabilitation Center of Edison, NJ. Dr. McCagg prescribed a therapy program which consisted of two days a week, for several months.

In December, 1981, I was again elected Captain of the Squad.

Returned to work at Paul's Trucking Corp. in March, 1982. Worked there for approximately two (2) months and was then layed-off (sic) due to work slowdown.

During these weeks of my truck driving, a friend worked for Berta Electric. He covered all service calls and worked with me on my days off from trucking.

Cathy decided she would go for her NJ Articulated Vehicle license at Action Academy. She completed her training approx. late May, early June ë82.

Cathy was in process of looking at 125 Durham Avenue, talking to contractors about needed repairs to the house, and discussing sale price with Carol Carlin of the MacPherson Real Estate Agency.

Carol Carlin had originally called me about 125 Durham Avenue, as it was listed as a "handyman's special". Carol had called Gail and I on several occasions with information about "Handyman Specials" in the Metuchen-Edison-Woodbridge-Highland Park areas, and had taken us to some of these "specials". Our intentions were to obtain a second mortgage on 7 East Walnut Street, purchase, repair and sell a "special" and then pay off the two (2) mortgages on 7 East Walnut Street from the profits of this transaction. This would allow us to finish repairs and renovations on our house, sell it, and be able to afford a farm and land on which to live, and raise our children, off the land.

I contacted Michael Mandell and Charlie Weissenburger for repair guesstimates on 125 Durham Avenue. I also spoke to Cathy about loaning me the cash to buy said house. After receiving projected costs from Mike Mandell (Plumber) and Charlie Weissenburger (Carpenter), I told Cathy it would not be feasible for me to buy and repair house and then attempt to sell it at a profit as the market value would be less than costs incurred thru purchase and repair.

However, Cathy had received a notice from her landlord that her lease was due for renewal, and that a rent increase would also take place at time of renewal. We then discussed the pros and cons of her purchasing the house, and repairing it and living in it, versus staying in her apartment and paying over $500 per month for something she could not sell, nor recoup any of her monies paid out. We discussed this matter on several occasions, one of which she met Carol Carlin who made arrangements to show Cathy the house, property(s) and rental bungalow located to the rear of main house.

I suggested to Cathy that we could save her some money by doing some of the repairs and/or renovations through Berta Electrical Contractors. This would obtain various materials, supplies, or services at "contractor's cost" for which she would then reimburse Berta Electric. (i.e. - backhoe digger for removing old oil tank and grading entire property.)

After considering the above mentioned pros and cons, estimates from contractors, etc., Cathy decided to purchase, repair and renovate, and live in the house at 125 Durham Avenue. Metuchen NJ. As stated above, repairs commenced soon after the closing proceedings, and continued through the next several months.

During the renovations, I spoke to the owners of See-More Television & Appliance Center of Metuchen, N.J. and informed them that I was working on the Durham Avenue house with Mike Mandell, and would need a full selection of appliances for this house. I asked if they would work a good price deal, better than usual, for the homeowner due to the large quantity of appliances. I was assured that a good price deal would be worked out when the time came. Subsequently, Cathy and I visited this store, and Gilbert conducted the sale to Cathy Warner for all appliances needed. (i.e. - kitchen stove, refrigerator, dishwasher, two (2) air conditioners, clothes washer & dryer & dehumidifier.) All of these items were then price checked at Tops Appliance City of Edison, NJ. The prices at Tops were again based on quantity of items and contractor's cost as they were at See-More's. While bottom line total cost at Tops was approximately $20 to $30 less expensive than that of See-More's, I recommended to Cathy that she deal with See-More TV & Appliances as their follow-up and customer service were very good.

In December, 1982, I was re-elected to the office of Captain for the Rescue Squad.

I informed Cathy that I would soon be getting separated from Gail and staying at the Squad House and occasionally staying at her house.

I separated from Gail for three (3) weeks in January, 1983. After several discussions with Gail about our current situation, I returned to my house, my wife, and my family. This decision was made by myself, after realizing that I loved my wife and children and wanted them more than my current relationship and a future (long term) with Cathy Warner.

In early May, 1983, I was involved in an auto accident which totally destroyed my Ford van and broke my right wrist and several ribs. I was sent home on the 10th, and told to return on the 11th, for an arm/wrist cast as the swelling should be reduced by then.

When I returned on the 11th for the cast, my entire rib cage shifted back into its proper position, causing severe trauma. This condition resulted in my being admitted to J.F.K. Medical Center for four (4) days. It was during this admission period that tests revealed approx. 8 multiple rib fractures.

While being admitted on the 11th, my wife returned to the hospital to take me home, and was informed by Dr. Medina that he was admitting me for further tests."

Voices — Dennis Malinowsky

"I knew Gene since we were in the third grade. We lived down the street from each other, on Grove Avenue in Edison. I don't recall actually where we met. But I originally moved to Edison and I had come in the middle of third grade. Somewhere between the 3rd and 5th grade is where I met him. He was really close with another guy, Kenny. They were really tight.

One of my first recollections was when we couldn't have been any more than 9 or 10 years old. We were together for a while as friends, and then there were some problems between Kenny and myself, having a little brawl in my kitchen in the summertime. The feud started out between Gene and I, but Kenny was there to finish the job. As I recall, there was something about newspapers. We used to play softball between Tommy Rees' uncle's house and the Semenza's, right off the corner of Grove Avenue and Twin Oaks Drive. There was a skinny little lot there and we used to play softball. I remember something had transpired and we were busting Gene's chops . . . it was something about the newspapers Gene delivered and we wouldn't let him go near them. There were only five or six papers there. I remember his father came and got them, and then it ended up with me and Kenny rolling on my kitchen floor. I remember my brother Bradley was there. It was kid's stuff, it meant nothing. Maybe it started with a water gun or something like that. It was absolutely nothing that anyone would take note of except a 9- or 10-year-old.

"I remember after a while Kenny and Gene started talking about these Mafia families and being rather proud of their Italian heritage. They were mentioning various Italian names. As far as I know, they could have been anyone walking down the street; what did I know, a Polish kid from Perth Amboy? Later on, 20 years later, you find that Gene was spreading stories about being a Mafia hit man. I saw more and more coincidences of that nature: Gene told me that his father had to leave Italy because of the Black Hand, they were after him. Gene also told me that his father had made him head of the house, head of the family; this was after the first set of heart problems.

"Gene's mother ran the house, but Gene's father, being the man, was the head of the house. Now, that in itself is a contradiction in terms. And basically, I think that's when some of the problems started with Gene. Gene was the youngest of the family. His brothers were out of the house by the time he was reaching puberty, they were already married and had moved away. He was brought up with his father, who was considerably more laid back; his mother, who was the disciplinarian, and his two sisters. The sisters were older than him, so, if they were like his mother, it was like being raised by three mothers. Maybe that's what started this; Gene hearing his father telling him, 'yeah, women're just out there to nail' and then maybe questioning, if he's this macho man, how come the mother and sisters are taking the lead? And if they're taking the lead and giving the discipline and dad isn't, did they take it away from him? Maybe Gene decided he was gonna get back at women for that.

"If he looked up to his father as being the head of the family, and his mom was the vocal head, the one who would be seen as being the head of the family, I often wondered if his hatred and use of women did not actually come from his family life. He would tell me, like, if mom was making sauce and you went over and took the pot top off, he said, 'she ain't big, and she ain't strong, but them knuckles are bony and when she whacks you across your face, you know it.' You got the feeling from him that she was the one who ruled the roost. Pop was inside, enjoying the baseball game, and mom was always the go-getter, keeping things organized.

"Gene, as early as 10 or 11 years old . . . when you start to reach puberty, you get into that 'Johnny Appleseed' time in your life with girls, and Kenny and Gene and myself were exactly the same. But it had become an obsession with Gene. He was always looking for another conquest, and that's all it was. Gene always said that sex was just sex, it had nothing to do with love. In that way, he was giving himself an excuse, but he was also giving them an excuse.

"Gene and I had shared girlfriends, Cathy was one of them. It was always funny, wherever Gene was, there was a loose woman nearby, you could count on that. It was funny back then 'cause there wasn't anything you could catch that you couldn't get rid of. The worst that could happen is that you could go to a doctor and be embarrassed and get a shot of penicillin, and that's the end of it. Not that that ever occurred.

"At 11 or 12 years old, I think we had parted, because we had gotten into a debate about his newspaper route, or something. And then we really didn't get back in each other's company until we joined the first aid squad. And by then, Gene's life had already been formulated. Gene had married his first wife, Kathy, and had his first son, Gene, Jr. They had an apartment in Trafalgar Gardens, off Oak Tree Road.

"Gene and Kathy started having problems; she was very laid back and prissy, a little prissy. She was a little laid back and not dead set into reality as Gene was. He was from a family of farmers and killing and skinning rabbits, and more worldly than someone who was brought up in suburbia. I remember one occasion where little Gene was running a temperature, and Kathy could not bring herself to using a rectal thermometer on the boy, it was just beyond her. However, he had been running a high fever. And Gene came home from work, and said, 'what's the boy's temperature?' That was the term that he and his father both used, 'the boy'. Not to mean it in a derogatory sense, it was just a word. And she said, 'he's okay.' 'Yeah, but what's his temperature?' 'Don't worry about it, he's okay.' And the long and the short of it was that she never took his temperature. The boy could (the boy, I'm right back to it again), Gene Jr. could have really been physically harmed had the temperature gone up again, because she wouldn't have known.

"Gene at one point had a landscaping business. This was right after high school. I helped him out sometimes, but right away I started to find out that working with Gene didn't pay. Because if you went for supplies with him, and it took him three hours, well, he didn't count that as work. 'But you were taking up my time, and you stood there bullshitting with the guy for God knows how long!' But that was a lesson well-learned. I still remember sometimes working with Gene, and afterwords we would go into his mom's house, wash up, sit down at the kitchen table and have something to eat. The window was always open, the breeze was coming through . . . it was a very warm, homey atmosphere.

"After his landscaping business, I think he was working for Metropolitan Talc in South Plainfield, in the laboratory. What had actually transpired I think was that his wife, Kathy's, father worked there. Gene became an electrician working in that job. He did electrical work and he did some talc sampling, just maintenance. This was about the same time that he and Kathy were starting to have problems. But for the year or two years that he worked at the plant where his father-in-law worked, it seemed as if he was holding down a pretty decent job. But it seemed to get worse and worse as time went on. He started to work for American Hospital Supply as a trucker, and he was let go from there for sleeping on the job, having too many automobile accidents. I don't recall why he left Metropolitan Talc.

"He always wanted to be a leader, but never had it within himself to be a leader. He was 13 years old and never made it to the major leagues in baseball, he was never athletic. He got involved in Boy Scouts and then with a church group, the Order of DeMolay group, and he was always the big kid with the little kids, again, a power thing. And that seemed to be the beginning. After that, it was one woman after another after another. And these woman had herpes and one thing after another, and he was still jumping the shit out of them.

"Gene was a slob, but he was a meticulous slob! This is Gene walking out of the house: He'd walk out the front door and lock the door with the keys, pick up his keys — he had two huge rings of keys — and he'd fix them until they were right, and then he'd put them on his belt. And then he'd walk toward the bannister or whatever, and he'd pick his foot up and he'd pull up his sock, and he'd untie his shoe and tie it again, and fix his other sock and tie that boot again. Then he'd reach into his pocket and pull out a handkerchief and wipe the perspiration off his face, fold up the handkerchief and put that back into his pocket, properly. He was very very meticulous about the way he kept things. Then he'd fix the dog's chain when it was tangled. It would take him 10 minutes to get out of the house!

"And even getting out of his truck! Everything in his truck, was put in a place in a proper order; that's why it took him a half hour to get out of the truck. He would open the doors and he had to fix everything and get it right, before he moved on to the next thing. That's what stopped him from getting ahead.

"He would be like that whenever he was at a job. He spent more time putzing than he would working. That's another way he would get into a rut. His mother was very meticulous. If you were to look in his drawers, everything was the way it was supposed to be. If I was at his apartment, and used an ashtray, he knew it. His house was a wreck, and he had fleas, from the dogs, but that was because of Gail, in his opinion. She was the wife: wife is house, man is work. But, he never worked, he was always out finding another woman. It's amazing, absolutely amazing.

"There was another girl from Sayreville that Gene got pregnant, this was back in the '70s, before Gail and before Cathy. She wanted to have an abortion, and I went down to the parents of a girl I was seeing, Jan, and we explained things to them, so they let Jan stay with Gene and I at his apartment, because in the morning we were leaving to take her into New York. But she opted out last minute, and quite evidently she had the child. I saw her a number of years later in a car wash.

"He had no problem with getting women pregnant; the more kids the merrier.

"I was the best man at his marriage to Kathy. I remember standing in the anteway just before he walked out. They hadn't started the bridal march yet, and I looked at Gene and said, 'Hey, bud, this ain't gonna fuckin' make it. So let's drop it here, we'll get in the car, we'll book out to your brother's place in Ohio, and fuck it.' And he said, 'No, bud, I'm gonna go through with this and give it a shot.' All you had to do was know both of them and you knew it wasn't going to work. He was hard core rough, and she was prim and proper. They were just miles and miles apart.

"When he divorced his first wife, she charged cruelty. He was out fucking around. He slapped her around sometimes. He hit her around a couple of times. He would always start to play, and then the play would get rougher and rougher and then it became a power thing, until it got really rough and somebody got hurt or he got pissed off. I remember him telling me about one time where he and his wife were having some kind of argument in the kitchen. The kitchen was very narrow and walked out into the dining area. They were having words and he had turned his back, and she was cooking. He had noticed that there was a knife on the counter next to where she was cooking. He told me that he saw out of the corner of his eye her reach in that direction and he felt something on his back. What it wound up to be was a wooden spoon, she had the spoon part in her hand and the other part hit him in the back. When he felt that, he just reacted; he turned around and backhanded her. He said it was the old story of the two sounds; me hitting her and her hitting the floor, ha ha ha. Gene wanted to be the ruler, but Kathy knew that you couldn't rule if you couldn't get your act together. I think there were problems even at work, and Kathy's father must have been talking to her mother and I think her grandmother.

"He was in the process of divorcing Kathy, he left the apartment and he got himself an apartment in Elizabeth, working at St. Elizabeth's Hospital or Muhlenberg, and that's when he met Cathy Warner; she was a nursing student or had just gotten out of nursing school. He had brought her back to this area, or she followed him back to this area. Cathy was married and then divorced very young and very quickly. Cathy then had come into this area and Gene was seeing her; would go over to her apartment. Cathy was so much in love with him, she would do anything for him. So if they were around a group of his friends, and he said, 'hey take them on, they're my buddies, go ahead, go with them,' she would. It was no problem for her.

"Finally, Gene and Cathy had stopped seeing each other, because Gene had met his now wife, Gail, and Cathy met John Warner. When she got married to John, I thought that was the perfect couple, because he'd do anything for her, and she would reciprocate in kind. She was still carrying a torch for Gene, though.

"I guess she figured, well, John's not Gene, but he's almost everything I want in a man, so you take what you can get. Perfection doesn't exist. They were happy. When she was married to John at that time, she was his. She wasn't seeing Gene on the side, that I know of. I think he would have told me. That would have been another one of Gene's conquests, to prove that he was a man.

"We used to call him Big John. He was very very special. You ever crossed him, you were in deep shit, but you really had to go a way to cross him. And Big John was big. Anyway, Dawn Farnell told me she remembers speaking with Cathy just before Cathy was going to make a decision with regard to who she wanted: 'John would give me a family, John would give me a home, John is a good man, there's no problem with money, he works. Gene doesn't work, he's out whoring around all the time, he treats me like shit . . . but I love Gene.' It wound up that Gene stayed with Gail and Cathy married John, and then John died.

"I remember going to John's funeral and a day or two after the funeral, as I recall it, I was working as a sanitary inspector in Metuchen and I saw Gene — Gene and I would run into each other because he'd be conducting his business as an electrician, and be in his blue Ford van, and he'd be driving up one way on a street and I'd be driving the other, and we'd just say hello to each other — he stopped, beeped the horn and turned around, and I'm thinking, *'what the fuck's the matter with this guy?'* He says, 'Guess who's back in town? It's Tingley!' He had already been over there, John wasn't even cold in the grave yet!

"And that's when Gene started getting money from her. Quite evidently there was a lot of money that had crossed hands. She paid off the van, and she was handing him money continuously. That was after John's death, because John had left Cathy a sizeable fortune.

"This brings back another story: I knew these guys named Pete and Chuck, they were cousins. Pete was working over at an electronics supply house in South Plainfield. He had a cousin who had a hair salon. Gene did some electrical work there and we got to know each other, and we went down there and one night, we were just sitting around drinking some beer after the shop had closed, laughing and telling stories, and Pete told us a story about this guy who was a con artist, who took money from this woman and somehow Pete played a small role in the deception. And I really think that may have been where Gene may have gotten the idea to run this scam on Cathy. He may have already been borrowing money from her, but maybe this put the twinkle in his eye. A little seed in his mind to go for bigger and better things, I don't know.

"Gene was strapped, I mean busted flat. There were times when he didn't have a toilet in the house because the toilet broke and they were going in buckets and stuff. There were times when he would have five and 10 dollars and he would go down to the Big T Plaza on Route 1 and get diesel to put into the furnace so they would have heat and hot water for the night.

"He never got around to finishing things. His work as an electrician . . . when he would wire a main panel, it was beautiful, that's how well done it was; it was actually a work of art. But it took him a horrendously long time to do it, and he could not charge for it. Half the time he didn't finish writing out what he had spent on the job, so he really didn't have the records, the guy didn't get charged right, and it wound up that come the end of the week, there was nothing left after expenses. But if someone were there to guide him and show him, do this and do this and do that, and if he could take orders, he would have made out well. I remember going with him up to Big T and getting five gallon cans. I knew he was strapped; I remember having conversations with Chuck, saying, 'I'll give him the money, but I won't loan it to him. If I loan it to him, I ain't gonna get it back and it's gonna stir the shit up.' And I told him, 'Look Chuck, you ain't exactly wealthy, do what you can do if you can help the guy out, but I don't know where the hell he's gonna get the money from, but he's got to learn a lesson. He's got to come on hard times and maybe straighten his act out.' Quite evidently, that's when he started getting more and more out of Cathy.

"I remember sitting with Dawn (because Dawn and I had gone out quite a while) and Gene, in Cathy's apartment, this is after John's death, knowing that she was teetering on the edge of going off the deep end, she was very close to padded room time. She was seeing a 'classical Freudian psychologist, couch and all', that's the way she described him. After about a year and a half, two years, she had started to learn how to say no. At any rate, sitting there with Dawn, we told Gene, look, she's on the edge, don't be playing with her mind, because she's gonna kill herself, we know it. And he said no, I honestly do love her, I really do. I remember him saying that like it was yesterday.

"Gene was an amiable kind of person. He knew people in high school that I went to high school with, that I didn't know. And knew them well. That's one of the reasons why he started to fall down on that electrical business, because if he went to a deli, he would see somebody he knew, he would find a woman to talk to. He would go over to Cathy's house for lunch and wind up being there all afternoon. He'd take Cathy with him and they'd wind up fooling around in the truck, or wherever. Most of the time he spent cleaning and picking up.

"He tried to get into the Navy, but they rejected him because he had trick knees. He had to get orthotics and they wouldn't let him in.

"He talked Kenny and this other guy, Emil, into going down for the physical. And Emil and Gene didn't get in, and Kenny got sucked in! They told me a story and Kenny swears to it: You know you go for your physical and everybody's in line? Emil was a laid back kind of guy and not really paying attention. So the sergeant or whomever said, bend over and spread your cheeks. And Emil said, what? And he said, bend over and spread your cheeks! What? The guy jumped into his shit, and Emil bent over and did like this (inserts fingers into his mouth and spreads his cheeks). There they are, standing bear assed naked, laughing like horses asses!

"Gene could be bullied. He was not what you would call a very physical person. He was a menacing sight, if you didn't know him, and maybe that's how he got along. He always wanted to be a man's man. I never saw him get bullied, but I saw the results of it. When he had moved out of the apartment he had with his first wife, he started giving some guy who lived above him some shit; the guy didn't have rugs and he could hear him clomping around, and the guy would complain that Gene's stereo was too loud, and Gene hauled off and tried to give him a shot, but the guy broke his nose.

"Gene was a good friend, a real good friend. I could tell you right now that I would trust him with my life to this day, without hesitation."

Voices — Pat Bauer

"I didn't like Gene when I first met him; I thought he was very slovenly in appearance, I thought he was very dominant, very forceful. His appearance drove me insane. He was so sloppy. Sometimes he shaved his head. And when you come from somebody who was so clean cut, and my Dad was always so clean cut and so appearance conscious, and my husband John was a Marine. The first Rescue Squad meeting I sat in at was January of '82. They bring you down and you're interviewed by the trustees and the captain; they just ask you questions, what are you going to give to the squad, how much time do you have, what are your qualifications, why do you want to join the squad? Gene asked me if I was any relation to Alena Bauer, I turned to him and said, how do you know my daughter? He said, I didn't mean to upset you, she dates my brother-in-law, Vin Nuzzo. When Gene asked me if I was any relation to Alena, I thought, what is this big huge, scrounge doing asking about her?

"I started to change my opinion of him after a while, I started to appreciate that the guy knew what he was doing. He did know what he was doing. I went almost a whole year on that squad before I got into the EMT class. But then he taught us advanced first aid. But other than the fact that he was an excellent teacher with a lot of knowledge, he never did anything to single me out. He showed me where I was wrong with certain bandages, or showed me how to do it the right way, but it was just like the interest of a squad captain.

"There were disputes about how the squad was run, but a lot of it was between Gene, George Taylor and this one guy. And this one guy, they used to call him God; he walked around there like he thought he was God: this was going to be done this way and this was going to be done that way. At one point, Gene had asked me to be a trustee, it was prior to my having anything to do with him. He said we need somebody who has a little bit of intelligence and can make a decent decision. So I became a trustee, and I was trying to work with this guy, and I could hear the hassles all the time were between him and George and Gene. I wasn't really on the squad long enough to form an opinion. I was a temporary trustee, just filling in for somebody who was out on extended sick leave. And then when I started dealing with this guy, it was like, what's he pulling here? I realized that the guy they were calling God, in my opinion, was pulling some fancy stuff. He used to order things for himself and have it billed through the squad, so he used to take advantage of the squad discount. He'd pay the squad back, but usually the company would have to chase the squad for a long time. So it was like if you didn't know the part was actually going to him, you would wonder, is he trying to screw the squad or did he actually take anything from the squad. He was the one whose certifications weren't up to date; he was a first aid instructor, but he would pass people who shouldn't have passed, stupid things. Then, when I became an instructor, I would say things like, I'm not passing this guy, and he would say, no, you have to because he's so and so's son. And I would say no, he didn't pass the test. He used to say to me, you better learn to play the game. So it was things like that that made me realize that God had it out for Gene and George. So the side I kind of leaned to was theirs. They may have been tough, but they would go through it and say, your CPR has to be renewed, get a new card, take a course. They were on top of stuff like that. So there was somebody who really wasn't that good at first aid, who was knocking two guys who really were superb.

"They were too tough. They used to say they ran the squad with an iron fist and yes, they did. There were two guys who were supposed to be on duty one night, and who had never shown up for duty, but showed up to a call drunk. They had taken a walkie talkie from the building. There were five people on the crew and three of us had gone out on the call, which was a legal crew. It was like, here we are trying to do our thing and here are these two guys giggling a mile a minute, high as kites. That's the one time they say that Berta took this one guy and literally threw him up against the truck. I didn't see it, but if it did happen, it was warranted.

His judgment in a lot of respects was excellent: he made sure the truck was right, he made sure the first aid supplies were there, he made sure everybody's training was there. He participated in a lot of squad activities, like he tried to make the squad the best thing he could.

Voices — R.

"I first met Gene when I joined the squad in 1972. He was an easygoing guy. Gene is a likeable person. He'd do anything for anybody. When I first met him, he was divorced from his first wife. Then I met Cathy Warner because Gene was going out with her. And then she joined the squad, and then six months later, Gail joined the squad, and then he married Gail. And he was fooling around with Cathy, I knew that, that was obvious. I knew he was going out with Cathy, and he was going out with Gail at the same time. And while he was going out with them, he was going out with at least four others that I knew of. That was Gene. His reputation, that's the way he was. First aiders, we're all different, we come from all walks of life; you ignore things unless it's too obvious in the organization, then you try to get it out of the organization.

"He worked when he wanted to work. He was a decent electrician, supposedly. He did my back porch for me. In fact, he was dating Cathy at that time, because Cathy used to come over with him when he was doing the wiring. That was sometime in the '70s.

"Everybody knew he chased everything with a skirt. Gene chased women left and right. If a new woman came on the squad, he was after her. I don't care if she was short, tall, skinny or fat, he chased them, period. It was just a conquest, that's all it was. Gene was never a good-looking guy. He had a line. I don't know what it was.

"Gene was very animalistic with women. He treated women like they were his play toys, like he could do anything he wanted with any woman he wanted, in front of anybody. I saw him walk up to Gail before they were married and say, hey look at this, and squeeze her breasts, in front of other people. You don't want to see that, you don't need that. I'm a lot older than Gene, figured he was ignorant, and let it go at that.

"Berta caught Patty Bauer at the perfect time, and he had a line of crap, he seemed to catch any girl at the perfect time. I remember, there was a guy on the squad years before Patty come on. He broke up with his wife, and they did eventually get a divorce. But first they got separated. The day after they got separated, Berta was over there with her. If I had walked out on my wife, he'd be knocking the door over trying to get in. That's the way he was.

"We had this nurse on, I can't remember her name, but my God, he hounddogged her so bad, she finally just quit. And of course the young girls, in plain English, he got them. He just got them. He'd wear them down, beat them down, but he got them. That's why I keep saying Patty was a class act, he just got to her at the right time. There was no other way.

"I don't even know what he would do. All of a sudden he would be leaving with one of them for whatever reason. And then of course he had a few slobs. There was a girl he fooled around with, she happens to be happily married today, she wasn't a slob, she was a nurse. Her parents threw her out of the house when she got pregnant. Gene and Gail took her in, knowing that it was Gene's kid. And then Gene and Gail wanted to adopt the kid. After that, she got back into her house, he was still chasing her. This is after she lived in his house. How he reaches them, I have no idea.

"I don't know how much Gail knew about him when they first went out because, again, Gene's got a line of crap. But as time went on, she knew where he was at, but it didn't seem to bother her.

"So that weekend, he went away with Patty, and the same day he came back, he took his family to the seashore. And that was totally out of character for Gene.

"Nobody knew that he was seeing Patty. I went to EMT school with

Patty, and I never even knew. Patty was a classy person, Gene was not. We used to go to school together, and finally, I stopped waiting on them. I said to my wife, 'I can't wait for Gene and Patty, they get there so late, I didn't get any pre-study time.' But for a good six or seven weeks initially, we were going to school together. But I didn't suspect that anything was happening at all.

"He was a top-of-the-line first aider. He could learn anything, and he could teach. We had one call on Grove Avenue, this guy was driving drunk and he hit a tree or something. His left leg was just about detached, and he was trapped in the car, and Gene went right in through where the windshield was and got him. Six months later the guy walked out of the hospital; I didn't think he would walk because the skin was just hanging there. I remember I was just handing Gene pillows and Gene was just putting pillows between the guy's legs, and then trying to put some kind of a bandage over it. We wrapped him in a sheet and pulled him in the sheet right up through the windshield, and then we put a board under him. The guy was so drunk, he didn't even know he was hurt. And there was a cop on the call, we called him Cookie. Anyway, he was standing there and this victim says, what are you staring at? There's nothing wrong with me!

"Gail was always a tough person. She had a pretty good body. She was like the kind who didn't need anybody. She looked like the kind who if you crossed her would kick the hell out of you.

"As captain of the rescue squad, Gene was a nice guy, you could get away with murder. You didn't have to worry about getting in trouble with Gene. But it wasn't run like an organization. Even though we're all volunteers, there has to be somebody in charge and people have to know there are certain things expected of them at all times. And once you start getting lax in these areas, it's no good. That's the way it was with Gene.

"I'd go on a call with my crew, I'd let my crew do all the work and I'd support them, that gives them an opportunity to learn. But when you go on a call with Gene, Gene was always doing it all. You can only learn so much by watching Joe Blow. At some point, you got to put this to work, too.

"And you can't set rules and then break them, and Gene broke every rule there was. You can't have weapons in the room, and he had a shotgun; there's no such thing as sex in the building, and Christ, he lived with it;

you're not supposed to smoke pot, and he would. Needless to say, we got a lot stricter in a lot of areas (after he left).

"Gene wanted to be captain for the power of it. Mermelstein was captain when I joined, and Gene was the assistant. Mermelstein stayed captain for a few years, and then Berta became captain while I was on the squad, and then he was gone and then George Taylor became captain, and it became a Berta-Taylor thing for years. I left in 1979, didn't come back until '83, and when I came back it was still Berta and Taylor.

"Gene's attitude was, you do what I say, and that's it. You didn't question Gene, you just did what he said. If you didn't like it, he'd suspend you. But, again, he was so lackadaisical in so many other things. It was not the kind of organization you would let your daughters join when he was captain. If they did join, and you heard some of the stuff that went on, you'd make them quit.

"He had no morals. He enjoyed being a hero, he enjoyed being a leader. Other than that, I guess he felt he could do no wrong, he could do what he wanted to do. And he did for most of his life. Even when he was married, he did what he wanted.

"The Parsonage Diner is where the squad members hung out in those days, the squad was down the street from there. You'll find our squad at the Parsonage Diner even now. I know he was always there. One time, there was four or five of us there, we were there before the other members got there, we were done eating. In the meantime, maybe 10 or 12 more come in. So they got a table with us and they ordered, so Gene says, 'I'll pay the tab.' So, fine, this guy's being a sport. I forget who it was at our table that give him the tab, but then Gene got the tab from the other table. Ours was nine or 10 bucks, but the other table was probably about 25 dollars or so. So Gene takes that tab, crumbles it up and throws it on the floor. When I heard it, I was fit to be tied. It was embarrassing."

Voices — Donna Tokar

"He didn't like me. After a while, whenever I would go to Cathy's house, he would leave. And I said, 'Cathy, what's up with this? He doesn't even stay in the same room with me?' She said, 'you know, he didn't expect you to come over and we were supposed to go out.' I said, 'I'll leave,' and she said, 'no, that's all right'. But it wasn't that, he probably just didn't like me. He was a jerk. Like he would say, 'when's the last time you went out', or, 'when's the last time you had a date?' you know what I mean? When's the last time I had sex? you know what I mean? I was like, believe me, I don't need you! I had been engaged, too. And I used to say, he's the greatest guy. And he was, he was so nice to me. And I think that used to aggravate Gene, that I used to talk so nice about my husband. Gene wanted everybody to fall on the ground before him and just think that he was wonderful. He wanted everybody to be like Cathy. So many people were like that with him.

"I don't understand how he could stay at Cathy's house for so long. What was he telling his wife? That he was at the rescue squad on call?

"She used to think going with him in his truck was the greatest thing. They used to sleep in the cab. They used to go to different states, that's what she used to tell me. Everything she told me I took with a grain of salt. He was probably horrible to her, but she never used to complain about him. If anybody didn't know him, they would think that Gene Berta was a saint. She would tell them and they would believe it.

"They used to go look for trucks. The price was ridiculous, I said, 'don't even think about it, how are you ever going to afford that?' She said, 'I have money.' And she said you could do so much in it, you can sleep in it . . . I said, you better be able to set up house in it! With furniture, and a maid.

"I wanted Cathy to go to the shore with me that weekend. She wouldn't tell me she was going with Gene. We were supposed to go to the Aztec Motel. I kind of knew that he was going with her, and I wanted her to go with me instead. She wanted to go to the Aztec, she picked that place. I don't know why she wanted to go there, I had never been there before.

"I used to talk to her every single solitary day. One time, I didn't talk to her one day, so I called her the next day but there was no answer. And she was always home, if she wasn't at work, she was at home. And if she wasn't home, she was with me. Or pretty much she was with me. I called her, I called her, I called her, I called her. I go to her apartment, she's not there. I'm banging on the door, banging on the door, she's not there. I'm thinking, 'what if she slipped in the bathtub or something and was dead?' I was frantic. And then she called me when she got home. I said, 'where were you?' She goes, 'I went in the truck for the weekend with Gene' to do . . .' whatever they do in that truck. I said, 'Cathy, I talk to you, and then you're gone the next day and you don't even say you're leaving? I thought something happened to you!' She said, 'I'm sorry.' I said, 'I talk to you every day, you've gotta think that I'm gonna think something happened to you.' She goes, 'I didn't even think.' I said, 'From now on, you call me when you're leaving and you call me when you get back so I know you got back safe. Because nobody keeps in contact with you, you don't work any specific shift, nobody's gonna miss you at work.' So she did after that.

"When she didn't answer the door that day, I thought she was dead in the bathtub. And I said, for some reason, Cathy, there's something about you and that bathtub. I used to dream of her taking a shower, or that she was in the bathtub and she would fall, always fall in the bathtub. Only this was before she was killed. It's a weird thing. I said to her once, 'If anything happens to you in the bathtub, and you die in the bathtub, would you come back so I could say I told you so?' I never had that dream again after she was killed."

Voices — Joy Niemiera

"He scared me before I met him. I remember one time her telling me that he had beat her. Any man who beats a woman, in my book, is not worth it. Also, they took these shooting courses or whatever, and I knew that she had this gun, and it's just my own personal belief that you just don't have these in your home and we would have fights about this. I just felt that it was too dangerous. I never saw the gun. I knew that she kept it in her bedroom in the top night stand drawer. I remember her and I just going 'round and 'round about guns, and her saying, 'Oh, Gene thinks it's good that I have a gun.' It was from John's gas station. They would go out shooting."

Casting the Net

IT WAS IN LAW SCHOOL that Thomas Kapsak decided he wanted to pursue a career as a trial lawyer; of all the courses he took, the ones involving litigation were the ones to which he was most attracted.

"My wife thought I was crazy," he recalled, "because she didn't think I had the right personality to be a trial lawyer. A lot of people think trial lawyers are flamboyant, and some are. But you don't have to be. You need to like the challenge of combat and be able to think and act on your feet."

Contrary to his wife's opinion, Kapsak felt his low-key personality suited the courtroom, especially in his role as a prosecutor. "There's so much pressure in the factual patterns of a case that if you're already high-strung, the pressure could become a little too much."

Kapsak's first job after graduating from law school was with a Middlesex County, New Jersey law firm, for which he handled negligence cases. These weren't the meaty cases he had fantasized about trying while in school, but at least he was given the opportunity to fine-tune his profession before a judge and jury.

That practice would serve him well. Several years later, in 1969, Kapsak learned of an opening for an attorney in the office of then-Middlesex County

Prosecutor Ed Dolan. Kapsak immediately applied for the job.

Already building a reputation as a tenacious attorney, Kapsak used that trait to its fullest in pursuing the position in Dolan's office. By his own admission, he haunted Dolan's office, continually making appearances and inquiring about the job. In 1970, his strategy paid off; he was hired as a Middlesex County Assistant Prosecutor.

Kapsak and the 11 other assistant prosecutors — all of whom worked part-time until the mid-1970s, when they were made full staff members — spent their time bringing different types of criminal cases to court. By the time he joined Dolan's staff, Kapsak had already had more than 50 trials under his belt, making him one of the more experienced attorneys in the office.

Kapsak quickly established a reputation among his colleagues as a hard worker and a gifted litigator. During his tenure, Kapsak headed every department in the Prosecutor's Office at least once.

After 10 years of bringing varied types of criminal cases to court, Kapsak in 1980 was assigned exclusively to homicide. It was an assignment he took to heart.

The Second Assistant Prosecutor believed that an important part of any murder investigation is getting to know the victim's family. Indeed, he prided himself on the relationships which he built over the years.

"When you deal with a victim's family close-up — you sit with them, you listen to their grief, you cry with them — you become very motivated," he explained. "I don't distance myself from the family. After you see so much of this stuff, you're able to maintain a professional approach, but not a clinical approach. I think my involvement with the family makes me more motivated and makes me a better prosecutor. When it's four in the morning and I'm still working, it's because I'm close to the family."

Every murder investigation headed by Tom Kapsak was really two investigations: county detectives looked for evidence which will lead to the arrest of a suspect, and Kapsak looked for information he could bring to a jury to convict the accused. It was because of his belief that experts should do what they do best that Kapsak did not immediately respond to the scene of a homicide.

"I do go to the scene at some point," he said, "I want to get a feel for the scene, but I don't go there and tell the investigating detectives what to do."

Although Kapsak had been presented with many difficult cases throughout his career, it was in 1982 that he had to face what was perhaps his greatest challenge.

As a young man, his father — Thomas Kapsak, Sr. — competed as a semi-professional boxer. One of the holdovers from his boxing days was Kapsak Sr.'s habit of walking five or six miles each day around his native South Plainfield. One evening in 1982, while he was taking such a walk, the elder Kapsak crossed a street with what he thought was the green light. In actuality, the light was red for traffic in one direction and green for the other; a motorist who had the green light and didn't see the dark-clothed Kapsak struck the 69-year-old man, killing him.

"That was a difficult time because one of the things I do is supervise the death-by-auto unit," Kapsak recalled. "So my unit had to investigate my father's death. Then we had to decide what to do with it, and we decided it was not a chargeable offense, which was not easy to explain to my family. The team consulted me; ordinarily I would have been directly involved in the decision, but because it was my father, I didn't want to be. But before the decision was made, they consulted me, and of course I agreed that it was the right decision. But it was a hard time for me."

Yet another great challenge awaited Tom Kapsak in that hot July of 1983.

July 17, 1983

Rosemary Cascella had an uneasy feeling about her when she walked into Middlesex General Hospital's main floor nurse's lounge at 7:30 that morning. Rosemary was still slightly spooked by the mysterious male voice that had answered Cathy's phone the day before; something, she felt, wasn't right. Trying to push any negative thoughts out of her mind, she joined the other day shift nurses in receiving their patient reports from the departing night shift. She noted with a small grin that her friend, Merelyn, hadn't come in yet. "She must have had a late night," Rosemary joked to herself.

"Excuse me, everyone, can I have your attention please? I have an announcement to make." Rosemary looked toward the front of the room. She saw her supervisor, Nancy Wilson, standing with two men she recognized as hospital administrators. Nancy didn't look happy.

"I've got some terrible news," Wilson said. "I've been told that one of our fellow nurses, Cathy Warner, was found dead in her house yesterday. The first indications are that she was murdered."

Rosemary heard faint cries of disbelief and shock from the women and men around her, but she was struck speechless. She looked around for the other nurses on Four Tower. Where the hell was Merelyn?

"I don't have all the details," Wilson continued, her voice rising above a growing wave of conversation. "I'd just like to ask you to not discuss this with anyone, especially the patients. And if you are contacted by any member of the police or the county prosecutor's office, please give them all the assistance you can."

Tears welled in Rosemary's eyes as she absorbed the enormity of what she had just been told.

"Cathy's dead? Murdered? Who would want to do such a thing?" she asked herself, although a part of her knew the answer. She suddenly felt claustrophobic; her chest tightened, making it difficult for her to breathe. "I've got to get out of here," she told herself aloud. "I've got to get some air."

Slowly, she made her way through the clustering nurses to the closed door. As she pushed it open, Rosemary nearly ran headfirst into Merelyn Daniel. Wordlessly, Rosemary pushed her friend back into the hallway, a look of pure terror in her eyes.

"Rosemary, what's wrong? What happened?"

Steeling herself as best she could, Rosemary took a deep breath and told her friend the terrible news: "Merelyn, Cathy's dead."

Merelyn Daniel's jaw dropped, her eyes opened wide and her expressive face became a mask of disbelief.

"What do you mean, she's dead?" Her eyes searched Rosemary's face for some indication that this was a joke.

"Somebody killed her." Rosemary had to force out the sentence.

Daniel shook her head, her eyes welling with tears. "You know who killed her," she sobbed, not caring that she was crying in public, in the hallway, in front of patients and their families. "You know who killed her!"

Unable to hold back any longer, Rosemary hugged her friend and burst out in tears.

The nurses had been told to not speak with anyone, but by mid afternoon, that became almost impossible. Merelyn tried her best to keep her composure, but all she wanted to do was go home. Before she started her shift, she called her husband, Kenny, who still worked in their native New York City.

"Kenny," she said, still crying, "I was right! I was right, somebody killed Cathy!"

"What! Who told you that?" Kenny had known Cathy, too and the news of her death affected him as well; Cathy Warner had been a dinner guest at the Daniel home many times. In fact, earlier that summer, Cathy had helped Kenny assemble and set up a swing set in their backyard. She had come to his aid when he could not figure out how to mix the cement he wanted to use to secure the poles in the ground. "I'm just a city boy, I don't know stuff like this," he had joked at the time.

"The supervisor made an announcement this morning. Oh Kenny, I knew something was wrong! I should have gone to her house Saturday."

"Now you just take it easy, baby, just take it easy. Did they say what they want you to do?"

"They told us not to talk to anyone except the police. But Kenny, I can't work today. I just don't know if I can get through the day!"

"Well, you just do your best. Just do like they say and come right home when you get off, okay?"

"Okay, I'll try. See you later."

Merelyn always felt better when she spoke with her husband; he was her rock, he kept her together.

Hanging up the phone, Merelyn saw Rosemary Cascella coming down the hall toward the nurse's station. Merelyn could tell from the look in Rosemary's eyes that she couldn't yet talk about the horrible fate that had befallen their friend.

That entire day, Merelyn Daniel felt as though she were operating on remote control, just going through the motions of performing the routine daily tasks. She couldn't permit her mind to wander, for to do so would be too painful. What she found most difficult to accept was what she had found out later in the morning; that, judging by the rate of decomposition of Cathy's body, police thought she had been dead for at least several days, maybe as long as a week. "I can't believe that an entire week had gone by and no one from her family had tried to call Cathy, nobody even suspected anything was wrong," she thought. "I never knew how alone she really was."

Although the nurses weren't supposed to speak about Cathy Warner's death with the patients, they could do nothing about the patients broaching the subject.

"Excuse me nurse," one elderly patient said to Merelyn, as the nurse was checking her charts. "I just heard on the radio that a woman named Cathy Warner was murdered, and that she was a nurse here. Isn't she the girl that worked with you?"

Merelyn didn't know what to say, so she lied.

"No, that's not her, it's just somebody with the same name." She didn't care if the woman believed her or not. Afraid that she would burst out crying again, Merelyn hastily retreated from the room.

Shortly after 11 a.m., Metuchen Police Lieutenant Edward Studnicki received a visit from Sgt. Allan Demcoe of the Middlesex County Park Police. Demcoe and his wife, Janet, were longtime friends of both Cathy Warner and Gene Berta. Demcoe had called the police department the day before, saying he had heard about Warner's death, but he would not reveal the source of his information.

"I just dropped by to tell you that I remember Cathy telling us that her first husband tried to reconcile with her sometime this past year," Demcoe said.

"And would you have a name and address on him?" Studnicki asked.

"Bill Tingley. I think he lives with his mother in Edison. I just remember Cathy telling us that he wanted to get back together with her, but she wasn't too interested."

"Okay," Studnicki said, still a little annoyed at Demcoe for not telling him how he had heard about the death, although he had been repeatedly asked to do so. "I'll pass it on."

At about 11:30 a.m., Studnicki was told he had a call from Sgt. Salamone. Salamone, Studnicki remembered, was at Perth Amboy General Hospital, overseeing the autopsy on Cathy Warner.

"She was killed, lieutenant, shot," Salamone said. "The M.E found an entry hole in the back of her head, and a corresponding exit hole under her left eye. He said there was too much damage to tell the exact caliber, but he guessed it was a handgun. The official cause of death is, wait a minute, I got it here — cerebral laceration and hemorrhage and a fractured skull, due to the gunshot wound."

"I just can't figure it," Studnicki said, shaking his head. "Who would want to kill her?"

"I don't know lieutenant, but he must be one sick son of a bitch. From what we saw yesterday, we think she may have been shot somewhere else and then put in the tub after she was dead."

"Christ . . . she was such a nice girl. I can't believe something like that could happen right next door to me."

"Zimmerman asked me to ask you to call her family and have them come down to headquarters so they could be told and interviewed."

"Okay, I'll take care of it. See you when you get back."

As he replaced the receiver, Studnicki tried to remember the last time he had seen Cathy Warner alive. It had been several weeks ago, he thought, when she was working in her front yard. She was always working around that house, trying to fix it up, but she was never too busy to not stop and talk with you. "Such a nice girl," he muttered aloud. "It's not fair."

It took him 15 minutes of calling, but Studnicki was finally able to reach one of the Neals at home. It was Cathy's brother, Gary.

"Hello Mr. Neal, this is Lieutenant Studnicki from the Metuchen Police Department. I was wondering if you and your family could come down to headquarters as soon as possible; some investigators from the county Prosecutor's office have some questions for you."

"Well, my parents are out making funeral arrangements, but as soon as they get home I'll tell them, and we'll be down. Is that okay?"

"That will be fine, Mr. Neal. We'll see you then."

The Neals — Richard, Gloria, son Gary and daughter Mary Beth — arrived at police headquarters at about 1:30 p.m. Once they announced themselves to Studnicki, he ushered them into a small meeting room, where they were introduced to Allan Rockoff, the Middlesex County Prosecutor. Rockoff, a former Superior Court judge with a slight resemblance to Edward G. Robinson, had been named to his new post just two months before. This was the first major case to fall under his tutelage.

Rockoff had also been informed earlier that day of the autopsy's results. He had delegated to himself the task of breaking the news to the Neals; investigators had been careful up to that point to not mention the possibility of murder to the family.

Clad in a conservative grey suit, Rockoff stared at the four bereaved family members as he grappled for the correct way to tell them that Catherine had been murdered. He could see that Gloria Neal and her other daughter, Mary Beth, had been crying by the tell-tale redness around their eyes. Gary Neal and his father simply looked helpless and stunned.

Rockoff decided the best way to go about it was the most direct.

"We received the autopsy report earlier this morning," he began, careful to catch the eye of each Neal as he spoke, finally resting on Richard. "Our medical examiner determined that your daughter was shot . . ."

A gasp erupted from Gloria Neal. She looked as though she might faint. Teary-eyed once more, Mary Beth clutched her mother's arm to give her support as the older woman stared uncomprehendingly at the Prosecutor.

"Shot!? Shot? Who would want to shoot her? I don't understand!" she said, as fresh tears rolled from her eyes. Silently, from his position next to her, Gloria's husband wrapped his arm around her shoulders and pulled her close. She buried her face in his shoulder as she sobbed, "Who would want to shoot Cathy? Who?"

"I know this is very difficult for you, and I assure you we will do everything we can to catch the person responsible for this," he told the family. "Since this is now officially a murder investigation, it would help us if you could think back and remember anything that could help us; who Cathy's friends were, who she dated, anyone she may have had a problem with. Lieutenant Zimmerman will be contacting you for a statement soon. I just want you to know that we are doing everything we can to find the person that killed your daughter."

"We'll do whatever we can to help," Mary Beth assured him.

Thinking that the family would want some privacy, Rockoff excused himself.

"Shot her?" Richard Neal thought, as he watched Rockoff leave the room. "Who does she know that carries a gun? Who does she know with a gun?"

Zimmerman had arrived at Metuchen police headquarters while Rockoff was breaking the news to the Neals. He saw the prosecutor leave the small conference room and silently shut the door, quickly cutting off the muffled sobs emanating from the room's interior.

"Give them a few minutes, Joe," the prosecutor said.

Zimmerman waited about 10 minutes, then softly knocked on the door.

"I'm sorry to disturb you," he began, "but there are just a few things that I have to ask you. This isn't anything formal, we'll probably be asking you to make an official statement in a couple of days. But I just need to know a few things now, just so we can start somewhere."

Gloria Neal dabbed at her reddened eyes and blew her already-raw nose.

"Okay lieutenant, what do you need to know?"

Zimmerman asked the family questions that by this time had become rote in his investigations: Who were your daughter's friends, boyfriends, acquaintances? When did you see her last? Do you know anyone who'd want to harm her? It was always a painful sight to watch a murder victim's family suffer through these kinds of memories, but, Zimmerman knew, it was a necessary evil.

Detective John Haley, a Middlesex County Detectives' identification officer, filed the following description of the body, after the autopsy:

"The body of the victim was found in the bathtub of the downstairs bathroom. The nude body was found partially in water, the head of the victim was towards the right side, this side would be the deep end of the tub where the faucets are located. The body was decomposed and covered with maggots.

"The knees of the victim were bent so as to fit into the tub. The high water mark on the side of the tub would indicate that water was over the head completely at one time. The hands of the victim appeared to have been bound with trash bag ties, but closer examination revealed that these ties were not secured in a manner to hold the hands. The water was not running and the stopper was in a closed position.

"Prior to beginning the autopsy, Dr. Shuster removed a ring from the left ring finger and a Timex watch from the left wrist. These items were turned over to the undersigned by Dr. Shuster. The time on the watch was 3:03 and the date was the tenth.

"The autopsy revealed a bullet wound to the head of the victim. An entry hole was visible in the rear of the victim's head, and an exit hole was visible below the left eye."

Dr. Shuster' best guess was that Catherine Neal Warner's death occurred sometime after July 14, 1983. But, owing to the advanced decomposition of the body, Shuster found it hard to be more specific.

Shuster had removed some blood, fingernail clippings and head and pubic hair from the body and gave them to the detectives, who would then send them to the State Police laboratory for analysis. The doctor also removed several maggots from the body, instructing that they should be turned over to Dr. Louis Vasvary, a Rutgers University entomologist. Since Shuster could not be positive about the exact date Cathy Warner was killed, he thought Vasvary could help by studying how far the maggots' growth cycle had progressed. More maggots would later be removed from the crime scene for further study.

Back at Metuchen Police Headquarters, the investigators weighed their options.

"I think we need to go talk to her friends," Watson said. "I think we need to find out more about this Gene Berta." Watson still had a bad taste in his mouth from the interview the night before.

"Well, we've got a few names to go on, they were given to us by her parents," Zimmerman said. "And there were some names and addresses in an address book I found in her bedroom. That's as good a place as any to start."

The team was somewhat aided in their task by the fact that Cathy Warner was a sociable person who spoke to several of her friends at least every day. For the most part, Cathy knew that she could confide in her friends — although she didn't feel comfortable talking about Berta to them because she knew they didn't like him — but she also knew they would be there for her when she needed consoling.

The group of women Cathy Warner considered her best friends were those with whom she worked at Middlesex General's "Four Tower" and, before that, at John F. Kennedy Memorial Hospital. The county detectives and Metuchen police were able to find those women and speak to them within seven days of Cathy's body being discovered.

Among the first of Cathy's friends to be contacted was Rosemary Cascella, who had moved with her new husband to Edison. Sgt. Salamone spoke with Mrs. Cascella later that afternoon, after she had returned home from work.

Rosemary, still in shock from learning about Cathy's death earlier that morning, invited the officer in.

"I'm sorry about this," Salamone began, "I know this is tough, but I really need to know whatever you can tell me about Mrs. Warner."

"Okay," Rosemary said, dabbing at her eyes, "what do you want to know?"

"Well, can you tell me when was the last time you saw her?"

"June 25th, that was when I got married," Rosemary said, briefly smiling through her tears. "She looked so pretty in the dress she wore. She helped me plan my wedding, you know."

Then her eyes opened wide, as though she had had a revelation.

"I have a picture of her from that!" Rosemary bolted up from her couch and ran into her bedroom, emerging several minutes later with a color photograph, which she handed to the officer.

The picture was of four people, two couples, seated around a table. It was from the Cascella's wedding reception the month before. Rosemary identified everyone in the photo.

"That's Cathy, that's Gene, and next to them is Merelyn Daniel, another nurse at the hospital, and her husband Kenny. They all had such a good time that day."

Salamone hid his surprise at seeing Berta pictured with Warner, it seemed to go against how Berta had described his relationship with the dead woman Saturday night.

"So you didn't see her after you got back from your honeymoon?"

"I tried to call her when I got back, on the eighth, but she didn't answer the phone," Cascella said. "Cathy and the other nurses were going to have a party for me when I got back; I was supposed to be in that day, but I decided I wanted to wait until Monday to come back, try and stretch out the honeymoon, you know?"

"And when did you try to call her?"

"I think I called her twice, at about 5 o'clock and then at 7 o'clock. She didn't answer either time."

"Did you try contacting her after that?"

"Oh yes," the nurse said, wiping her eyes with a fresh tissue. "I called her at least once every day for the next week. She never answered."

Later that evening, Zimmerman, Salamone and Watson knocked on the door of Mary Ann Burns of Woodbridge. Burns met Cathy Warner about nine years before, when they both worked at John F. Kennedy Memorial Hospital in Edison. Burns was still employed there when her friend was killed.

"We were good friends," a tearful Burns told the men. "She and her husband John lived in the same apartment complex in Edison as me and my husband."

"Mrs. Burns, did you know of any men Cathy might have dated in the past?" Zimmerman asked.

"There were several, I think," she said. "She dated a few guys after she got divorced and up until the time she met John Warner, but none of them were anything serious."

"And do you know who she'd been dating recently?"

"Well, about a year ago she told me she was dating this guy named Gene."

"I see," Zimmerman said, glancing over to Watson. This was the first time Zimmerman and Watson were made aware of Berta's name being linked to Warner's by a friend, and it seemed to directly contradict Berta's assertion from the night before, that his and Cathy Warner's relationship had been casual. "What can you tell me about Gene?"

"All I know about him is he's married and has kids; I don't think Cathy wanted me to know too much about him. I mean, I only met him a couple of times; Cathy brought him over here."

"Do you remember when she did that last?"

Mary Ann Burns knitted her brow, trying to remember. "I think it was about three months ago, I'm not really sure. I remember the last time he was here, he told this story about how his backyard neighbor's dog tried to get over the fence to get at his dog, so he got his gun and shot the other dog. He thought it was funny."

Zimmerman could see that Burns was getting progressively more upset, he wanted to end the interview as soon as he could.

"Okay, Mrs. Burns, can you tell us the last time you saw or spoke to Cathy?"

"I spoke to her on the phone about two weeks ago," she said. "Cathy said things were going badly with her and Gene and that they were going away together to try and straighten things out. She said they had to get away from Gene's wife to be able to think things out and decide what to do."

"In all the times you spoke with her, did Cathy ever tell you how she felt about Gene Berta?"

"She really loved him," Burns said, starting to cry again. After several minutes, she regained her composure. "I'm sorry, I just can't believe she's dead. I remember that she even learned how to drive a tractor trailer so that she and Gene could buy their own truck.

"But Cathy was really depressed about the relationship since Gene had that car accident, back in May; he went home to recuperate with his wife. Cathy said she started to see the light after the confrontation with Gene's wife at the hospital. She said she thought that Gene might not really be leaving his wife for her and the thought really depressed her because she wanted to marry Gene and have kids."

"Just one more thing, Mrs. Burns, and then we'll leave you; did you know Cathy was going away?"

"Oh yes. In fact, Cathy said she would call me when she got back and tell me what she and Gene had decided."

"And did she?"

"No, I never heard from her again."

Donna Tokar, another nurse from JFK, was next on the detectives' list. The trio spoke with her at about 9 p.m.

Tokar had already heard the tragic news from her mother and had pretty much composed herself by the time the detectives arrived. She invited them in, motioning to two seats in her living room.

"I first met Cathy about two and a half years ago," she said, answering

Zimmerman's first question. "Cathy had had a very hard life: her second husband died about three years ago, and she had trouble with her parents over her first husband."

"Why was that?" Zimmerman interrupted.

"They just didn't approve of him," she replied.

"Did Cathy tell you about any men she had been dating recently?"

"Well, I know she's dating a guy named Gene Berta," she answered.

Repeating a question that would become very familiar to him in the next several weeks, Zimmerman asked, "What can you tell us about Gene?"

"He's married, was married once before, and he has a bunch of children," Tokar said. "As far as I know, Cathy's been dating him for a long time. He goes over her house a lot, sometimes he even brings his son, Gene Jr., along. He's about 12, I think."

"And how had that relationship been going?"

"Okay, I guess, until about May," Tokar replied. She then recounted the story of the confrontation between Cathy Warner and Gail Berta in Gene's hospital room, a tale the detectives would hear a number of times.

"Cathy was very sad after she found out that Gene was living at his house. I remember that while Gene was still in the hospital, Cathy gave me a charm that he had given her and told me to give it back to him, and she told me to tell him that she wanted her keys back. And I remember, she put the charm in an envelope with a letter. I guess it was supposed to be something that was really significant to them. So I brought it back to him; he was just laying in bed and I said, 'Cathy wanted me to give this to you.' Then I asked him what he was doing. Gene told me that he was going back with his wife. I just looked at him."

"But as far as you knew, before that, they had a pretty strong relationship?" Watson asked.

"Well, yeah. They even set a tentative date to get married, I think it was June of 1984. Cathy told me that after they were married, they were going to move out west and buy a farm."

"What else can you tell me about Gene, Donna?" Zimmerman asked.

"Well, I think he's a sex maniac," she said. "He even made a pass at me once. He was so possessive; he tried to get Cathy pregnant while he was still living with his wife."

"Can you tell me when you last spoke with Cathy?"

"She called me on the Fourth of July to tell me she couldn't go to the shore with me that weekend because she was going to Virginia to be with her sister," she answered.

"Uh-huh. And was she just going there for the day, or was she going to spend some time there?"

"No, she was there for the whole weekend."

"Have you tried to contact her since then?"

"Yeah, I tried to call her at least once a day, every day, since July 11, which is when she told me she would be back from her trip."

While the county detectives and Salamone were conducting their interviews, Sgt. Sardone and Lt. Studnicki spoke to Samuel Harris, one of Cathy's neighbors. The officers asked Mr. Harris to come to police headquarters for the interview.

"Okay, Mr. Harris," Studnicki began, "how long have you lived on Durham Avenue?"

"I been here about 10 years," Harris replied.

"Did you ever see your neighbor, Mrs. Warner?"

"Oh yeah, I would see Cathy once in a while, usually when she was leaving or coming home."

"Can you remember the last time you saw her?"

"It was on July 4, between 8 o'clock and 8:30. She was standing in her yard. I come out, and we talked for awhile. Cathy said she was going on a trip and that she needed to get her head together. She asked me to watch her house for her. I said I would."

"Is there anything else you can tell me, did you notice anything strange about the house?"

"Well, I saw her car parked at the end of the driveway one day, I think it was July 6. That was something she never did before."

"July 6, you're sure about the date?"

"Yeah, I'm sure it was July 6, cuz' I was still resting from hurting my eye the day before."

"Okay, and did Mrs. Warner have a lot of visitors; anyone who kept coming back?"

"Well, there was this fella in a blue van who kept coming back. I didn't get his name, though. He used to help renovate the house."

Voices — Merelyn Daniel

"Cathy had a patient who she took care of, that was her patient. Everybody has a favorite patient. This man was semi-comatose, he was a big man. Cathy would go in there and the only time Cathy asked you for help was to flip him over. She did total care on him. The week after we found out Cathy died, he died.

"I guess if she had a family where they called each other everyday or knew her activities, the first two days that they didn't hear from her, they would have investigated. But they weren't close. I didn't meet Cathy's family until her memorial services. As a matter of fact, I didn't know that Cathy had brothers or sisters until after she was dead. And then I realized the estrangement of her family when her mother thought Cathy was at work and Cathy had been dead for a week. From what we gathered, there was no contact between Cathy and her mother.

"The part that I found hard was that she was there a whole week and nobody from her family even suspected that anything was the matter. Then you know just how alone she was."

Monday, July 18, 1983

The group of men who assembled at the Metuchen Police Headquarters that Monday morning knew they had quite a task on their hands. The investigation of this case was being spearheaded by the Middlesex County Prosecutor's Office, as is the rule with all major crimes which occur in that county. The gathering included Prosecutor Rockoff, Second Assistant Prosecutor Kapsak, and the county detectives assigned to the Major Crimes Unit: Zimmerman, Watson, and identification officers John Haley and Sgt. Casimir Smerecki. Also in attendance were Studnicki, Salamone and Sardone, who would handle the investigation from the Metuchen side.

The only thing the detectives were certain of was that a single gunshot to the back of the head had ended Cathy Warner's life. They were not sure where it happened, they were not sure when it happened or why, and, most importantly, they were not sure who did it, although the county detectives were beginning to form suspicions on the latter question. But, as Kapsak reminded them all, while suspicions can be exploited to their fullest during an investigation, they are absolutely worthless in a courtroom.

The meeting commenced with a briefing from the local police and county detectives on what they had found over the previous two days, beginning with the discovery of Warner's body, through the autopsy results and up to the interviews the detectives had conducted Sunday evening. Zimmerman filled his colleagues in on the discussions he and Watson had with Berta and Bauer.

"That guy didn't even blink an eye when we told him she was dead!" Watson said. "You should have seen this guy! He's as cold as ice. And an arrogant bastard."

"And he denied he and Warner had a relationship, even though she had paid for this trip to Minnesota and had lent him $10,000?" Kapsak asked.

"That's what he said," Zimmerman replied. "And the friends we spoke with yesterday said they had been together for a long time. One of them said they had even set a date to get married! And Berta told us he knew her "casually". What do you think, lieutenant? You knew them both."

"Well, I just knew Cathy Warner to say hello," Studnicki told him. "Berta's been on the rescue squad for what, 17, 18 years? Christ, he was just named 'Man of the Year' a couple months ago! I just can't imagine a guy like that doing something like this. But I guess people have killed for less."

"I don't know," Watson mused, "I think this Berta guy's handing us a load of bull. His story just doesn't check out. He expects us to believe that Cathy Warner made all the reservations, paid for everything, then just calmly accepted the fact that she wasn't going? Especially when she told at least one of her friends they were going to get married? I think there's more to this than he's saying. And I think that Bauer woman knows something, too."

"Relax Denny," Zimmerman told the young detective, "we'll find out what they know, you've just got to give it time."

Zimmerman often found himself having to harness in the energetic Watson, but he didn't mind. He knew that given time, Watson would prove to be a top-notch investigator.

"All right," Kapsak said, stroking the back of his head with his right hand as he studied the preliminary notes he had taken on a yellow legal pad. "What we need to do is talk to her family, her friends, the other nurses on her floor, everyone we can find who was connected with her in some way. Find out what we can about who she dated; maybe there's a jilted lover in her recent past. From what you've told me, it looks like whoever killed her knew her: no signs of a struggle, and all the doors were locked. Joe and Denny, I guess you'd better check out the rest of Mr. Berta's story. Let's see if we can find out anything else he hasn't told us."

"In the meantime," Rockoff said, "I spoke with the press yesterday, the story should be in today's papers. I figure that if we publicize this, maybe someone who saw or heard something will read the paper and contact us."

Kapsak closed his manilla folder and scanned the room's occupants. "I'm sure this isn't news to you, but this is going to be a tough one, gentlemen."

The story hit the local newspapers on July 18 and would receive almost daily coverage in the weeks to follow. Although the county detectives had already poked some holes in the story given to them by Gene Berta and, privately at least, were keeping him at the forefront of their attention, the information released by Rockoff was that there were no suspects and, as of yet, no clues. As is usual in investigations of this type, police were stingy with information; there was no mention of the airline tickets, nor of the voided check, nor of the food scattered around the victim's car. Because Cathy Warner was found with her hands partially bound, there was speculation on the part of some reporters that she had been killed somewhere else and her body transported to her home after the fact.

News of Cathy Warner's death was also broadcast over local radio stations. Pat Bauer's car radio was regularly tuned in to a Central New Jersey easy listening station, WCTC; she preferred the softer music during her commute to and from work. It was on her way to her job that morning that she heard the announcement: a 29-year-old Metuchen nurse had been found dead in her bathtub, an autopsy revealed that she had been murdered, a single gunshot to the head. The nurse's name was Catherine Neal Warner.

A wave of panic enveloped Pat Bauer when she heard the victim's name — Cathy Warner! Feeling herself getting dizzy, she quickly pulled to the side of the road and turned up the radio's volume, hoping to hear more.

"That's the girl George told me Gene was seeing!" she said to herself aloud. "She lived right across the street from the Durham Cafe! Oh Gene, you've done it this time."

Once at work, Pat expected to receive a call from Gene. She didn't. Nor would she hear from him the entire week.

The county detectives and Metuchen police had been given their assignments: Zimmerman and Watson would start talking to Cathy Warner's friends, while Salamone and Sardone would begin their investigation within the borders of Metuchen, although they would also periodically accompany the county detectives. The detectives wanted to question anyone who knew Cathy Warner, from family to acquaintances to lifelong friends. Based on their initial hunch that Warner was killed by someone she knew, the investigators understood that they had to piece her life together as completely as possible, develop as great an understanding of the people in her life as they could so that eventually they might be able to focus in on one person — her murderer. But Dennis Watson's gut was telling him they'd already met the man.

Every last detail had to be checked; anything the police found in the house had to be researched, anything a detective was told had to be double checked. To Denny Watson, this was forensic Nirvana.

Sgt. Salamone spoke with the Metuchen Postmaster, Richard Huff, early in the morning of July 18. Having information which lead him to believe that Cathy Warner had planned a trip, Salamone wanted to find out if she had made the standard arrangements.

"Yup, here it is right here, sergeant," Huff said, as he returned to the front counter carrying a small green card. "Cathy Warner placed a "hold' on her mail from July 9 through July 23."

"When was that placed?"

"The date here is July 8. And it's signed by Cathy Warner."

"I think I'd like to take that with me, Mr. Huff. Do you mind?"

Huff said he didn't, and Salamone left with his prize. He would later turn the card over to the county detectives.

"It's a great day for a drive down to the shore, huh guys?"

But Joe Zimmerman, Ralph Salamone and Dennis Watson were not heading south to lie on the sand and improve their tans. They were on their way to Seaside Heights to check out some of the things Berta had told them Saturday night, and also to follow up on information Zimmerman had been given by the Neal family on Sunday.

Seaside Heights, a popular New Jersey shore area, is located about 20 miles south of Asbury Park. The trio drove in silence, each absorbed in his private thoughts.

The detectives' first stop was at the Surf Side Motel, where they met with the manager, Caroline O'Kinsky. Mary Beth Neal had told Zimmerman that it was at the Surf Side where she had stayed with her sister the last time she had seen her alive. O'Kinsky gave them a registration card made out to Cathy Warner of 125 Durham Avenue, Metuchen, for the dates June 24 through June 27.

The investigators then proceeded to the Aztec Motel, which was located on the Seaside Heights boardwalk. After checking her records, the hotel's manager, Diane Buzzard, told them that on June 24, a Gene Berta made reservations for the dates July 11 through July 14 and left a cash deposit of $72. Berta gave as his home address 125 Durham Avenue, Metuchen.

While at the Aztec, the detectives also spoke with Jeffrey Wain, the desk clerk who was on duty early in the morning of July 12, when Berta and his wife checked in.

"I was told by the guy I relieved that a Mr. Berta had called in late that night and asked us to hold his room," Wain recalled. "Mr. Berta said he was at the airport, and he would be down here as soon as he could. Then, when he finally checked in, I asked him something about the airport and he freaked out. He made it a point to tell me that he wasn't in the airport, he was just driving by it. I noticed his wife looked at him kind of funny."

"Didn't that old Mr. Jones say he had a son?" Zimmerman asked Watson as he steered their car onto the northbound lane of the Garden State Parkway.

"You mean the guy who lives in the shack? Yeah, he said his son visited him a couple weeks ago. Said he lives somewhere in Metuchen. I think I've got the address here in my notes."

"Well, then. I think we should pay the young Mr. Jones a visit."

Kenneth Jones invited the two detectives into his home and offered them something to drink. Both declined. Jones had spoken to his father over the weekend and learned about Cathy Warner's murder. This, he said, was a visit he had been expecting.

Zimmerman had no time for chit chat, he knew there was much more ground to cover.

"Mr. Jones, can you tell me the last time you saw Mrs. Warner alive?"

"Well, I was visiting my father on July fifth when Cathy Warner came over and asked my father to watch her house for her. She said she was going on vacation. And then she said she needed the rent by the fourteenth so she could pay her taxes."

"Your father told us this happened on July 12," Zimmerman said.

"No, I know it was the fifth," Jones replied. "I remember I asked her how her Fourth was, and she said it was terrible because she had to work."

"Do you remember your father ever mentioning anything about a guy named Gene Berta?"

"Gene Berta? Well, he knew about him, but he really didn't see him that much. One time he told me he gave Berta the rent check because Cathy was in the shower, but that was about it. They never really sat down and talked."

"Okay, one other thing, Mr. Jones, in the times that you visited your father, did you ever notice where Cathy Warner parked her car?"

Jones thought for a minute. "Yeah. She always parked in the front of the driveway, near the porch."

After their interview with Jones, the trio decided to split up; Watson would return to the county office to make some phone calls, Salamone would remain in Metuchen, and Zimmerman would pay a visit to the Menlo Park Travel Agency in Edison's Menlo Park Mall.

Zimmerman arrived at the mall about 15 minutes later. He asked to speak with the manager; he was soon greeted by Joseph Valitutto, the travel agency's president. Valitutto lead Zimmerman to his desk, then motioned for him to sit down.

"How can I help you?" he asked, folding his hands in front of himself on the desktop.

Zimmerman reached into his coat pocket and removed Cathy Warner's picture identification badge, placing it near Valitutto's arm.

"Do you recall this woman booking a flight through here? Her name is Catherine Warner."

"Oh yes," Valitutto said. "I helped her myself. Hold on, I think I should have a file on her." Valitutto opened a desk drawer, flipped to the "Ws", then pulled out a manilla file folder.

"Here she is. She came to the agency twice," Valitutto reported as he fingered through the papers. "The first time was in the middle of June. She asked for general information about Minnesota, things like pricing and lodging. The second time she came in was during the week of June 27, when she paid for and picked up the airline tickets."

"What names were the tickets made out to?"

Valitutto glanced at the file, then said, "the tickets were made out in the names of C. Warner and G. Berta. As I said, I was the one who wrote the tickets for her. I also made reservations for her at the Best Western Thunderbird Motel in Minneapolis and reserved a Hertz rental car for her, all through the American Airlines computer here."

"Did she tell you where she was going in Minnesota, or why she was going there?"

"All she said was that she was going to Moose Lake," Valitutto said. "She didn't tell me why she was going."

"United Farm Agency, Natalie speaking. How may I help you?"

"Hello, this is Detective Dennis Watson from the Middlesex, New Jersey county prosecutor's office. I'm conducting an investigation, and I was hoping you could supply me with some information?"

"What kind of information do you need, detective?"

"I was wondering if you have any records on a Eugene Berta. He would have been there during the weekend of July 8 through the eleventh of this year."

"One second and I'll check our records," she said. She was back on the line several minutes later.

"Yes, our records show that Eugene Berta signed an agreement of sale on July 11 to purchase an 80 acre tract in Birch Creek Township, Pine

County, for $29,500, and that he left as a deposit a personal check for $3,000."

The detectives made it a point at the conclusion of each interview with a friend of Cathy Warner's to ask if they knew of any other people who might have some information. As a result, the investigators' "To See" list was growing larger each day. And, concurrently, so was the list of potential suspects.

George Salagi, Cathy Warner's newspaper delivery man, told Sgt. Salamone that he picked up a newspaper hold notice during his delivery on the morning of July 8. The hold was to be placed from July 8 through July 15, he recalled. He couldn't answer any questions about Cathy Warner, he explained, because he never met her. "She always left her payments in the mailbox," he said.

One of the things of which detectives were somewhat certain early on in the investigation was that whoever killed Cathy Warner had a key to her house. Based on that, they wanted to speak with anyone who she might have given a key. Because Cathy had extensive renovations to her home prior to her moving in, detectives thought a logical place to start would be with the contractors who were hired to do the work.

What the investigators found was that while there were several contractors working on the house at the same time — including Berta Electric — none of them, except for Gene Berta, admitted to having retained any of her keys.

Michael Mandell of Metuchen, who was hired for plumbing work, recounted the story of how he was originally approached by Berta for an estimate on the house because, Berta said, he was going to buy it.

"He said he was thinking of buying the house as an investment, but he didn't want his wife to know," Mandell told Sgt. Salamone. "I knew he didn't have the money to buy a house, hell, he didn't have two nickels to rub together."

It was some time later, Mandell said, when Gene took him to the house and he first met Cathy Warner.

"She bought the house instead. It needed a lot of work, though. She paid me about $8,000 alone; I think she spent about $30,000 all together for the repairs."

"Did you ever see Cathy Warner after the repairs were finished?" Salamone asked.

"Well, I had a Christmas party last year, and Gene and Cathy were there," he said. "I remember she was very friendly, very cordial to everyone, especially the men."

"And when was the last time you spoke with her?"

"That was about a month ago. She called me because she needed someone to remove a big tank from her back yard. I told her I didn't do that.

"I read in the paper that her father found her," Mandell added. "You know, I'm surprised Gene didn't find her body, he was always around her house."

Tuesday, July 19, 1983

Dennis Watson began his day by interviewing Dawn Farnell, a longtime friend of Cathy Warner's. Farnell and Warner knew each other for 25 years, having grown up together in South Plainfield. The last time Dawn saw her friend was the day after Thanksgiving, 1982, during the 10th reunion of their high school class. Cathy was accompanied to the event by Gene Berta.

"I didn't know him very well," Farnell said, when she was asked about Berta. "All I knew is that he was married and had children, and that he was supposed to be leaving his wife for Cathy."

"Did you ever spend any time together with the two of them?"

"Sure; three summers ago, Cathy and I went down to Seaside Heights, we stayed at a place called the Aztec Motel. Gene came down later with a friend named Dennis Malinowsky to visit us."

"Did you see Cathy and Gene together a lot?"

"Not really, the last three years I only saw them together about a dozen times."

"What are your impressions of Mr. Berta?" Watson asked.

"I always found him to be crude and intimidating," she answered, without hesitation.

"What did he do to make you feel that way?"

"Well, he always used obscene language," she said. "And, I don't know, it was just the way he looked at you."

"I understand they were talking about getting married."

"I doubt he was ever serious about that. When you get down to it, I always thought he was just leading Cathy on."

Later in the day, Watson caught up with Dennis Malinowsky at his Edison home. Malinowsky was a friend of both Cathy Warner's and Gene Berta's.

"How long have you known Mr. Berta?" Watson asked.

"Geez, I've known Gene for about 20 years," Malinowsky replied. "I met him while I was on the rescue squad. As a matter of fact, that's where I met Cathy, too."

"So you knew Cathy before she married John Warner?"

"Yeah. You know, she married that guy, but I know she was still in love with Gene. I mean, her whole life revolved around Gene and what he did. All she wanted was for Gene to divorce Gail and marry her. After a while, Gene said he would. Then they started talking about getting out of New Jersey, maybe buying a farm or a tractor trailer."

"What else can you tell me about Mr. Berta? How is he set financially?"

"Well, I know he's always broke," Malinowsky said. "He's always falling behind on the payments for his mortgage and his van."

"Do you know if he owns any weapons, any handguns?"

"The only guns I know about are a .22 calibre rifle and a shotgun."

Concluding his interview with Malinowsky, Watson returned to his office in New Brunswick. He wanted to make some more phone calls to round out the details of Berta's Minnesota trip.

The first call he placed was to the Best Western Thunderbird Motel in Minneapolis. Speaking with the owner, Rod Wallace, and his executive secretary, Patricia Anderson, Watson learned that a reservation for a double room was made on June 22, 1983 by American Airlines through the Menlo Park Travel Agency and Best Western for Friday, July 8, 1983, in the names of Ms. C. Warner and guaranteed to Ms. Warner's MasterCard number.

Under a section on the reservation card labelled "special information" appeared the name, "G. Berta".

"Was that reservation used?" Watson asked.

"No," Anderson told him. "The reservation was cancelled on July 8 at 7:32 our time, that's Central Standard Time. There's a notation under the cancellation which says "Self', which means the cancellation was called in by the person who made the reservations."

Checking a time zone map, Watson determined that 7:32 p.m. Central Standard Time was 5:32 p.m. in Metuchen.

The detective's next call was to the Howard Johnson Hotel in Newark, where he spoke with Max Houston, the hotel's manager. Houston told Watson that his records showed a Mr. and Mrs. Geno Berta of Grove Avenue, Edison, checking in on July 8, 1983 and vacating before noon the next day. The room, Houston noted, was paid for in cash.

Joe Zimmerman walked into Dennis Watson's office just as Watson hung up the phone.

"It's time for us to speak with the Neals," he said. "I just called them, they're all waiting for us at their house."

"Yeah," Watson said. "I'd like to hear what they can tell us about this Gene Berta. This guy's story's starting to stink up the room."

Although they were briefly interviewed the day Cathy Warner's body was discovered, the detectives felt it better to wait a few days, until the shock had worn off, to take a formal statement from the Neal family. When they arrived at the house, Zimmerman explained to the family that they would interview each of them individually. He introduced the third member of their party, Investigator John Mumber, a Certified Shorthand Reporter, after which Mrs. Neal suggested they use the kitchen for the interviews. The rest of the family would wait in the living room.

The first family member called in was Mary Elizabeth — called Mary Beth — whom Berta claimed Cathy was going to visit when he last saw her on July 8.

Mary Beth was, at that time, a seven-year veteran of the U.S. Army, stationed at Anacostia Naval Station in Pennsylvania. She had recently moved to Blue Ridge Summit, Pa., from Alexandria, Virginia.

Mary Beth Neal told Zimmerman the last time she saw her sister alive had been June 27, after she and Cathy had returned from spending the weekend at Seaside Heights. Also down there that weekend, she said, was Gene Berta.

Cathy and Gene arrived at about 10 p.m., Friday, the 24th, Mary Beth said, adding that she didn't get there until 2 p.m. Saturday.

"Did the three of you stay at Seaside Heights all day Saturday?" Zimmerman asked.

"Yeah, till about dinnertime. Then Gene and Cathy went, came back up here to go to Rosemary's wedding. But I stayed in the area, down the shore."

"Okay. And did they come back to Seaside Heights?"

"Cathy came back alone."

Mary Beth said the only reason Berta accompanied Warner down to the shore was that Mary Beth could not make it down that Friday, as had originally been planned. Berta was there to keep Cathy company.

When Cathy and Mary Beth returned to South Plainfield, Mary Beth said, Cathy Warner went back to her house, "but she sort of figured we were going to have a cookout or something, so she called up and came back and had a cookout."

"When did you go back to the Army down in Alexandria, Virginia?"

"I left about 8 at night, I think."

"Now, from the time you left on the 27th until right now, did you ever see Cathy again or talk to her?"

"I know I didn't see her, but I don't remember if we spoke on the phone or not."

"Did Cathy, from the 27th until today, did she ever go back or did she ever come down to Virginia to visit you?"

"No, she didn't."

"And you would be certain of that?"

"Yeah, 'cause she had — she could have called work. They're there 24 hours a day and they would have gotten a message to me."

Zimmerman then asked Mary Beth Neal if her sister, while they were in Seaside, had mentioned any future plans for revisiting the shore.

"Yeah. She mentioned that she and Gene were planning on going down in like about two or three weeks. She had already made reservations and stuff, and I think it was at the Surf Side again."

Mary Beth told Zimmerman that she first met Gene Berta — who she described as Cathy's boyfriend — about five or six years before, when he was "between wives." Although she didn't think that Gene Berta lived at her sister's house, Mary Beth Neal was certain that he slept at the house "here and there" and that some of his belongings were kept there.

"How would you describe this Gene Berta?" Zimmerman asked.

"I never liked him because of the fact that he was married and because he — he was one of those Italian macho, everything he does is right and no female could even, you know, compete with him," she said.

Mary Beth Neal told Zimmerman that her sister was financially well-off and that she had several investments but that, as far as Mary Beth knew, Cathy never loaned anyone money.

"Did your sister ever talk to you about her future?"

"Yeah ... she was hoping that Gene would get a divorce and then they would go live somewhere away, and she didn't even care if she wasn't going to be a nurse anymore."

"Was this your sister's own belief or was Gene part of this picture?"

"He talked about the farm they were going to buy a lot, but I never saw him do nothing towards getting a divorce. It don't take three years to get a divorce."

"Did he ever talk about buying a farm?" Zimmerman continued. "Did you ever hear him talk about buying a farm or marrying your sister?"

"He told me that a number of times he really loved her," Mary Beth replied. "And the only stuff he talked about the farm was jokes about milking the cows and slopping the hogs."

"And how did you feel about this conversation, did you believe him?"

"I didn't, no. I seen too many times, if he wanted a divorce, he would have gone ahead and got a lawyer and got a separation and started the proceedings."

Zimmerman asked Mary Beth Neal if her sister had ever mentioned any other man that she dated, to which Neal replied that Cathy had seen an optometrist "a lot".

"Did (Cathy) ever mention to you that it was completely over with (Berta)?"

"Yeah, a couple of times," she replied. "The last time was just before we went down the shore. And that's what I told you, I was surprised to learn that he was going to be there."

Mary Beth Neal told Zimmerman that Cathy and Gene knew about her plans to move from Virginia to Pennsylvania, and about the fact that she was planning on keeping her old apartment through the month of July. She said they also knew she was planning on moving her belongings out of the old apartment during the July 4th weekend.

"She wanted to be there, but ... she had to work that weekend. But Gene offered to come out and help me move stuff. And I told him since the truck and everything wasn't firmed up, it wouldn't be worth it for him to come out. I didn't really want him to, anyway."

"If your sister Cathy was going to come down to Virginia or Pennsylvania to see you, would she call ahead of time and alert you and make arrangements?"

"She always had before, and she visited me quite a bit. She did talk sometimes about wanting to just put her stuff in the car and pop up at the door one day, but she knew that, you know, she wouldn't really know where to catch me."

Her sister never really had problems with anyone, Mary Beth Neal told Zimmerman, except for Ed Jones not paying his rent and her next door neighbor, Sam Harris, "getting a little too nosy or familiar." But, she added, those were more along the lines of inconveniences.

"Do you know of anyone who has keys for (Cathy's house)?" Zimmerman asked her.

"I don't have firsthand knowledge of that," Mary Beth replied, "but what I wanted to say before, when Cathy lived in the apartment in Edison? When I'd stay with her, we'd come home and there would be a note on her refrigerator from Gene. So I know, you know, it was routine for him — he had a key there, and he'd just stop in when she wasn't there, not knowing that she wasn't there, leave a note and she'd leave notes for him."

Gary Neal told the investigators that the last time he saw his sister Cathy alive was about a month before, after she had been involved in a motor vehicle accident.

"I think I seen her right that next weekend, but I'm not sure of the date," he said.

"Would it be unusual for you to go a month without hearing or talking or seeing your sister Catherine?" Zimmerman asked.

"No, it wasn't unusual at all," Neal told him. "I work nights, so I'm usually gone when everybody else is around."

Neal recounted the events of July 16 for Zimmerman, saying that prior to his sister's body being discovered, the only thing he and officer Sardone found unusual in the house was that someone had defecated in the upstairs bathroom and had not flushed the toilet.

"After we checked all the rooms, the doors and underneath the bed, everything seemed in order," Neal recalled. "We found suitcases at that time that were packed. And then my father started pounding on the wall because he can't yell because of his condition. He usually pounds on the wall to get your attention. And then both of us went downstairs."

"And when you were downstairs, did you talk with your father?"

"He motioned me to stay back and not come in towards him. I went the second time, he just said, 'stay right where you are.' And then the officer went and looked in the bathroom."

Neal told Zimmerman that as far as he knew, his sister had no reason to believe that anyone she knew would harm her. When asked if he knew of any of her acquaintances, Neal said, "Just casual, several of her acquaintances. I don't know if they're real involved, but I know some of her acquaintances."

"And could you tell me who they are?"

"Gene is one."

"If you do know their last names, it would help us a lot," Zimmerman prodded.

"I heard it mentioned, I really don't know his last name . . ."

"Gene; how well do you know this person?"

"Not very well at all. I've only seen him a handful of times."

"What type of friend was he of your sister's; was he a casual friend or a boyfriend . . ."

"Boyfriend."

"What did you yourself know about Gene?"

"I knew he worked as an electrician," Neal told him. "He worked on the rescue squad. He did drive occasionally, Paul's Trucking, he drove for them occasionally."

Neal said he knew Gene was married and that while Gene didn't actually live at Cathy's house, he was there quite often.

"Did Gene ever come to this house here at Maple Avenue?"

"I think he was here one time," Neal said. "It was quite a while ago, though. And that was it, he was not allowed in this house."

"You say he was not allowed in the house, by who?" Zimmerman asked.

"The wishes of my mother. She does not approve of the relationship."

But Cathy Neal Warner was intent on continuing her relationship with Gene regardless of her mother's wishes, Gary Neal remembered.

"She spoke of going, finishing up her master's degree. She had got an articulated license, and at one time they were looking at buying a tractor."

"They, meaning who?"

"Gene and Cathy. That never came about, though, 'cause I went with them to look at the truck. And she had mentioned something about moving out of state. Exactly what, I'm not . . . That would have been with Gene, they would move out of state and buy some land somewhere; I wasn't sure of the whole details of that, though."

"From the conversations," Zimmerman asked Gary Neal, "from what you say about looking at the tractor also with them, did you have reason to believe that your sister and/or Gene believed . . . I mean, did you believe that they were eventually going to get married?"

"The way they talked — the way my sister talked, I should say — that's what I was led to believe. But it didn't seem like it was ever going to come about anyway. Several times I've heard it mentioned of him supposedly getting a divorce. In fact, this past January, he was supposed to be separated. But that, as far as I know, it never came about."

By this time, Dennis Watson knew in his gut that Gene Berta had killed Cathy Warner. "Any man who would lie like he did Saturday has to be guilty," he thought to himself. "He had to be trying to cover up for himself." But Watson also knew they were a long way from being able to charge Berta with anything. "I've just got to be patient," he told himself, echoing

Zimmerman's instruction. "Just be patient."

"Did you ever see or hear your sister Cathy mention anything about weapons?" Zimmerman asked Gary Neal.

"Well, at the time of her motor vehicle accident, there was an officer who took care of the case at the time, a Metuchen police officer," Neal answered. "I'm not sure of his name, I believe it was Jim. She had spoke with him that he was going to handle some of the details of the accident. He was going to drop off the motor vehicle report and help her out, whatever way he can. She had mentioned that he stopped by the house several times and she would talk about, like, him coming — I think he might have had, like, dinner or something like that, just stopping by after the shift. And she mentioned something about him taking the belt off, the whole thing off. She seemed a little impressed with the, you know, I guess the uniform and the gun, handcuffs and all that."

Neal also said that Cathy had never spoken to him about going away on a vacation and that she had never given him a set of keys to her house.

Next to be questioned was Cathy Neal Warner's mother, Gloria.

After going through several background questions, Zimmerman asked Mrs. Neal if she could remember any of the men her daughter dated between the time of her divorce from her first husband, Bill Tingley, and her marriage to John Warner.

"Well she dated several people, but I don't know who they were," she answered.

"Is there anybody that she dated then that you may think of their names right now, like if she's been going out with them again since John died?"

Gloria Neal could not mask the distaste from her voice. "Well, she was involved with this Gene, whoever he is; the electrician or something they tell me he was."

"Before she married John, she was going out with Gene?"

"Yes."

"Do you know Gene's last name?"

"I've heard it, but I don't have any idea what it was," Gloria Neal said.

Mrs. Neal was then asked to recount the events of Saturday, July 16, beginning with the phone call from Middlesex General Hospital, which she did.

"When was the last time that you and Cathy were talking or that you were together? When's the last time you saw her?" Zimmerman asked.

"I believe it was July the Fourth, when she called after work and said, 'Are we having a cookout?'" Mrs. Neal answered. "And I said yes. And we had a little barbecue, and that's the last time I saw her. Whether I talked to her since then, I honestly don't remember."

Mrs. Neal said her daughter arrived sometime between 4 p.m. and 6 p.m. on July 4, and stayed until midnight. After the cookout, Gloria and Richard Neal and Cathy Warner had gone to North Branch Park to see the annual fireworks display.

"Did she mention to you about going away on vacation anywhere?" Zimmerman asked.

"No."

After Mrs. Neal told Zimmerman that she worked at Muhlenberg Hospital in the billing department, the detective asked her if she had been or was a patient at the hospital any time during the previous six months.

"No," Gloria Neal said.

"Did (Cathy) ever mention to you of ever having any problems with any neighbors, or co-workers at work even?"

"No, she seemed to get along fairly well with everybody," Gloria Neal said, missing the irony of her answer. "Everybody has their normal disagreements. She never told me about the little things. But I know there was somebody living in that little house behind her, and she wanted him out of there. But who it is, I have no idea; I've never seen him and don't know his name. She said he's a little old drunk that lives back there."

"Did she ever mention of having any kind of disagreement or any problems that arose in an argument or something?"

"No. She just mentioned that he used to walk in the door if she didn't close it, you know, if the door wasn't locked or closed or something. He was always walking in the door like he lived there. I've never seen him and I never saw him do it, so I'm just telling you what she said."

Zimmerman knew that Mrs. Neal was speaking about Edward Jones. Based on his frailty and his predilection toward alcohol, the investigators had already dismissed him as a suspect. Zimmerman was more interested in delving into Cathy Warner's relationships.

"Had she . . . to your knowledge, do you know of anybody that she had been dating more recently, in the past year, let's say?"

"The only one I've heard of is Gene."

"Have you ever met Gene?"

"He's been here," Gloria Neal said, again failing to hide the distaste she felt for the man. "He came here once. Cathy came to stay with us because she had her, her wisdom teeth out, so she stayed with us for a week. And he came to see her, and I wasn't going to let him in. I asked him who he was, and he said Gene. And I wasn't going to let him come in, and she got a little upset. So I said okay, for a minute. So she was on the sofa and he talked to her for a minute, and then he left."

"Being that he had only been here that one time, could you tell me why you felt that way towards him?"

"I don't like him," Gloria Neal answered.

"Everybody that ever knew Gene always told Cathy he was no good," she continued. "And I'm of the old-fashioned school; if you're married, you're married. You ain't showing up at somebody else's place, either one or the other."

Gloria Neal told the investigators that her daughter would have liked to have married again. "I heard her mention one time that he was going to get divorced, and they were planning on getting married. And I told her right then, I didn't approve. And she was her own person, so she'd have to do what she wanted to do. But I never yet heard of anybody doing that . . . It was a subject of conflict between us. So she finally decided not to mention him at all because she knew how I felt."

Gloria Neal also told Zimmerman that she had never seen a gun in her daughter's house, nor did she ever hear Cathy mention one.

"Okay, Mrs. Neal, that's it. Would you send your husband in, please?"

The strain of the past few days was vividly displayed on the face of the man who sat before the three county detectives. Zimmerman promised him it would be quick, then told him to just take his time and answer the questions as completely as he could. Because of the laryngectomy, the detectives found themselves straining to hear what the bereaved father said.

Following Neal's recounting of the phone call and the discovery of his daughter's body, Zimmerman asked Neal of there was anything else he could remember that would help the police in their investigation.

"Two things," he answered. "You told us at the end of our last meeting she was shot. I was kind of dumbfounded. I thought, who owns a gun, who carries a gun? But Cathy, when Cathy first got married, her husband Tingley. I remember when she first got married to Tingley, they used to shoot the shotgun off by the house at some target. But I don't know what. That rung a bell.

"Then I also remembered she had an accident, and the officer that took charge of the investigation, he frequented her house on a friendly basis, that's all. And I thought of a gun again. Who the heck carries a gun?" He sighed heavily and shook his head. "That's the only thoughts."

Sgt. Salamone received a message that Mary Ann Burns had called him. Rather than call her back, Salamone decided to go to her house and speak with her.

"I wanted to tell you that I remembered Cathy once told me that she had a gun," Burns said, after letting the officer in. "It was earlier this year; I was at her house and we were talking about her living alone and how she had to be careful. And then Cathy told me she wasn't scared because she had protection, a gun that she kept in the drawer of the night table next to her bed."

"Can you describe the gun?" Salamone asked.

"I never saw it," she replied. "Cathy told me that her husband had kept the gun at his gas station.

Zimmerman, Watson and Salamone regrouped later that afternoon. They filled each other in on what they had found out, then decided to make several more stops before calling it a day.

Their first interview was with Dr. Richard Borden, a Woodbridge optometrist with an office in the Woodbridge Mall, a short distance from Metuchen. Borden told the detectives that he had known Cathy Warner since 1979, when she came to his office, accompanied by her husband John, to be fitted for contact lenses. Borden said he and Cathy dated several times after her husband's death.

"My wife and I were having . . . difficulties," he explained. "We just went out for a couple of lunches, one dinner and a rock concert" But Borden maintained that he was just giving a "lonely girl" a "sympathetic ear". He said that in mid-1980, after a few dates, Cathy wanted to get closer with him, but he backed off.

"I knew she had an old friend named Gene who had reentered the picture," Borden told the detectives, "and I thought this gave me an excuse to bow out of the relationship."

"Did you see her again after you 'bowed out?' " Zimmerman asked.

"She came in for treatment in early 1983 and showed me pictures of the house she had bought. She told me that she was still dating Gene, and that he was going to get a divorce and that they had plans for the future. She said she was just waiting for him to separate, and that he was going to fix his house up and sell it."

"Do you remember the last time you saw her?"

"That was about the fifteenth of June," the doctor said. "We passed each other in the mall and talked for a few minutes. I don't really remember what we said, it was just small talk."

Merelyn Daniel was probably the last of Cathy Warner's friends to see her alive. A fellow nurse at Middlesex General's Four Tower, Daniel described herself as a good friend of Cathy's, but she reiterated pretty much the same scanty information the rest of Warner's friends provided about her love life: that she was dating a man named Gene — whom Daniel had only met twice, and for whom she did not care — who worked at the first aid squad and who was married and had children, and who was also supposed to be getting a divorce so he and Cathy could get married and start a family.

"She called him her 'Teddy Bear.' " Daniel told the detectives.

Daniel also repeated the events of the previous May, when Cathy and Gail Berta ran into each other at Gene's bedside.

"She found out that Gene was lying about leaving home and filing for a divorce," Daniel told the detectives. "Cathy was very upset and broke up with him, but she still didn't go out with anyone else. She even took all his things out of her house and left them on his porch, and then sent a message to Gene that she wanted her keys back. I heard that his wife took the keys back, and they sat down and had a long talk.

"And then, I don't know, it must have been a few weeks or a month, Cathy told me that she and Gene were getting back together. I told her she was crazy, that she could do better than that idiot, but she said she had things under control and that she was only giving him a certain time frame, I think it was six months, to get a divorce. And she said that if he didn't get divorced by then, then it was over."

"How did she act before the day she was supposed to be going away?" Zimmerman asked.

"She acted jovial the whole week before," Daniel said. "She was glad to be getting the time off."

Daniel told detectives that Cathy had arranged to leave work early, at 3 p.m., on July 8 so she could catch her flight.

"But at about a quarter after two, she told me she had to leave now, because her mother had been taken to Muhlenberg Hospital. I told her to call me and let me know what was happening with her mother. She didn't call, so I did, at about 8:30 that night. I never got an answer."

Another former co-worker, Joy Niemiera, was the group's last interview that evening. It was Niemiera, who worked with Cathy from 1977 to 1978 at JFK, who told the detectives that Cathy had been seeing a psychiatrist at the hospital's mental health center to help her cope with her husband John's death.

Joy had been devastated when her mother-in-law had called her on the 18th with the news that Cathy Warner had been murdered.

"Isn't that Catherine Warner your girlfriend?" she had asked.

"Cathy? Yes, why do you ask?

"Well, I don't know how to tell you this, but I think she's been murdered! I read about in the paper today."

"Oh my God, no" Joy remembered the terrible feeling that overcame her the week before, as she and her husband were travelling to Massachusetts. "Mom, I've got to go, I'll call you later."

Joy barely made it back to the kitchen table after she hung up the phone;

her grief was beyond anything she had experienced in her life. A wracking pain in her stomach doubled her over as she sat on her kitchen chair; her tears flowed freely, brought on as much by the tremendous sense of loss she felt at her friend's death as her overwhelming feeling of guilt for having hung up on Cathy several weeks earlier.

"She should have listened to me," Joy sobbed, "she should have listened to me."

Zimmerman thought Niemiera did not look at all well when she opened the door for the detectives. The fact that she was about eight months pregnant contributed to his impression, but the woman looked as though she hadn't slept for quite a while. As though she were reading his mind, Niemiera apologized for her appearance as she led the men into her living room.

"I know I must look like a mess," she said, as she struggled into a chair. "It's just that I loved Cathy so much, she was such a good friend to me."

"I understand how you feel, Mrs. Niemiera," Zimmerman told her. "We'll try to get this over with as quickly as we can."

Niemiera told the detectives that although she heard much about Gene, she only met him once at Cathy Warner's house when she and her husband were helping Cathy paint. "He was there with his son," she said.

"Did you have any idea how she felt about him? Did she ever talk about the future with you?" Zimmerman asked.

"Cathy really wanted to marry Gene, but he always kept coming up with excuses why they couldn't," Niemiera told him. "Either his wife was pregnant, or he had to fix up his house before he left, or he wanted to buy a tractor trailer and get started in a business, or he wanted to go to paramedic school."

Outwardly, the nurse continued, Gene acted as if he were in complete agreement with Cathy's plan for them; they even attended a course at Middlesex County College in Edison on how to obtain a divorce.

"It was Gene's idea for Cathy to buy that house, too," she continued. "He wanted her to do that so they would have a place to live when he got his divorce."

"Did you ever know Cathy to lend Gene any money?"

"Cathy gave Gene a lot of money at different times," Niemiera answered. "She bailed him out of jail when he didn't make child support payments, and she also paid when he was in an accident with a rental truck. But she told me in April that she wanted to get her money back from him."

"Can you remember anything else that she might have told you about her relationship?"

"Well, she told me once that she had gone off the pill for a couple of months and she thought she was pregnant."

"How did Gene feel about that?"

"Gene said it was okay if she got pregnant."

"Did you ever hear of any arguments they had?" Zimmerman continued.

"I remember that Cathy was really upset a few months ago, I think it was the beginning of May," Niemiera said. "She met Gene's wife in the hospital after he was in an accident. She told me she went to visit her sister to think things over after that."

"Can you tell us when you last saw or spoke to Cathy, Joy?"

"We spoke on the phone about three weeks ago," she said. "Cathy told me she and Gene had just had a fight — she always called me after they'd had a fight — and that she wanted to get back together with him."

"So Cathy always called you after she and Gene fought?"

"Oh yes; one time she called and told me that Gene had punched her."

Attempting to develop information he had been given earlier in the day, Zimmerman asked, "Did you know of Cathy to own a gun?"

"Cathy told me that she had a gun, but I never saw it," Niemiera said. "She told me once, I think it was last year, that she had gone to a shooting range to learn how to fire one."

"I see. One more thing, do you know where Cathy usually parked her car?"

"Yeah, she always parked it at the front of the driveway. She said it was safer to get into the house at night through the front door."

Wednesday, July 20, 1983

A memorial service was held for Catherine Warner at 6 p.m. in St. Luke's Episcopal Church in Metuchen. Among those who gathered to remember Cathy were her immediate family, cousins, friends and two carloads of co-workers from Middlesex General.

The nurses from Four Tower sat together in a pew toward the front of the church. They were surrounded by the sounds of the grieving, sobs punctuated by the rector's voice as he spoke of Cathy's life, paying particular attention to her nursing career and the fact that she had cared for her second husband, John, while he was suffering from Hodgkin's Disease and then leukemia.

It was about that time that one of the nurses, curious to see who was in attendance, looked around to scan the church. She froze when her eyes fell upon a face she did not expect to see — Gene Berta. Instantly, she grabbed Rosemary Cascella's arm and, when Rosemary looked at her, gestured to the rear with her head. Rosemary's mouth dropped when she saw Berta, then she became enraged when she noticed that he was sitting next to an attractive blonde.

Rosemary tapped Merelyn Daniel on the shoulder and jerked her thumb back; Merelyn saw the fire in her friend's eyes and took a quick glance around, then slowly looked back at Rosemary and shook her head.

Leaning in close to Cascella, Merelyn whispered, "What is his problem? Do you believe he's here?"

"And who's that blonde he's got with him?" Rosemary asked. "Look at him, looking so sad, with that blonde on his arm."

"He probably went to her for consolation," Merelyn said.

At the conclusion of the service, the nurses filed past Berta and the blonde, Pat Bauer, without even looking at either one of them. "*I don't even know you,*" Merelyn thought. "*But I know you killed my friend.*"

Cathy's parents and sister and brother were standing on the steps outside the church, receiving the condolences of the mourners. Merelyn thought the entire family looked as though they were in a daze.

"I guess if I found one of my loved ones in that condition, I'd look the same," she thought.

Although they were Cathy's good friends, this was the first time Rosemary and Merelyn had ever met Cathy's family. Cathy very rarely spoke about her family; in fact, Merelyn didn't even know Cathy had had siblings.

Merelyn waited on the sidewalk in front of the church for the other nurses to finish speaking with the Neals. She noticed policemen stationed at the church doors, and also noticed two cops standing on lawns down the street. When the nurses were all gathered together, Merelyn made a suggestion: "Let's go to Captain G's and get some drinks. I, for one, need them."

Unbeknownst to the nurses and the other mourners, county detectives were videotaping them from across the street in a specially-outfitted van.

Zimmerman and Salamone walked together from the church to the Metuchen Police Headquarters parking lot.

"Did you see who Berta was there with?" Salamone asked.

"Yeah, Pat Bauer," Zimmerman said. "I don't know about this guy, he's either real stupid, or he's got balls as big as China."

The two investigators were about to part company when Zimmerman heard his name being called. It was Gene Berta; he was gesturing for them to come over to his car, which was also parked in the police department lot.

"I've been thinking since we last talked," Berta said. "There's a few things I remember, if you've got a minute."

"Sure," Zimmerman said. He was playing Mr. Affable. "What do you have?"

"Well, I knew that Cathy would occasionally go out with an eye doctor, or a guy who was either a producer or a director, but I don't know their names," Berta said.

"That's it?" Zimmerman asked.

"Yeah, that's it."

"You know Gene, I'm still a little confused about your relationship with Cathy Warner. You were going out with her too, right?"

"Yeah we were lovers, we were intimate, but we could both do as we pleased," he said.

"I see," Zimmerman said.

"Let me ask you something, Joe," Berta continued, assuming a familiarity the detective found discomfiting; "do you think I could get into Cathy's house? I've got a shotgun there that I'd like to get out."

"We found that, Gene," Zimmerman said, keeping the smile plastered on his face. "It's being checked out by our identification detectives."

"Oh, okay. I've also got a roll of pictures there that I took during the trip to Minnesota. I left them in the top drawer of Cathy's bureau, in her bedroom. Do you think I could get those?"

"Film? We searched that entire room, but we didn't find any film," Zimmerman told him.

Berta looked puzzled.

"You sure you looked in the right bureau? You go up the stairs to Cathy's bedroom, as you enter the door, the bureau would be on the left side of the room, against the wall."

"I know which one you're talking about. I searched it and the first two drawers were empty. But we'll look for it again."

"I'd appreciate it," Berta said. "Those pictures wouldn't be of any use to anybody; they were taken in Moose Lake and they only show some trees and land that I bought."

(Talking to Det. John Haley the next day, Zimmerman learned that

Haley had run across the roll of film in the bureau before Zimmerman arrived July 16 and had confiscated it and sent it off to be processed. Haley said he didn't know Zimmerman was looking for it).

"A farm, huh, Gene? You don't look like the farming type to me," Zimmerman said.

"Oh yeah, I used to live on a farm in Edison before it became built up," Berta told him. "I always wanted to buy a farm in Minnesota: you can raise cattle and grow different produce there; you know, live off the land. I planned to move there by 1985."

"Did you and Mrs. Warner ever talk about this?"

"I spoke to Cathy about it," Berta said, a little wary now. "I thought that if she wanted to go with me, I had no problem with that, but I was going to move by 1985, with or without her."

Then, to get the discussion back on a safer track, Berta said, "You know, I'm trying to remember anything I can that would help you in your investigation."

"I appreciate that, Gene," Zimmerman said. "You can do one thing for me, tell me again about the last time you saw her."

"Okay," he said, heaving a big sigh, preparing himself for a long recital. "On July 7, I stayed at her house overnight. I drove her to work the next day to the hospital."

"Was that in your car?"

"No, it was in her car."

"Okay, go on."

"After I let her off, I went back to Metuchen and did some things to prepare for my trip to Minnesota. I was at her house when she called me and asked me to pick her up."

"And what time was that?"

"That was, I guess about 1:30. Anyway, she wanted me to pick her up because she said she was getting out of work early. I drove back to the hospital in her car, then I used the downstairs phone to tell her I was there. She came down, and I drove us back to her house."

"Then we both prepared for our trips."

"Your trips?"

"Yeah, I was going to Minnesota, and Cathy was going down to Virginia to visit her sister."

"And how long did you have these plans, Gene?"

"I guess about two weeks."

"And Mrs. Warner knew you were going to Minnesota?"

"She not only knew, she made all the arrangements."

"Then I drove Cathy to the MetroPark train station that night . . ."

"Do you recall what time it was, Gene?"

"I don't know the exact time, somewhere in the early evening I guess," Berta said. "She was going to catch a train to Virginia. I parked the car in the daily lot, put $1 in the envelope or coin slot they have there; I figured that would be enough for parking because Saturday and Sunday are free."

"Do you remember what Mrs. Warner had with her when you dropped her off at the station?"

"Yeah, she had two suitcases, one large one and one that was much smaller, with a flower pattern. She packed her clothes in the larger one and toiletries in the other one. And the last time I saw her, she was walking toward the station."

"And what did you do after you dropped Mrs. Warner off?"

"I called Pat Bauer and told her to come pick me up. I had made plans with her to go with me to Minnesota. So Pat picked me up at the train station and we drove to Newark Airport. But we missed our flight, so we stayed at the Howard Johnson's, right there by the airport. And then, the next morning, we flew to Minnesota."

Zimmerman already picked out several inconsistencies between this story and what he had been told Saturday night. But he sensed that Berta was the verbose type, so he wanted to let him keep talking.

"Okay, then what happened when you got to Minnesota?" he asked.

"Well, I met with a realtor, and he took me out to look at a farm in Moose Lake. And I met him again the next day, Sunday, and looked at some more farms. And on Monday, I made a deal for an 80-acre spread. After that, Pat and I flew back to Newark, we drove back to the MetroPark station and then I took Cathy's car back to her house."

"You drove her car back to her house? Where did you park it?"

"I parked it in the back of the driveway, and went in the house by the side door," Berta told him. "That was the closest door to where I parked.

"I went up into the kitchen, then used the phone to call a cab."

"Was that a local cab company?"

"Yeah, the Metuchen cab service, the ones who park by the railroad station. Anyway, when I went back inside I brought her suitcase inside . . . I mean my suitcase."

"I took the garbage out and then ..."

"Can you tell me exactly what you did when you took out the garbage?"

"Yeah. I went out the side door, grabbed the can on the side of the house and took it to the front of the house, out by the curb. Then I went back inside, made sure I locked both locks, went back to the kitchen, saw the cab and left the house."

Anticipating Zimmerman's request to explain exactly how he left the house, Berta said, "I took my suitcase out the front door, set it on the porch, locked the front door, both locks, got into the taxi and then went to my house. When I got there, I picked up my wife and we went to the Aztec Motel in Seaside Heights. We stayed there until the 14th."

"Okay, Gene, I appreciate that," Zimmerman said. "Oh, one more thing, did you ever go upstairs that night, when you got back from Minnesota?"

"No," Berta said, "I never went upstairs at all."

"Okay Gene, thanks for the information. You have a good day, now."

Driving down Route 27, Gene saw his friend, Dennis Malinowsky, walking down the street. Malinowsky had also attended the memorial service.

"Hey Dennis," Berta yelled, as he pulled over. "Come on, I'll give you a ride.

Zimmerman later caught up with Watson and related his conversation with Berta.

"Oh, man, lieutenant, I'm telling you, this guy did it! I know it!" Watson's exuberance was always a source of amusement to Zimmerman.

"Calm down Denny, if he's the one, we'll get him. But we've got to make sure, first. We've got to rule out everyone else, we can't get tunnel vision here."

Watson knew Zimmerman was right, but he still couldn't wait for the day he took Berta in. A day Watson knew would come.

"Listen, let's go back to Metuchen and talk with that cab driver," Zimmerman said. "Let's see what he's got to tell us."

Richard Guidetta of Edison was the taxi driver who picked Gene Berta up at 125 Durham Avenue late in the evening of July 11. Guidetta told Zimmerman and Watson that when he arrived at the Durham address, he stopped in front of the house and blew his horn.

"Some guy stuck his head out the door and hollered that he'd be right out," Guidetta said. "About four or five minutes later, the guy came out the front door and got in the back seat behind me. All he said was, "Take me to 19 East Walnut Street'.

"So I drove him there, he paid the buck fifty, and got out."

"Did the man say anything to you?" Watson asked.

"No, the whole ride, I only talked about the weather and he didn't say a thing."

"Can you describe the man?" asked Zimmerman.

"Not really. I didn't even see the guy because he sat right behind me. But I think he was black, because when he leaned over to pay me from the back seat, his hand was dark."

Thursday, July 21, 1983

Proceeding down the list of men with whom Cathy Warner had had relationships, Zimmerman and Watson interviewed William Tingley, Cathy's first husband.

Tingley and Cathy Neal had met while in high school; they became sweethearts and married shortly after Tingley's graduation in 1971. Cathy's mother wasted in no time in letting her daughter know how she felt about the coupling; when Cathy announced that she was engaged, Gloria Neal locked her out of the house.

The Tingleys did not stay married long, however, as Tingley told the two detectives.

"We were married about nine months when I found out she was seeing another man at work," Tingley said. "I filed for divorce. We were separated for a year and a half before it went through."

"Had you seen or talked to Cathy lately?" Zimmerman asked.

"No, I haven't spoken to her since last year. I just called her up just to say hi, how you doing."

"So you never went to her house?"

"I didn't even know she had a house until I read about it in the paper,"

Tingley said. "I went to the memorial service yesterday, then, I guess out of curiosity, I just drove by it."

"Okay; can you tell me if you knew of any men Cathy had been dating recently?"

"Well, a friend of mine who works on the rescue squad told me that she was dating a man named Gene Berta, but I've never met the guy. I really can't tell you anything about him."

"Okay, Mr. Tingley, that's all we needed to know for now. We'll get back in touch with you if we have any questions."

Once they were back in their car, Watson turned to his partner.

"Well, what do you think? Jealous ex-husband wanting to get back with the victim, she refuses and he shoots her?"

"No," Zimmerman said. "I don't see him doing that. It's been 10 years since they were divorced, I doubt he feels anything that strong."

"But he did say he called her last year . . ."

"So the guy hit a low spot, he wanted to capture a bit of his past. Haven't you ever thought of doing that, calling up an old girlfriend out of the blue? Nah, I don't think he's our man. Besides, I thought you were hot on Berta?"

"Well, like you said, you can't get tunnel vision, right? Although I still think Berta's guilty as sin."

Having arrived back at his office, Watson found a note on his desk, a message that Dennis Malinowsky had called him. He dialed the number he was given, then made arrangements to meet Malinowsky in 30 minutes at his home.

"I called you because I had a long talk with Gene yesterday, after Cathy's memorial service," Malinowsky told the detective, once they had settled in the former's living room. "He told me some things I thought you should know."

"I'm all ears," Watson said, as he pulled out a small note pad.

"Gene told me that Cathy and Gail had a big blow out at Middlesex General last May," Malinowsky began. "They both came to visit him in the hospital after his accident, and they both showed up at the same time! Can you believe it?"

"I'm sure it must have been quite a scene. Let me ask you something, did Gene ever tell you that he had a key to Cathy's house?"

"Yeah. In fact, Gene told me that a lot of times, after he and Cathy would fight, she'd take the key back and then give it back to him when they made up."

"Did he ever mention anything to you about his plans for the future?"

"Yeah, he said he wanted to buy a farm out in Minnesota and move out there, but without his wife. He even said that he'd take all his kids with him, if Gail would let him.

"I'm trying to get a handle on this guy," Watson said, appearing to want to draw Malinowski into his confidence. "What can you tell me about him?"

"You know, sitting here thinking about it, I remember one time, geez, it must have been back in 1978 or so, Gene picked me up at the MetroPark train station and gave me a ride home," Malinowski said. "He looked kind of raggedy, and I asked him if he'd been working. He said that he and about four or five guys had just hit four states. When I asked him what he did, he just said, "you don't want to know. Nothing I haven't been into for a while.'

"But he used to say weird things like that all the time. About a year later, I was at his house on Aylin Street, that he used to rent. Anyway, we're in the garage, and he picks up a piece of electrical cord, about three inches long. There was a plug on one end, and the other end was bare, you know, just the wires sticking out? So he picks up the end with the plug, sticks it in a socket, and watches the other end spark! I say, "Gene, what are you doing?' He just looks real weird and says, "don't ask'."

"He sounds like a pretty mysterious guy," Watson said. "Did you ever see him lose his temper?"

"Yeah, once," Malinowsky answered. "It was when he was thrown out of his Aylin Street house because he didn't pay the rent, I think it was 1979. He was really mad; this other electrician, his name was "Chuck' or 'Junior', or something like that, told me that Gene asked him to drive him while he offed his landlord. So this other guy says, 'but Gene, if you do that, you'll be the number one suspect.' And Gene says, 'no I won't, I won't be around when it happens'."

"What can you tell me about Cathy Warner?"

"Cathy, she was a case. She had an eight-year obsession for Gene,"

Malinowsky said, shaking his head. "She always talked about buying a farm and running away with him. The last time I saw her — it was last summer, we were at the shore — I told her she was stupid because she couldn't see how Gene was just leading her on. She didn't want to hear it."

Nothing that Watson had learned in the past five days had dissuaded him from his original impression, that Gene Berta had murdered Cathy Warner. In fact, the more he heard how in love Cathy Warner was with Berta, and how Berta was just using her, the more convinced he became that his gut instinct was correct.

Back in his office, Watson was cleaning up some notes of what Malinowsky had told him when his telephone rang. On the line was a Patrolman Ostenberg from the Moose Lake, Minn. police department. "Maybe he'll have some more good news," Watson thought.

"Hello detective, I just wanted to tell you that I spoke with Gary Neumann, that's N-E-U-M-A-N-N, out at the United Farm Agency today. He's the realtor who sold your Mister Berta that farm? He told me that he got a phone call from Mister Berta on July 8, and that Berta told him then that he could not make his flight connections and would be there the next day, instead. He said that Berta got there to his office on July 9, at around 3 o'clock, and he had a curvy blonde on his arm."

"Did he describe the blonde?"

"Yeah, he said she was in her 30s, approximately 5'5", about 110 pounds. Neumann said he didn't remember her name, but he did remember that Berta kept calling her "honey'."

"Well, he's a romantic guy," Watson said.

"Whatever. So Neumann showed the happy couple some land on July 9 and also on July 10. He said he got them a motel room at the Northwoods Motel, in Barnum. That's not too far from Moose Lake. He said on Sunday night, that would be the tenth, Berta and his blonde stayed at the Moose Lake Motel. Now, to save you a phone call, I already checked with the Northwoods and verified that mister Berta and a guest stayed there on the ninth. The registration card said they were driving a rented Mercury, from Hertz. Do you want Mister Berta's address?"

"Sure, why not?"

"Okay, it's 625 Grove Avenue, Edison. Now, getting back to Mister Neumann. He said that on July 11, Berta gave him a check for $3,000, for a deposit on the property, with the balance due in 90 days."

"Do you have a total price on the farm?"

"Yeah, it was twenty-nine five. Mister Neumann asked Berta if he would have a problem paying the balance in 90 days, and Berta said no because he was going to sell his home in New Jersey or take out a second mortgage against it, but he would have the money."

"Neumann also remembered that Berta asked him to cut down all the hay on the property, and he asked about the specifications for installing bathrooms inside the house and in a lean-to that was against the house."

"Anything else?" Watson asked, impressed with the policeman's thoroughness.

"Yeah. Neumann said that one day, while they were driving around, they passed Mercy Hospital, which is right near Moose Lake. Mister Berta asked Neumann if there was an ambulance service there. When Neumann said yes, Berta said he and the blonde would have to apply because they were both ambulance attendants."

"Hey Denny, I've got a hot date tonight." Joe Zimmerman was standing in the doorway of Watson's office, holding a half-empty cup of coffee.

"Oh yeah? Who's the lucky girl?"

"Pat Bauer." Zimmerman said. "I asked her to meet me at Metuchen headquarters at about 7 o'clock."

"A hot date in a police station? Gee, lieutenant, you sure know how to treat a girl!"

Zimmerman noticed that Pat Bauer seemed nervous as he greeted her in Metuchen's police headquarters. The detective rose from his seat as Bauer was escorted into the small conference room, the same room where Gene Berta had been questioned on July 16th. Bauer was sharply dressed — she wore a well-tailored summer-weight business suit; Zimmerman guessed that she had come here straight from work.

"Okay, Mrs. Bauer . . "

"Oh, you can call me Patty."

"Okay, Patty," Zimmerman continued. "I asked you here tonight because I'm a little unclear about your relationship with Mr. Berta and also about the trip you two took during the weekend of July 8 through the eleventh."

Pat Bauer paid rapt attention to what Zimmerman was saying. Although she was nervous, she felt on slightly steadier ground than when she had first met the detective at the rescue squad headquarters. She'd since found out that she had gone to school in New Brunswick with Zimmerman's older sister.

"Now Pat, you work for the Edison Rescue Squad Number 2, is that right?"

"Yes, I'm the corresponding secretary."

"Did you know Cathy Warner from the squad?"

"No, I didn't know she was a member until other members told me. I never met her, she was gone when I joined."

"And how did you learn that she had been killed?"

"I heard it on the radio, I think it was Monday morning."

"And you had no contact at all with Cathy Warner?"

"No, other than our mutual friend, Gene Berta," Bauer replied.

"Now, I understand that you and Mister Berta spent some time together on the weekend of July 8; why don't you tell me how that came about?"

"You want it from the beginning?"

"That would be fine."

"Okay. Well, it really started out with us just talking, you know? Sometime before Valentine's Day, Gene and I had a long talk about my marriage, I told him that I had found out my husband was cheating on me, and that he moved out, and all the other stuff. Gene said that if I ever needed a person to talk to, that I could call on him. And that was important to me, because I felt like I didn't have anywhere to turn.

"Anyway, I remember Valentine's Day because we had a squad meeting that day, and Gene was late. And I said to him, you know, Gene, you're the captain, you're not supposed to be late! And he told me that the reason he was late was that he stopped to buy me a Valentine's Day card, which he gave to me. I thought that was really special, because I didn't think I had any reason to remember Valentine's Day."

Bauer was smiling now, quickly warming up to the subject.

"After that, we met a lot of times; we spent hours just talking about ourselves, what we wanted, that kind of thing."

"Where did you and Mister Berta usually meet?"

"Most of the time we met in the lot at MetroPark train station," she said.

"And during the course of these meetings with Mister Berta, did you become more than friends?"

Momentarily shocked by the question, Bauer said, "Yes, after a while we became . . . intimate."

"Okay, Mrs. Bauer, go on."

"Well, the next big thing I remember happening was about the beginning of May. I was transporting a patient to JFK emergency room with another squad member — George Taylor. As we brought the stretcher in, George brushed up against a bed that was in the next cubicle; I couldn't see who it was because there was a curtain around it. So I heard someone say, "Ouch!' from behind the curtain, and I thought I recognized the voice. I looked behind, and there was Gene, lying on the bed! He told me that he had just been in an auto accident, down on Route 27."

"So we talked for a few minutes, and then Gene asked me to call George over. I waved goodbye and left the hospital."

"And did you know why Gene wanted to talk to George?"

"Well, later that night, my friend Cheryl — she works on the squad, too — came over to my house. We chatted for a few minutes, and then she said, "Patty, did you hear what happened today over in the emergency room at JFK?' And I said no, what? So she started to tell me that Gene had asked George Taylor to call his girlfriend and tell her that he had an accident; she must have seen the shocked look on my face, because I was thinking, 'Wait, I'm his girlfriend, and I already knew!'. So Cheryl said to me, 'Patty, you did know Gene had a girlfriend, didn't you?'

"I didn't say anything, I mean I couldn't, so Cheryl just continued with her story. She said that Gene's wife, Gail, had also been called to the hospital. She got there a few minutes before his girlfriend did. Then I guess there was this big blowup between the wife and the girlfriend, and the girlfriend went running out of the hospital in tears."

"Did Cheryl tell you the name of the girlfriend?" Zimmerman asked.

"No, she didn't know it. Neither did I, I mean, I thought I was it! So, we were still talking about it when my phone rang. It was Gene; he sounded like he had been drugged up."

"What did he say to you?"

"Oh, just nonsense," Bauer answered. "Pat, Pat Bauer; I love you, I love you. I tried talking with him, but nothing of any substance came from the conversation."

"Did you hear from him after that?"

"Yes, he called me the next morning. He asked me if I knew where he was, and I said, no, Gene, and I don't want to know. I thought he was home, but he told me he had been admitted to the hospital. He kept telling me that he loved me, so I said, how could you, Gene? I heard about what happened in the hospital yesterday between your wife and your girlfriend!

"And he told me to not worry about that, that it was all over. I took that to mean it was all over between him and his girlfriend.

"So Gene asked me to come visit him, and I did; in fact, I think I visited him all five nights he was there."

"Was Gail also visiting him?"

"As far as I knew, yes."

"What did you and Gene talk about in the hospital?"

"Gene told me that he and his wife didn't get along and that he was thinking about divorcing her. He told me there was just nothing between him and his wife."

"Did he ever mention anything about moving away, maybe to the Midwest?"

Bauer hesitated long enough to light the cigarette she had placed in her mouth. "Yes," she said, taking a deep drag and blowing the smoke out forcefully, in the air away from Zimmerman. "One time when we were talking, he said he was thinking about buying a farm in Minnesota and moving there, and he wanted to know if I would think about moving with him. I really don't remember how I answered; we both left it an open subject."

"Okay. Did the subject of Mr. Berta and yourself moving to Minnesota come up again?"

"Yes, it was around the end of June, either the 22nd or the 29th," she said. "I remember he called me early in the morning, at about 6:30. He was talking in a kind of a low whisper. He said he was making plans to go to Minnesota, and wanted to know if I was going with him. He asked me if I had any time off coming to me, and I said I did. Then I thought about it for a few minutes, and finally said that I would go with him. He said he'd call me back as soon as he made the arrangements."

"When did he tell you the details of your trip?"

"Oh, I don't remember the exact date. He said we'd leave on July 8, and that he would call me sometime in the early evening that day to tell me what time."

"Did he tell you anything more about the trip on that occasion?"

"No, the rest of the conversation was just about what we would wear. He said he was bringing a couple pair of jeans and two pair of dress pants in case we wanted to go out during the evening, He suggested that I bring the same, and that I not forget to pack a bathing suit."

"Okay, I want to bring you to July 8, now, Pat. Tell me what happened then."

"Well, Gene called me at about nine-fifteen or nine-thirty that night and asked me if I was ready to meet with him. I told him I was all packed, and then he told me to meet him at twenty to ten at MetroPark, which I did."

"How do you remember that he said meet him at twenty to ten?" Zimmerman asked.

"Because when I talked to Gene, he said let's synchronize our watches at 9:30. I left my house at nine-thirty and I deliberately took my time because I was annoyed with him."

"And why were you annoyed with him?"

"Because there was nothing definite going the way it was supposed to be."

"So Gene was waiting for you when you got to the train station?"

"Yes; I saw Gene waiting for me in the parking lot when I pulled in."

"Did you know how he got to the station?" Zimmerman asked.

"No. I thought maybe he drove his wife's car and I didn't want to know anything about his wife. I completely blocked that subject out of my head.

"So Gene got in my car, and we drove to the Howard Johnson Motel in Newark, near the airport which is where Gene said he wanted to start our trip. We had dinner and stayed overnight; I think we got up around 5:30 the next morning."

"What time was your flight?"

"It was around 7 a.m., I think; 7:10. We had to make a stopover in Pittsburgh. When we landed in Minnesota, we rented a car at the airport and drove to Moose Lake."

"Do you know how far Moose Lake is from the airport, Pat?"

"Yeah, it was about 110 miles. Anyway, once we got to Moose Lake, we met with a realtor and went out to look at some properties. That night, the realtor arranged for us to stay in a motel in another town, I think it was called Barnum, like the circus? So we stayed there that night, and the next day we met with the realtor again, and looked at some more properties."

"Did you stay in Barnum that night, also?"

"No, we made our own reservations in Moose Lake. Gene said he wanted to be closer to the town. So the next day, that was Monday, we met with the realtor to make a decision on which property to buy; by that time, we narrowed the choices down to two farms.

"Gene kept asking me if he should buy the 160-acre farm or the 80-acre farm. I said, why are you asking me? You're the one who's buying it. He said, I know, but you're going to have to live there, too."

Bauer laughed. "I call that the 'we' weekend," she said, eliciting a smile from Zimmerman. "Gene kept saying, 'we'll do this together' to everything!

"Eventually, we decided on buying the 80-acre farm. It had one house on it, two fireplaces and two outhouses."

"Did Gene take any pictures of the trip?" Zimmerman asked, recalling Berta's strange request of the day before.

"Yeah, he did," Bauer said, smiling. "Gene brought a small camera; he took a bunch of pictures of the property." Then, shyly, she added, "about four or five of them are of me."

"What happened after Gene bought the land?"

"We drove back to Minneapolis and flew back to Newark Airport. We got my car, then we drove back to MetroPark."

"What time did you arrive back at the train station?"

"I guess I dropped Gene off sometime between 10:15 and 10:30 that night."

"Did you ask him how he was going to get home?"

"Nope."

"Okay; when did you hear from Gene again?"

"I didn't hear from him again until last Friday," she said. "He asked me how things were going, and I said I'd had a hectic week. He said he was coming down to the rescue squad, but he pulled up just as I was responding to a call, so we didn't get a chance to talk."

"Did you see Mr. Berta after that?"

"Yes, the next day. We were working together at the squad."

"Okay, Mrs. Bauer, just a few more questions." Zimmerman was getting around to the most delicate part of his interview. "What kind of man is Gene Berta? I mean, do you think he's capable of killing someone? Do you think he killed Cathy Warner?"

"Nope. I don't think he could. He's captain of the first aid squad for God's sake!"

"Did you know Cathy Warner?"

"No, I never met her."

"Did you know that Gene was seeing her?"

"Nope."

"Did Gail Berta know her?"

"She might have, I think they were in the squad at the same time."

"What can you tell me about Gail Berta, based on what you've seen of her?"

Pat Bauer thought a moment. "Gail is a rock," she said, finally. "She is a very hard person. I never really associated with her, she just wasn't my cup of tea."

Friday, July 22, 1983

"So how was your hot date last night?" Dennis Watson settled into a metal chair he had placed in front of Joe Zimmerman's desk. The chair was one of those military-issue types, silver steel made slightly less uncomfortable by green Naugahyde padding on the seat and backrest.

"Great," Zimmerman smiled. "Patty was a little more forthcoming, but I still got the feeling she was holding something back. This Berta's a smooth operator, Denny. Bauer told me that he was late getting to a meeting on Valentine's Day, and when she asked him why, he said he had to stop off and buy her a Valentine's Day card!"

"He's a regular Hallmark," Watson said. "He knows just what to say and how to say it."

"She's really the key to this, I think. There's a lot more that went on that weekend than what she and Berta have told us. I think if we work on her, we may be able to break down the barrier and get her to tell us everything. The trouble is, I think she loves the guy."

"But he's a murderer! Doesn't she know that?"

"Well, she may know it, but I don't think she wants to believe it, Denny."

"Sooner or later, we're going to prove it to her."

"Well, we may do that. Listen, let's go over to the Berta house and see if we can talk to the missus. I'm dying to know what she's got to say about all this."

"Yeah," Watson agreed. "I wonder if she knows her husband's such a playboy?"

Gene Berta may have played the playboy, but his home was far from a mansion. The two-story house was in dire need of repair; shingles hung loosely from the outside walls, flapping in the cool summer breeze. Various items used in construction were scattered about the yard: a ladder, a wheelbarrow, sawhorses.

"This is a real fixer-upper, hey lieutenant?" Watson asked. "Ten grand would go a long way to making this liveable."

Zimmerman nodded his agreement.

Gail Berta was more the type of woman the detectives expected to see linked with Gene Berta — short, pudgy, with brown eyes and shoulder-length black hair framing her large, angular face.

The detectives introduced themselves, flashed their badges, and asked if they could speak with her for a few minutes.

"We're investigating the murder of Cathy Warner," Zimmerman told her.

Gail Berta invited them in the house. The house's interior looked as unkempt as its exterior. The room was musty, littered with clothes, boxes, toys and just plain junk. Along one wall, close to the front door, was a doorless, open space crammed with an assortment of coats, shoes, boots, scarves and hats.

Watson noticed black smears and handprints on the walls and, peeking into the kitchen, could see about a week's worth of dishes piled in the sink, as well as cereal boxes and bowls on the kitchen table. "I can't believe they've got little kids in here," he thought to himself. "I'm glad I don't have to go to the bathroom."

The three made themselves comfortable in the living room. Gail didn't offer the officers anything to drink; neither one would have accepted, even if she had.

In response to Zimmerman's first question, Gail Berta told the detectives that she had been a member of the Edison Rescue Squad for the past eight years.

Zimmerman didn't want to remain in that squalor any longer than he had to, so he decided to come right to the point.

"Mrs. Berta, did you know that your husband was having an affair with Cathy Warner?" he asked.

"Yes, I did," she said. Watson noticed that Gail Berta was assuming the same haughty attitude that her husband had displayed the week before in Metuchen police headquarters. That fact didn't escape Zimmerman's notice, either.

"I understand you and she had a . . . confrontation in May? Why don't you tell me about that."

"It was on May 3rd," Gail Berta said matter-of-factly. "She showed up in Gene's hospital room, then left. Later, we met at her house to talk about her affair with Gene, and her future. She said that she put Gene on a pedestal and that she wanted to marry him. But she agreed that as far as Gene was concerned, I had won and she lost." Both detectives noticed a victorious smirk on Gail Berta's face.

"Okay. Now, you and your husband took a trip to Seaside Heights the week of the eleventh, is that correct?"

"Yes."

"How long ago did you make those plans?"

"We made reservations on June 26 at the Aztec Motel. The reservations were for July 11 through July 14. Gene was going to surprise me with the trip, like a second honeymoon, but he let it slip that day."

"Okay, and can you tell me what you did on July 11, when you left for your trip?"

"We left the house at about 11 o'clock that night. We got a late start because Gene didn't get home until about 10:30."

"How did you travel?"

"We drove my car."

"Did you go straight to the shore from here?"

"No. The first stop we made was at the Foodtown here in town to buy some magazines, some candy and some gum, and then we stopped at the squad headquarters so Gene could drop off a walkie-talkie. Then we drove to the Garden State Parkway, and headed south."

"What time did you get to the motel?"

"I guess it was between 12:30 and 1 in the morning," she said.

"Do you remember the room you stayed in?"

"It was room 104," she answered tersely.

"Okay, you have four little girls, right? Did you take them on the trip with you?"

"No, we had made arrangements with our babysitter about two weeks in advance to take care of them.

"We stayed there until 14th. We checked out at around 11 in the morning, then drove right to the rescue squad."

"What time did you get there?"

"About 12:30. Then we went straight home."

"Okay, Mrs. Berta. Can you tell me where you and your husband were the weekend of July 8 through 11?"

"I was at home with the kids; Gene was somewhere in the Carolinas, with his buddies."

"In the Carolinas?" Zimmerman asked, shooting a glance at Watson. "Do you know why he went there?"

"No."

"Does your husband usually go away for the weekend without telling you where he's going?"

"It's not unusual for Gene to go away on weekends with his buddies."

"I see. Uh, Mrs. Berta, can you tell me what luggage you took on that trip to Seaside?"

"We only took one piece of luggage," she said. "The suitcase that Gene had taken on his trip. He emptied it and put both our clothes in it."

"When did you first meet Mrs. Warner, Mrs. Berta?"

"I met her the first time in 1974, at the rescue squad."

"And did you get along with her? Did you like her?"

"No, I didn't," Gail Berta answered. "She was a tramp."

Zimmerman and Watson's next appointment was for 5:30 p.m., at the home of Kathy Valia, the Bertas' babysitter. On the way, the two detectives stopped at the MetroPark Train station to inspect its parking lot system.

Kathy Valia appeared well-poised for a girl of 15. She confirmed that she had babysat for the Bertas' while they were in their shore trip.

"When did they first ask you to babysit, Kathy?" Zimmerman asked.

"About the end of June," the girl replied. "She said that she and her husband were going down to the shore for a few days."

"Did Mrs. Berta tell you about any other trips she or her husband would be taking?"

"Yeah, she said they were going to go to Minnesota to look for land later this month or next month. That's where I thought Mr. Berta was when he came home Monday, night, but he told me that the trip had been postponed."

"Okay, now, do you remember when you got to the Bertas' house on July 11?"

"Mrs. Berta picked me up at the roller rink, the United Skates of America, at about 7 o'clock," the girl replied. "We went to her house and waited for Mr. Berta to come home."

"And what time did he get there?"

"I guess it was about 11."

"Well, that's something new," Dennis Watson said when he and Zimmerman had returned to their car. "Gene and Gail were talking about moving to Minnesota? I thought that was all Gene's plan."

"So did I," Zimmerman replied. "I guess we'd better go pay another visit to the good Mrs. Berta.

"Don't worry Denny, I'll take this one by myself," Zimmerman said, as he exited the car parked in Berta's driveway.

"What do you want now?" Gail said, not even making an effort to conceal the hostility in her voice.

"Well, there was just one more question I forgot to ask you, Mrs. Berta," Zimmerman said, as he climbed the steps to the front porch. "Mind if I come in?"

"Yes, I do," Gail Berta said. "I can hear you good enough from there."

"Okay, have it your way. I just wanted to know if you and your husband had ever talked about moving out of the Metuchen area."

"Well, yeah, We've both talked about it. We had planned to get out of here by 1985."

"Did you have anywhere specific you wanted to go?"

"We looked at a lot of maps and then we sent away for some information from Minnesota. Gene and I decided we wanted to buy a farm, near a town called Moose Head Lake."

"Sounds nice," Zimmerman said, forcing a smile. "Is it a large piece of land?"

"Yeah, about 80 acres," Gail Berta answered. "It's got a bigger house than this."

"That must cost a pretty penny."

"No, just about $29,500."

"Have you seen this land yet?"

"No, Gene and I were going to look at it in June, but we cancelled because of the problem they had with dioxin. We didn't want to leave the kids."

"The Carolinas?" Thomas Kapsak was speechless. "She told you he went to the Carolinas with his buddies? What buddies?"

"Well, she didn't seem like she believed it too much, herself," Zimmerman said. He and Watson had dropped in on Kapsak when they returned from their interviews with Gail Berta. "She said it wasn't unusual for him to go down to the Carolinas with his buddies."

"And she said they had been planning for a while to move to Minnesota, huh?" Kapsak asked.

"Yeah, Moose Head Lake," Zimmerman said, with a laugh. "If she's lying, she could at least get the town's name right!"

"Gene probably told her what to say to cover his own ass," Watson said. "This guy's operating on everybody," he added. "Cathy Warner, Pat Bauer, and his wife!"

"He's been lying to too many people for too long," Kapsak said. "Sooner or later, it's going to trip him up."

"I just want to be there when he falls," Watson said.

Kapsak told the detectives that he had appeared in court earlier that day and won a court order to obtain the past six months' toll records of Gene

Berta's home telephone from New Jersey Bell. Because they didn't want to alert Berta that the investigation was beginning to center around him, the order also prohibited New Jersey Bell from notifying Berta that his records had been released.

"I think we need to get together and review where we are so far," Kapsak said. "Let's meet in about an hour at John Haley's office and go over what we've got. We'll be able to get a look at the evidence he's been able to pick up so far. I'll let the rest of the team and the Prosecutor know, so they can sit in."

Pat Bauer glared at the telephone receiver for a few moments before hanging up the phone. She had called Gene's house, looking for him, and Gail Berta had just hung up on her. She was in the first aid squad headquarters' basement, having driven there straight from work.

Bauer had found it nearly impossible to concentrate the entire morning at work; "*Thank God for summer hours,*" she thought to herself. "*I never would have made it through a full day.*" Pat's company allowed its employees to go home at 12:30 p.m. on Fridays during the summer.

Bauer paced the rec room floor; she was getting nervous and needed some answers from Gene, right away. She didn't understand why that detective had asked her so many questions about Gene and their trip and about Cathy Warner.

"*I wonder if they think Gene killed her,*" Pat thought. She remembered reading in the newspaper that the medical examiner said Warner had been killed at least three or four days before she was discovered.

"*He was with me the whole weekend,*" she thought. "*He couldn't have killed her.*"

Then, looking down at the phone, Pat murmured, "Gene, hurry up and call me, I really need to see you."

Her plea was answered at about 2 p.m., when Gene finally called.

"Hey babe, I got the message that you called. What's up?"

"Gene, I'm at the squad. I need you to get down here right away."

"What's the problem? Is something wrong?"

"Gene, just get down here now. I need to talk to you."

Berta arrived at squad headquarters about 20 minutes later. He was greeted by a panicked Pat Bauer.

"Come on Gene, let's go for a ride."

"What . . . what is going on, Pat?"

"Don't ask any questions, just follow me."

Pat Bauer didn't speak for the first 10 minutes of their ride. She was frantically trying to arrange her thoughts, trying to make sense out of the senseless situation in which she found herself.

"That girl who got murdered last week, that was the girl you were going out with, wasn't it?" Her tone was cold, her voice sharp; there was none of the softness to which Gene had become accustomed.

Gene didn't like the way this conversation started.

"Do you think I did it?"

"No," she shook her head to emphasize her answer. "I don't see how you could have because you were with me at the time. But the point is, Gene, I don't want to become involved in anything like this; I mean, here I am going away with you and all of a sudden you're not calling me anymore."

"Oh, babe, I'm . . ." But Pat Bauer didn't give him a chance to finish. She had been preparing what she was going to say for an hour, and she was damn well going to get it out before he could sweet talk her.

"And I'm getting nervous about all these prosecutors talking to me. I need you here for support, Gene. They kept asking me for proof that I was there with you, so I told them about the pictures you took."

By this time, Pat had steered the car to their usual meeting spot, the MetroPark train station parking lot. She switched off the ignition and turned in her seat toward Gene, who had a quizzical look on his face.

"What pictures?" he asked.

"The pictures! The pictures you took out at the farm — you know, with me in that stupid swing — and in the motel, Gene, when I was in that towel, those pictures!"

Berta burst out laughing.

"I didn't take any pictures of you in the motel, Patty. I was just fooling around. There wasn't any film in the camera!" Berta seemed quite pleased with himself over the joke he had played on his lover.

"But Patty, why did you tell them about the film?"

"Because they wanted proof that I was there."

"Well, I don't have that film anymore. I put it back at Cathy's."

Pat Bauer felt the first sensation of a cold rage burning in her stomach.

"What do you mean, back at Cathy's?" she asked him, her tone growing even icier.

"When I left you that night we got back, I went over to her house and left the film there."

Bauer was furious.

"You left me and went to be with another girl?"

"Yeah," Gene answered, dumbfounded by her reaction. "What's the problem?"

"What's the problem? WHAT'S THE PROBLEM?" Pat Bauer slammed her palms down on the steering wheel as she spat out each word. "First my husband cheats on me, then my boyfriend cheats on me, and you want to know what the problem is? You bastard! You were with her when I was across the street waiting and waiting for you! The trip is in her name, you go to her house after I drop you off, and you want to know what the problem is?"

Berta didn't answer. He just stared at her.

Pat Bauer was near tears. What he had done to her, she felt, was the ultimate disgrace.

"That's it Gene, leave me alone," she said, facing forward in her seat. "I don't want anything to do with you. I don't want to see you, I don't want you to contact me, I'm just going to forget you."

"No, Patty, I'm not leaving you alone. I'm still going to see you."

"Didn't you just hear me? I said I don't want anything to do with you! I told you on the plane that I couldn't hack a relationship with you if you were just going to run around behind my back. And you said I had nothing to worry about, then you go over her house as soon as you're through with me! I don't believe you!"

"Patty," he began; he attempted to take her hand in his, but she yanked it away. "Patty I'm not leaving you alone; I'm going to start a new life with you, don't you see?"

"All I see is that I'm never having anything to do with you again, ever!"

"Oh, Patty, you're going to put an end to a beautiful love story. Don't do this."

"Oh, Gene, stop it. You don't believe that any more than I do!"

"But Patty, yes I do! I took you to Minnesota with me and you helped me buy that farm — our farm. You and I are going to have a whole new life together, Patty. One little incident shouldn't ruin all that."

"But it's not just one little incident, Gene. You're going to do this again and again, and you'll always have some excuse. No, this is it, I'm through. We're through."

Upon making her pronouncement, Pat Bauer started her car and steered out of the MetroPark lot, driving in teary silence back to the rescue squad headquarters. She pulled up next to Gene's car and put hers in park, not turning off the engine.

"Get out, Gene. And don't ever talk to me again." Pat Bauer stared straight ahead, waiting to hear the car door close.

Having no other alternative, Berta got out, slammed the door shut and walked back into the squad building.

More good news was waiting for Berta when he walked inside. In his mailbox was a phone message: "Gene, call Joe Zimmerman, Midd. Cty. Pros. Office."

Berta called Zimmerman as requested. Zimmerman told him that there were a few more things he needed to clear up, and suggested they meet the following afternoon at Metuchen Police headquarters. Berta agreed.

Zimmerman was all smiles when he walked into John Haley's office. The county identification bureau was located in a long, two-story building behind a diner on Route 1 South in North Brunswick. The walls needed a paint job and the floor was in ill repair, but, as John Haley was fond of saying, "it's a little cluttered, but it's home."

The meeting had just begun when Zimmerman joined the group: Besides Kapsak and Haley, there was assembled Dennis Watson, Casimir Smerecki, John Nagle and Prosecutor Allan Rockoff.

"I made an appointment to speak with Mr. Berta tomorrow at Metuchen PD," Zimmerman told the group. "I think, to be on the safe side, I should Mirandize him."

The Miranda warning — the set of instructions usually given to a prisoner when an arrest is made — is sometimes given in a non-custodial setting, especially when investigators believe they are close to making an arrest.

The news was music to Dennis Watson's ears.

"You think we're getting close, Joe?" Rockoff asked.

"Yeah, I do," Zimmerman said, as he settled into a chair. "There are just too many inconsistencies in his stories. First he tells me that he knew Cathy Warner slightly, then all her friends — and some of his — tell us that they had this long affair that lasted about 10 years, and that they were talking about getting married. Then he changed his story from last Saturday to Wednesday, especially the part about not going upstairs when he went back to the Warner house on the eleventh. I'm gonna talk to him in detail tomorrow to see if he changes it again."

"And there was the way he reacted to her death in the first place," Watson chimed in. "Real cold, like he never even met her."

"I think Mirandizing him is a good idea," Kapsak said, "but remember, we don't have anything yet that is strong enough for an arrest, let alone a conviction. We don't have a weapon, we don't have a bullet, we don't even know for sure where she was killed, there are no eyewitnesses; it's pretty thin. Just because he lied about how close he was to her, I don't think we can take that into a court and have a jury believe, beyond a reasonable doubt, that he killed her.

"Let's just take a little time and see what we do have," the assistant prosecutor suggested. "These are the possibilities," he said, counting off on his fingers as he enunciated each option.

"Number one, Cathy Warner's murderer could have been another lover with access to her house. Number two, the murderer could have been a stranger who forced his way in. And, number three, the murderer could have been Gene Berta."

"I take door number three," Dennis Watson said, raising his hand.

"I think we have to rule out the second scenario," Joe Zimmerman said. "We went through that house top to bottom. Everything was in order, her clothes were still packed in the suitcases, the whole place was locked up tight as a drum. There were no signs of forced entry, no broken windows —

other than the one the brother broke to get in — no signs of the doors being jimmied, nothing."

"I have to agree," Haley told him. "It looks to me like she knew whoever killed her."

"My gut keeps telling me Berta," Watson said. "This guy just ain't acting right. His stories don't jibe."

"What do you think, Joe?" Kapsak asked.

Zimmerman shook his head. "I'm inclined to agree with Denny; I mean, the guy acted like he knew she was dead, and he wasn't supposed to know. And then when I told him, he acted like he didn't even care! So I think this guy Berta is going to need some close watching, but I don't want to eliminate the other possibilities, not just yet. There are a couple of other people we need to check out — his wife, for one — before we can lock on to one person. Remember, he wasn't the only one with a key to her house, some of those workmen had keys, too."

"But they hadn't been there for a while," Watson countered.

"Yeah, but Denny, anything is possible."

"John," Kapsak said, turning to John Haley, the county identification officer, "what do you have in the way of physical evidence?"

Haley and a number of I.D. officers had been combing Cathy Warner's house for the past week, tagging and bagging anything they found that might prove useful. Haley had personally been to the house every day since Cathy Warner's body was discovered. Some days, all he would do was walk around, looking. So far, the investigators hadn't found the main items for which they were looking: a gun, a bullet, and some indication of where she was killed.

Haley referred to a list he kept on a yellow legal pad as he made his presentation. He would sometimes stop in his recitation to elucidate the significance of a particular piece of evidence, most of which he pulled out of a cardboard box.

"I'm going to start from the beginning so we're all clear on what we've found so far that might be important," he explained.

"The first night, we found two packed suitcases. They were both on her bed, and indicated that she had either been planning on a trip, or had just come back from one. The itinerary we found in her purse showed that the trip was to Minnesota, with a G. Berta. There were no tickets in the itinerary, which leads us to believe that they were used.

"Downstairs, on the kitchen table, we found a number of things, one of which was a small calendar. Looking through it, you notice that every day is crossed off with a horizontal slash; every day through and including July 7. There were also notations in the boxes for a number of days, indicating that she used the calendar as a diary. The box for July 8 held the notation, "NA 4:45 p.,' which we think means a flight that was supposed to leave Newark Airport at 4:45 p.m. On the eleventh, it looks like she wrote the words "Aztec' and "July 4th'. We're not sure what that means yet. Other stuff that was found on the table included department store and other bills, returned checks, old check registers, letters, pictures of what looks like the different stages of the remodeling on her house and a blank note pad that is labelled, "Things To Do Today'.

"The most significant thing we found in her purse was her checkbook; as we all know, that's where the $5,000 voided check was found. There was also another "Things To Do Today' list with different chores on it. It looks like things she had to do before her trip."

Haley reached into the box and pulled out a clear plastic bag with the slip of paper inside. He passed it around so the men assembled in the room could read its contents:

"Pick up end of June 30th — plane tickets. Call ahead — charge card or check.
Pay for car + hotel there
Flight to Minneapolis 7/8 early eve.
Rent a car 7/8 - 7/11
Hotel room Minneapolis 7/8
Moose Lake 7/9 7/10
Return flight Nwk 7/11 afternoon
US Air 4:45 -7:24 Pittsburgh $125

Northwest 5:15p - 8:02 p $139
3:25 p - 5:02 p

Hertz - Intermediate size
22.90 per day
Aries, Citation, Concord, Zephyr, Omega

Best Western - $52 double Mastercard
Call before 4p (TRAVEL AGENT) that day (we arrive) if need to
cancel
Moose Lake
1400 Mobil Guide."

"It's obvious she was going on a trip, and that she was making all the arrangements," Kapsak said. "And, based on what Mr. Berta has told us so far, I think it's pretty obvious that the trip he took is the one she was planning."

"Here's something else you might like to see," Haley said, as he retrieved another plastic bag from the box.

It was another note, undated, and simply addressed, "Hi Hon:

"If you want, here's $300 cash. Put it in the bank now. Just make sure I remember to pull out more for shore.

Love You,

Me.

P.S. In case you didn't see my other note, Rosemary says you can come to the wedding if you change your mind."

"We've also got the note that Cathy Warner probably wrote on July 8, when she was being told that her mother was taken to the hospital," Haley said, bringing out another plastic bag.

On one side of this piece of paper was written, "Mother to hospital, chest pain - thought MI - GB attack." The other side contained notes about several of Cathy Warner's patients.

"We're going to have to check with her friends and make sure that's her handwriting," Zimmerman noted.

"Yeah," Kapsak agreed. "Eventually, if we decide that Berta is our man, we'll probably want to get a handwriting sample from him."

"We also took a number of articles of clothing," Haley said, continuing his litany, "including a dress that matches the description of one Berta said Mrs. Warner was wearing the last time her saw her. We also have several nurse's uniforms, underwear and assorted jewelry and shoes.

"As I went back to the house during the past week, I noticed there were several areas in the basement, the steps and in the kitchen that held what looked to me like blood stains," Haley continued. "The first thing I noticed was a stain in a crack in the stairs from the basement to the kitchen. Then I saw another stain which looked like blood on the kick plate of the top basement stair, this would be the one leading into the kitchen. There were also some droplets on a trash can liner in the kitchen and along the wall of the basement steps."

"Do you have any idea where she was shot, John?" Rockoff asked.

"That's what's so damn frustrating about this, we're not sure. I personally think she was killed in the house, but I couldn't tell you where. We know she wasn't shot in her bathroom, because there's no bullet hole anywhere — which there should have been because the bullet went through her head — there's no blood — except for what was in the tub — and there's no bullet. We even pulled the drain trap in the tub, nothing. And I doubt that she was killed somewhere outside of her home and brought in; I think someone would have seen the killer carrying a large and bulky bundle.

"Did you check the walls up in her bedroom for bullet holes?" the prosecutor asked.

"We've gone over that house from top to bottom and haven't found a thing. I took a bunch of photos that haven't come back yet, I'm expecting them in about a week or two. I wasn't shooting anything in particular, just trying to get a sense of the house."

"Well, the presence of bloodstains in the basement would lead me to believe that she might have been killed there," Zimmerman said.

"Like I said, we've been down there a number of times and have come up empty handed. To tell you the truth, the walls down there are so pitted and scarred, even if there was a bullet hole in one of them, it would be next to impossible to find."

"So we're still left looking at the basic questions," Watson said. "Who, when, where and why. I think we've got the who, and I have a pretty good idea of the why. We have to work on the when and the where."

Kapsak picked up the calendar that was found on Cathy Warner's kitchen table, the one with all the days crossed off.

"I think this and statements from her co-workers are going to help us with the when," he said. "I talked to Dr. Shuster, and he told me that he could not be certain when Catherine was killed. He said his best guess was three or four days before she was found, but, because of the advanced state of decomposition, he said he could be wrong. That's why he wanted those maggot samples taken to that Rutgers entomologist. He thought an analysis of them would help confirm the date of death.

"Now, the last day crossed off on this calendar is July 7. We know she was alive July the eighth, but she obviously wasn't alive to cross it off her calendar. Let's take this a little further and speculate a bit. She was last seen on the eighth, Berta admits that he was with her on the eighth, in her house. If we can show that she was killed in her house, then get some additional corroboration that she was killed on the eighth, I think we've got our man.

"What about that stuff that was found around her car?" Kapsak asked Zimmerman. "Have we gotten anywhere with that?"

"That's been a dead end so far," the detective replied. "Sgt. Salamone in Metuchen took the meat and rolls to some local stores, but didn't come up with anything."

"Let's dig a little deeper into that," Kapsak suggested. "Try to find out where those rolls were baked, maybe there's something on the packaging that can tell us when. If they were planted, they were supposed to make us think she was attacked on her way from the grocer's. We're going to have to be able to dispute that in court.

"Okay, here's what I'd like to do," Kapsak said, bringing the discussion to an end. "Let's keep concentrating on her friends, maybe they can tell us more about Cathy and Berta's relationship; maybe one of them will remember someone else she was dating, a jilted lover, or something like that. Right now, we don't really have any evidence, other than a body and some circumstantial stuff. We're going to need a lot more than that.

"It seems to me that if the time comes when we arrest Mr. Berta and bring him to trial, we're really going to have to focus on the relationship if I'm going to convince a jury that he killed her. So far, we know we have a married man who was making a lot of promises to Cathy Warner and extracting money from her on the basis of those promises, apparently with no intention of ever keeping them. We need to establish just how in love with him she was and how much money he was getting from her. And we're going to have to prove that he never intended to spend his life with her. And to do that, we're going to have to rely on her friends."

The investigators sighed. A week into the case, and they knew they were just scratching the surface. And they also knew that in murder cases, the longer it takes to gather enough evidence to make an arrest, the less likely there will even be an arrest.

"We're still digging at the house, Tom," Haley said. He and Smerecki had been to the house several times over the past week, having left with a number of items that were currently being analyzed in the State Police lab.

"Well, until anything positive comes from that, let's just play it cool," Rockoff suggested. He held up his right hand, the thumb and forefinger less than an inch apart. "We're this close, we don't want to blow it."

"Okay," Zimmerman said. "I'll let you know what Mr. Berta has to say tomorrow."

Saturday, July 23, 1983

Gene Berta arrived at police headquarters on time at 1 p.m., having been brought to the station by Sgt. Salamone. Joe Zimmerman had already been there about 15 minutes, he wanted to settle himself in the conference room to get his thoughts together.

Zimmerman thought Berta seemed mildly surprised when he was told he was going to be given his rights under the Miranda Act. Although he had been reciting these rights for years, Zimmerman still read from a card; when he was finished, he had Berta sign and date the card, certifying that he was properly given his rights and that he understood them.

"I don't understand this, Joe, am I a suspect?" Berta looked genuinely unsuspecting of the answer.

"Well, according to the information that we have you were the last one to see Cathy Warner alive. You can take that any way you want."

"Okay, Gene," Zimmerman began, "I'm going to ask you once again to describe for me your relationship with Cathy Warner."

"Fine," was all Berta would say.

"Can you tell me when your first met her?"

"We met back in 1973."

"And then you started dating, is that correct?"

"Yeah, we dated for a while. Of course, that ended when I married Gail."

"Gail was your first wife?"

"No, she is my second. Anyway, Cathy didn't take it too hard; she married John Warner shortly after I got married."

"And did you and Cathy Warner resume your relationship after that?"

"John Warner died in 1980," Berta answered. "We started seeing each other after that."

"This was an intimate relationship?"

"Yeah, we were intimate."

"What can you tell me about Cathy Warner, Mr. Berta? What kind of person was she?"

Berta leaned back in his chair, crossed his arms in front of his chest and thought a few moments. A smile slowly crept across his face.

"She was a nice piece of ass," he said. "In the beginning, when she was a member of the rescue squad and after she was just divorced from her first husband, she'd go to bed with just about any man attached to the squad."

The detective shuffled through some papers as he hastily charted a new course to follow in his interrogation.

"Okay, Mr. Berta; do you remember at any time telling Cathy Warner that your marriage to Gail was a 'distant' relationship?"

"I remember saying that, yeah," Berta answered. "I think it was after her second husband died."

"I see. Let's talk about Pat Bauer for a few minutes, okay?"

Berta smiled.

"When did you start dating her?"

"We started seeing each other in February of this year," Berta answered.

"Before you started dating Mrs. Bauer, did you tell Cathy Warner that you were going to leave your wife?"

"Yeah, I guess it was around January. I told her that I was going to file for a divorce. We talked about that a lot. Cathy told me she wanted to marry me and have a baby." Berta laughed. "Did you know she used to go to a psychiatrist? Really! Over at JFK. I went with her a couple of times. I remember one time the psychiatrist asked her if she wanted to have a baby out of love, or just so she could have a tighter reign on me." Berta laughed again.

"Where did you stay those times you moved out of your house?"

"Sometimes I stayed at the squad, other times I stayed at Cathy's house. She wanted me to move in permanently, but I didn't want to."

"How long did you bounce back and forth between the squad headquarters and Mrs. Warner's house?"

"About three weeks. After that, I moved back with my wife."

"Okay, so about three weeks after you told Mrs. Warner that you were going to file for a divorce, you moved back in with your wife, right?"

"Right."

"Did you tell Mrs. Warner that you had gone back to your wife?"

"No," Berta said, matter-of-factly. "She didn't need to know."

"And this continued until the first week of May, when you were involved in a serious motor vehicle accident, is that correct?"

"Yes, that's right."

"Okay, why don't you tell me what happened at the hospital that day? After you were taken to Middlesex General."

"Well, that day I was involved in a two-car collision that killed the other driver," Berta began. "One of the nurses at the hospital called my wife, but I didn't know that. Then I asked a friend of mine to call Cathy and tell her that I was there. Then Cathy and Gail showed up in the emergency room at the same time, and there was a little scene.

"I found out later that Cathy went back home, got all my clothes that I kept there and threw them on my front porch. Gail went over her house later and had a long talk with her."

"Did you contact Mrs. Warner after that incident?"

"Yeah, I called her. I asked her why she tossed all my clothes. She said she did it because she felt I wasn't being sincere, seeing as how she found out that day that I had moved back into my house with Gail. So when I got out of the hospital, I called her. We met in a parking lot and we had a long talk about our relationship."

"And what resulted from that?"

"Well, we started up again. We resumed the intimate relationship that we had before my accident."

"And did you stay over her house with any frequency after that?"

"Yeah," Berta smiled. "I was over her house probably as much as I was at my own house."

"Okay, Gene. Let's talk about Minnesota. Did you and Mrs. Warner ever discuss moving there?"

"Yeah, I had some conversations with Cathy about moving there."

"Did you ever ask her for money so you could buy a farm?"

"One time I asked her for $10,000 that I could use as a deposit on land. I wanted to use whatever other money I had to fix up my house here and sell it."

"When did Mrs. Warner give you the money?"

"We went down to Seaside Heights, down to the Surfside Motel, the weekend Rosemary got married. I guess it was June 24. Anyway, she gave me a check there for $5,000."

"Why only $5,000?"

"Cathy said she went to the bank to draw out the entire $10,000, but someone at the bank said that because it was in a money market account, it would be better for her, in terms of interest, to take out half now and half later. I got the second $5,000 on July 7."

"Now, while you were in Seaside Heights that weekend, did you go to any other motel and make reservations for a future trip?"

"Yeah, at the Aztec. We were walking down the boardwalk, and Cathy wanted to go into this store to look at shirts. So while she did that, I went to the Aztec and booked a room for July 11 through the fourteenth. I gave them a cash deposit."

"Whose name and address did you use?"

Berta looked puzzled as he answered the question.

"I gave them my name and Cathy's address."

"Did Cathy know about these reservations?"

"No, at the time, she didn't know."

Zimmerman flashed on the calendar that was sitting on Cathy Warner's kitchen table the day her body was found. On it, penciled in the box for July 11, was the word "Aztec". She obviously thought she was going there, too, the detective told himself.

"So you and Cathy spent that weekend alone in Seaside Heights?"

"No, Cathy's sister, Mary Beth showed up the next day, the 25th," Berta said. "Cathy and Mary Beth had made plans some time before, I don't know when, though.

"So later that day, Cathy and I came back up here to go to Rosemary's wedding. Mary Beth stayed at the motel. After the wedding, Cathy went back with her sister, and I went home."

"Do you know when Mrs. Warner made the reservations for the trip to Minnesota?"

"It was sometime during the last week of June. She got them at the Menlo Park Travel Agency."

"If she knew she wasn't going, why do you suppose she made the reservations in her name?"

"I don't know! I told you, I never understood why she made the reservations in both our names . . ."

"Even though she paid for the tickets and made all the reservations," Zimmerman interrupted.

Berta glared at the detective. "I told her I was going alone, and not with her! I don't understand what was in her mind when she made the reservations."

"Okay Gene," Zimmerman said, unaffected by Berta's short outburst. "Let's skip ahead to July 7th. Now, you told me before that you spent that night at Cathy Warner's house, correct?"

"Right." Berta had somewhat regained his composure. "I spent that night with her, because she wanted me to drive her to work the next day. In fact, we were a little late, and I got pulled over by a cop in Highland Park. I think the only reason we didn't get a ticket is because I flashed the cop my rescue squad I.D. and told him that we were on a call. Then the cop got another call, and he took off.

"Gene, it's very important that we know exactly what happened that day, so I'm going to ask you to describe for me, with as much detail as you can, what you did and what Mrs. Warner did on July 8."

Berta folded his hands and placed the on the table top in front of him; he was the picture of self-control. "Well, after I dropped her off at the hospital, I stopped at a one-hour cleaners, then went back to Cathy's house to prepare for my trip. I did some odd jobs around the house, you know, I straightened up, washed the sheets and pillowcases, that sort of thing."

"Oh, I forgot to tell you, Cathy brought some food with her to work that day. The nurses were having a welcome back party for Rosemary. She also took an envelope that had $50 in it. It was a gift to Rosemary from the other nurses. Cathy told me later that Rosemary didn't come back to work that day, but she didn't tell me what happened to the food or money."

"So about 1:30, Cathy called me at her house and told me she was ready to leave. So I got in her car and drove to the hospital, and when I got there I called her. She came down to the ground floor to meet me, we got in her car and I drove us back to her house."

"And at this time, Mrs. Warner knew she was not going to Minnesota with you, right?"

"Yeah, well, when we got home, she gave me a little grief about that," Berta said. Zimmerman thought he looked a little uneasy. "We had a hassle about that, about me going to Minnesota without her. But the night before, she had decided to go to Virginia to visit her sister. Anyway, once I quieted her down, we went upstairs, made love and then we fell asleep."

"You made love and then fell asleep?"

"Yeah," Berta smiled again.

"Okay, then what happened?"

"Well, I woke up at about 7 that night. I knew right away that I had missed my flight, so I called the airline to change my reservations. Then we got dressed, and I drove Cathy down to the MetroPark train station at about quarter after nine and dropped her off in front of the station."

"Do you remember what she was carrying? What kind of suitcases?"

"She was carrying a large suitcase, a small suitcase and her pocketbook."

"And what was she wearing?"

Berta tipped his head back and closed his eyes, as if he was willing the picture of her walking away back into his mind.

"She was wearing a bluish-purple skirt, it was sorta long; it had an elastic waistband. I think it was cotton. And she had on a terry cloth blouse, it was either light yellow or beige. It had those thin straps, so her shoulders were bare."

"Do you know if she had any money with her?"

"Yeah, we each bought traveler's checks for our trips. I think Cathy got $200, I got $300."

"Did you know how long Mrs. Warner was going to be staying in Virginia?"

"Nope, she didn't tell me. All she told me on that Thursday was that she was going down there."

"What did you do after you dropped Mrs. Warner off at the station?"

"I parked her car in the daily lot, then called Pat Bauer at her house and asked her to come and pick me up," Berta answered.

"You had your own set of keys to Cathy's car?"

"Yeah, she gave me a set and she kept a set. I think she took hers with her. Anyway, Patty showed up and we drove up to the Howard Johnson's motel in Newark, near the airport. We spent the night there and took a flight to Minnesota early the next morning.

"Once we got to Minnesota, we met with a realtor and he showed us property on the ninth, tenth and eleventh," Berta continued. "On the last day, I signed a contract to buy 80 acres of farmland.

"After I signed the contract, Patty and I flew back to New Jersey. Pat drove us back to MetroPark, which is where she dropped me off."

"And what time was that?"

"That was about 10 o'clock. After Pat left, I took Cathy's car back to her house."

"And where did you park it?"

"In the driveway."

"Where, exactly, in the driveway?"

"Near the back, where I always park it."

"So I went back into the house . . ."

"Do you remember which door you entered through?"

"Yeah, it was the side door, near the driveway." Berta paused, waiting for Zimmerman to ask him how many steps he went up, or something equally useful. When no follow-up question came, Berta continued. "I went into the kitchen and called a cab. While I was waiting, I noticed the garbage hadn't been taken out, so I did, I took it out to the curb. Then I went back into the house and locked the side door. After that, I went up to Cathy's bedroom and put a roll of film in her bureau drawer. That was the film I was telling you about, with the pictures of the farmland in Minnesota. There will probably be some pictures of Pat Bauer on there, too. Then I went back downstairs, saw the cab, locked the front door and went home."

"Okay Gene, what did you do then?"

"I went home, and then Gail and I left for Seaside Heights. We stayed at the Aztec until the fourteenth."

"When you returned, did you speak to Cathy Warner?"

"Nope, I just stayed around my house and did some work."

"Did you even try to contact her?"

"No. I never even went near her house again."

"Had you ever been to Minnesota before, Gene?"

"No, that was my first time."

"How did you find out about Moose Lake?"

"I wrote to a company and told them I wanted to purchase property in different states and Minnesota was one of them," he replied. "The company mailed me back maps and brochures. After looking at them, I decided I was interested in Moose Lake."

"When are you planning on moving?"

"I want to get out of here as soon as I can," Berta told him. "It's just not healthy to be around here, all that dioxin in Edison at the landfill."

"Have you decided who you're going to take with you to Minnesota?"

"No," Berta said, "I'm not sure.

Zimmerman studied Berta as the man absorbed what he had been told. "Gene, let me ask you this; would you be willing to take a polygraph test?"

"Depends. What kind of questions would you ask?"

"Oh, the questions would be very specific," Zimmerman told him. "This won't be a fishing expedition. I'll ask you questions like, "Did you kill Catherine? Do you know for sure who killed Catherine? Did you arrange to have her killed?'"

"Okay, I guess that wouldn't be a problem. When do you want to do it?"

"How's Tuesday, that would be the 26th?"

"That sounds okay."

"All right, let's make it 9 a.m. on the 26th. We'll do it here, at police headquarters. I'll get Sgt. Salamone to give you a ride here, okay?"

"Sounds fine," Berta answered.

By the time he arrived home, Berta had come to a decision: it was time to call a lawyer. The best one he knew was a man he had used before, Morris Brown of the prestigious Middlesex County firm of Wilentz, Goldman & Spitzer. Berta called Brown and, luckily finding him in his office, related the events of the past week, ending with his agreeing to take a polygraph test the following Tuesday.

"First of all, Gene, you're not taking that test," Brown said. "If they've all but said you're a suspect, or even the prime suspect, I don't want you doing anything that would help them."

"But I already made the appointment with Zimmerman."

"Don't worry about that, I'll take care of it. You just sit tight, understand? Wait 'till I get back to you."

"All right, I'll wait for your call."

The attorney didn't lose any time. His first task was to place a call to Joe Zimmerman.

Zimmerman, meanwhile, was feeling pretty good with himself. He had just stopped short of telling Berta that he was their prime suspect, and the fool was still willing to help them drive more nails into his coffin. "I knew this guy was a talker when I first met him," he said to himself.

That jovial mood evaporated when Zimmerman returned to his office to find a message from a "Mr. Brown from the Wilentz firm" waiting on his desk. "Regarding Gene Berta and the Cathy Warner murder," it read.

"Who the hell is Mr. Brown?" Zimmerman muttered as he dialed Brown's number.

"Detective Zimmerman, I just wanted to inform you that I am Gene Berta's attorney. I understand you and he made an appointment for a polygraph test next week?"

"Yes," Zimmerman said, "that's right."

"Well, my client won't be there. To be honest with you, I don't have much information on polygraphs or on this case, so I'm going to want to confer with some other attorneys in my firm."

"Do you have any idea when we'll be able to reschedule?"

"I'll try to get back to you later next week," Brown said. "Maybe

Wednesday. I don't know how quickly I'll be able to get the information I need."

Zimmerman slowly replaced the phone on its cradle and stared at the instrument for several minutes.

"Mr. Berta's getting smarter," he said, an appreciative grin creasing his face. "Or maybe he's just getting scared."

Merelyn Daniel sat at a table in Middlesex General's nurses' lounge as Sgt. Salamone pulled over a chair. The woman's large eyes showed a sadness that had not ebbed in the week following the discovery of her friend's dead body.

"Mrs. Daniel, you mentioned before about a party the nurses had on July 8. Can you tell me more about that?"

"Well, it was a party for Rosemary, Rosemary Cascella. She had just gotten married, and we were going to throw a little get together for her when she came back from her honeymoon."

"And this was going to be held in the hospital?"

"Yeah, it was going to be in the nurse's lounge, here, at about 11:30. We were all supposed to bring food and we had all kicked in some money, about $50, to give her as a gift."

"And what was Cathy supposed to bring," Salamone asked, half expecting the woman to answer "hamburgers and hot dogs."

"Cathy was bringing cold cuts. And she held the money because she was going to get a nice card to put it in."

"And something happened that day, you didn't have the party?"

"No," Daniel shook her head. "Rosemary called in sick that day. But we ate the food anyway," she added with a laugh. "I took the money and the card and told Cathy that I would give it to Rosemary when I saw her, because Cathy was going to be away then." At the mention of Cathy Warner's trip — the trip she never lived to take — Merelyn's eyes filled with tears.

"That's all for now, Mrs. Daniel," Salamone said, rising to leave. "You've been very helpful." Merelyn nodded her head in response, quietly sobbing as the officer turned and left the room.

Salamone's next stop was John F. Kennedy Medical Center in Edison, where he spoke with Janet Demcoe. Demcoe worked with Cathy Warner at JFK; she and her husband, Al, a Middlesex County Park policeman, had remained friendly with Warner after she had left the hospital.

"I last saw her about a month ago," Demcoe told Salamone. "It was about the time that Gene had had his accident; she told me that he was moving back in with his wife."

"Did you know if Cathy was seeing any other men?"

"No, I think Gene was her only boyfriend. I understood that he was staying on and off at her house, which is why it was such a shock to her when she found out that he was moving back home."

"Did Cathy ever mention anything to you about owning a gun?"

"You know, she did once. I think it was in January, she told me that she had a gun and that she used to go target shooting with her late husband. I told her that I would go target shooting with Al, but his gun is too big for my hand. And she said that John's gun fit right in her hand."

"Do you recall what kind of gun it was? Was it a handgun, a shotgun?"

"I never saw it, but my husband said it was a revolver."

Al Demcoe later told investigators that he had known Cathy Neal Warner, her current boyfriend, Gene Berta, and her late husband, John Warner, for nearly 10 years. Demcoe said that he had dated Cathy Warner before either of them were married.

"Then she started dating John, and I just dropped out of the picture. I didn't want to lose John's friendship over a girl. But we stayed friends with them and we used to visit a lot," he said.

July 25, 1983

It was a bright summery Monday morning in Metuchen when Sgt. Salamone walked into McPherson Realty and asked to speak with Carol Carlin. Carlin confirmed that she was the person who sold Cathy Warner the house at 125 Durham Avenue.

"I don't think she made the decision alone, though," Carlin said.

"What do you mean by that?" Salamone asked.

"Well, every time I saw her, she had this man with her, Gene, I think his name was. He was a big man; long hair, a shaggy beard."

"Did she tell you what this man was to her?"

"No, not really. From the way he was talking, he looked like he was advising her on which house to buy."

"Did Mrs. Warner have any other . . .'advisors'?"

"No, just Gene. Well, she had workmen in, you know, plumbers, electricians, carpenters, to give her estimates on how much it would cost to fix the place up — I think she ended up spending something like $30,000 on renovations — but Gene seemed to be the only one who was helping her decide to buy the house."

"Okay. Did you ever see or hear from Mrs. Warner after she bought the house?"

Carlin thought for a minute. "Yes, she called me not too long ago, I think it was near the end of June," she answered. "She asked me to give her an estimate of the house's sale price." Carlin let go a slight chuckle. "I talked to her about it the next day. I told her I didn't think she would get back all the money in renovations she put into it."

"Did she mention why she wanted to sell? Did she say she was moving?"

"No, she didn't say anything like that. All she told me was that she wanted an idea of what she could get for the house if she sold it."

Salamone and Watson paid a visit to another Metuchen real estate agent later that afternoon. Robert Nann Jr. owned an agency bearing his name; he told the two investigators that he had known Cathy Warner from the time her late husband John owned the Metuchen Exxon station.

"I was dating a neighbor of John and Cathy's around the time John got sick," Nann recalled. "Her name was Sue Colitre. We became really close after John died."

"Did you know of any men that Mrs. Warner dated after the death of her husband?" Watson asked.

"Yeah, there were a couple that I knew about," he said. "She saw this eye doctor for awhile, I can't remember his name. Then she dated this sleazy guy named Gene Berta. He lives somewhere in town."

"Do you know how she felt about Gene?" he asked.

"It sounded like she thought they had some kind of future together. I remember, after John died, I suggested that Cathy take the inheritance and invest it in a small home. But Cathy didn't want to, she said she wanted to wait until after Gene got a divorce.

"Then there was one time when Cathy, Sue and I had dinner together one night. We were just shooting the bull about a lot of things, and we started talking about Gene and Cathy. Sue and I both told Cathy that she should stop seeing Gene, that he wasn't right for her. Well, the next day, in walks Gene Berta. He comes up to me and tells me to mind my own business and that he never wanted me to speak to Cathy again."

"Did he threaten you?" Salamone asked.

"No, he didn't come right out and say anything, but the inference was there. And it wasn't too long after that that Cathy called Sue and told her that she couldn't be our friend anymore after what we had said about Gene. Can you believe it?"

"When was the last time you saw Mrs. Warner?"

"I think it was in January," he answered. "I was rushed to Middlesex General because I got a fish bone caught in my throat. Pretty damn embarrassing. Cathy was there, we talked for a few minutes, and that was it."

"Is there anything else you can tell us about Gene or Cathy?"

"Well, only that I once had Gene do some electrical work for me at a house I rent out. The tenant told me that he kept making passes at her. That's why I told Cathy that he wasn't any good for her; she deserved a guy who wouldn't be out fooling around all the time."

The detectives visited Nann's former tenant — Margie Smith — later that afternoon, after he had provided them with her name and new address. Smith remembered Berta, telling the detectives that the incident happened about three years before.

"He was making the repairs and he kept making innuendos about wanting to go out with me," she said. "He told me he was married, but that he and his wife had an arrangement and each of them went their own way." Smith said she declined Berta's offer.

"Then, about a week later, I came home and found a rose with a note from him on my front door. He called me that night and asked me out again, but I told him no. The guy was such a creep."

Joy Niemiera had a normal day with her son, Greg, which is to say she was exhausted. She had lost count of the number of seizures the infant had suffered, the minutes he had scared her half to death when he stopped breathing. It was times like these when she missed her friend Cathy the most because Cathy always seemed to know what to do to relieve the mother's suffering.

After checking on Greg one more time, Joy flopped into a chair, let out a sigh and stroked her bulging belly. Thoughts of her unborn daughter, who's name would be Heather, filled Joy's mind.

The shrill ringing of the phone snapped Joy out of her daydream. Struggling to her feet, Joy lumbered into the living room and picked up the receiver.

"Hello?"

Joy distinctly heard the sound of heavy breathing. "*Great,*" she thought, "*this is just what I need.*"

"Hello? Who is this?"

The only response was continued heavy breathing.

"Who is this?"

The breathing stopped. In its place came a soft, yet threatening voice.

"I'm going to get you."

Wednesday, July 27, 1983

It had occurred to the investigators that there were most likely four key interviews of all those conducted: Gene Berta, Gail Berta, Pat Bauer and John Bauer. The first three had already been contacted; the only one who remained was John Bauer. That task fell to Zimmerman, Watson and Salamone.

Involving a fellow police officer in a murder investigation is always tricky business. The decision had been made to interview Bauer at Edison police headquarters; Zimmerman thought it best that he lead the discussion. Watson and Salamone agreed.

The four men met in an empty interrogation room. Zimmerman decided to keep it light, approach Bauer as a fellow officer seeking information, even though, in a broad sense, he was a suspect.

Bauer told the trio that he and Pat had been separated for some time when, on the fifth of July, she called him to tell him that she had just been hired by the Warner Cosmetics Company of Somerset.

"I told her we should celebrate, and then asked her if I could take her out to dinner," Bauer recalled. "She said yes, and we decided to go to Claire and Coby's, in Old Bridge."

"So the dinner was going okay, and then Pat said that she was going to Houston to visit a friend of hers. She said her friend was having marital problems, like we were, and that she was going so they could both cry on each other's shoulders."

"Uh-huh. And did she tell you when she was going to leave?" Zimmerman asked.

"Yeah, she said she had scheduled a flight for July 8, and that she would be back on the eleventh. So I said I'd take her to the airport, so that we could bring Andy along, and she acted real weird. She got all defensive, and said no, that she wanted to go by herself. I've been a cop too long to ignore a performance like that." Bauer's comment drew chuckles from the three investigators.

"Did she tell you when she was going to leave?" Zimmerman asked.

"I was over at the house at about 1 o'clock," he answered. "She said she was taking a 3:30 flight with Continental. She said she was on stand-by."

"Did you take her to the airport?"

"No, she didn't want me to, so I just left the house."

"Alright. You said before that you had been a cop too long to ignore how she acted when she told you she wanted to go to the airport alone. Did you do anything about it?"

Bauer's face broke out in a sheepish grin. He had used his police skills to perform some marital spying.

"Yeah, I tried to find out where she went. First, I called the Port Authority police at Newark Airport and asked them to look for her car. I gave them a description and the license plate number. They called me back a little while later and told me they found the car in the parking lot. I told them it was part of an investigation. So then I called Continental and Eastern airlines, because I knew they have flights to Houston, but neither of them had her listed as a passenger. So after a while, I called the people Pat was supposed to be visiting. Get this: I talked to the husband, and he told me that not only was Pat not there, he didn't even know she was supposed to be visiting!"

Zimmerman saw the anger flash in Bauer's eyes, so he quickly interjected a question.

"What happened when Pat got back? Oh, before that, do you remember what time she got home?"

"She got home at about 9:30 on the night of the eleventh. I was waiting for her." Zimmerman saw the anger disappear, to be replaced by a look of sadness. "I asked her where she went. She said it was none of my business. Then she told me to leave the house, and I said no, I wasn't going to leave because I lived there, too. Patty said if I didn't leave, she would call the police. I just laughed and said, go ahead. So she called the police; they came, we talked it over and I left. But I talked to my lawyer the next day and he told me to move back in, so I did. I moved back in while she was at work. I was putting my stuff in the bedroom closet, and I noticed that her bags were just laying there and that she hadn't unpacked them yet. I figured, if I looked in them, I would probably find out where she went and who she went with. Then I just, well, I searched them." Bauer looked a little embarrassed as he made his confession.

Zimmerman noticed the look, but didn't care.

"Did you find anything?"

"Sure did. I found luggage tags from the Menlo Park Travel Agency, over in the Menlo Park Mall. I went over there, to see if they had some record of her tickets, but they told me she wasn't listed anywhere."

"Is there anything else you can tell us?"

"No, that's really all that happened. I just remember I was furious because I thought she was going away with another man," Bauer said, trying to explain his subterfuge. "I mean, if you thought your wife was fooling around and you found out she lied to you about a trip she took, wouldn't you want to find out everything you could about it?"

"Yeah," Zimmerman said, "I suppose I would."

"Denny, let's run over to Warner Cosmetics and ask Pat Bauer about her husband finding the luggage tags," Zimmerman suggested, after he and Watson had left police headquarters. "I don't think she told us about that." Salamone took his leave, saying that he had some other matters which needed attention.

Pat Bauer was incredulous when she was told of her two visitors.

"Detectives? Here?" she said, hoping the receptionist had made a mistake or that this was some practical joke. *"Those bastards!"* she thought, as she picked up her purse and prepared to meet them in a conference room. *"I can't believe they have the gall to come here!"* She had been spooked by the detectives — Zimmerman in particular — ever since that first interview at the rescue squad headquarters. The two hours she spent with Zimmerman in the Metuchen police station had unsettled her nerves to the point where she called her brother, a public defender in New York City, told him what was happening and asked him his advice.

"Just answer the questions they ask you, Patty; don't volunteer anything," he had said.

She wasted no time in lacing into Zimmerman when she walked into the room where he and Watson had been ushered.

"How dare you come to where I work and ask for me like this! What am I supposed to say if someone asks me why two detectives were talking to me here? I can't believe you would do this!"

Zimmerman tried to calm her down.

"Look Patty, we're sorry if we caused you any embarrassment, but we just spoke to your husband and we had a few things to ask you, that's all. This won't take long."

A new emotion swept over Pat Bauer when Zimmerman said they had been talking to John: rage had been replaced by panic. *"God,"* she thought, *"what did he tell them that they had to rush over here?"*

"Do you mind if I have a cigarette?" she asked, not waiting for the detectives' reply before she reached into her bag. She willed her hand to stop shaking as she placed the cigarette between her lips. Zimmerman lit the end with a silver lighter he had fished out of his jacket pocket.

"Okay," she said, blowing two long streams of smoke from her nostrils as she sat down opposite Zimmerman, "what do you want to know?"

"After you returned from the trip with Gene, did your husband ever ask you about the Menlo Park Travel Agency?"

Bauer's eyes grew wide. "Yeah, he did!" she said, her nervousness now replaced with an air of wonderment. "And he really confused me, he kept saying, I know where you went, I know where you went! I know about the Menlo Park Travel and I know where you went. And that really confused me, because I didn't know how he found out about that. Did he tell you?"

As he had done in the past, Zimmerman ignored Bauer's question and pressed on with his own.

"Pat, do you remember when Gene told you the time and date that you were leaving for Minnesota?"

"Well, we made plans to go in June, and I know he told me we were going on July 8, but he never really told what time we were leaving," she answered, as she stubbed out her cigarette and reached in her purse for another.

"Was there ever any conversation that day about when you were leaving?" Zimmerman punctuated his question by flipping closed the top of his lighter after Bauer had lit her cigarette.

She looked down at the table, gathering her thoughts for a moment. "I remember getting a call from Gene at about seven that morning," she said. "We spoke about the trip, and then he said he would call me later and we would go over the final plans. Then he called me at around nine, and we had pretty much the same conversation . . ."

"And he still hadn't told you when you were leaving?"

"No, not yet. He called again at ten, but I said I couldn't talk to him because John was home. Then he called me again, later in the afternoon. He said he wanted to make sure that I was still going, but he still didn't tell me when we were leaving."

"Okay, and what did you do after that last conversation, the one in the afternoon?"

"I took my son, Andy, over to my sister's house. She was going to be watching him over the weekend."

"And did Gene call you again that day?"

"Yes, he called me at about seven that night," Bauer said. She was calmer now, the nicotine had succeeded in settling her nerves. Watson noticed that the pace of her speech had slowed down somewhat, but she still exhibited a nervous tick he had witnessed before: she would constantly flick imaginary ashes off of the table top.

"Did he tell you his plans then?"

"No, and I was getting angry about that," she said. "He asked me if I was still going, and then he asked me if I loved him and trusted him. I said yes, and he said he would call me in a little while."

"And did he?"

"Yeah, he called me later that night and told me the final plans for the trip."

"Pat, do you still have those luggage tags?"

"Yeah, I think they're still on my suitcases. Do you want them?"

"Yeah," Zimmerman said, "if you can find them. Just give me a call and we'll come pick them up."

"It's Kohen, K-O-H-E-N; my name is Jean, but all my friends call me Jennie." Dennis Watson gave what he hoped was an appreciative smile as he noted the spelling of "Jennie's" last name. They were sitting at a booth in a Woodbridge Mall pizza parlor; Kohen was Dr. Richard Borden's assistant and had agreed to meet with Watson after she left work. Watson quickly assessed the woman who sat across from him, nibbling on a slice of pizza; prim, her hair tied back in a bun, with a reassuring face and an easy smile. Watson watched her as she sipped her drink before asking his first question.

"I want to thank you for meeting me like this, Jennie," he began. "I just have a few questions. Can you tell me when you first met Cathy Warner?"

"I guess it was in 1979, after her first visit. She and her late husband had come in. We became friends rather quickly. I remember in October of 1979, my husband was badly injured in a fall at the Meadowlands. Cathy was so sweet, she always gave me medical advice, you know, things that I could do to make him more comfortable. She even offered to be his private duty nurse. She was so helpful. I felt so indebted to her. Such a sweet girl."

"Did she ever tell you anything about her personal life?"

"Well, let me think," Kohen said, as she took another bite of pizza. "I knew that she was dating a man named Gene and that he was an older, married man, with children."

"Did she ever talk about Gene?"

"She told me that he was an electrician and that he also drove a truck. You know, Cathy told me she even took lessons to drive a tractor trailer, and that she had gotten her license. I guess they were going to drive around together, or something."

"Okay, was there anything else she told you; any other men she dated?"

"No, Gene was the only one she told me about."

"When was the last time you saw Cathy?"

"About two months ago," Kohen said, as she took another sip of her soda. "She and I got together for lunch. We had a nice conversation."

"Do you remember what you talked about?"

"Mainly about Gene. Gene and children, and his children." A wistful look came into Kohen's eyes. "Cathy always wanted to have children," she said, shaking her head. "She told me she bought the house on Durham Avenue so she could set down some roots for when she and Gene got married."

"Is there anything else you can tell me, anything that she might have told you about Gene?"

"Well, there was something, but I really can't remember it exactly." Kohen knitted her brow as she probed her memory. "It was something about Mrs. Berta; either Cathy had offered $10,000 to Mrs. Berta or Mrs. Berta had demanded $10,000 in exchange for Cathy to take their two children when she and Gene got married."

Thursday, July 28, 1983

Joe Zimmerman and Dennis Watson found themselves driving along Main Street, Metuchen, on their way back to New Brunswick.

"What do you say we drive past Berta's house and see if he's in?" Zimmerman suggested. "There's something I need to ask him."

"Mind telling me your brainstorm?" Watson asked.

"Our Mr. Berta is not being entirely truthful with his wife," Zimmerman said. "For instance, he hasn't told her yet that he is the owner of 80 prime acres in Moose Lake, Minnesota. That's got to be a sore spot with him; I'd just like to see what happens when I bring it up, that's all."

"Sounds good to me," a smiling Dennis Watson said. "I'd love to see the guy shit in his pants."

Zimmerman turned onto Walnut and immediately saw Berta on a ladder, painting his house. "I wonder who's money he used to buy the paint?" Watson quipped.

Zimmerman and Watson exited their car and walked over to Berta. "How you doing, Gene?" Zimmerman yelled up at Berta, squinting to keep the sun out of his eyes. "Mind coming down to Earth so we can talk to you for a few minutes?"

Berta sighed — he made it extra loud so the detectives could hear it — balanced his brush on the rim of the paint can and slowly descended the ladder. He brushed off his overalls, then asked what he could do for the gentleman.

"Well, I just wanted to tell you that I've spoken to Morris Brown, and he told me that he was your lawyer," Zimmerman began. "That's pretty high-powered representation you've got." Zimmerman let his eyes wander over Berta's unkempt house and property, hoping his gesture was obvious enough for Berta to catch the irony in his statement. "He also told me that you weren't going to take that polygraph test that we had set up, but he would arrange to do it another time."

"Well, he's the lawyer," Berta said, clearly not interested in conversation.

"Have you talked to him lately about that? Do you know when you'll be taking it? Morris told me he would get back to me, but he hasn't yet."

"I don't know, I still have to talk to him," Berta replied, wiping the sweat off his brow with his sleeve. "I think I'm supposed to take it in New York City. But when I find out, either I'll call you or Morris will."

"Okay, that's fair enough," Zimmerman said, trying to sound affable. He knew Brown's strategy was to have Berta take the test in New York, then either agree or refuse to take a polygraph with Zimmerman, depending upon the first test's results.

"Ah, Gene, you were around when Cathy Warner was making the arrangements for her trip, right?"

"Yeah, most of them," Berta answered warily, not knowing where Zimmerman was headed.

"She put a hold on her mail for the week, right?"

"Yeah, she asked me to fill out the card, so I did. I left it at the post office."

"And when you got back on the eleventh, she wasn't home?"

"No, I thought she was still in Virginia."

"How'd you get into the house? Do you have a set of keys?"

"Yeah. Cathy gave me a set when she moved in."

"There's something else I've been wondering about, Gene," Zimmerman said, trying to sound casual. "How are you going to tell Gail that you already bought farmland in Minnesota?"

Berta did not bat an eye. "I already told her," he said. "I told her that when I got back from Moose Lake."

Watson had to suppress the impulse to call Berta a lying S.O.B. He abruptly turned on his heel and walked back to the car.

"Oh, I see. Okay, Gene, we'll be seeing you," Zimmerman said. He smiled at Berta and watched him ascend the ladder before walking back to his car.

Berta waited until the detectives left before calling Morris Brown and telling him about the visit. Brown was on the phone to Thomas Kapsak within five minutes.

"My client, Gene Berta, just informed me that two of your detectives were harassing him. I don't have to remind you that they've already Mirandized him, and they shouldn't be talking to him at all. Now I'm going to say this once: you tell them to lay off, or I'll haul your ass into court."

"Mr. Brown, I can assure you that our detectives are not harassing your client. But I will get in touch with them and find out what went on," Kapsak said. To himself, he said, "I can also assure you that the last thing you want to see is your client in court."

"That guy's a lying bastard, Joe, telling us he told his wife about buying the farm. She had no idea that he bought that land."

Watson was livid. He hated the fact that Berta was toying with them and getting away with it. It was all he could do to just stare out his window as the two drove back to New Brunswick.

"I know Denny, I know," Zimmerman was more amused than anything else. "I was just throwing a wedge in," he explained. "I knew that Berta hasn't told Gail everything, Gail has no idea how much she is being deceived. I just did that because I wanted to let Gene know that it probably would come out some day and I wanted to find out how he would answer it."

Just then a call came over the car's two-way radio; Kapsak was asking Zimmerman to call in on a "land line," a regular telephone.

Zimmerman pulled into a gas station and walked to a pay phone. Watson remained in the car, mulling over what his mentor had explained. "I still want to nail this guy," he said to himself. "I want this guy put away."

Zimmerman returned to the car several minutes later, looking mildly perturbed.

"What was that all about?"

"Seems like Mr. Berta called his attorney after we left and complained about police harassment," Zimmerman said. "Tom asked me why we went over to talk to him, and I just said I had a few questions to ask him. Then he brought up the Miranda, and I told him that Berta didn't tell us to leave."

"No," Watson agreed, "he was perfectly willing to answer our questions. He probably realized that he said the wrong thing when he told you he already told Gail about buying that land, and he ran to his lawyer for protection. What an idiot."

Zimmerman repeated his explanation to Kapsak when he and Watson arrived back in the office; Kapsak agreed that he had no problems. But he suggested that he call Morris Brown, just to set the record straight.

Zimmerman went back to his own office before calling Brown.

"I just want you to know, detective, that if this matter does come to court, I will have any conversation that you had with my client stricken from the record and rendered inadmissible as a result of your violating my client's rights under the Miranda decision," Morris Brown told the detective.

"Just hold on a second, counsellor," Zimmerman said. "First of all, I didn't violate anyone's rights. Your client had every opportunity to tell me to leave, he didn't. He answered every question I asked, and not once did he invoke his Miranda rights."

"I'm telling you I don't want you speaking with him any more."

"That"s not your decision, Mr. Brown. I have to hear it from Mr. Berta. If I have occasion to visit him again, and he consents to speak with me, I'm going to question him, as is provided in Miranda. If he tells me to go away, he's not answering any more questions, then I'll leave. But, as I'm sure you know, that has to come from him."

Watson, who had been listening to his supervisor's end of the conversation, silently applauded Zimmerman as he hung up the phone.

"Man," he laughed, "you sounded just like Perry Mason!"

Acting on information given to them by Joy Niemiera, Salamone and Watson interviewed Dr. David Rogoff, Cathy Warner's psychologist at John

F. Kennedy Medical Center in Edison. Rogoff had been Warner's therapist for several years, up until 1982.

"Did Mrs. Warner ever tell you of anyone that she was afraid of, or that had threatened her?" Watson asked.

"No, she never mentioned anything to me about having any enemies; she never said she was afraid of anyone hurting her," Rogoff answered. "About the only thing that was complicating her life at the time was her relationship with her boyfriend."

"Did she ever tell you his name?"

"Yes," Rogoff said, peeking into his file. "His name was Gene Berta. I remember her saying that he was married, and I think he has children."

"Did she ever tell you how serious this relationship was?"

"As I recall, it was pretty serious," the doctor answered. "I know he spent a lot of time at her house, I think he even had a key. Cathy used to tell me that he was going to divorce his wife and marry her; in fact, he even sat in on one of her sessions. He told me the same thing, that he was going to leave his wife and settle down with Cathy. Then I asked him why it was taking him so long to do it, and he became very evasive. He always seemed to have an excuse."

"Were there any other men that you knew of Cathy Warner seeing after her husband died?"

"There was just one that I remember," Rogoff said. "Cathy told me she had a brief affair with an eye doctor.

"You know, Cathy desperately wanted to have a baby. She was afraid she was getting too old to give birth."

"Did she ever tell you how she was going to resolve her relationship with Gene Berta?"

"No, she stopped being a patient of mine in 1982," Rogoff said. "When she left, she still hadn't resolved it."

July 29, 1983

"The guy's lying through his teeth, I know it!" Dennis Watson bolted out of his chair and paced Tom Kapsak's office. "Every time he opens his mouth, he tells us another whopper. He's got to know that we're checking up on him!"

Watson, Zimmerman, Haley and several other investigators, as well as Prosecutor Allan Rockoff, were assembled in the second assistant prosecutor's office for their regular weekly meeting to discuss the investigation.

"He told you that he'd already spoken to Gail about buying the land in Minnesota?" Kapsak asked Zimmerman.

"That's right. But when we talked to Gail, she didn't know anything about it. Remember, she thought he was in the Carolinas!"

"Okay, what else have we found out?" Kapsak asked.

Zimmerman recounted the interviews he and Watson had held with Berta, John Bauer, Dr. Rogoff, Robert Nann and Jane Kostu, as well as the interviews conducted by Sgt. Salamone with Merelyn Daniel, Janet Demcoe and Carol Carlin.

"How did Berta act when you read him his rights?" Kapsak asked.

"He just wanted to know if he was a suspect," Zimmerman answered. "He was real cool."

"What I don't understand is how the hell can a guy like that, a guy who hasn't got a pot to piss in, how can a guy like that afford a law firm like Wilentz?" Watson said.

"He's probably got a few grand left over from what Cathy Warner gave him," Zimmerman offered. "I'm sure he's dipping into that."

"I can't believe his balls," Watson marvelled. "This guy probably killed her, then he uses money she gave him to defend himself! Money she thought was going to be used to start a new life for herself!"

"What about John Bauer, do you see him as a suspect?" Kapsak asked Zimmerman.

"No, I don't think so," the detective answered. "He was pretty steamed about the thought of his wife going away with another man, but he didn't know who the other guy was, so he would have had no way to connect him with Cathy Warner."

"But didn't he keep telling Pat Bauer that he knew where she went and who she was with?" Rockoff asked.

"He said that, but at first all he knew was that she didn't go to Texas," Zimmerman answered. "He didn't find out about Minnesota until he found her luggage tags. And anyway, he still didn't know who she went with. No, I don't see him as a suspect at all."

"What about this eye doctor, have you followed through on that?" Kapsak asked.

"Yeah, he was interviewed last week," Zimmerman replied. "He went out with her a couple of times, when he and his wife weren't getting along. That was a while ago. I don't think there's anything there."

"Well, maybe he wanted to resume their relationship, and she didn't, so he got mad and killed her in the heat of passion," Rockoff suggested.

"There's really no foundation to that," Zimmerman told him. "Cathy never said anything to her friends about him bugging her, and I'm sure she would have. Hell, she might even have said something to Gene, if that was the case. No, I believe what he said, he just went out with her for a short time, until he got his head together."

"Right now, the only person that's really a plausible suspect is Gene

Berta," Watson added. "Everybody we've talked to, all of Cathy Warner's friends, are telling us how she was in love with the guy, how all she wanted to do was marry him, settle down and have a family."

"And then," Zimmerman interjected, "when I asked him to describe her, the first thing out of his mouth is, she was a nice piece of ass! He didn't care about her, all he cared about was her money."

"We got this guy lying to Cathy Warner, to his own wife, and to Pat Bauer," Watson said. "You lie that much, sooner or later you start mixing up your stories."

"Well, the fact that Cathy Warner was in love with him isn't enough for an arrest," Kapsak said. "John, have you been able to find anything else over at the house?"

"Nothing like a bullet, if that's what you mean," John Haley said. "We've taken some more stuff from the house to be analyzed, things like the kitchen door, the shower curtain from downstairs, a camera and some film." He paused to consult his notes. "A 12-gauge shotgun that will probably turn out to be Berta's — besides, from what Dr. Shuster said, that's not the murder weapon anyway — cellar sweepings, things like that. But as far as hard, tangible evidence goes, we haven't been able to come up with anything. I mean, me and Cas have been on our hands and knees going through that basement. There's just nothing there."

"So we still don't know where she was killed, right?" Kapsak asked. Haley answered by shaking his head, a look of frustration on his face.

"Well, all I can tell you is that we've got to keep on trying," Kapsak said. "If we can't prove where she was killed, we don't have anything to take into court. All the pieces to this puzzle are just too important by themselves, we've got to have the whole thing, or we have nothing at all."

Voices — R.

"After Cathy was murdered, it was amazing, Gene became a home man. For a guy that was never home, now he was always home. I think I seen him a total of three times after Cathy's murder, until the time he was arrested. He might have been down there maybe half a dozen times after that. But Gene was normally down every day; he would come down six o'clock at night, and he wouldn't leave "till 2 o'clock in the morning. Now these times, he'd come down 7 or 8 o'clock at night, and by 10 or 11 he was gone. None of that was normal. But I attributed that to, okay, he's a suspect, and he's walking a tight rope now.

"I never saw a woman stand up to him. I remember when he was pawning his wife off on everybody. He would say, "why don't you sleep with my wife?' Because he was cheating with so many other people at that point in time, that I guess it was bothering him. I don't think she liked it when they first got married, but after a while, she probably said, to hell with it, what's the difference? And they both did their thing.

"They stayed married to each other, I guess they slept together. They had orgies. They both smoked pot, and that they did quite regularly. He invited me to one of the orgies; I said, "hey, I'm a married man, I'm sorry.'

I happen to know that one time, there was Gene, there was Gail, there was this girl named E. from the squad, and there was Gene's old Navy buddy, I don't remember his name. About eight months after the initial orgy, that guy married that girl E. and they moved to Pennsylvania. He would come back and talk about that stuff, but who the hell wanted to hear about what you did in bed? Nobody wanted to know. But that was Gene.

"That's when they lived in Metuchen, they had a water bed. There was no room for anything else in the bedroom, it was just a water bed. The bad feature I remember about the whole situation was that they didn't have any children of their own at the time, just the two girls from Gail's first marriage. Those kids would walk around and curse, they were nasty brats. But that was the parents' fault. I mean, the kids couldn't have been unaware of what was going on sexually, and the parents would smoke pot with the kids sitting right in the room. How the hell they survived through all that is beyond me.

"They moved around a lot; they had a place in Edison, on Farm Haven Road, then they had a place in Metuchen, just before St. Joe's high school, one of them side blocks. That's where the orgies went on.

"He had total command of Cathy. In other words, if you were sitting here and she was over there — as God is my witness, I saw this happen — and you were looking at her, he'd say, 'what are you looking at her for?' And you'd say, 'Well, she's nice, I'm looking at her.' He'd say, 'You want to go to bed with her?' 'Sure, I'd love to!' 'Hey Cathy . . . (he gestures).' Anybody . . . if you were his friend and you liked what you saw in Cathy . . . hey, no problem. And she did whatever you said. She was sick at that time. She was Gene's slave. This girl was Gene's love slave, there were no two ways about it.

Voices — Dennis Malinowsky

"It was a good time, we were close, we really were. But things were getting worse and worse and worse with Gene. This was after John's death.

"Gene used to bring Cathy around to some of the jobs with him. Ford's Jewelers, Barry Berman, the owner? Gene did an electrical job for Barry, and rewired the new left section of the store. That was one of the last times that Cathy had actually gone out on a job with him. That was when, whatever the date was, when I started to distance myself from them, because Dawn (Farnell) and I were seeing more and more of each other, and this whole problem with Gene and Cathy was starting to wear on us both. I think with Dawn starting a business, and myself being involved and working also, we really didn't have all that much time. I just had a bad feeling.

"Gene was always fond of guns. They were hunters, farmers. His father used to work at the arsenal. They always had guns. He had a hammer shotgun, external hammer, a beautiful piece. That's where I was introduced to guns. I remember them showing me jars of different kinds of bullets.

"Gene had this one shotgun, he called it Grandpa. Every morning, a crow or a catbird would be in a tree outside his bedroom window, making a lot of noise and waking him up, and it pissed him off to no end. So one week, he took Grandpa upstairs with him, and he would get up in the morning to get it, but he could never get a shot at the damn thing. But then one morning, he looks out the window and there's the bird, but he couldn't get the right angle from the window. So he grabs two shells and the shotgun. He's running down the stairs, and he clicks the shotgun open, and puts one shell in each barrel. He gets down to the base of the stairs, and there's a big rounded post there, so he grabs ahold of it with one hand to swing himself around. As he swung around, he snapped the gun closed with the other hand, but at the same time, the safety comes off, and both rounds go into the floor. But that wasn't the worst of it; the worst of it was the pellets went through the floor and into his mother's pickling jars in the basement! He told me, 'she kicked my ass for an hour! And I got the ear job.' She comes running over, 'what happened? What happened? What happened?' 'Oh, the goddamned safety come off and the gun went off.' And she goes, 'My pickling room!' Because they had a coal bin that they had turned into a pickling room and that's where she kept her jarred stuff. She goes running downstairs and comes back up, grabs him by the ear and says, 'come here.' He was down there picking that stuff up with a wheelbarrow.

"He was always mischievous. He hated cats, used to plink them with his guns. That's part of the time I started to back away. He had the .22 and I had bought him a scope for it. I had just gotten back from the military. He bought the house in '78, he was trying to get some squirrels that had nested in the eves. He got them all. He could shoot, but I wouldn't call him a marksman. What does it take to deal with a .22? I never knew him to have a handgun.

"We were always mischievous kids, but nothing that I would call criminal. But as I look back, he always did have that 'get back, get even vendetta' shit. And I find that a lot of people are that way. Quite evidently, his got a little blown out of proportion. He got a little bit strung out with his own importance, or his need to be important.

"I remember when he was being evicted from the house on Aylin Street, he was going to torch a place his landlord owned, just because his landlord was throwing him out. We were in the garage, and he took a piece of electrical zip cord with a plug on one end. He shorted two ends together, then he plugged it in and it sparked. And I said, 'What the fuck you doing, you gonna burn something down?' He said, 'It's better you don't know.' As a matter of fact, I remember hearing Gail saying something about that. So, I guess he was getting thrown out of there, so he was going to do the get-back.

"I knew Gail and her family after Gene had started dating her. That's a strange bunch. Her father had done time, he was a small-time crook. Perhaps that's where Gene could have gotten his intros into doing whatever he had to do to get money. Ursula (Ushie) was her younger sister. Then there was a brother who was in between Ursula and Gail. Then there was a young one. He had a learning disability; he started smoking pot at a young age. I said to him, "you're fucking burned out already, you're never gonna go nowhere.' And he went running into Gail, 'Am I burnt out? Am I burnt out?' But you could see where Gail had a family that was more like a bunch of independent individuals living in the same house. Whenever I was there, I felt like something was always going to explode, even though there was nothing happening."

"That rescue squad was a regular Peyton Place, that's for sure. There was another girl there, M.S., she had Gene's baby. I was not at the meeting when she announced that she was pregnant. Gene and another guy were. They were in the back of the room, and somebody had said that when she said she was pregnant and she was going to be taking a leave of absence, everybody turned around and looked at those two. Later they said, well, Dennis isn't here, so we know it's got to be one of you three motherfuckers. So, I said, 'swear to God, it wasn't me!' She was always so prim and proper. And then R. told me she wasn't so prim and proper, and he knew. This is when he was separated from his wife. Quite evidently, everybody would sleep around with everybody else.

"There was another girl, I don't remember her name, but her husband was a park ranger and he had a gun, so you had to be in and out of there quick. But when you're young and you want to sow your Johnny Appleseed, you're thinking with another part of your anatomy other than your cranium. It's all a part of growing up. Most guys would stay away from married women, but when there's an open invitation . . . For me it was just one time, I said, I can't handle this anymore. I think it was about that time that I started reflecting and just wondering, what the hell are you doing? And was it really all worth that? I guess I was about 23 or so when I started thinking more and more and more about some of the nonsense that I would pull off — who are you hurting and, while it was fun while it lasted, what kind of hurt did you put on their head?

"This might be how rescue squads are, I can't see how this would be so atypical. Where there's men and where there's women, there's going to be fooling around. I hear there was more to it than I knew of. It was just that there were a bunch of young guys out whoring around. Gene seemed to attract all the pùtas. Then everybody shared, 'cuz he didn't mind, so why the hell not?

"The orgies were with Bart and Gene and a woman named E.. This is my understanding: Kenny was around at that time. Gene and Gail lived on Aylin Street, and this E. got involved with Gene and the squad and whatever, and quite evidently what happened was, I think it started with Bart and it wound up going to Kenny, or it was Gene, Kenny and Bart and Gail and this E.. That's how things got started. As I recall the story that Gene told, his wife was getting peeved because the guys were paying E. more attention than her.

"Kenny had been in the service and left an Oriental girl behind. E. was his first girlfriend since being out of the service. And they decided to get married. Kenny and Gene had a parting of the ways because of E. I think this whole thing of the orgies was what brought Kenny and E. together, and Gene wanted to continue with them, and Kenny didn't, and I think, love being as blind as it is, Gene probably told him, look, man, she isn't worth it. That was it, Kenny didn't want to hear it and he was gone.

"I also heard he (Gene) wasn't shy about sharing his wife. I didn't, however I heard stories that that wasn't a problem. Gail and I had spoken of it, but I opted out. I though she was a nice girl, but I didn't find her all that attractive, and it was just too close to home; you don't shit where you eat. Gene and I were close friends, I didn't know what his feelings were and that was just about the time when my ideals started to change."

Monday, August 1, 1983

Dennis Watson sat at his desk, his pencil tapping an irregular tattoo while he idly stared at the notes he had hastily scribbled during a conversation with a United Airlines booking agent. Watson wanted to check out Berta's assertion that he had been able to change his reservations with one day's notice. He found out that there were 12 flights daily from Newark International Airport to Chicago's O'Hare, from where a passenger could easily board another plane to Minnesota. Watson was also told that a passenger could easily switch reservations from one flight to another, providing there was room. That was as specific as he could get, though; when pressed about the existence of any records of July 9, 1983, the airline's representative told Watson that United did not keep that kind of information on file.

"Patty? This is Cheryl. Listen, can I come over? I've got something really important to tell you."

"Sure, Cheryl, come on. I'm not doing anything."

"Okay, I'm at the Menlo Mall. I'll be there in a few minutes."

Pat Bauer was perplexed.

"What could be so important that she would have to come from a mall to tell me?" she thought. "This is really getting too weird for me."

The fact that it was close to 9 p.m. didn't faze Pat Bauer in the least; strange things had been happening ever since she came back from Minnesota with Gene. The scariest of all was that big black car that Pat noticed driving up and down her street several times each night. The first time she saw it, all she could think of were the times when Gene used to hint that he had Mafia connections; Pat thought that maybe he had sent some of his Mafia buddies to keep an eye on her. Or worse. It had gotten to the point, she once confided in Cheryl, that she was afraid to drive down Route 287 to go to work.

Pat had the coffee ready for Cheryl when she arrived 15 minutes later. Cheryl's face was beet red.

"I'm so mad!" she said, as she poured cream into her coffee. "I was walking through the mall when that cop, Danny Cannavo, you know him? He comes up to me and he starts talking about you, saying what a nut you were."

"What?" Pat nearly dropped her coffee mug.

"Yeah! He said he was at your house the other day when you and John were fighting, and that you were screaming at everybody and saying fuck this and fuck that. 'That Pat's a kook,' he said.

"I don't believe this. He wasn't there!"

"Yeah! But listen! So I said to him, 'gee Danny, that's funny, I was there, but I didn't see you.' So he starts backing off, and mumbling something about being outside. So I said, 'you know what, Danny? I'm going to go see Patty and tell her what you said. You're supposed to be her friend'."

"That bastard! I'll get him!" Pat was livid. If Cannavo was making up stories about her, she could be pretty certain that others were, too. "I've got to put a stop to this, quick, before someone believes this crap."

"Well, he didn't look too happy when I told him I was going to tell you."

"He's not going to be too happy when I complain to his boss, either."

Tuesday, August 2, — Monday, August 8, 1983

Dennis Watson performed the majority of the footwork during the first week of August. On Tuesday, August 2, he met with Jerry Celentano of South Plainfield, whose name police had found on a note the day Cathy Warner's body was discovered. The note, which was found in the dead woman's mailbox, read, "Let me know if I can help," and was signed by Celentano.

"Yeah, that's me," Celentano said, as he handed the slip of paper back to Watson. "She called me and asked if I could remove an empty oil tank from her back yard, but I said no because I didn't have anything to carry it in. So a few weeks later, I was riding with a friend of mine, in his pickup, and we ended up in her neighborhood. So I said to my friend, 'You want to make some quick money?' and I told him about the oil tank. I said, 'Let's go over to this girl's house and see if she still needs it moved.' He said yes, so we drove over to her house.

"We drove up, and I saw her car in the driveway, so I went and knocked on the door. Nobody answered, so I waited a few minutes, then I wrote that note and stuck it in her mailbox."

"Do you remember exactly when you were at her house?" Watson asked.

"Yeah, it was a couple of weeks ago, I guess it would have been July 12th."

"By any chance, do you recall where her car was parked, its position in the driveway?"

"It was at the back end of the driveway, kind of on the grass."

Watson returned to his office pleased with his work. He had gathered another piece of corroborating evidence that could be used to show that Cathy Warner was dead at least four days before her body was found.

Watson spent the remainder of the day attending to minor tasks, writing his report and trying to tie up loose ends. At one point, he came across Cathy Warner's phone bills. Noticing several long-distance numbers, Watson punched out the first number on his phone. "You never know what you're going to find," he told himself.

The first call was to Pat Vanderway of the RLM Agency, a Pompton Lakes insurance broker. Vanderway told Watson that Cathy Warner held several insurance policies through her agency.

The next call was to Judy Kenner of Old Bridge, whose father, Robert, owned a scrap metal business. Kenner recalled that a woman called her father around the end of June and asked whether he could pick up an oil tank. She was told that he worked only for large companies.

The final call was to Ronald Syme, Cathy Warner's accountant. She had called his Caldwell office on June 30 to inquire about her estimated quarterly income tax, he told Watson.

On Wednesday, August 3, Watson and Kapsak went to the First National Bank branch in Metuchen, where they met Beverly Kodila, the senior platform representative.

"We checked our withdrawal records on the account and found something you might find interesting," Kodila told the pair as she led them into her office. "Not everyone is aware of this, but every time you make a withdrawal from our automatic teller machine, we have a closed-circuit television camera recording the transaction. This is so we have some way to identify a person who might steal a money card and use it to gain access to an account, or who may commit some vandalism to the machine."

On her desk, with the screen facing two visitor's chairs, sat a portable videotape viewer. Kodila removed a cassette from its case, inserted it into the viewer and turned the machine on.

"Why, it's our friend Gene!" Watson said, with mock surprise. "Looks like he needs some money."

"When was this taken?" Kapsak asked.

"The date and time are stamped on the film," Kodila said. "This tape was taken at 12:21 a.m., July 12th."

"He looks like it's just another day at the bank," Watson opined.

"Gail was probably waiting for him in the car," Kapsak added. "I can't believe she never even wondered where he was getting all this money."

"Well, sometimes people don't ask questions because they don't want to know," Watson said. "I get the feeling most of the women involved with Gene Berta were like that."

"Except Cathy Warner," Kapsak mused.

The assistant prosecutor and detective thanked Kodila for her efforts and left the bank.

"Well, that's another lie Mr. Berta has ensnared himself in," Kapsak told Watson as they walked down Main Street. "He and Gail said they arrived at Seaside Heights by 12:30; unless the Concorde flies to Seaside Heights, I'd say they were off by at least an hour."

"For some reason, he didn't want us to know that he got that money," Watson said. "I'll give you three guesses what that reason is."

"Patty? It's Cheryl. You're not going to believe this, but I'm at the Menlo Mall again and I ran into that jerk Cannavo."

"Now what did he say?"

"I can't tell you over the phone, I'll be there in a couple of minutes."

Pat looked at the clock, it was about 6:50 p.m. Cheryl arrived at her house before seven.

Bauer noticed that her friend looked pale, and that he hands were slightly shaking as she accepted her coffee.

"So now what did he say?" Pat asked. Mad as she was, she hadn't followed through on her threat to complain to Cannavo's boss.

"Oh, Patty, this is terrible. He saw me walking through the mall, and he comes up to me and says, 'Just a word to the wise; you go back and tell your girlfriend that they know she bought the ice. They found her fingerprints, and they know that she's the one who killed Cathy Warner.' "

"WHAT!" Pat Bauer bolted upright, knocking over her chair. "He said I was the one who killed her! I didn't kill anybody! I didn't even know who she was!"

Cheryl jumped up and tried to calm her friend, who had by now burst into tears.

"I don't understand! Who is doing this to me? Why do they say these things, Cheryl, why are they trying to hurt me? I didn't kill her! Why would I kill her?"

"I know you didn't Patty, I know you didn't. I just wanted to tell you what he said so you'd know what is going on."

"I know I don't have to take this shit," Pat said, as she wiped the tears from her eyes with a napkin. She walked into the kitchen and opened the cover of her address book. Inside she found a card given to her by Joe Zimmerman.

Glancing at the clock, which read 7:30, Pat dialed Zimmerman's number.

"Middlesex County Prosecutor's Office."

"Hello, I need to speak with Joe Zimmerman."

"I'm sorry ma'am, but Lieutenant Zimmerman is gone for the day. Can I take a message and have him get back to you in the morning?"

"NO!" Pat felt another wave of hysterics coming on. "You don't understand! I gotta talk to him tonight! He's gotta call me. This is Patty Bauer."

"Can you tell me what this is in reference to?"

"The Cathy Warner murder."

"Alright. I'll see if I can get in touch with him and have him call you."

"Thanks for nothing," Pat said as she hung up the phone. She walked back into her dining room. "He wasn't there, but the security guard or whoever's there is going to try to get in touch with him. I don't believe this happening to me."

About five minutes passed before the phone rang.

"Hello?"

"Hi Patty. Joe Zimmerman here. What can I do for you?"

"Oh Joe, thank God you called! I want to know what's going on. Some Edison cop just told a friend of mine that you guys were getting ready to arrest me because you found my fingerprints in Cathy Warner's house, and you knew that I bought the ice! What's going on? What ice?"

"Whoa, whoa, Patty, slow down a minute. Now who said this?"

"This Edison cop. He ran into a friend of mine at the Menlo Park Mall, and said all those things to her. Are they true? Am I really the one you think killed her?"

"Listen Patty, just relax. You're not a suspect, okay? We didn't find any of your fingerprints in the house, and I don't know what he's talking about when he says you bought the ice. I don't know what that means."

"Well, that's what this guy is going around saying."

Zimmerman recognized his chance to make an ally out of Pat Bauer.

"Listen Patty, if you'll cooperate with us, I'll take care of this. I'll make him stop saying that stuff."

"Well, okay. Okay, I'll cooperate."

"Great. First, what's this guy's name?"

"Cannavo. Danny Cannavo."

"And he's an Edison cop?"

"Yeah. My husband knows him."

"Okay. Don't worry about this anymore. I'll take care of it."

"Thanks, Joe. I really appreciate it."

Assembled in the Edison Chief of Police's office the next day, August 4, was the chief, Robert Henna, Joe Zimmerman, Dennis Watson, Danny Cannavo and John Bauer. Although none of the officers knew what the meeting was about, Cannavo looked quite ill at ease.

Zimmerman, wearing his fiercest mask, walked up to Cannavo, who was seated.

"You!" he said, pointing directly at Cannavo. "You have got a big mouth!"

"What? I . . ."

"I don't want to hear it," Zimmerman said. "You are interfering in an investigation, and I don't like it. And I can assure you, if I don't like it, the prosecutor doesn't like it, either."

"You mind telling me what you're talking about?" Cannavo said.

"The other night, you went up to a friend of Pat Bauer's in the Menlo Mall and told her that she better tell Pat to watch out, because 'they' know that she bought the ice, and 'they' found her fingerprints in Cathy Warner's house, and that 'they' know she killed Cathy Warner!"

"What!" John Bauer had risen to his feet, his fists clenched, staring at his brother officer. "Where do you get off saying that?"

Cannavo remained silent and seated.

"This is what you're going to do," Zimmerman continued. "First, you're going to keep your mouth shut about this investigation because you don't know what you're talking about. Second, you're going to go to Pat Bauer and apologize for saying those stupid things about her."

"I'm not apologizing to anybody, " Cannavo said.

Bauer, enraged by the thought that this man had been bad mouthing his wife, strode over to Cannavo, picked him up by his lapels and smashed him back against a wall, his face just inches from Cannavo's.

"You will apologize" Bauer hissed.

"But she's playing around on you," Cannavo said, a slight tremor in his voice.

"She's still my wife, and you will apologize!"

Bauer held Cannavo against the wall for several minutes, just staring into his eyes. Then feeling himself weakening, he let Cannavo go, stepped back and walked out of the room.

"If I were you, I'd listen to him," Zimmerman said.

Joy Niemiera was about at the end of her patience. She had spent the past half hour on the phone with a New Jersey Bell representative, trying to convince him that she needed a tap on her phone line.

"Listen," she said, trying to stay calm. "I have been getting threatening phone calls regularly for over a week. I talked to the prosecutor's office in Middlesex County, and they thought I should have a tap put on my phone. I don't understand why you can't do it!"

"Ma'am, I'm trying to explain, we are in the middle of a strike, it's all we can do to maintain our normal operation. Now, unless this is a dire emergency, and I don't think someone just calling qualifies as that, I'm afraid there is nothing I can do for you right now. Have you contacted the local police?"

"Oh, what good is that going to do me? Having cops hanging around here. He'll just wait until I'm alone, that's all." Niemiera had told the same thing to Kapsak when she had contacted him several days before, panic stricken, to tell him about the calls. Kapsak had suggested that she get police protection and also have a tap placed on her phone. She rejected the first idea, but thought the notion of a phone tap was good.

Hanging up the phone, Joy considered her options. "I've got to have some protection," she thought. "I'll talk to Greg, maybe we can get a dog or something."

Kapsak announced his decision on Friday, August 5.

"I think we should go for an arrest next week. I think we should pick up Gene Berta."

Thomas Kapsak caught his team off guard. A huge smile lit up Dennis Watson's face.

"Oh man, this is it!" he said, practically leaping from his chair. "When do you want to do it?"

"As early next week as possible; I don't see any reason to delay it," Kapsak answered.

"Are you sure we've got enough to make it stick?" asked Prosecutor Allan Rockoff. "I wouldn't want to go through all this and then have it backfire."

"Well, let's look at what we've got," Kapsak said. "Actually, let's first look at what we don't have. We don't have a witness, we don't have a weapon, we don't have a bullet. But, we do have a lot of other stuff."

Turning to Watson and Zimmerman, Kapsak said, "You guys have interviewed what, about 80 people by now? And what is the common thread — Cathy Warner was head over heels in love with Gene Berta, and Gene Berta couldn't have cared less. Here was a man who was making promises to her, promises that he never intended to keep, and was getting money from Cathy Warner on the basis of those promises. We know from talking to her friends that Cathy fully expected to be going to Minnesota with Gene, even up to the day she was killed. She made the plans, she paid for everything. That trip was very, very important to her. And then Gene ends up going with another woman, not even his wife? There was no way that Cathy Warner was going to stand for that.

"We know that the last day Cathy was at work was July the eighth," Kapsak continued. "Not one person who knew her said they saw her after the eighth. And Gene Berta has admitted that he was in the house with her on the eighth, and that she had given him a hard time about not going on the trip."

"We had a little hassle," Zimmerman recited.

"We also know that Cathy had a gun, a handgun, that no one has been able to find," Kapsak added. "What probably happened was she threatened to stop payment on a check that she had given Berta, and then he got mad and killed her."

"I can see him doing that," Watson mused. "I can see a guy like him getting so mad at a woman who would defy him that he would kill her. That's just the type of guy he is. I can even see them fighting."

"When do you think he killed her?" Rockoff asked his assistant prosecutor.

"It was July 8," Kapsak said. "I know the ME said she was killed three or four days before she was found, but he also told me he could be wrong. I think when we get the final report from the entomologist, I think we're going to find out those maggots were more than a few days old. And really, the maggots are just part of it. There's the calendar that was found on her kitchen table; she had crossed every day off until July 7. We found three years' worth of calendars in her house, every single day was crossed off. And I was talking to her mother last week, she told me that she herself had been in the habit of crossing off days for the past 30 years! She said she would do it each morning, cross off the previous day. Cathy obviously picked up the habit from her. And the reason why the eighth is not crossed off is that Cathy wasn't alive on the ninth to do it. Then there are her friends; several of them told us that they spoke to Cathy every single day, either in person or on the telephone. Not one of them heard from or saw Cathy after the eighth. Not one.

"And finally, there's the issue of the keys. The only person we spoke with who admitted to having keys to her house was Gene Berta. She didn't even give her parents a set! And whoever killed her had to have had keys because the house was locked up tight. I just don't see how there could be any other suspect. Do any of you?"

The room was silent.

"So you're absolutely sure about your evidence?" Rockoff asked.

"Absolutely? No. All we've got is circumstantial stuff. I'd rather have something a little more concrete, but I think that for now, we have to charge him. We can work on developing the case later, but I think it's important to charge him now. Let him know he hasn't gotten away with anything."

"You think money was the only reason he killed her?" Watson asked Kapsak.

"Yes, Denny," Kapsak answered. "You've seen his house, even his friends said he never had two nickels to rub together; Gene Berta's financial picture is muddy at best. Cathy Warner, on the other hand, was quite well off. I think he saw Cathy Warner as the solution to his financial problems, and when she threatened to cut him off, I think he snapped."

Kapsak looked around the room. "So we get him next week, right? I think that what we should do between now and then is tie up any loose ends. I'm going to need all the information I can get when I go before a judge for an arrest warrant."

"Unfortunately, I'm not going to be around to join in the fun," Zimmerman said. "I've got a conference in Atlanta to go to."

"Don't worry, lieutenant, I'll take pictures," Watson joked.

On the following Monday, August 8, Dennis Watson spoke with another of Cathy Warner's neighbors, Dorothy Gierlich.

"Do you remember seeing anything unusual about Mrs. Warner's house from about July 8th through the 16th?" he asked.

"Well, I do remember one thing," she replied. "There were two nights, I think the Tuesday and Wednesday before her body was found; I noticed an upstairs light was on both of those nights. I thought at first that she was home, but I didn't see her car. It was very strange."

"Did you usually see her car when she was home?"

"Oh yes; she always parked it at the front of her driveway."

Pat Bauer was sitting in a booth at the Parsonage Diner in Edison with several other squad members that evening when she saw Danny Cannavo walk in. She smiled to herself, amused at the story she had been told earlier in the week by Joe Zimmerman about the incident at Edison police headquarters. And she was mildly surprised by her husband's actions, she didn't think he cared that much about her. But the best part of it was when Joe Zimmerman told her that Cannavo had been ordered to apologize to her. "*This*," she thought, "*ought to be good.*"

Cannavo saw Bauer as he walked in the diner, but he did not immediately acknowledge her. He waited until he had ordered his dinner before pushing himself away from his table and walking over to Bauer's booth.

The squad members' conversation stopped abruptly as Cannavo appeared at Bauer's side.

"Patty, I want to talk to you."

"I've got nothing to say to you." Bauer wasn't going to let him off the hook easily.

"Well, I have something to say to you."

"You can say it here. You never cared about where you shot your mouth off before."

Cannavo bristled, but held his tongue. Then with a shit-eating grin, he bent at the waist and leaned his head close to Bauer's, until his mouth was just opposite her ear.

"You're a murderer's girlfriend," Cannavo whispered before quickly straightening up and walking away.

"You bastard !" Bauer hissed under her breath. "You have *had* it!"

Patricia Bauer — In her own words

"I WAS ONE of eight children, there were six girls and two boys. I had a Catholic school education, I went to St. Peter's in New Brunswick. I was a cheerleader, I was a twirler. I was a good student. The distinction I had was when I graduated from school, I had a 98.3 average. I didn't finish college. I went to college part-time after getting out of high school. I was going to go to Trenton State, I wanted to be an English teacher. Then I wound up going to Berkley Secretarial, and I wound up getting a job at Revlon. Then I went to Middlesex County College, and I took a couple courses at Rutgers, just to get them.

"My daughter Alena was born in 1962, she is illegitimate. She lived here. That's why I never went to Trenton State. I graduated from high school in 1961. I didn't even know I was pregnant. I was going with somebody, I didn't know anything about sex. I think that's why my parents were so protective, they knew how naive I was. I really didn't date. The guy who is her father is somebody who I honestly, truly believed I loved. But my mother says that had she let us get married, we probably would have been fine. I loved him, but I had no conception of what was going on. When I found out I was pregnant, they gave me an option of what I wanted to do. I didn't know what to do, I didn't know the first thing about what was going on. So I went to Scranton, there was a home for unwed mothers up there. I stayed at my aunt's house first. I didn't want to give the baby up for adoption. My mother said, well, you're 18, you can do what you want. So when I had the baby, I said I want to come home, and my father said, okay. And that was it. It was before things like that happened. At that point, My father worked days and my mother worked nights, so there was always somebody around. They felt that I was a wonderful mother, but I was too young to do it all by myself. And they were right. So I raised her with my mother and father's help. And she was the apple of their eyes.

"Marriage never really entered into it. The boy's parents made the mistake of saying to my father, well, he ruined her, he'll have to marry her. And that was the end of that. When I came back, I wasn't sure how I felt. They didn't want me to see him, so I didn't. The he started seeing another girl, and I got furious, so I started seeing him on the sly. So then he said, do you want to get married, and I thought, may parents would shoot me if I married him, so I said I can't. And he said, if you don't marry me, I'm going to marry somebody else. So that was it.

"Everybody in the family accepted her. She was adorable as a child, so that made it easier. And then, I was working, I had a decent job and my salary was good, so I spent it on her. She was well-dressed and she was a smart little girl.

"My oldest sister has her doctorate in biology, she's a prominent world scientist, so she travels around the world. My brother is vice president for Eastman-Kodak, so he's also a prominent business person. Everyone else is pretty much local; my sister is nursing supervisor at Robert Wood Johnson University Hospital; I have a younger brother and sister who are twins. My youngest brother is a lawyer.

"My mother, Lillian, a registered nurse, did private duty and worked in local hospitals. She was the nursing supervisor at Parker Memorial Home in

New Brunswick. Once, I was teaching a first aid course down at the squad and she got in on the first aid course and took it. She doesn't preach God but she's a firm believer that the Lord is there and will help you. We went to 9 o'clock Mass every Sunday. Until my mother turned 80, I didn't know how old she was. I didn't know how old my father was until he died.

"My Dad came from a big family, I guess there was about 18 kids. He always said he was 35, and my mother was always 29. He had this white hair, he never looked his age. He and his sister were the only ones that were alive, all the others had died of heart conditions. My godfather was 27, had a heart attack and died. But they said the only thing that kept my father going was his heart. His name was Walter. In Pennsylvania, his name was Walter Conley; his father died and his mother remarried. The man that she married, his name was Moore, and he adopted all the kids.

"My Dad was the superintendent for Mack motors. Mack closed the plant in 1963 or '64, it was on Jersey Avenue in New Brunswick. We lived in Scranton when we were born; my father used to go to New Brunswick, and come back to Scranton on the weekend. Then he moved us all to Franklin. He was a professional football player, years and years ago. Don't know the team. He had broken his legs a number of times; when he was at Mack one time, he was in a fight and a bunch of guys went after him and pushed him. Another guy got the ambulance there and got everything taken care of. He came and knocked on my mother's door to take him to the hospital.

"After the plant closed down, my Father went to work for Tony Yelencsics (the late long-time Mayor of Edison Township) as a service manager at Boro Motors (Yelencsics' business). When they opened up Dayton Ford, he went there as a service manager. He was at Dayton Ford when he got sick; he had some kind of virus, and he passed out. He slumped down and his knees went up in the air, and when he did, his leg broke. It was just so far beyond repair that they amputated it. Then they put in the fake hip. It wouldn't take, so they ended up doing three total hip replacements. None of them worked, so they finally just removed his pelvis. And to go from a guy who was so very active to one who was bedridden, he just couldn't handle it.

So he said, put me back in the hospital and you do something to make me walk. So we got this one doctor who said, let's see what we can do.

"So they put him in the hospital, and a therapist came in and said, are you Mr. Moore? And he said yeah. And the therapist said, I understand you want to walk. Here's a guy who had been bedridden for almost three years, and who only had one leg. And my father said, yeah, I do. And he said, well, let's see if we can get you up. So they pivoted him on a chair and stood him up. And my father said it was the greatest thing he'd ever felt. But what had happened was that his remaining leg had atrophied and the bone just crumbled. My mother came into the hospital 10 or 15 minutes later and took one look at him and started screaming, get me a nurse, get me a surgeon! His remaining leg is broken! So she said, get him out of here, I want him home. Then the doctor came in and looked at my Mom and said, you're right, his leg is broken. He said, you want to do some x-rays? And she said no, I want him out.

"They brought him home and a bone fragment got loose in his blood stream and he had a stroke and he died. And he died at home. But that was what he wanted and that was what my mother wanted; he was out of it — it was about three weeks from the time she took him out of the hospital to the time he died. He didn't recognize anybody, but a few hours before he died, it seemed like everything cleared. I had been over there and I was baby sitting because it was really tough on my mother. He was horrible at first, and then I guess he came to. And then he kept apologizing, he kept saying, you know, I love you kids and I love your Mom and all that. And I thought oh, look at this, he's getting better. And then Mommy came home, I guess it was about 11, and she looked and she said, how was he? And I said he was a little miserable in the beginning, but then he kind of calmed down and we were sitting in there talking for awhile. And she said, well, he's resting comfortable now, you can go home, go get a good night's sleep. I should have realized that something was wrong, but I wasn't involved with the first aid squad, So . . .

"I went home. She cleaned him up and about an hour later he died. But he was conscious; she said it was very peaceful and she was just sitting there. It's strange, you know, she had two dogs and my sister was back at home and she had a dog, and I guess because he was home all the time, the dogs loved him. So the three of them used to hang around by his bed. My mother said it was five to one and she knew that his breathing pattern had changed (once you know what's going on, you know the signs of death), she said she knew that he was going to go; and all of a sudden he sat up and he said, I love you, or something like that, and then he just laid back down and died. And the dogs went crazy; they started barking and growling, as though someone had come into the room. My mother said when he sat up, he actually opened up his eyes and looked, almost as if he saw something. The dogs kept it up so much so that the neighbor thought something was wrong and called police. My brother-in-law got the call and he came flying down in the police car. He had a key to the house, and he let himself in. He said, do you want me to call an ambulance, and Mommy said no, I'm just going to clean him up. She called us at six in the morning and told us to come over and say goodbye to your father. About seven in the morning, she called the doctor, and the doctor came over and pronounced him dead. He was 78.

"I met my husband August 15, 1968. I remember the day because it was a Holy Day of Obligation. I had made the dress that I had on, it was nice dress. He was an Edison cop, they were working security at Revlon because Revlon was building an addition onto the plant, so a lot of cops were working there. My girlfriend had met somebody, and the two of us were coming up from break, and the guy that she had met had just come through and he had this guy with him. So she stopped, she introduced me to this guy, and he introduced me to John. At the time, his badge number was 50, and I don't know why, but I looked at him and thought, he's probably 50 years old. So I really wasn't interested, but I ran into him two or three more times. And he kept saying to me, have coffee with me, sit in the cafeteria and have coffee with me. We thought we were the hot shots of the credit department at Revlon, so we did whatever we wanted. I was seeing somebody else at the time, and one thing led to another, and we were going out. And before I knew it, we were going out pretty steadily. We got married, December, 1970. It was a little over two years after we met. I continued to work, and he was married before, and he had three kids. He was in the middle of getting divorced when I met him. I was a little leery about getting involved with somebody who was married, but he was a good guy.

"He was a patrolman; it was exciting. He used to call me in the middle of the night. And you'd come out of work and the police car would flag you down, silly things like that. My father didn't like him. He used to go to Boro Motors, and my father used to call him a chiseler because he used to try to get him to reduce the price of his work. I guess after a while he kind of accepted it. Well, I was in a pretty nasty car accident on Route 1 before I had met him, and at the time, this was in 1968, when the case was going to come to court — we were suing for $100,000, which at that time was like a million — my father said a couple times to me, all that guy wants you for is your money. But I had been working for a couple years, and I used to have savings bonds taken out of my check, so I had a couple thousand dollars, and of course the possibility of getting $50,000, that was a lot of money.

"So, John and I used to have these horrendous fights, and my father used to say, he's after your money. And one time I said to John, you just want me for my money, and he said, oh get out of here. Your father doesn't like the fact that I was married before, and he wants you to get married in a Catholic church. That's what he doesn't like. My mother said you do what makes you happy, your father will love you no matter what. And he did. I was afraid he wasn't going to give me away. So we had a big fight, I guess it was about August, and we broke up. I didn't see him for about three weeks. I went to court, and even though we were suing for about $100,000, my lawyer said to me, you'll probably only get about $10,000. Well, it came time to go to court, and I think I wound up with $52,000, but by the time the lawyer took his cut, I had $28,000. And my mother said to me, just watch it, just watch it. And sure enough, I got home from court that day and John called. And he said, oh I can't stand it without you, I love you . . . My mother said, just don't mention that money. Of course I told him. So he decided we should get married. I got the money sometime in October. At that point, he wanted to go out and look for houses. We went out and must have looked at 25 houses; we fought about every single one of them, because he wanted this and I wanted that. I knew what I wanted; his wife lived in a small house that looked like everybody else's, and I wanted a big house. My parent's always told us, aim high, you'll get your mark — you're a Moore, you deserve the best of everything. That's probably what half of our arguments were about; he would settle for a lot of things, and I would always say, I want what I want, and if I can't get what I want, I'm willing to wait. He didn't, he wanted everything now.

"So finally, we saw this one house, we walked in and I said, this is it. It was a gorgeous house, they wanted $35,000, I had $28,000 and he decided we'd put $25,000 down, which was fine. I had a couple thousand in the bank and a couple savings bonds. By the time we bargained, it turned out to be $36,500. The first year we were married, our combined salaries were $25,000. He still had to support the three kids and he had to pay half the expenses on his other house. My salary paid the mortgage on our house, and the gas and electric and everything; it was difficult. The house was in Edison, off New Durham Road. We lived there for four years.

"When I got pregnant, I wound up with a lot of pregnancy problems, and I was about 4 months pregnant, and I had to leave work on a medical disability. I had Andrew in August of 1972.

"We got divorced in 1974. We were split up to October 1, 1977. When we got divorced, I sold the house and moved to the other side of town, off Woodbridge Avenue. It was about a mile from Middlesex County College and the Kin-Buc landfill. So I didn't see John for about the first six months after we got divorced, then I called him and we started dating again. And when we were separated is when he came down with Hodgkins and that's when he met Cathy and John Warner.

"When we were divorced and started dating, he was living at his mother's and with some other woman. He was very easy; he was a nice looking guy, and he needed companionship. So he met this other woman the day we got divorced and moved in with her. I don't know that much about her except for the fact that she used to come to my house all the time and bang on the door and scream and yell; didn't I realize that she was good for him and I was not? Women are strange. I have too much pride for that. But she was one in a series. I thought that he was doing that once or twice when we were first married, people would say things to me. But then if I asked him if he was, he would say, don't be ridiculous; I'm home here at night. Which he was, but also was at work during the day and that's when he carried on.

"We remarried on August 1, 1977. My mother was fine, my father came to the wedding, he was sick at the time. My mother and John always got along, though; I think he loved my mother. My father seemed to get along with him, but didn't like him. I knew it. It's funny because when I decided to get a divorce, I had gone back to my father, and I said Daddy, I think I want a divorce. And he said, a divorce? What are you going to do? He said, Why? Does he beat you? No. Do you love him? I don't think so. Well, whatever you do, I'm behind you. And that was it. And I said, Ma, can I move back home? No. But Ma! No. We remarried because I loved him. I loved him and I hated him. I hated the way he made me feel and I hated what he did to me, but when he was sick, he kind of reverted into a nice guy. In 1975, he got Hodgkins and went through the whole treatment. By 1976, they considered him cured. The first five years, he had to go every six months for an exam to see if anything had come back, and every single time he went he was clear.

"It was tough. His first wife was very vicious. The kids were very demanding. We didn't have any money. I wasn't working. It was a total struggle. He was very dominating. He was a Marine, then he became a cop. My parents didn't fight; I mean, they fought, but there was a lot of mutual respect. My father, you would think, ruled the roost, but my mother did. They didn't verbally abuse each other; John was verbally abusive in a lot of ways. And I don't think it was him so much as it was the job. I guess I just wasn't used to it, but I really couldn't deal with it. He wanted a little wife who would sit home and make bread and clean the house. My house was neat, but he would come around and actually inspect. He was very nice looking, very insecure, and he needed constant reassurance, and I didn't come from a family where we needed that. I guess we're very strong; there were so many of us, so you had to be strong individuals in order to have somebody recognize you. But he used to drive me crazy; when he didn't get constant reassurance, he would get verbally abusive. He didn't curse and he didn't drink, but I always thought he ran around.

"John was in the Marines, served in Korea; he told me he was a drill sergeant. He joined the force in 1966. The woman who was the local Democratic party representative happens to be best of friends with John's mother. And she went to school with Tony Yelencsics. John was out of the Marine Corps, he was in the Marine Reserves and he was working in Westinghouse, and he just decided that he wanted to be a cop. He was in the Edison Memorial Day Parade, marching as part of a unit for the Marines, he said to this woman, I want to be a cop. And she said, let me introduce you to Tony. And she brought him up to Tony, and Tony said, I was a Marine myself, And John said, well I'm a Marine that wants to be part of Edison township's police department. Tony said, be at my office Monday morning, and that was it. After the Memorial Day Parade, June 6 he became a police officer. So that's how it works, it's always been that way.

"He always said he was on the F Squad in the Police Department, after the TV show, 'F Troop.' In front of a crowd, he was funnier than anything you ever saw. And when we would go out with people, he would tell these stories about how awful his wife (me) was, and the tears would be welling down your face you'd be laughing so hard. I got to the point where I knew it wasn't personal. He was a comic in front of a crowd. He would tell stories, like, Pat makes him this big breakfast, she gives him hot Tang and Pop Tarts. And how I love him so much that I used to sew hearts on his bullet proof vest so everybody would know where to aim. It was stupid stuff, but he would have these people rolling. He would have accidents with the police car; he'd back into things. Or he'd lose the keys to the police car. And he was a sergeant; that's how he got his firewood. He would pull the driver over and say, see this badge, it says Edison police. You gonna drive through my township, put the wood in the back of my car. But he never took money. A couple of times, you know how the cops hang out at Dunkin Donuts, one time he was in the Plaza Diner, and a former councilman came in and made a crack, and John said to him, do you eat dinner in your car? What makes you think that I'm any different from you, I should eat dinner in my car? Or don't you think I'm entitled to sit at a table? I do my job.

"In a lot of respects he was right, he believed that policemen were the law. And he went by the law. He used to brag that he never gave tickets to Edison residents, because that was the town that he protected, that was his town. What he would do is he would offer them alternatives; since I stopped you for speeding, what are you going to do for the town of Edison? One of his big things is he would make them walk up and down Route 1 and pick up the trash. He would follow behind them in the police car. But people from out of town, forget it.

"No matter what it was, everything was an accusation. And when we had gone to the first counselor, like a marriage counsellor type of thing, he tried to explain that this is what you do, you bring the job home with you. I had said to him everything is an accusation; you never would say to me, did you make supper? You would always say, you didn't make supper yet! He was very gruff. He said can you imagine what a policeman's life would be like if a jewelry store just got held up and this guy comes running out and John walked up to him and said, hey, did you rob that jewelry store there? He said you don't say that, you say, you! You robbed that jewelry store there. You have to be direct. And that was what he used to bring home. So you try and understand that, and you can to a point, but once in a while you have to say, give me a break. And, I have a nice job at Revlon, and I'm good at what I do, but in front of him, I crumbled. He was so overpowering. Finally I took a course in self assertiveness, and he used to tell everyone it was the ruination of a good woman. Because if he said the sky was blue, I said the sky was blue. And if he said, one and one are three, I would say John said one and one are three. The strange part about it is I don't remember that much of my own existence. I guess, it was just so involved with him. I could function at work, but no other part of me functioned. I was always in the background; I don't think I had a thought that didn't come from him, other than my job.

"This was my entire relationship, until . . . my mother was out in Somerset, and his mother was here, it had to be after his father died. It was when I joined the rescue squad, 1981 or 1982. January of 1982, but maybe the year before is when I took the first aid course. I decided to take a first aid course in case anything happened to his mother, I wanted to take CPR. So I took CPR at Iselin First Aid Squad, and I got a 100 on it. And Iselin said to me, anyone who registers for a first aid course, we generally notify the local first aid squad. So the squad called me and said would I be interested in becoming a member, or would I be interested in taking other courses. So I thought about it and I thought about it, and I said to John, maybe I'll join the Edison Rescue Squad. And he said, oh, that would be a good idea, that way I'll make lieutenant. That had plenty to do with it; it's just like, you join the Democratic organization in Edison and that way you'll get promoted, and you do.

"The second marriage, nothing changed. People don't change. We would fight and go back and fight and go back. It got to the point where we just accepted it. My mother used to tell me, all you have to do is praise him and you could wind him around your finger. And girlfriends used to laugh and say, you've got him right where you want him, as long as you talk to him sweetly. He betrayed my image of what I thought he was. He comes across as very strong, domineering; they say he reminded me of my father. He probably did appearance wise, everything else . . . But he didn't have a shred of understanding, whereas my father did. An example: One time I had gotten a C in one subject, a subject that I happened to be very good in. My father was furious. He said to me, you got a C? I said, yeah. He said, get out of my sight. It was like, aren't you going to punish me, you can't use the telephone for the next week and no going out on Friday night, that kind of thing. And he said, no, I don't want to be bothered by it, It was devastation; I said, Daddy, hit me!, hit me! Daddy don't do this to me! Do anything to me but don't do this to me! He said, get out of here. And then my mother — once the kids were fighting, and she said, I can't stand this, I can't stand this anymore! And she ran upstairs and said, I'm going to flush myself down the toilet! And she went into the bathroom, locked the door and flushed the toilet and wouldn't answer. We stood there screaming: please Mommy!!

Don't do this! I had to be like 13 years old at the time. We laugh about it now.

"John was funny, he was home at night, unless he had to go to a meeting or something, but he found ways to run around. For somebody who never ticketed anybody, he had to go to court a lot. But he also worked split shifts, and always came home right on time. But you find out stuff afterwords. There was this one couple that he met; it was a guy from town who is very well-to-do. He was married, and his wife is the woman who my husband ended up fooling around with for five years at the end. They asked us to double date, so we had gone out to a movie, and then they wanted to go out to dinner afterwords. Well, we didn't have that much money, so we said, no, let's call it a night. And they said, no let's go for a couple drinks. They wound up insisting we go, and the guy picked up the tab. So I said, the next time we go, we'll pick up the tab. So we saved for a couple weeks and we invited them back out again, and they wanted to go to this real fancy restaurant. So we did go and we paid. She started calling me all the time, why don't you do this with me, why don't you go shopping with me? And initially, it was like, okay, I'll go with you. John was friends with her husband. Then they would invite us over their house, and she and her husband would fight; they were like nitpicky at each other. And it used to drive me crazy. I would come home from work and he would say, Rachel called you, Rachel called.

"So that was going on and then John's daughter had a big fight with her mother and she moved in with us. Then there was the two other kids, they didn't want to live with their mother, they wanted to live with us. All of a sudden I had all these kids. And it was like every Sunday and every holiday. But I got along with the kids, so it was okay. Then his daughter decided to get married. John didn't like the guy, I didn't like the guy. He was my age, he was like 18 years older than John's daughter. The guy had money, but he was giving her a rough time. So she wound up getting married, that was a touchy situation; her mother would call and end up screaming. Then his younger son joined the Navy. There were a lot of things going on.

"Then one day I was at work, and this Rachel's husband called me. And he said, I just spent the morning with John and I guess he's a little upset over the doctor's appointment he has to go to. I said, he's not upset over the doctor's appointment. He said, oh yes he is. You know, we had a couple drinks and that's when it came out. And I said, I just don't understand. And he said, well, maybe there's a lot you don't understand, you know he's been going out with my wife. In fact, that was one of the things we talked about today, and what we'd like to do is you move in with me and he'll move in with her. So I said to him, drop dead. I hung up, I left work, I came home. I guess it was right before we split up. I came home, John was home, and he says to me, what are you dong home? And I said, Joe just called me. He said, what did he call you about? So I said he told me he was here with you all morning, you were very upset about going to the doctor's, and that you're having an affair with his wife and that you want his wife to move in here and you want me to move in there with him. And he said, that's a lie. I'll prove it to you that's a lie. I'll call Rachel and you can listen in, I said, I don't want to do that, I don't understand what's going on. She calls here all the time, she's not somebody I'm all that crazy about, I don't understand why we always have to go out with them, we can't afford this. But he said, I'll prove it to you. With that, he picked up the phone, he dialed her number and he said to me, get on. And I knew I shouldn't have done it, but I did. And he said, Rachel, your husband called Pat at work and told her that we were having an affair, and that he wants her to move in there and you to move in here with me. And she started laughing, and she said, don't you think it's about time she found out? I said, you will hear from my lawyer! and I hung up the phone. I said to him, get out. Well, he wouldn't. There was arguing, we were screaming, next thing you know, in comes the other guy, and everybody was yelling at me. And I said forget it, I'm leaving. So I took off, and I went over to my mother's and called a lawyer. And I told the lawyer this is what happened. So he said to me, what do you want to do? And I said, get a divorce, I'm not going through this.

"John had gotten a lawyer, and the two worked out a deal. We wouldn't get divorced right away, we would have a separation and he would move out. He moved out, and the girl moved out on her husband. But he had a lot of money, so she was suing him for divorce and she claimed he was beating her and all kinds of cruelty. Part of the settlement was he bought her a house. She moved into the house and John moved in with her. So it was at that point, I was already on the first aid squad, that I became involved with Gene.

"Gene was just there. A lot of things were going on, John would come down to the first aid squad with his police car, he would ride around the squad. Everybody knew him, there's no disputing car 5. The police radio was always on because you have to have constant contact with the police, so we could always tell what was going on. The policemen would have to identify themselves, so you'd hear Car 5 and there was no mistaking John's voice because he had a Brooklyn accent. A lot of the first aid people knew what the cops were doing, so they would monitor the calls and there was a lot of talk. So Gene would always make sure the radio was down, or if anybody started to say anything, he would say knock it off, that somebody's personal business and that doesn't get discussed here. There was the one time when John was up at Ashbrook Swim Club in Car 5, and apparently his girlfriend had gone up there to meet him, and the cops had also gone up there. And they were making a joke about it on the radio, about catching Car 5. And it was on at the squad house, the radio was on and you could hear all of this going on. I happened to walk in, I heard part of it. He walked in and he said, turn that off, nobody has to listen to that, there's no need to do this. He was just protective in a lot of things.

"Then Valentine's Day came, that was the first time he did anything. We were going off to the EMT class and he was late. And when he did get there, it was five minutes after class started, he said, I was deliberately late because I wanted to give you something. So he gave me the nicest Valentine, he said, I just wanted you to know that somebody's thinking about you. And that's what I needed at the time.

"Alena had already moved out by the time I started seeing Gene. She quit high school the year she turned 18. She took off. She wouldn't talk to me, but she would talk to John. We had a lot of mother/daughter hassles. She was a difficult teenager. So she was seeing Gail's brother, and Gail's sister lived in Key West. She was very bright, but she got in with the wrong crowd. She started skipping school, she started going out with V.N., they would have fights, he would come to the house and do stupid things. Things like that we would fight about, back and forth.

"Gene and George Taylor would trade years being captain of the squad. They didn't want it to seem like there was one man rule there. They were friends, but I think they were also enemies to a degree. One would make a play for this girl, one would make a play for that girl, but they would also fool around together. Once, after EMT class, when I had gone down there, I used to go to class after work, so I would go dressed up, I would still be in a suit. One time when we had come back from class, I was still in a suit and I had gone down to the first aid squad, George had said, you know, she's never been initiated, let's initiate her. Gene said no. He said nothing else, it never came up again. I was afraid that someone would think that I was going out with him, which I was by this time.

"My first call, I was on a call with Gail Berta. A guy on Inman Avenue that was on a motorcycle was hit by a car. There were people in the car that were injured, and all I remember is that I had CPR and standard first aid, and they put a guy on a longboard and they put him in the rig, and they said to me, okay, sit with him. Believe me, I watched that guy just to make sure his chest was moving because I was in hysterics. I was really afraid. I was panic-stricken. My next call was a guy with chest pains at a restaurant, that was a call that I was on with Gene. We got in there and he said to me, he needs some oxygen, four liters would be good, then we did it. Then he said to me, okay Patty, get me a blood pressure, and I had never taken a blood pressure before. So I put the cup on the wrong way, and of course he put it on the right way; he said, sometimes these things are hard to figure out. And then he said, listen and tell me what you hear, so I did and I told him what I heard, and he said, Hmm. So I said, why don't you recheck that? And he did, and he said to me, you were right, trust your instincts. It was just like everything he did really gave you confidence, really bolstered you.

"Then there was one time when we were on a motor vehicle accident and there were five or six people involved. And I was only on the squad one month and I had only been on maybe five or six calls. There were two MICUs that were there, and there was another girl and myself who were with this patient, she had only been on the squad about two months longer than me, so I guess we had a patient that wasn't that bad. Of course, we didn't know it. We had done everything that we thought we should have done for this guy. He was talking to us but it was freezing cold. We put him on the long board, tied him up and secured him, put his arm in a splint, and we just talked to him, tried to keep him calm. The rest of the call, the people must have really been screwing up, because we had two ambulances there and Gene was not on the crew, and he wound up coming to the scene in his own car. When we got back to the building, he was screaming from here to Kingdom Come, at everybody who did anything wrong. This was done wrong and that was done wrong and then he said, and then we got two people who are brand new on this squad and who don't know anything, and they were the only two who had the common sense to know what to do. He did everything in his power to praise you.

"The only thing that gave me any indication that he had an interest in me was on my birthday, January 30. I was on duty that night, and I was down the first aid squad. He had gone to Clara Barton's installation dinner, and he came back to the first aid squad, and he had that leisure suit on, and it was a blue leisure suit, and he had this flowered Hawaiian print shirt on, it was so grotesque. By that time they should have burned those suits. Everybody was horsing around at the building, and it was myself and another guy, it was his birthday also. John and I had just split up, this was maybe two weeks after the Rachel and Joe incident. I was on duty on the squad, and they had told him it was my birthday, so he said, you know what the captain is entitled to? And I said what? And he said, he is entitled to a kiss. And I said all right, so I leaned over and I gave him my cheek and he said to me, I don't take cheeks. I said, oh my God! I was scared stiff. So I kind of looked away.

"The following week, he said to me, I was able to pull some strings and get you into the EMT class. And I was so thankful; I really wanted to get into that class, and I thought he pulled all the strings in the world. Then the following week was Valentine's Day, and that's when he gave me the card. And I guess that's when I thought, this guy is very nice. And we went out that night, after EMT class, and we went to Dunkin' Donuts, and we went and sat at MetroPark train station, and I don't think I got home until 2 o'clock. We talked and we talked. He was really polite, he didn't try to kiss me, he didn't try anything. He kept saying if there ever is anything you need, I've been through this before. We went to class every Monday and Thursday, and I was on duty Saturday nights, so it was like I knew that I would see him Monday, Thursday and Saturday. Of course, once I started seeing him, I would see him every night, or just about every night. I don't know how he heard that I had split with my husband, I'm sure there was local gossip.

"I used to meet him in the morning at a local deli, and we would just sit and have coffee and talk. But it wasn't like I was meeting him, initially. I used to go to that deli and then he was just there; I had never seen him there before, but all of a sudden he was there. Initially, I never thought it was planned, I thought it was accidental. Sometimes I would go there at 7:45 and sometimes I would go there at 7:55, and he was always just pulling in at the same time I was.

"It was funny because he didn't smoke, and I did, and he said to me smoking isn't healthy for you. And I said to him, do you like it? And he said, no I don't. So I said I won't smoke. So I just quit, and it never bothered me.

"We went out to dinner twice. He took me a couple of times to things he had to go to for presentations from squads, or state functions. I only dated him for about five months. Most of the time he just came over to my house. We'd go to the diner, but I was always on duty Saturday night. I don't think we ever went to the movies.

"He was over here one night, and we were watching television, and we were sitting down in the family room. Gene had a walkie talkie with him, and I guess John was on duty, and he had a habit of patrolling the street. One time he stopped and came inside the house and Gene was here. And I had heard the police car pull up, Gene hid in the closet down there. John had a walkie talkie and Gene had a walkie talkie, and the walkie talkie went off, and John looked down at his walkie talkie and started fiddling with the volume.

"We kept our affair secret only because it wasn't any of anybody's business, second, I was still married. The funny part was, they used to say, oh, Gene must be out with his girlfriend because he didn't answer his pager, or they'd call him at home and Gail would say he's out. And I thought, they think he's seeing somebody, well let them! He was with me. One time they had called him for an accident, apparently it was pretty bad. And they kept talking that they couldn't get him, and he didn't come home until 2 o'clock in the morning, and he was out with his girlfriend. He was here and I knew it. It was hard for me to go out because Andrew was young, so he just came over here and watched TV; a couple times I cooked, made dinner or something."

Accused

August 9, 1983

JOHN HALEY AND CASIMIR SMERECKI met Thomas Kapsak as the latter was walking into his office, having come from a meeting with the prosecutor. Both detectives wore huge grins.

"What are you two looking so smug about?" Kapsak asked, as he walked past the men into his office.

"This," Haley said, pointing to a slim manilla envelope. "I think you're going to like what you see."

Haley dropped the envelope on Kapsak's desk, then joined Smerecki in pulling up a chair and sitting down. Haley looked as though he would burst out laughing any minute.

"What am I looking for?" Kapsak said as he thumbed through the photos. The pictures were of Cathy Warner's basement, taken the day her body was discovered.

"Look at the one showing the front of the washing machine on the left," Smerecki said. "Tell us what you see."

Kapsak studied the photo for several minutes.

"It looks like a big stain . . . A BLOOD STAIN!" he said, his eyes widening with the revelation. "Right there in front of the machine! Why didn't we see that before?"

"There're so many shadows down there," Haley said, "lots of things get past the naked eye. But when you shoot a strobe light on them, everything gets illuminated."

"You think that's blood, John?"

"Well, it sure looks like it could be. It looks like that area was wiped clean, like somebody scrubbed it."

"That's probably where she was killed," Smerecki pointed out.

"I could see him doing that," Kapsak said. "I could see him killing her in the basement and carrying her upstairs to the bathroom."

Haley leaned over the front of Kapsak's desk and fished through the pile of photos. He selected one and handed it to the second assistant prosecutor.

"Look at the bottom of the machine, what do you see there?" he asked.

"Looks like a streak of blood, like something bloody was slapped against the front of the machine," Kapsak answered. "So if he was wiping up the floor, the corner of whatever he was using could have left that streak on the machine, right?"

"You got it," Haley said. He turned his head to look at Smerecki, then turned back to Kapsak. "And if we test that blood, and it comes up A Positive, like Cathy Warner's then we know she was definitely killed in the basement. I think we need to go back to that house one more time, don't you?"

Before the pictures had come back, Smerecki and Haley had not held out too much hope of finding anything new in the house; they and other county identification officers had literally been combing it on their hands and knees for several weeks, unsuccessfully looking for anything that would have given them a clue of where Cathy Warner was killed. In fact, Haley had been to the house for 11 consecutive days. Sometimes he would just walk around the house, not really knowing what he was looking for.

But even with the photos, the detectives weren't certain of what they would find.

"There's got to be something there," Smerecki said, as the two detectives drove from New Brunswick to Metuchen. "There's got to be something in that basement, something near where we saw that big blood stain. But I don't know, we've swept and vacuumed just about every square inch of that basement, and haven't found anything yet. This guy was pretty slick."

Haley had personally placed padlocks on all the doors of Warner's house when the investigation ended on the night of July 16. Three keys were needed to open the doors, all of which were in Haley's possession.

"All right, John, let's go see what we've got," Smerecki said, after the two were inside the house. The small home was eerily silent; as if to not disturb the peacefulness, the two detectives quietly rushed through the kitchen and descended into the basement.

Smerecki and Haley reacquainted themselves with the cluttered cellar. Scattered about the musty room were lawn and garden tools, paint cans, workbenches, old furniture and newspapers. Ghostly shadows played against the walls, cast by the lone light bulb which hung naked from the ceiling. The detectives split up, Haley moving to the rear of the basement and Smerecki to the front, the side which fronted New Durham Avenue.

Picture in hand, Haley stood near the center of the basement, in front of the washer and dryer, facing the wall which ran parallel with the driveway. He knelt down and ran his hands over the large spot which had discolored part of the floor. "I can't believe I didn't see this," Haley muttered. "This definitely looks like somebody mopped something up here. This has got to be blood."

Removing a hammer and chisel from a bag he brought into the house, Haley carefully chipped away a chunk of the floor, then placed it in a plastic bag. Smerecki stood over him, a thoughtful look on his face.

"This is definitely where she was killed, John," Smerecki said. "Cement is a very porous material, the blood probably was absorbed right into it. He tried to clean it up, but he couldn't get it all."

"I hope he didn't use any kind of harsh cleanser," Haley said. "That would probably break down whatever blood was left."

"I don't think you'll have that problem, I bet that comes back positive."

Haley stood up, scanning the wall directly in front of him. "Okay, so we know she was shot, and we're pretty sure she was shot here," he said. "So there should be a bullet hole somewhere."

Smerecki walked away, leaving Haley standing in the center of the floor. "She would have been standing up, so the hole would probably be pretty high. Unless he was standing at the top of the steps, and he shot her at an angle . . . hmmm." The detective reached into his bag and pulled out a flashlight, then played its beam along the wall. He was frustrated in his search for a bullet hole by a fact that he had observed earlier: the walls were so pitted, finding one specific hole was nearly impossible.

Kneeling down, the detective played the flashlight along the same path, from left to right along the wall, except this time he concentrated his search to the bottom portion of the wall. Haley's pulse quickened as the beam rested on a piece of plywood that was leaning up against the wall, in front of a wooden ladder back chair. The beam highlighted a hole in the lower right hand side of the wood; Haley froze as he recognized the hole's outline.

"Jesus Christ! Sarge, c'mere, look at this!"

Smerecki ran over to Haley, who by now was down on both knees, directly in front of the chair fingering a hole in the wood. Smerecki estimated that the wood measured roughly three feet high by a foot and a half wide. Haley aimed his flashlight at the hole, then asked Smerecki what he thought the hole resembled.

"It looks like a bullet that went through sideways," he answered. "I think we got the son of a bitch."

Haley felt a month's worth of frustration seep from his body, replaced by indescribable relief. He hastily stood up and grabbed his camera, handing the strobe flash to Smerecki. "Let's get some pictures," he suggested.

After taking three snapshots, Haley placed the camera on the floor and walked back over to the chair. "With any luck, there's a bullet back there," he said.

Smerecki carefully grabbed the chair by its sides and pulled it away from the wall. He then flipped the plywood forward, revealing five folded corrugated boxes. Smerecki knelt down and whistled between his teeth. "Looks like the bullet went clean through the wood and these boxes," he said. Smerecki retrieved a tape measure from the detectives' bag of tools and placed it below the hole; it measured 3/4 of an inch long by 3/8 of an inch wide.

"Okay, before we do anything, let's take some more pictures," the sergeant said.

Haley snapped several shots of the plywood, the hole and the general area surrounding the wood, making sure to get different angles.

"Let's take a closer look and see what we've got here," Smerecki said when Haley finished. He carefully flipped the boxes back against the wall, focusing his attention on the plywood.

Viewing the hole from the rear, the detectives saw that it was splintered outward: a classic indication of an exit hole.

Haley pointed to the first cardboard box; "Look at that, Sarge, that hole is in line with the one in the wood." Haley and Semerecki found the same to be true with all the boxes. A close look at the cinder block wall directly behind the wood and boxes revealed a nick, somewhat resembling the shape of the holes.

The two detectives looked at each other and smiled broadly. Four weeks of intense investigation had come down to a barely-noticeable hole in a piece of wood.

"I don't believe this," Haley said. "If I hadn't knelt down and used this flashlight, we never would have found that."

"Sometimes it's just dumb luck," Smerecki said. "You just can't explain it."

Smerecki dropped to his knees again and studied the hole in the plywood. "Any guess about what we find when we test this stuff, John?"

"If this doesn't come up positive for lead, I'll eat this chair," Haley answered.

The detectives placed the cardboard and plywood back in its place so that more photos could be taken. Haley was lining up another shot when he noticed something odd about the ladderback chair. Once again down on one knee, Haley focused his attention on two rungs underneath the chair's seat. Looking closely, he saw a nick on the chair's top rung, directly in line with the hole in the plywood and similar in length to it.

Haley felt another rush of excitement.

"I think we found what we need, Sarge," Haley said. "This is going to put us over the top! We're going to get that bastard!"

"All right, why don't we see if there's a bullet lying around here," Smerecki suggested.

The detectives crawled around on their hands and knees for a half hour, sifting through whatever dirt and debris was left on the floor. Finding nothing near the area of the chair, they decided to look behind the washer and dryer, pulling the two appliances from their resting spots against the wall, into the middle of the basement.

A search of that area was equally fruitless.

"It's no use," Haley said. "He must have found the bullet and taken it with him. You know, for a guy who was so thorough, he sure did a sloppy job after all."

"Yeah, well, they all usually` make at least one mistake," Smerecki said as he and Haley pushed the machines back to their places. "That's why they get caught."

"Hey, what's this?" Smerecki said, walking back to the chair and wood. He stood close up to the cinder block wall, squinted his eyes, and pointed to several stains on the wall. "What does that look like to you?"

"Looks like it could be blood," Haley said, joining him at the wall. "Could be splashes from the bullet's impact. Let's pull some pieces out of the wall and send them down to the lab to be analyzed with the other stuff."

"There's something else I want to take, too," Smerecki said as he walked across the floor and under the staircase. He emerged carrying a long white radiator cover. Walking back to Haley, Smerecki pointed to several red dots on the cover. "I bet that's blood," he said.

"So from how it looks, he killed her down here, then carried her upstairs into the bathroom," Haley observed. "This is one cool cucumber."

There were other pieces of evidence seized from different parts of the house before the detectives left: a partially filled bottle of scotch was taken from the kitchen, as was a letter to Cathy Warner's accountant, and Haley removed the chrome bathtub stopper handle from the downstairs bathroom. Working upstairs in Cathy Warner's bedroom, Smerecki found a checkbook register from March 1980 to September 1980. One particular entry caught his eye; it was check number 161, made out to Berta, ET, in the amount of $4,250.

The detectives walked back to their car, evidence in tow, happier than they had been in weeks.

"I can't believe we missed this for four weeks," Haley said. "It was right in front of our faces the whole time!"

"Well, just be glad we had that picture of the floor," Smerecki told him. "Otherwise, we may not have even thought about looking there."

The normally staid Thomas Kapsak was elated when Smerecki reported what he and Haley had found. Their information, plus news he had received earlier in the day from Dr. Louis Vasvary, the Rutgers University entomologist who was analyzing the maggots found on Cathy Warner's body, spurred him to call Prosecutor Allen Rockoff and the remainder of the investigative team to arrange an impromptu strategy session.

The detectives and lawyers were assembled in Rockoff's office twenty minutes later. It was the meeting for which each of them had been hoping since July 16.

"I think we can pick him up tomorrow," Kapsak said. "I know I've got enough to get a warrant."

"It's too bad Joe isn't here," Watson said. "He'd love to be in on this."

Kapsak turned the meeting over to Smerecki, who told the assembly of the suspected bullet holes and large bloodstain found in the basement.

"I did a quick analysis of the chair, the plywood and what we think is the bullet hole," Smerecki said. "The mark on the chair strut is a foot above the floor, the first bullet hole, in the plywood, is about seven and three-eights off the bottom. The last hole, in the last of the cardboard boxes that were stacked behind the plywood, is six inches off the ground. All of the holes line up and, if you were to stick a rod in from the front to the back, you would see a definite downward path. On top of that, there are wood splinters in each of the holes in the cardboard, which tells us that the holes were made at the same time."

"We didn't find a bullet, but this is the next best thing," Haley added. "This stuff was sitting right in front of that big stain we found. That's got to be where she was standing when he shot her."

"We've got the place, and we've got the approximate day, too" Kapsak added. "I spoke on the phone today with Dr. Vasvary at Rutgers. He finished his analysis of the maggots and told me that based on the conditions in the basement and the bathroom, they were between six and seven days old. That brings us back to the weekend. Put that together with the fact that no one heard from Cathy Warner after July 8, and that the last day she crossed off on her calendar was July 7, and I think we can make a strong, and I admit circumstantial, case that she was killed on July 8. Plus, we have Berta's admission that he was with her on the eighth. Now add that all up with what the friends have been telling us, and I think we have Gene Berta murdering Cathy Warner sometime in the afternoon of July 8. He killed her in her basement, undressed her, and then put her in her tub and filled it with water. And while Cathy Warner lay rotting in her tub, Gene Berta was out spending her money, first with Pat Bauer, and then with his wife. That's the case we have, and that's the case I think I can take to the jury."

"You feel comfortable with that, Tom?" Rockoff asked.

"I know it's going to take a little more work, but, yes, I feel comfortable with what we have," Kapsak answered.

"He probably killed her as soon as he brought her home from work, right?" Smerecki asked.

"That's what I'm thinking," Kapsak answered.

"So then she must have been wearing her uniform at the time. Somewhere, there's got to be a bloody uniform, or maybe parts of one."

"But didn't Berta say he took the garbage out Monday night when he got back to her house?" Watson interjected.

"Yeah, he did. You're thinking that maybe he stuffed the uniform in the garbage bag and then tossed it," Smerecki said. "That could be, he could have done that. But let's take that one step further. Every one of those nurses had on a name tag. If she was wearing her uniform when he killed her, she probably still had it on. So that means she should have been wearing the name tag. That's one thing I'll look for when I go back to the house."

"And a stethoscope," Watson said. "Nurses always carry them around, too."

"That's a good thought, Denny," Kapsak said. "Cas, you should probably go back to the scene in the next couple of days to find those things."

"Sounds good to me," Smerecki agreed. "But that still only looks at one of the questions. There are others we've got to answer, like, what gun did he use?" Smerecki said, continuing his train of thought. "There are no records of him buying a handgun recently, and we weren't able to find a bullet."

"We know Cathy Warner had a gun, and we haven't been able to find it," Kapsak agreed. "Berta probably used Cathy's gun, then got rid of it in when he went on his trip. It's probably sitting at the bottom of Moose Lake."

Wednesday, August 10, 1983

Gene Berta was painting his porch, his back facing the front of his house, when he heard the car pull into his driveway. He turned around to face Dennis Watson and several officers he had not yet met — county investigator Lawrence Nagle and Metuchen police Sgt. Matthew Siecinski and Det. Robert Kolbus.

Watson, who had been anticipating this moment since the first time he had met Gene Berta, felt strangely numb. The feeling of victory to which he had looked forward for so many weeks was not within him. Wordlessly, he reached into his inside jacket pocket and pulled out a piece of folded white paper.

"We've got a warrant for your arrest Gene, let's go."

"I don't fucking believe this," he said. "You guys really think I killed her? You are making a big mistake."

Watson responded by removing the special card which contained a suspect's rights under the Miranda Act; he began to read from the card as the two Metuchen officers approached Berta. Berta had been Mirandized before, but Watson was taking no chances.

The Metuchen officers searched Berta as he stood on the porch; he did not take his eyes off Watson as he was read his rights.

"Do you understand these rights as I have read them to you?" Watson finished.

"I speak English," Berta answered. He shot Watson his best "fuck you" look, but the detective remained unfazed.

"Okay Gene, do you mind signing this?" Watson held out the rights card from which he had just read; he was motioning for Berta to acknowledge that he had been properly read his rights.

"Fuck you, I signed one of those for Joe Zimmerman, I'm not going to sign another one."

"Have it your way," Watson said, as he printed "Refused to sign rights card" on the signature line. He looked at his watch and noted the time: 2:10 p.m.

"Where are you taking me?" Berta asked.

"First, we're going to take you to Metuchen PD to be booked," Watson told him. "Then we'll take you into New Brunswick for your arraignment."

"You mind if I make a couple of calls before we go? I need to call my lawyer and my mother. Someone's got to watch my kids."

"Sure, go ahead," Watson said.

Berta walked back into his house, followed by the four officers. Watson was astounded at Berta's cocky attitude as the accused murderer spoke on the phone.

"Morris? This is Gene Berta. Listen, the detectives are here, they've got this warrant and they're taking me in. Nah, I'll be out of there in a couple of hours. This is a bunch of bullshit, they've got nobody else, so they pick on me. It's nothing, I just wanted to let you know. Okay, I understand. See you."

Berta's next call was to his mother; he asked her to come over and watch his children.

Eugenia Berta arrived at 7 East Walnut about 20 minutes later. Looking dazed and bewildered, she glanced at the four men — two in police uniforms and two in plain clothes — and asked her son what this was all about.

"Well, these men are here to arrest me, mom. But it's nothing. It's just a stupid mix up. I'll be back in no time. Gail should be home later, would you tell her what happened?"

"Sure Gene, I'll tell her."

"C'mon Gene, we've got to go," Watson said.

Berta said good-bye to his daughters, then preceded the men out of the house. Watson had already decided to not handcuff Berta in the house, he didn't want to unduly upset his mother and daughters.

"Wait a minute, Gene," Watson said as Berta was preparing to enter the car. "We've got to make it official."

Siecinski reached behind his back, into a pouch on his belt, and pulled out his handcuffs; Berta rolled his eyes when he saw what was happening.

"Do we really need to do this?" he asked. "It's not like I'm going to run away."

"S.O.P. Gene," Watson said. "We've gotta do it."

Berta was escorted into the Metuchen Police Department, handcuffed, by Siecinski and Kolbus with Watson and Nagle tagging along behind. Watson marvelled at Berta's attitude; rather than being embarrassed by his circumstances, Berta adopted an aggressive posture. He wore the usual put-upon look which Watson had grown to hate, acting as though he hadn't a care in the world.

The booking officers put Berta through the drill: Fingerprints, mug shots and the requisite vital information for the arrest report.

When their tasks were completed, the Metuchen officers officially turned Berta over to the county detectives for the ride into New Brunswick. Watson replaced Berta's handcuffs, asking, "That's not too tight, is it Gene?" Berta did not answer; indeed he remained silent throughout the entire trip.

"How'd it go?" Tom Kapsak asked Watson as the latter entered his office.

"Piece of cake," Watson answered. "Real smooth. He didn't say anything, he just looked real arrogant the whole time. That's typical for him, though. He just acted like we were wasting his time."

"Okay. Now that we've got him, I've got to work on keeping him in prison. I'm going to try to get the judge to set a high bail; I don't doubt for a minute that if he had the chance, Gene Berta would try to skip out.

"We're going to need to get search warrants right away for his house and his car," Kapsak continued. "He may have hidden the gun there, or there may be some bloody clothing somewhere. I'm going to need you to testify; it'll probably be in the next few days."

"Just let me know," Watson said as he turned to walk out of Kapsak's office. "I'll see you at the arraignment."

Even as his colleagues were arresting their suspect, Casimir Smerecki was working to strengthen the case against Gene Berta. Smerecki began what would turn out to be a series of tests on the items found the day before in Cathy Warner's basement. In addition to the chair, the plywood and the corrugated boxes, Smerecki and Haley confiscated a Star-Ledger newspaper dated July 8, 1983, which was the topmost of a pile of newspapers on the chair; a brown paper bag, which was sitting on top of the newspaper, a white box and an empty sugar box.

At this point, Smerecki was looking only for fingerprints but his search was fruitless. He found no prints on the plywood, corrugated boxes, brown paper bag or sugar box; on the white box he found one print, but that was identified as being John Haley's. However, Smerecki did find two partial prints on the center of the chair's backrest and also several partial prints on the front page of the newspaper.

The partial prints he found were of little value for several reasons: First, police did not as yet have Gene Berta's fingerprints to use as a control; second, since they were only partial prints, there was no way of telling whether they would match Berta's at all. And third, the fact that they did not have any prints from Cathy Warner, due to the advanced decomposition of her hands, left wide open the possibility that any of the unidentified prints could be hers.

And looking for Cathy Warner's name tags turned into a bigger job than Smerecki had envisioned. Before he and John Haley returned to Cathy Warner's house later that day, Smerecki called the state police laboratory in Sea Girt, where he had sent several uniforms found at the scene for analysis, and asked the lab technician if any name tags were attached to the articles. The answer was no.

Back at 125 Durham Avenue, Smerecki and Haley carefully checked every place they could think of where Cathy Warner might have stored the tags. Smerecki's detail work paid off in the bedroom; he found six name tags — in the name of Tingley, R.N. — in the bottom drawer of Warner's night table. He found two more name tags — in the name of Warner, R.N. — in the top, left-hand drawer of Warner's mirrored bureau. And, in the same drawer, he found four stethoscopes, two of which had "Cathy Warner" written on their name tags.

"How many of these things did this girl have?" Smerecki asked himself.

Continuing to search the bedroom, Smerecki found and seized a number of pieces of jewelry — mainly gold and silver chains and the wedding ring given to her by John Warner — and a collection of coins: Eisenhower dollars, buffalo nickels and various period and foreign coins. Smerecki also found three more two-piece nurse's uniforms in Cathy Warner's bedroom closet, along with a clean pair of white nurse's shoes.

A more interesting finding awaited Smerecki when he partially closed the open bedroom door. On the floor, hidden behind the door, were a second pair of nurse's shoes, a small reddish-brown stain on the left shoe spoiling its pristine whiteness.

Smerecki's sense of victory increased as he retrieved the shoes and placed them in a bag. "This could be what we're looking for," he thought. The detective was convinced that once analyzed, the small stain would show positive for blood; if there was enough of it to register a reading.

"Hey Sarge, I think I found something in here!" Haley summoned Smerecki from the kitchen.

Descending to the first floor, Smerecki placed his bag filled with shoes, name tags and coins on the kitchen table before walking over to the back door, where Haley was standing.

"Look at this window curtain," Haley said, pointing to a piece of plastic-looking material with brown and tan stripes that was held against the door's window with a piece of masking tape in each corner. "This has the same pattern of the shower and window curtains that're in the bathroom where she was found."

"Yeah, looks like somebody just threw it up and taped it there," Smerecki said. "You know, I remember seeing a roll of masking tape in the basement. Let me go get that, and you take down the bathroom window curtain."

Smerecki ran down to the basement to find that his memory was correct; near the stairs, on a makeshift table comprised of two saw horses and a piece of plywood, was a thick roll of masking tape. Smerecki knew that the state police lab technicians would be able to find any fingerprints on the tape, and could also determine if the pieces attached to the back door curtain came from this roll.

"Okay John, let's go," Smerecki said. "I think we've got enough for now."

Kapsak received in the mail the written report of Dr. Louis Vasvary, the Rutgers entomologist who had examined the maggots found on Cathy Warner's body. Vasvary had already given Kapsak an oral report, but he went into greater detail in his letter.

"The black blowfly, a species common throughout the United States, undergoes four stages (instars) of growth: the egg, maggot (or larva), pupa and, finally, the adult, Vasvarry explained in his report. Eggs are laid on decaying animal matter and hatch into larvae between eight and 52 hours later, depending on the temperature of their environment.

"At the optimum temperature of 99 F. hatching occurs after 8.13 hours," the scientist continued. "Larval stages require 4 to 15 days, again depending upon temperature, before they enter the pupal stage. Pupae require 3 to 13 days to transform from larvae to adult flies. The total development period, egg to adult requires 10 to 25 days.

"Therefore, third instar larvae collected from the body and face were judged to be between 4 to 6 days old. If an additional 8 to 16 hours are added for the egg stage, the body became infested 4.3 to 4.6 days to 6.3 or 6.6 days prior to the time samples were collected."

The key phrase in Vasvary's report was "optimum temperature." As the scientist had explained to Kapsak, his findings were based on the assumption of a constant temperature of 99 degrees, which, of course, wasn't the case in Cathy Warner's death. Although the daytime highs were in the upper 90's, temperatures cooled off when night fell, leading to an average temperature of between 75 degrees and 80 degrees during the eight days Cathy Warner's body lay first in her basement, then in her tub.

Based on that information, Vasvary said, hatching would have occurred sometime between seven and nine days before the samples were taken.

Vasvary's findings strengthened Kapsak's conclusion that the eggs were laid sometime during the weekend of July 8 through 11. And for the eggs to have been laid at all, Cathy Warner would have to have been already lying dead and decomposing in her first-floor bathtub on July 11 when Gene Berta, by his own admission, was in her house.

"It's all adding up," Kapsak thought, as he filed the report. "It's coming together like a jigsaw puzzle."

Allan Rockoff greeted the bevy of reporters assembled in his outer office, then slipped on his black, horn-rimmed glasses and removed a prepared statement from his inside jacket pocket.

"We have made an arrest in the murder investigation of Catherine Warner, the nurse who was found dead in her home last month," he began. "We have the suspect in custody and he is now awaiting arraignment, which should be later this afternoon before Judge Nicola. The suspect is Eugene Thomas Berta . . ."

Rockoff was interrupted by an outburst from a member of the press corps.

"Oh no, not Gene Berta!" a woman cried out with shocked disbelief. It was Jean Whiston, the editor of a local weekly newspaper, who had known Berta and his family for many years.

Rockoff paused several minutes while the reporters quieted down.

"The suspect is Eugene Thomas Berta, age 34, of 7 East Walnut Street, Metuchen. Mr. Berta is married and has five children, four of whom live at home. He also has a son by a previous marriage who lives with his mother. He was arrested at 2:10 p.m. today, by investigators from the Middlesex County Prosecutor's Office and the Metuchen Police Department. Mr. Berta has also been charged with possession of a deadly weapon for unlawful purposes.

As he had been throughout the investigation, Rockoff was sparing with the information he released to the press.

"Do you still believe that she was killed somewhere outside of her house and then carried into the tub?" a reporter asked.

"No," Rockoff answered. "We now believe that she was killed somewhere in the house."

"What made you change your theory?"

"I'm not at liberty to go into too much detail at this time," Rockoff answered. "Her whereabouts are part of the evidence that will be presented to the grand jury."

"Did you find a weapon?" asked another reporter.

"I'm not at liberty to answer that, either," he replied.

"Was he your main suspect?"

"Mr. Berta was one of a number of individuals who were looked at very closely," Rockoff said.

"Did he confess to the murder?"

"No, we have no confession.

"The arraignment is scheduled in about an hour," Rockoff added, before he dismissed the reporters and disappeared into his office.

All eyes were on Thomas Kapsak as he stood before Superior Court Judge George Nicola.

"Judge, at this time the State asks for a bail of $1 million, with no 10 percent option." Kapsak's request elicited a gasp from the onlookers in the courtroom and an incredulous glare from Morris Brown. Berta merely smiled to himself. The 10 percent option allowed a defendant to post 10 percent of the bail before being released.

"Your honor," Brown began, "I would have to object. That seems like an unreasonably high amount."

"Judge, the State believes the bail is justified for several reasons," Kapsak countered. "First, the suspect has stated several times that he plans to move to Moose Lake, Minnesota, and that he in fact has purchased a farm there, with money given to him by the victim, Catherine Warner. Second, the State feels that the vicious nature of this crime warrants a high bail. The defendant told the victim that he was going to Minnesota with another woman after the victim had made all the arrangements and, in fact, had paid for the trip. On July 8, they argued in her home. She was never seen alive again after July 8. The victim's body was found in her house on July

16, 1983. Considering these facts, the State feels that Mr. Berta represents a considerable risk of flight if he is released on bail."

Brown rose once again to protest.

"Your honor, the statement of probable cause for the arrest of my client contains a quantum leap of fact and logic between the assertion that Catherine Warner and Eugene Berta argued and that she was last seen alive on July 8 and the complaint charging my client with a very serious crime.

"Investigators questioned my client repeatedly for a week without any indication that they thought he would run away," Brown continued. "I might add that my client and his wife are long-time area residents, and that my client has a long and distinguished record of service to the community through his association with the rescue squad. I would also add that my client has been recognized for his volunteer work by the Edison Kiwanis Club, which this year named him their 'Man of the Year.' In light of those facts, and considering the shallow complaint brought by the State, it would be unreasonable and unfair to incarcerate my client."

"Again, Your Honor," Kapsak retorted, "I would reiterate the State's position and remind the court that the defendant is facing a possible death sentence and that he has recently purchased land in Minnesota with the intention of moving there."

"All right," Nicola said, ending the debate. "I'm going to set bail at $500,000, with no 10 percent. The defendant will be remanded to the Middlesex County Adult Detention Center. I'm also going to schedule a probable cause hearing for next Wednesday, that would be August 17, at 9 a.m. in this courtroom. Will that be any problem?"

"Your Honor, I would request that we move the probable cause hearing to a closer date" Brown said.

"The 17th is really the earliest I would be prepared for a hearing, judge," Kapsak said. "This is a very complicated case, it's not a one or two witness case. It's a very complicated, circumstantial case. I have to arrange for the appearance of several witnesses, one of whom is in the Army in Virginia. I don't think there's any possible way I can be prepared before next week."

"Okay, the 17th stands," Nicola decided. "Court is adjourned."

Casimir Smerecki, meanwhile, was back in his office, toying with the Timex watch found on Cathy Warner's wrist. He noticed that the watch was of the wind-up variety, with a sweep-second hand and a day-date window. The sergeant noted the time shown on the watch was 3:14, and the number appearing in the date window was 10.

"The question is, is that 3:14 a.m. or 3:14 p.m.?" Smerecki asked himself. "But I can't worry about it now," he thought, glancing at a pile of papers sitting on the corner of his desk; at the top of the pile was a report from the state police laboratory; it held both good and bad news.

The good news was that a hair found on the washing machine was identified as matching a test hair from Cathy Warner's head. That information could be used to help prove she was killed in her basement. The bad news was that no fragments of bullets or bone were found in any of the cellar floor sweepings that had been collected over the past month.

"This guy really cleaned himself up well," Smerecki thought.

Part of the frustration felt by Smerecki and the other detectives stemmed from the fact that very few of the items they had collected from the house and submitted to the state police for analysis resulted in any meaningful evidence. Red stains found on a white radiator cover, a piece of the cellar stairs, the gold kick plate at the top of the cellar staircase and the white trash can liner from the kitchen had come back labelled "NR", meaning there was no reaction when a reagent designed to react with blood was applied to the items.

Certain items had tested positive for blood — the pieces of the cellar floor, the drain traps in the tub and cellar sink and a sample of the wall along the cellar staircase being the most important. Those results, coupled with the more recent find of the bullet holes, showed that Catherine Neal Warner had been killed in the basement of her home and carried upstairs to her first floor bathroom tub.

Thursday, August 11, 1983

Casimir Smerecki returned to 125 Durham Avenue to make one last-ditch effort to find a bullet or a bullet fragment. He found it hard to believe that a person could have found every single piece of a lead projectile that had first passed through a human head and then slammed against a cinder block wall. There had to be something left to find!

Back in the house's basement, Smerecki examined every item he found along the room's front and side walls. After his inspection, he placed the items out of the way, in an area under the front porch. He also moved out the washer and dryer, examining the floor under the two appliances. Finally, he swept and sifted the entire area one more time.

Nothing.

While he was in the basement, Smerecki noticed that a window at the bottom of the stairs — facing the driveway — was covered with a white towel with a floral print. Pushing the towel aside, Smerecki whistled through his teeth when he saw several red stains on the towel. He also noticed that from his vantage point, he could see directly into Metuchen police Lt. Ed Studnicki's living room.

"If I can see in, Studnicki could see out. Berta probably knew that, too," Smerecki told himself. He walked up the stairs to the kitchen phone and called Studnicki asking him to come over to the Warner house with a camera.

Studnicki arrived a short time later, his Polaroid instant camera in hand. Smerecki asked that they go over to Studnicki's house to take the pictures, and explained why.

Smerecki took several photos, then thanked Studnicki for his time and left the house.

"Cheryl, I'm telling you, I can't believe Gene would do anything like that. I mean, he's the rescue squad captain, for God's sake! He's supposed to save lives, not take them!" Pat Bauer was sitting across her dining room table, sharing coffee with her friend Cheryl. The pair's get-togethers had become almost a nightly ritual since Pat had returned from Minnesota.

"I don't know, Patty," Cheryl said, taking a sip from her cup. "There are some pretty weird stories flying around the squad about him. He was into some pretty strange stuff."

"Oh, you can't believe all those things," Bauer told her friend, waving her hand dismissively. "Gene probably started half those rumors himself."

Just then the phone rang. Pat glanced at her clock as she walked into the kitchen, it was 8:30 p.m.

"Hello?"

"Hello, may I speak to Patricia Bauer, Please?" Pat did not recognize the voice on the other end.

"This is Patricia Bauer. What can I do for you?"

"Mrs. Bauer, I'm sorry for calling you so late in the evening. My name is Roscoe Meagher, I'm from the office of Morris Brown, of the Wilentz firm? We're representing Gene Berta."

"Oh, yes. What can I do for you?"

"Well, I know you're a good friend of Gene's, and I can tell you he needs all the friends he can get now. I was just wondering if you were on his side with this murder thing?"

"Well, yes, of course I am!" Bauer said. "I don't believe for a minute that he did it."

"That's great, he'll be happy to hear that. Listen, I think it's important that we get together as soon as possible. We'll need a statement from you, is that all right? It's really important that we get as much evidence as we can."

"Sure, that's fine," Pat answered. Turning to Cheryl, she pantomimed smoking, then pointed to her cigarettes and lighter lying on the dining room table. Cheryl pulled out a cigarette, lit it, then brought it to her friend.

"When do you want to meet?" Bauer asked. The cigarette's tip glowed bright red as she sucked down a deep drag.

"Well, I thought we could get together tomorrow night, about 9:30?"

"Well, that's kind of late, but okay," Bauer said, haltingly. "Should we meet in your office?"

"No, that won't be necessary," the voice said, a little too quickly. "Let's meet someplace neutral, say, the Greenwood Manor parking lot? Do you know where that is"

"The Greenwood Manor parking lot?" Bauer had to repeat his suggestion out loud to make sure she hadn't misheard what Meagher said. "I never heard of it." The voice gave her simple instructions from her house.

"Okay," Bauer said, when he had finished. "I should be able to find it."

"Great. See you at 9:30 tomorrow." The line went dead before Pat could answer.

Bauer stood in the kitchen, staring at the phone with a puzzled look on her face.

"What's the matter, Patty, who was that?"

"Some guy who said he was working with Gene's lawyer. He said he wanted to get a statement from me tomorrow night, at 9:30 in the Greenwood Manor parking lot! Doesn't that sound a little strange to you?"

"You bet it does," Cheryl said, a look of fear in her eyes. "Patty, please don't go. It's probably a trick that Gene cooked up; he probably wants to have you bumped off so you can't testify."

"Oh, Cheryl, please . . ."

"Don't oh Cheryl me, Pat Bauer. You know as well as I do that Gene is in the Mafia!"

"Cheryl, Gene is not in the Mafia," Bauer retorted, as she settled back into her seat at the dining room table. "Besides, why would he want me out of the way?"

"I don't know, Patty, but you better watch out. Berta's up to something."

"Okay, okay, I'll tell you what; tomorrow I'll call Gene's lawyer and double-check, make sure this guy really is who he says he is. Will that make you feel better?"

"Yes," Cheryl said. "It would."

Friday, August 12, 1983

Smerecki gathered together a number of items he and Haley had found at Cathy Warner's house—the name tags and stethoscopes he had found in her drawers, as well as the white slip of paper on which was written information Cathy was given about her mother on July 8—and bundled them in a brown paper bag. Earlier that morning, the detective had spoken to Arnold Nachinsky, head of Middlesex General's nursing department, about the tags. Nachinsky had suggested that Smerecki bring the articles in question to the hospital, when Nachinsky would be better able to identify them.

"Well, I should tell you that we issued new photo I.D. cards to all our personnel on May second and third of this year," Nachinsky told the detective. "We changed the format from a photo and the individual's information in a horizontal position to a vertical position. We collected the old tags when we issued the new ones."

"Okay, Mr. Nachinsky, let me show you a couple of things here," Smerecki said, as he pulled from his bag a blue and white name tag, and a photo I.D. card laid out in a vertical format. The card was found in Cathy

Warner's bedroom early in the investigation. "Are these what you are using now?"

"Yes, they are," the official said. "These are what everyone is using. We haven't changed the name tags in about six or seven years. They've been the same blue and white colors for that long."

"I see," Smerecki said, gazing thoughtfully at the tags. "Mr. Nachinsky, there are a few nurses that used to work with Mrs. Warner that I'd like to speak to. Would that be possible now?"

"Certainly, follow me."

Nachinsky lead the detective to the Four Tower nurse's station, and introduced him to Mary Bacorn, the assistant head nurse.

Smerecki told the nurse what his business there was, and then asked to speak with the head nurse, Janina Stevens, and Rosemary Cascella.

"I'm sorry, but they're both off today," Bacorn told him. "Rosemary would be a good person to talk to; she and Cathy were very close, almost like sisters."

"Did you know Cathy?"

"Oh yeah," Bacorn said. "In fact, we had lunch on the day she was supposed to go on vacation."

"What time was that?"

"That was about 12:30. I remember Cathy got a phone call sometime about 1 o'clock, and then she made a call of her own. The last time I saw her, she was leaving, or maybe getting ready to leave. That must have been around 2 o'clock."

"Mrs. Bacorn, let me show you something." Again, Smerecki reached into his brown bag, pulling out the folded slip of white paper. On the side he showed her was written:

Andrews 31-1
Bracchi 37-2
Blodgett 38-1
Perrone 38-2

Then, written across the fold, was the information about Gloria Neal being taken to Muhlenberg Hospital with a possible heart attack.

"Can you tell who wrote these words?" Smerecki asked.

Bacorn took the paper from the detective and examined it closely for several minutes. Finally, she handed it back to him, slowly shaking her head.

"No, I don't recognize the handwriting," Bacorn said. "But I do know that those names were patients."

"Were they Mrs. Warner's patients?"

"I don't know," Bacorn told him. "All I remember is that they were patients on the floor. I don't remember who's they were."

Pat Bauer was in her office at Revlon. It was mid-morning, as good a time as any, she thought, to call Brown and follow through on the promise she had made to Cheryl — and herself — the night before.

But her blood ran cold when Brown told her that no one from his office had contacted her.

When she gave him the name of the man who called her, Brown told Bauer that no one by that name worked for the firm.

"What did he tell you?" Brown asked.

"Well, he wanted to take a statement from me. He made arrangements to meet him tonight at 9:30 in the Greenwood Manor parking lot."

"Okay, look. Don't you go there. I want you to come to my office as soon as you can, I'll talk to you. When can you come in?"

"I guess I could come in after work today, around 5:30 or 6 o'clock?"

"That will be fine, I'll see you then."

Pat Bauer was shaking. "Who the hell called me last night?" she thought. "Who could it have been?"

Monday, August 15, 1983

Joy Niemiera felt an uneasy relief; it had been several days since the last threatening phone call, but she didn't really trust that they were over. She and her husband Greg had decided against bringing the Trenton police in on their problem, they opted instead to buy a dog, which they did. Joy had been receiving at least two terrifying calls a week since Cathy Warner's body was found; although she didn't recognize the voice, she knew who was tormenting her.

In fact, during one of the last calls, Joy's anger at the constant intrusions had emboldened her; before the caller could hang up, she screamed, "Gene, you cut that out!" and then slammed the receiver down.

Although she had tried to discount their seriousness, Joy found herself affected by the calls: She was more alert when she was outside, and on more than one occasion she caught herself double- or triple-checking the door and window locks before retiring at night. It had reached the point where she hesitated answering the telephone out of fear that the phantom caller — probably Gene Berta, she thought — would be on the other end of the line.

So when several days had passed with no calls, Joy become curious and decided to call Tom Kapsak to see how the case was progressing.

"Oh yes, hello Mrs. Niemiera, how are you?" Kapsak sounded as though he was not surprised to hear from her.

"Well, remember I called you a few weeks ago about those calls? I haven't had any for a few days, and I was wondering what was happening with the case."

"Haven't you heard?" Kapsak sounded genuinely surprised. "We arrested Gene Berta last week."

"You arrested him?" Joy felt a chill go down her spine. "Where is he?"

"He's in the county lockup. He's been there since we picked him up last Wednesday. The judge set a half-a-million dollar bail, so I don't think he's going to be getting out soon."

"You mean he hasn't been on the street since last Wednesday?" Joy asked, a hint of shock in her voice.

"That's right."

"My God, that's about when those calls stopped!"

Niemiera, stunned by the news that, to her, confirmed Berta was the one making the threatening phone calls, quickly regained her composure.

"So he really did it; he killed Cathy?" she asked.

"We think so. We've got a lot of evidence, thanks to you and some other of Cathy's friends. But there's still some more information we have to work out. There are still some holes that have to be filled."

"I knew he had done it! I knew he killed her!" Joy said. "I just can't believe that someone who Cathy loved so much would do this to her. I can't believe someone would be so heartless."

"I've been in this job a long time, Mrs. Niemiera," Kapsak said, "and I've learned one thing: Anyone is capable of anything."

Morris Brown appeared before Judge Nicola that afternoon, seeking to get his client released on his own recognizance or, failing that, at least effecting a reduction in his bail to a more manageable level. Brown submitted a statement from Eugenia Berta which detailed her son's life, stressing his lifelong commitment to the community and paying particular attention to his civic services.

"My son has never had any difficulty with the law in any criminal situation," Eugenia Berta testified. "He has an excellent reputation in and around the Metuchen-Edison area and there are many respected people in the community, including police officers, hospital personnel and others, who will vouch for his good character."

Brown argued that the accident Berta suffered in May had left him unable to earn a living and had forced him to apply for welfare. Under the circumstances, Brown told the judge, a $500,000 bail was totally unreasonable.

The judge agreed with Brown, lowering Berta's bail to $150,000. But Nicola did not give Brown everything he wanted; the judge still refused to make the 10 percent option available to the defendant.

"Don't worry Gene," his mother yelled to him as he was led out of the courtroom by sheriff's deputies. "We'll get you out of there soon."

Casimir Smerecki was back at Middlesex General Hospital, speaking with Janina Stephens — Cathy Warner's supervisor — Rosemary Cascella and Rhonda Lane. Smerecki was told on Friday that the nurses would be in this day. He showed them the same slip of paper he had displayed to Mary Bacorn, and asked them if they knew what the names meant.

"Oh yes," Stephens said. "These are patients on the floor. As a matter of fact, that one, Bracchi, was discharged on July 8."

"Do you know who wrote these names down?" Smerecki asked.

"No, but it was probably Cathy, it looks like her handwriting."

"Yeah, that definitely looks like Cathy's handwriting," Cascella said. Lane nodded her agreement.

Back in his office, Smerecki noticed that the Timex watch he had examined the week before had completely stopped running. He wound it fully again, then set it aside after noting the time was 3:14 and the dater was still on 10. Next to those numbers, he jotted down the actual time the test began: 11:30 a.m.

Early in the afternoon, Watson interviewed James Sumka, a longtime friend of both Berta's and Warner's. Sumka, who was an instructor of forensic science at John Jay College in New York City, was a member of Edison Rescue Squad from 1972 to 1978. Sumka had also acted as a witness for Berta at his second marriage.

"I'm just trying to get a handle on this guy," Watson told Sumka. "Is there anything you can you tell me about him, something that would kind of give me an idea of what kind of guy he is?"

"Well, he's careful," Sumka said. "As long as I've known Gene Berta, he's always covered his tail well. He's always looking out for himself."

"Do you know if he owns any guns?"

"Well, I know he used to carry a shotgun around with him," Sumka said. "I saw that one, and I recently heard that he was carrying around a .22, but I never saw it."

"Do you think he killed Cathy Warner?" Watson asked bluntly. "Do you think he's the kind of man who would shoot a woman?"

"No, I don't think he did it," Sumka answered. "That's not like Gene. I don't think that's the way he would have done it, anyway."

"What do you mean?"

"Well, I mean, I'm sure he was joking, but Gene once told me that if he ever killed anybody, he would cut up the body, put the pieces in Hefty bags and scatter them all over. That way, the chances of the body ever being found were slim. But, see, Gene was always saying crazy shit like that. Sometimes he's pretty hard to figure out."

Later that afternoon, Thomas Kapsak was in what some regarded as his natural environment: a courtroom.

The presiding judge was George J. Nicola; Kapsak was there that afternoon to apply for a warrant to search Gene Berta's home and 1979 Ford van.

"What we would like to look for, your Honor, is any gun, any firearm, bloodstained clothing or rags or any sort of material that would wipe up blood, and keys to the house and car of Catherine Warner of 125 Durham Avenue, in Metuchen and her vehicle, which is a black Ford Mustang, 1981," Kapsak said. "If I may proceed, your Honor . . ."

"Yes," Nicola interjected, "who will be your first witness?"

"Dennis Watson."

After reviewing Watson's tenure with the county, Kapsak lead the detective through a recap of all the evidence that was found and of his involvement in the investigation. Kapsak paid particular attention to the statements made by Berta to Watson and Zimmerman, detailing his relationship with Cathy Warner and his actions on the weekend of July 8.

Watson also pointed out that the autopsy revealed Cathy Warner had been shot and that no gun had been found, even though friends told police that she kept a handgun in her bedroom. It was his experience, Watson said, that head wounds cause extensive bleeding.

"Did you find any bloody clothes in the house, either belonging to Catherine Warner or anybody else?" Kapsak asked.

"There were no bloody clothes at all," Watson answered.

"Do you then want to search for bloody rags or towels or some sort of implement that could be used to wipe up blood?"

"Yes sir."

Kapsak's presentation took about 15 minutes. When he had finished, Nicola said, "The testimony furnished by Detective Dennis Watson clearly, sufficiently establishes that requisite probable cause finding so that a search warrant could be appropriately issued. And I so issue a search warrant to search the 1979 Ford van, registered to Berta Electric of Edison, as well as a two and a half story framed dwelling located at 7 East Walnut Street, Metuchen."

The search warrant approval was the last piece of business conducted by Nicola that day, he authorized the warrant at 4:30 p.m. Kapsak and Watson were in Kapsak's office half an hour later, preparing the detective for his role in the grand jury presentation Kapsak would deliver the next day, when Watson abruptly slapped his forehead.

"What's the matter, Denny, forget something?"

"I just remembered something someone told me," Watson said. "It might have been Pat Bauer, or someone else. They mentioned that all the squad members had lockers at the rescue squad. If Berta has anything incriminating, he might have stashed it there."

"Okay, don't worry about it. I'll call the judge first thing in the morning, and we'll get another search warrant for the locker. In the meantime, let's go over your testimony for tomorrow."

Tuesday, August 16, 1983

Thomas Kapsak quietly surveyed the 23 Grand Jurors after they had been seated in the Grand Jury Room, located on the 10th floor of the County Administration Building in New Brunswick. It was just before 9 a.m. This proceeding, Kapsak knew, would be the first test of his evidence: to convince the Grand Jury to hand down an indictment against Eugene Berta for murder based on the circumstantial information he would present.

The charges being considered were murder in the first degree and possession of a weapon for an unlawful purpose. To make his case, Kapsak would call six witnesses to the stand: Metuchen Police Sgt. Ralph Salamone; County Detectives John Haley, Casimir Smerecki and Dennis Watson; Janina Stevens and Pat Bauer.

Stepping up to the dais, Kapsak, as he had many times before, introduced himself to the Grand Jurors.

"My name is Tom Kapsak," he began. "I am one of the assistant prosecutors here in Middlesex County. My primary job is to supervise the Major Crimes Unit, which includes homicides, and I am here today to present evidence regarding the homicide of Cathy Warner, the nurse from Middlesex General Hospital, who was murdered in Metuchen a few weeks ago. The charges I am going to ask you to consider after you hear the evidence are murder and possession of a weapon for an unlawful purpose."

His brief statement concluded, Kapsak called his first witness, Sgt. Ralph Salamone.

Salamone related the events of July 16 to the jurors, telling how he was dispatched to Cathy Warner's house and, at Kapsak's prompting, describing in detail how the Neals and Officer Sardone had entered the house and how completely the house was locked. Salamone was on the stand for exactly four minutes when he was excused by Kapsak.

"Sergeant Salamone, that's all the questions I have," The second assistant prosecutor said. "Please stand by in case I need to recall you."

John Haley was next on Kapsak's list.

Haley briefly described to the jury his role in murder investigations, then focused on the evidence discovered by himself and the other investigators which lead them to their conclusions about when and where Cathy Warner was murdered.

In his questioning, Kapsak first zeroed in on the maggots found on Cathy Warner's body. Haley testified that samples of the maggots had been taken to an entomologist for analysis, who reported that they had been laid four and one-half to six and one-half days prior to the body being found. Kapsak knew, however, that even the maximum time period was not long enough for him to convince the jury that Berta killed Cathy Warner on July 8.

The entomologist, Haley testified, "also indicated that parts of the body that were under water would not be acceptable for the fly to lay eggs, or if the entire body was under water."

"What he was really telling you," Kapsak clarified, "was how long a period of time had passed from the time the eggs were first laid until the time the body was discovered and the maggots removed?"

"That's correct."

"If the body had been under water prior to that then the whole process wouldn't have started from the time of death?"

"He indicated the flies would not lay eggs on a body under water."

"Getting back to the time when you arrived at the scene, was the body, at least, partially under water?"

"Partially, yes."

"From the position of the body could you tell whether the head had been under water prior to the time you arrived, completely under water?"

"By looking at the level lines there was a little scum on the side of the bathtub, and it would indicate that the head would be entirely under water if it was below those lines, the way I found it."

"There was sort of a ring around the tub?"

"Yes."

"Which was higher than the level of the body?"

"That's correct."

"Indicating to you at some point the head had been under water?"

"That's right."

"The head was the area the maggots had attacked?"

"The head was completely covered."

"That would indicate, if I may, then that the body had been in the tub at least four and a half to six and a half days and probably longer?"

"At least that, yes."

After he described the autopsy results, Haley detailed the various blood stains he and other detectives had found throughout Cathy Warner's house. At Kapsak's request, Haley stepped up to a drawing board and outlined the interior of Cathy Warner's house. He noted the first floor bathroom, where her body was found, and also sketched in the basement and showed the location of the mysterious spot in front of the washer and dryer.

Haley was dismissed twenty minutes after taking the stand.

Next up was Casimir Smerecki, the county's senior identification officer. Smerecki described his mission on July 16 as being "concerned with the searching and possible location of the bullet, type of evidence, either a bullet mark or a spent bullet."

Kapsak brought Smerecki directly to the events of the prior week, when the suspected bullet holes were found in the chair rung, boxes and wood stored in the basement. Following the officer's description of what he saw, Kapsak asked him to amend Haley's sketch of the house with the approximate location of the chair, cardboard boxes and plywood.

"Can you indicate with a blue pen the direction of what you believed to be the bullet?"

"The direction would be south to north as indicated by the blue arrow," Smerecki said, as he drew the arrow.

"So that if a shot had been fired in front of the washer and dryer near where the stain was, it could very well have followed the path you found from the boxes and plywood?"

"Yes. All the evidence was in conjunction with the findings."

Smerecki then described his unsuccessful efforts to find a bullet.

"You mentioned also something about newspapers," Kapsak said, after Smerecki had finished his narrative. "Can you tell us again what you found with regard to the newspapers in the basement?"

"Yes. The newspapers on the chair were stacked as though a person would be saving them for a scrap collection. The top paper was a Star Ledger dated July the eighth. The newspaper directly below it was July the seventh. The below was July the sixth and so forth and so on. Each chronological date. The newspaper of July eighth appeared to have not been read. It was still folded neatly. I preserved it for fingerprints."

Turning to the jurors, Kapsak asked, "Does anyone here have any questions of Sergeant Smerecki?"

One juror raised his hand.

"In your opinion, could the bullet have ricocheted down and gone up, or did it just go down and that's it? In other words, when the bullet passed through the plywood and the cartons could it have bounced back up?"

"No way," Smerecki said, shaking his head. "Because the size of the plywood and the size of the cardboard boxes are — I will give you the measurement. The plywood is 34 three-quarters inches high and 18 and a half inches wide and three-quarter inches thick. The hole that appears in it is about six inches off the floor and about seven inches in from the nearest edge. The cardboard boxes, I have the measurements on them." Smerecki quickly flipped through his reports. "They are 32 inches high, 24 and three-quarter inches across and each box is at best three-eighths of an inch thick, and there are five of them. So by leaning up against the wall, in order to hold them in position, it would be impossible for the bullet to travel upwards."

Another grand juror raised her hand with a question.

"Would the bullet have been ordinarily expected, upon hitting the wall, to drop to the floor or ricochet?"

"It is passing through a lot of material," Smerecki explained. "You are almost passing through a phone book. There was an abrasion mark of lead appearing on the back of the mark. I feel it goes colliding downward and leaving a grayish-type of trail of lead that is being analyzed presently."

"Is it your belief," Kapsak interjected, "before the bullet hit that cardboard and plywood and that wall, that it had passed through the skull of Catherine Warner?"

"Yes," Smerecki answered, a solemn note to his voce. "That is my belief."

"It had gone through a lot of thick, hard materials before it hit the wall?"

"That's true. Also, it is traveling sideways at this point."

"Would you guess as to the calibre?" another juror asked.

"I can only estimate," Smerecki said. "I am not a ballistics man. It is fairly large, .28 (calibre), maybe .9 millimeters, somewhere in that neighborhood."

"Is it your belief," the juror asked, "that the bullet had been removed prior to any of the police officers arriving at the scene?"

"Yes."

"You said the bullet was travelling on an angle as it passed through," a third juror began, "striking the wall at an angle and it came back and slid down the cardboard. It was that type of angle?"

Smerecki looked puzzled. "I don't get your question," he said.

"If it was fired 90 degrees to the wall it wouldn't be passing on an angle. I am trying to follow through with what you mean by the angulation."

"Bullets do not always travel in a straight line," the officer explained. "After striking something they can be deflected. The exit wound on the body, according to Dr. Schuster in conversations I had with him, was not clean. The bullet had exited . . . not normal, let's say. It came out jagged. Its direction could have been changed within the person. Upon coming out from the person's body, striking the chair, it's going to be changed somewhat somewhere before striking the plywood. When it hits the plywood, it's travelling sideways instead of forward," Smerecki continued, using his outstretched hand as a visual aid. "The bullet is sideways. It's traveling in this direction, but sideways," he concluded, slowly pushing his hand out in front of his face.

"At this point," the juror asked, "it was going 90 degrees to the wall and possibly dropped with the gray mark on the cardboard?"

"You should have been there," Smerecki laughed.

"You would have expected it?"

"Absolutely."

The Grand Jury having no more questions, Smerecki was excused. He had been on the stand for 17 minutes.

Janina Stevens testified that Cathy Warner was originally scheduled to leave at 3 p.m. on Friday, July 8, but that she had approached Stevens at 2 p.m. and asked to leave because her mother had been taken to the hospital. Stevens also testified that Cathy had not returned, as planned, on July 15th.

Dennis Watson's testimony revolved around the evidence found at the house — including the itinerary and the check registers — and also interviews conducted with Cathy Warner's family and friends and with Gene Berta. Through his questioning, Kapsak brought out the facts that Cathy Warner had given large sums of money to Berta, and that she was financially better off than was Berta. He also questioned Watson as to the inconsistencies in Berta's characterization of his relationship with Warner, as opposed to that given by Cathy Warner's friends.

In response to Kapsak's questions, Watson related Berta's various depictions of July 8 and the several proceeding days.

"Did you find her apartment keys in her pocketbook?" asked a juror.

"Her house and car keys were on a ring which we found on the kitchen counter," Watson answered.

"What was the date he brought the film to the house?" another juror asked.

"Monday, July the 11th."

"There has been testimony about a lot of flies being in the house," the juror continued. "Did he make any comments about the house in general that there were any stenches or a lot of flies about the house?"

"He never mentioned any of that."

"Was it ascertained if she ever had a gun?" a juror asked.

"It was ascertained through friends of hers that she did have a handgun which was purchased by her late husband," Watson said. "According to the witness this handgun was kept in a night stand next to the bed. We didn't find it."

"During the course of your entire investigation, and I assume you spoke to many, many people, is that correct?" Kapsak asked.

"Yes, we did."

"Did you determine that anyone, aside from Gene Berta, had a motive to kill Cathy Warner?"

"Not really, no, sir."

Did you find anyone who had spoken to her or seen her alive past July 8, 1983?"

"No, sir."

"Was the story she told her nursing supervisor untrue?" a juror queried. "Did she have a mother who had a heart attack?"

"That was untrue, yes."

"She had received a phone call just before she told that to the nursing supervisor, is that correct?" Kapsak asked.

"Yes, sir. She received a phone call about 2 p.m., and talked with Mr. Berta. He acknowledged when he arrived at the hospital to pick her up he called. He remained downstairs and called up to the fourth floor where she worked."

"At around 2 p.m.?"

"When he arrived at around 2, 2:30, he said."

Kapsak wasted no time in calling his next witness: Patricia Bauer.

Kapsak had spoken with Bauer once, briefly, before her Grand Jury appearance. Based on the information he was given by Watson and Zimmerman, Kapsak adopted the posture that the police knew she was holding back information. He repeatedly told her that if she was not completely forthcoming with him, and if he found out she perjured herself, he would prosecute her.

She believed him.

A shaky Pat Bauer walked into the Grand Jury room. She had dressed in her best-looking business outfit, her arm encased in a plaster cast, the result of a fall down a flight of stairs a week earlier when she was making a rescue squad call. Unsmilingly — more out of fear than belligerence — Pat

Bauer took her seat. Sensing his witnesses' nervousness, Kapsak eased into the meat of his questioning, first asking several preliminary questions about where Bauer lived, her marital status and, most embarrassing to Bauer, whether she was dating Gene Berta. Bauer answered in short, to-the-point sentences. When he thought she was a little more comfortable, Kapsak zeroed in on the area about which he wanted Bauer to testify.

"At some point, did he (Berta) ask you to take a trip with him?"

"Yes, he did."

"To where?"

"Minnesota."

"When did he ask you to do that?"

"He told me around the end of May. He asked me to go in the beginning of June."

Kapsak wanted to convince the jury that even though he had Cathy Warner plan and pay for the Minnesota trip, he had no intention of ever taking her with him. Instead, he asked Pat Bauer to go a full month before its scheduled starting date.

Bauer told the jury that, right up until the last day, she had no idea exactly when she and Berta would be leaving for their trip.

"When did you find out exactly when you would be going, exactly what time you would be leaving?" Kapsak asked.

"Friday night."

"What did he say about it on Thursday? Did he tell you what time on Thursday."

"No, he said he was nervous. He wasn't really sure what he was going to do."

After several more questions, Kapsak asked, "What time did he tell you to be ready on Friday?"

"He didn't," Bauer answered. "He said he would call me and tell me what time to pick him up.

Bauer testified that Berta called her five or six times on Friday, beginning in the early morning and up until 9:30 p.m.

"During none of those conversations did he tell you what time you were leaving?"

"No."

"Did he give you any idea or details about where you were supposed to meet or at what airport or any details about how you were going?"

"He just said he would tell me when to pick him up."

At 9:30 p.m., Bauer testified, Berta called and said, "You got 10 minutes to pick me up, where we always meet."

"Where was that?" Kapsak asked.

"Down at MetroPark."

Kapsak quickly lead Bauer through the weekend, paying particular attention to the fact that Berta included Bauer in the selection of the farm he purchased.

"In fact," Kapsak asked, "did he suggest the property would be for the two of you?"

"He spoke in terms of 'we'," Bauer replied. "He never came right out and said, 'You and I are going to live here'."

Having made his point, Kapsak asked if any jurors had questions.

"What was his general mood while he was on the trip with you," one asked.

"He was in a good mood," Bauer told him. "We did a lot of laughing, a lot of talking."

Kapsak dismissed Bauer, thanking her for her time. Glancing at her watch, Bauer was startled to see that she had spent only 10 minutes on the stand.

"It seemed like an hour," she thought.

Kapsak used Watson to drive the final nail in Berta's coffin.

"Detective Watson, as part of your investigation did you learn that when Eugene Berta went to Minnesota he put a deposit on a farm, an 80-acre farm in Minnesota?"

"Yes, we did."

"The amount of the deposit was $3,000?"

"That's correct."

"Did you also get copies of the bank records to determine what his financial situation was?"

"Yes, we did."

"Absent the $10,000 he had gotten from Cathy Warner, would he have $3,000 to make a deposit?"

"No, sir," Watson answered. Kapsak could see the detective's testimony was having an impact on the jurors.

"She not only paid for the trip, but in effect paid for the deposit on the farm, is that fair to say?"

"Yes sir."

"He told you, did he not, that that had been his plan until he and Cathy Warner had made love and fallen asleep and didn't wake up until 7 o'clock, and he missed his flight?"

"That's what he said, yes sir."

"Did you obtain, from the telephone company, telephone records relating to Cathy Warner's telephone line?"

"Yes, we did."

"Did you learn from those telephone records he had called Moose Lake, Minnesota at 12:59 p.m.?"

"Yes."

"That would have been while Cathy Warner was still at work, and he was at the house alone?"

"That's correct."

"Long before he had to rearrange his plans about catching the flight to Minnesota?"

"Yes, sir."

Kapsak paused several minutes, shuffling papers, to let the jury absorb his question and Watson's answer.

"What was the nature of that telephone call to Minnesota?"

"At 12:59 on the eighth, he called the real estate agent, Mr. Newman, from United Farm Agency, a real estate agency in Moose Lake, Minnesota," Watson answered. "At that time he informed Mr. Newman he had missed his flight and would not be able to come there on the eighth, but he would be there the following day, on the ninth."

"He made the call at 12:59 even though his flight was not scheduled until 4:45?"

That's correct."

"At that time, according to what he told you, he was still intending to take the 4:45?"

"That's correct."

Following the questioning of Watson by several jurors seeking to clarify some of his testimony, Kapsak explained the state statutes covering murder and possession of a deadly weapon, and asked the jurors to begin their deliberations. "Feel free to ask me any questions," he added.

The members talked among themselves, but did not ask Kapsak any questions. Then, about half an hour after they had begun, the discussion ended. The foreman called for a show of hands regarding the first count, the murder of Catherine Neal Warner sometime between the dates of July 8, 1983 and July 16, 1983. All Kapsak needed was 12 votes. He stopped counting hands when he reached 12, although there were several more in the air.

The foreman called for a vote on the second count, possession of a dangerous weapon for unlawful purposes. Again, Kapsak stopped counting at 12.

"We got him, Denny," Kapsak told Watson as he stepped out of the jury room. "They voted to indict."

Watson was elated. "That ought to knock that smug look off his face."

"We've got an appointment with Judge Nicola at one," Kapsak continued. "This is for that additional search warrant."

"Okay, then we'll execute all of them this afternoon," Watson said. "If he's got anything incriminating, he may tell Gail to get rid of it now that it's all official."

The indictment notwithstanding, Gene Berta also received some good news that day. His wife and his father, Alexander, had put up their homes as collateral and had posted his bail; he was free to go home.

Berta and Gail left the Adult Correctional Center and went to the rescue squad headquarters. Once there, they went down to the rec room to talk.

"I don't want you running around anymore, Gene." Gail was trying hard to keep her tears in check. "I'll stick by you, but I've got to know I'm the only one you're sleeping with. It has to be that way."

"Sure babe," Berta assured her. "That's no problem. That's no problem. This whole mess has changed me. I'm committed to you and the kids, and to our marriage. I promise."

Kapsak and Watson were in front of Judge Nicola at about the same time Gene Berta was declaring his love for wife and family.

The hearing took less than five minutes; Kapsak simply asked Watson to describe the additional area he wanted to search.

"All right," Nicola said, after Watson had concluded his description. "I find probable cause to believe that materials in connection with this investigation could be in that locker and I grant the search warrants."

At about 2 p.m., County Detectives Lawrence Nagle, Watson and Haley, and Metuchen detectives Salamone and Robert Kolbus executed the search warrant at Berta's home. The house was exactly as Watson had seen it when he and Zimmerman interviewed Gail Berta: clothes strewn haphazardly, cans of paint everywhere, along with tools, tarpaulins and general dirt. Watson remembered the wall smudges and the overall dingy atmosphere. He could tell by the looks of disgust on his colleagues' faces that his opinion was shared.

The detectives began their search with the van, which was parked in the driveway. After a half hour, all they had confiscated was one .22 calibre round, which was found in the motor cover; a set of keys on a ring, found on the van's brake release, and a second set of keys on a ring, found on the motor cover.

"Okay, ma'am, we're going to search the house now," Nagle told Eugenia Berta, who was the only one home at the time. The woman had been standing on the porch, a perplexed look on her face, as the detectives scoured the van.

She'd already called Gene at the rescue squad, he and Gail were on their way home.

Nagle and Watson were upstairs, searching through the Bertas' bedroom.

"Geez, Larry, look at this. The guy's got an arsenal up here."

Watson was not far off. Four rifles were visible in the bedroom: a Powermaster 760 .177 calibre pellet rifle was hanging in plain view in a gun rack; a Ranger 16-gauge double-barreled shotgun was sitting in its case, in a corner of the room, next to the dresser; a Marlin 22-calibre bolt action rifle – with scope – was next to it, wrapped in foam rubber and a Savage Arms

22-calibre bolt action rifle was lying in its box, on the floor in front of the dresser.

"Take a look at this," Nagle said. He was looking through the dresser and had several drawers open. Three boxes of 22-calibre ammunition were in one drawer, next to a number of targets. On top of the dresser were two boxes of shotgun ammunition.

"This guy is really into guns," Watson remarked. "And by the looks of that target, he is a pretty good shot."

A cardboard box, on the floor at the foot of the bed, was opened, revealing a number of live and spent shotgun shells.

"What have we here?" Nagle said. Now he was standing in front of an end table, reaching in a drawer. His hand emerged holding a blackjack.

Watson, Kolbus and Nagle joined Salamone downstairs just as Gene and Gail Berta arrived home.

"What's going on here?" Gail Berta demanded. "What are you doing in my house?"

"We've got a search warrant, Mrs. Berta," Watson said, point to Gene's mother. "Your mother-in-law has it over there."

"This is bullshit, Gene, call Morris Brown. They can't just come in here when they feel like it! Make them stop!"

"Calm down Gail, I'll call Morris and get this straightened out." Berta climbed the steps to his bedroom, wanting to make the call in private.

"You're free to do whatever you want," Watson said. "Just don't interfere with our search. Watson noted that Gene Berta, for a change, was calm, but it was his wife who was in a combative mood.

"Another gun," Nagle said, walking out of the kitchen. He was holding a Winchester 12-gauge pump shotgun he had found in a box on the floor.

"Did you make sure you looked in my drawers, too?" Gail Berta yelled. "Did you get any thrills from my panties? Take a couple for yourself?"

Berta returned to the ground floor several minutes later, carrying a note pad and a pen.

"Calm down Gail, Morris says they can do this, but he told me to make sure I make a list of everything they take," Berta said. "We can start with the rifles."

"You're damn right we will," Gail screamed. "I don't want to see anything walking out of here that isn't on our list!"

"You can go ahead and make your list," Watson said, "but you're wasting your time. We're required to make a list and leave a copy of it with you anyway."

"That's okay, I'll make my own list."

"You're really being a jerk, Gene, but suit yourself," Watson told him.

"Don't forget to include this on your list, Mr. Berta" Nagle said. He was holding a plastic bag, inside of which was a small amount of what looked like a green, leafy plant. "I found it upstairs, in the bedroom."

Berta said nothing, instead busying himself with his list-making.

In addition to the weapons and the suspected marijuana, the investigators seized three keys to Ford Motor Co. autos, as well as a number of unidentified keys on a ring and Berta's firearms identification card. The search was completed by 3:20 p.m.

"What are all these keys for, Gene?" Watson asked.

"Well some of them are house keys, some are to mine and Gail's cars, and some are for the squad building, you know, the doors, my locker."

"This is for you," Nagle said, handing Berta the list of items that had been seized. "Have a good day."

"Did you get some good shots, John?" Watson asked. "Haley had followed the detectives around the house with a Polaroid camera, snapping photos of the evidence and the house in general.

"Yeah," he said. "I got one of a letter that looks like it was written from Gail to Gene. She says she'll stand by him if he stops fucking around."

"Everything a wife should be," Watson said. The officers were on their way to the rescue squad, where they arrived at about 10 minutes to four.

"We're from the Middlesex County Prosecutor's Office," Nagle told John Musicant, a squad member who met them at the door. "We have a warrant to search the locker of Gene Berta."

Having no other choice, Musicant let the officers in.

"It's number 17," Watson said, as the men walked down the row of lockers. "This is it," he said, pointing to a closed door bearing the name of Gene Berta.

"Open it, please," Nagle asked Musicant.

The opened door revealed an empty locker. Haley took a photo of the locker for the record.

"Okay, that's it," Nagle said, as he deposited the warrant on a shelf in the locker and shut the door. "We're finished here."

The detectives were met by George Taylor as they were leaving the building.

"What can I do for you?" Taylor asked. He had been alerted to the detective's presence by a squad member.

"Nothing, sir," Watson told him. "We just executed a search warrant for Gene Berta's locker. We left the paperwork in the locker."

Arriving back at the county building at about 4:30 p.m., Watson headed straight for Kapsak's office. Luckily, the second assistant prosecutor was still in.

"Hey, Denny," Kapsak said. "Find anything useful?"

"Well, we got a lot of guns and ammo," Watson told him. "I don't think we found the murder weapon, but we're going to check everything out. We also found a bunch of keys; house keys, car keys. We're gonna check to see if any of them open Cathy Warner's doors. Haley took a lot of pictures; you should see that place, it's a hole. They don't even have toilets!"

Kapsak made a face. "Why doesn't that surprise me? What about the locker?"

"That was a zero. He didn't have anything in there," Watson said, clearly disappointed.

"Well, we knew this wasn't going to be easy. Berta went to all the trouble of cleaning up that house and grabbing the bullet, there's no reason to think he would make things simple for us by leaving something in his house or locker."

"Anything happen over here?"

"No," Kapsak said. "Cas did some tests on the pieces of masking tape that Joe found in her kitchen. There weren't any fingerprints on it. Then he tried to match the fracture breaks of the pieces of tape with the roll that was in the basement, but there was no luck there, either.

"Jim O'Brien went back to the house yesterday," Kapsak continued. "He lifted some more latent prints and gathered up a bunch of bills and papers from Cathy Warner's bedroom. There may be something in them that will help us prove Gene Berta was using her for her money. Oh, he also took the window shade from the upstairs bedroom; he said he saw two stains on it that could have been blood. We'll be sending everything over to the FBI for analysis."

"So what do you think? Have we got a case?"

"Well, it's always tricky when all you have is circumstantial stuff," Kapsak told the detective. "If I want to convict Berta, and unless we can find a witness or a gun or something, I'm really going to have to prove motive. I'm going to have to make that jury believe that Cathy Warner really loved him, and all he wanted was her money. And the worst part about it is, you never know if you have enough evidence."

Voices — Merelyn Daniel

"When they arrested him, I wasn't even surprised. I just didn't understand why he killed her. I cannot understand why he had to kill her.

"What we couldn't understand was that Gene came to the memorial service. And we were saying, what is his problem? None of us talked to him, we acted like we didn't know him, nothing. No eye contact. He sat behind us, he came in after the services had started. One of the girls happened to turn around and see him. We couldn't believe it. He was just sitting there acting all sad like everybody else. The policeman told us that most murderers go to the services of the person they murdered, which is sick. After the service was over, we met Cathy's parents and sister and brother. They were kind of numb. The brother, he was like he was still in a daze. I guess if I walked in a house and found somebody I loved in that kind of condition, I guess . . . him and his father for the rest of their life will always have that picture. That had to be absolutely gruesome, and the smell had to be outrageous. That was one of the hottest weeks that we had and the house was all closed up. Her mother was very friendly, she introduced herself to us. We said that we were sorry and talked to her for a little while.

"I just know that she was a good person and she didn't deserve the things that happened to her."

Voices — Donna Tokar

"She had a gun, she got it from her husband. I think I saw it. She said she kept it in her room. For some reason, when I think I saw this gun, it wasn't a big gun., but it wasn't a little gun. Maybe I remember her telling me about the gun. I thought, why do you have a gun? It was because her husband was gone, and she didn't want anything to happen to her."

Voices — Joy Niemiera

"They asked me if I thought I knew who did this, and I of course said no, because I have a brother-in-law who's a policeman and he said, don't say anything. I had no proof that Gene did it, and I didn't know the facts, all I knew that Cathy was found dead. But the first name that popped into my head was Gene Berta. I didn't want it to be him because I didn't want to think that someone that Cathy loved and gave so much of herself to would have the heartlessness to murder her. But deep down, I guess that I knew it was him. I wasn't surprised when they arrested him."

Voices — Dennis Malinowsky

"I still can't believe that he was that cold, but I'll tell you something else: Chuck had gone out on a job with Gene, he told me, unless he was lying to me. Quite evidently, Chuck knew more than I did. Gene knew where my line was, so, being a friend, he didn't let me in on that part of his life that he knew I would disagree with, so that he wouldn't put himself into any kind of problems and he wouldn't put me into any mental turmoil.

"But Chuck had said one time at Pete's — I don't remember if we were drunked up that night or what; I don't mean sloppy drunk, just having a couple of beers and running off at the mouth. We never really got plastered plastered, just giddy. Gene was never a user of drugs or alcohol to any kind of extent to where you would say he was a drinker. He had the occasional beer or glass of wine with dinner, but that would be it— at any rate, Chuck said something about . . . maybe I just walked into the conversation: 'Yeah he got into the van with the bat, and he was laughing, and he said, 'you should have seen that mother fucker bleed'.' What do you draw from that? He rapped somebody in the back of the head with a baseball bat! Chuck's inference was, 'I knew the shit was going bad when he started to like it.' He said to do what you got to do is one thing, but to like it is something else. So in other words, Chuck was saying, the guy was in a scrape, a financial scrape, he had to do something dirty to get himself out of it, but he was starting to like it. So was he a hit man? Did he do a couple of jobs for somebody? Sounds like it to me."

"I remember getting drunked up one night — I was having trouble with one guy or another — we were on his porch and he was telling me, 'Well, whatever you do, don't be stupid enough to do it yourself, 'cuz you're too close to it.' And then Gail came out on the porch and said, 'Who you killing or blowing up now?' He just said, 'Shut up and get the fuck back in the house.'

"So what did he do? He went against his own rule and stuck it up his own ass. If he was involved in the mafia he could have done it as a return favor for somebody, but maybe he didn't have the reputation.

"I didn't talk to him after he was arrested. We talked at the memorial service. But that's part of the Mafia thing, you go to the funeral and you bring flowers to the person you murdered. That was part of the thing. We had asked him to go see a shrink because he had to get his shit together because his life was falling apart and he said, 'no, because there are some things in my life that I just can't talk to anybody about.' What they were, whether he was trying to allude to some of the things he had done, or whether it was just part of his imagination, I don't know."

Voices — R.

"I never knew him to have a handgun, he had a shotgun, he called it old Betsy. Years ago, we used to get calls to go into Potters Field, it was a bad area. We had a special gang who went into Potters. We had two guys who carried handguns and Gene carried a shotgun, and then there were two others. And the police knew it, although they might not openly admit it. I remember one day, Gene was sitting in the passenger's seat with the shotgun hanging out the window. He said, 'don't worry, we got you covered.' We always went in with two police cars. It was a bad area. One of us had a handgun, another had a handgun, Gene had his shotgun, and somebody else had them nunchuks. And of course, we all had a blackjack. Gene would always sit at the window with the shotgun."

Tightening The Noose

August 17, 1983

CASIMIR SMERECKI WAS in Joe Zimmerman's office when John Haley popped his head into the doorway.

"Sarge? You know that watch you've been testing? Well, I think it stopped."

"Be right back, Joe," Smerecki said as he looked at his own watch and hurried after Watson. It was 1:15 p.m.

Smerecki had been conducting informal tests on the watch found on Cathy Warner's body since the beginning of the investigation. But it wasn't until after Gene Berta had been arrested and several of Cathy Warner's nurse friends had been interviewed that the watch was considered a potentially significant piece of evidence.

A nurse's watch is a critical piece of her equipment, the investigators were told. Because the watch was used daily in checking patients' vital signs, it is of the utmost importance that it be kept in top working order. Cathy's watch, a Timex day/date model with a gold and silver-toned wristband and safety clasp, was of the wind-up variety. The nurses interviewed by police who had this type of watch told the investigators that winding it each and every morning became a ritual; they even did it when they were not on duty.

On August 15, Casimir Smerecki was contemplating those facts and toying with the watch when he realized that the watch could "tell" detectives when Cathy Warner had last wound it up—in other words, the last day Cathy Warner was alive.

The detective pulled out a sheet of paper and noted the actual time – 11:30 a.m. – and next to it wrote down the time and date that appeared on the watch's face – 3:14 and 10. He was pretty certain the "10" meant July 10, but he wasn't sure if the time was morning or afternoon. But he was certain that he would soon find out.

Smerecki wound the watch up taut, then followed the sweep second hand as it ticked around the dial. Satisfied that the watch was working, he put it on his desk and walked away.

Smerecki checked the watch periodically over the next three days, each time marking down the actual time and date, and then entering the time and date which appeared on the watch.

On August 16, at 8:32 a.m., Smerecki noticed that the time on the watch was 12:18 and that the dater had changed to "11". He calculated that the watch had been running for about 21 hours before the dater changed, which meant that when the watch stopped at 3:14, it was 3:14 a.m. on July 10.

"Now let's see how long this little bugger keeps running," he said.

The Timex had been running smoothly until Haley informed Smerecki that it had stopped.

"Let's see what we've got here," Smerecki said as he picked up the watch. The time on the watch was 2:55 and the dater had turned to "12".

"Do you know when this stopped?" he asked Haley.

"No, I just noticed it a few minutes ago."

"Okay, I think I can check it." Smerecki pulled out the paper on which he was noting the watch's progressions. He saw that the last time he had checked it was 8:30 that morning, and that the watch showed 12:15 and a date of "12".

"Looks like it ran for two hours and 40 minutes since the last time I checked," Smerecki said, placing the paper back on his desk. "So that means the watch ran for a total of . . . 47 hours and 41 minutes; just under two full days."

"So," Haley interjected, "if the watch had stopped at 3:14 a.m. on the 10th, that means it was last wound sometime in the early morning of July 8th!"

Smerecki smiled. "Like about 5:30 or so."

"Funny how we keep coming back to the eighth, isn't it?" Haley asked. "It's all adding up, Sarge; the watch was wound on the eighth, the days on the calendar are marked off up until the eighth, the last time she was seen was on the eighth, and the last time Berta said he saw her was on the eighth."

"And the trip was supposed to be on the eighth," Smerecki added. "This girl is helping us nail her own murderer!"

In speaking with several of Berta's friends, investigators learned that he had had a heavy high school romance with another Edison resident, P.M. Watson tracked P.M. down to an Edison apartment complex and interviewed her late that evening.

"Listen," she told the detective, after she reluctantly let him in her apartment, "I'll tell you what you want to know, but you've got to keep my name out of it."

"Well, I'm afraid I can't guarantee that, Miss," Watson said.

"Look, I finally found a great guy; we're engaged and are going to be married soon," she pleaded. "He doesn't know a lot about my past, and I want to keep it that way. There are some things I did that I'm not too proud of."

Watson sighed. He didn't want to blow a potential source, but he didn't want to mislead the woman, either.

"Okay, I'll see what I can do," Watson said. "I think I can arrange it so that the only way we'll call you is if we really need to. But that's the best I can offer you."

P.M. sat down heavily in an overstuffed couch and looked up at the detective with weary eyes.

"All right," she said, "what do you want to know?"

Watson was elated, but he kept it to himself. "First off, how long have you known Gene Berta?"

"God, I must have met him, oh, 15, 16 years ago," she answered.

"You went out in high school, right?"

"Yeah," she laughed. "In fact, we almost got married in 1967. I was a senior in high school, and we just ran off, we were going to get married. But my parents caught us and stopped us. I think we broke up shortly after that."

"Real strong relationship, huh?"

"Hey," the woman said, shrugging her shoulders, "what can I tell you? We were young."

"So did you stay in touch with each other after you broke up?"

"No, not really. I don't think I saw him again until, oh, 1975. We ran into each other in the Menlo Park Mall."

"Do you recall anything about that meeting?"

"Yeah, Gene said he was going through a divorce with his first wife. We started talking, and before I knew it, he asked me for my number. So I gave it to him, and he gave me his. We started dating again after that, but it didn't last long."

"You didn't want to run off and get married again?" Watson joked.

"Nah, it just wasn't there. Like I said, we were young. Thank God my parents stopped us."

"Okay," Watson said, getting the conversation back on track. "When was the next time you saw him?"

"It had to be a couple of years ago; yeah, I think it was 1981. This time *I* was the one going through the divorce. It was one of those things where I needed a lawyer, but I didn't know any, so I tried to think of people I knew who had gone through this. Then I remembered that Gene had been through a divorce, so I called him and asked him if he knew of a lawyer who could help me," she explained. "I asked him for some other advice, too."

"So you two met regularly to discuss your divorce?"

"Well, I don't know how regular it was. He gave me the name of a lawyer, and, like I said, I asked him for some help with some other things. And then we started dating *again*.

Then I got to the point where I really needed money because I wasn't working, and Gene suggested that I, well, . . ." Watson could see the hesitancy in her eyes. "This is the kind of stuff I can't have getting out; I mean, this could ruin me."

"I told you I'd do whatever I can to keep your name out of this," Watson assured her. "But I really need this information, I really need to know what kind of man Gene Berta is."

"I don't believe I'm telling you this," she said. "Gene said that if I really needed money, I could become a prostitute for him. So I did."

"So he acted as your pimp?" Watson tried, but failed, to keep the shock out of his voice.

"Yeah. He set me up about four times. Mostly parties at the firehouse. But Gene was there every time. He collected the money and then gave me my share after it was over."

"Were you the only one working for him like this?" Watson asked. He thought nothing he heard about Gene Berta could surprise him. This conversation was proving him wrong.

"No. He said he had other girls doing it too," P.M. said.

"So you would just work at parties?"

"Yeah, pretty much. But once, we were talking about his son, and he asked me, if and when the time came, would I take care of little Gene's . . . sexual needs."

"He asked you to sleep with his son!?"

"Yeah, but not right away. He said whenever Gene Jr. wanted to explore it. I didn't give him an answer. I mean, I wouldn't have done it!"

"Okay, is there anything else you can tell me, something that would show me what kind of a guy Gene Berta is?"

P.M. paused for a moment, gathering her thoughts.

"You know, now that I think about it, Gene was always hinting about being some kind of shady character." The remembrance brought a smile to P.M.'s face.

"Shady, huh," Watson said, answering her smile with his own. "What kind of things would he say?"

"Oh, well, like one time he told me he had to go away on business with another truck driver," she recalled. "He never really came out and said it, but he implied that he was a hit man because he would tell me that I would be surprised if I knew about the things he had done, and that he had a lot of contacts who could do things for him. And another time he told me that he saw to it that the father of Gail's two children never came around again, stuff like that. Oh, and once he bragged about shooting and castrating his neighbor's dog with a rifle."

"Did you believe him?"

"I don't know; you never could tell whether Gene was telling the truth or putting you on."

"Did you ever see him with any guns?"

"Yeah, he always bragged about keeping a loaded rifle in his van. I saw it a lot; he kept it wrapped up in a blanket."

"So you and he were dating, and you occasionally worked as a prostitute for him. How long did this go on?"

"Well, we were dating right up until after my divorce. That was in January of last year. But he still calls me. He asks me to work as a prostitute at parties at the fire house, and other places."

"You said you had asked him for advice, what kind of advice did he give you?"

"Well, I do remember one thing he told me when I was going through my divorce, and this goes back to what I was telling you about him hinting about a shady past. One time, we were talking about what you have to go through when you get a divorce, and he looked at me and said, you know, there are other ways to end a marriage than divorce. So I said, what do you mean? And he said, 'you could become a widow'."

"A widow?" Watson asked, his eyebrows arching.

"Yeah! He said it just like that! He told me my husband could be murdered for $3,000, but I told him I didn't want to do that."

"Did he ever bring up the subject again?"

"No, I don't remember him doing talking about it again."

"Okay. What words pop into your head when you think about Gene? I mean, how would you describe Gene?"

"Well, let's see; he's the kind of guy who likes to make people afraid of him, I guess that's why he always talked about his contacts. He's quick-tempered, intimidating and arrogant, but he can be a real charmer."

"Uh-huh. How do you think he would act if he was in a tense

situation?"

"I think if he was in a tense situation, he's the type of person who wouldn't panic; he's real cool-headed, like he's always thinking things out. "

August 18, 1983

Casimir Smerecki woke at his customary 5 a.m., taking care to not disturb his slumbering wife. Seated in his kitchen at about 5:30 a.m., he picked up the petite Timex watch found on Cathy Warner's lifeless wrist and set it to the correct time, then set the dater on "8". Finally, he wound the watch until he felt the spring was taut and placed it in his shirt's breast pocket before leaving for the office.

Smerecki checked the watch a number of times during the day, each time dutifully noting the actual time and the time and date which appeared on the watch. The last check he made was at 11:05 p.m., just before he retired for the evening. The watch was running smoothly.

August 20, 1983

At 8:19 a.m., Smerecki looked at the watch and noticed that it had stopped with the time reading 5:55 a.m. and the dater on "10". Reviewing his log, Smerecki saw that he had noted the dater had changed from "9" to "10" at 12:44 a.m., although the watch read 12:46.

"The watch, wound tight, ran 48 hrs. and 25 minutes," Smerecki noted at the bottom of his log.

"She must have wound it tight every day," Smerecki thought, as he picked up the watch. "But what would happen if she didn't?" To answer his own question, the detective set the time to 8:40 a.m. and the dater to "10" and wound the watch just until he started feeling tension in the spring.

"*I guess we'll find out,*" he thought.

August 22, 1983

County Investigator Lawrence Nagle walked over to Middlesex General Hospital in the late morning carrying the watch found on Cathy Warner's body. His mission was to see if Warner's closest friends at the hospital could identify it as being hers; if the prosecution could not determine that it was, they would lose one key piece of evidence in determining when she died.

Nagle took the elevator up to the fourth floor, then stopped at the nurses' station and asked for Janina Stevens. He was led to the small office occupied by Cathy Warner's former supervisor.

The investigator introduced himself, then asked Stevens if she could identify the watch as belonging to Cathy Warner.

"You know, I never really noticed what kind of watch she wore," Stevens told Nagle. "I really can't say that that one is hers. But you might have better luck with her friends; I think Merelyn and Mary are on the floor today."

Stevens called Merelyn Daniel and Mary Bacorn to her office, introduced them to Nagle and told them what he wanted. Nagle showed them the watch.

"That looks just like the one Cathy wore," Bacorn said. "I remember the gold and silver wrist band, and that funny clasp on the back."

"Yeah, I remember this," Daniels agreed. "Her watch had that day/date thing on the face. I even saw her wearing it on July 8. She kept looking at it as she was reporting out to me."

"You're sure this looks like the one she wore?" Nagle asked.

"Oh yeah, I'm positive," Daniels repeated. "I used to borrow it when I would forget my own watch."

The morning mail brought Thomas Kapsak some news for which he had been waiting: State Police scientists had tested the chair, plywood and corrugated boxes and found that the residue was "indicative of the nick and holes having been made by a lead projectile," according to a report written by Stephen M. Andrews, senior forensic chemist at the State Police lab.

Kapsak smiled to himself as he filed the report in a large brown folder labelled, "Warner, Catherine - Homicide". One more piece in the puzzle, he thought.

While the county detectives were trying to gather more evidence to prove Gene Berta's guilt, Berta was busily taking steps to prove his innocence. So it was that Berta found himself in Morris Brown's conference room that afternoon, secured to a special polygrapher's chair. Strapped around various parts of Berta's body were a series of measurement tools which were in turn connected to a special plotter: Two thin rubber numegraph tubes wrapped around Berta's chest and his stomach; these would be used to measure changes in his rate of breathing. The tubes' placement was to accommodate the two different types of "breathers" — those who breathe from the chest, and those who take deeper breaths, from the diaphragm. A cardio-cuff — similar to the device used by doctors to measure blood pressure — was placed on Berta's right arm and inflated. This was connected to the plotter pen which would record changes in Berta's pulse rate. And finally, the first two fingers of Berta's right hand were strapped to a special galvanic plate which would measure the amount of perspiration that escaped from his skin — the higher the level of stress, the greater the amount of perspiration released by the skin.

Berta's attorney had arranged for this session after Berta had cancelled the appointment in New York. Unable to get the same firm to travel to New Jersey, Morris Brown had been forced to find another firm.

Gary Charles of Truth Testing, Inc. had just finished strapping Berta to his machine when Brown and his colleague Barry Albin walked into the conference room. They would monitor the testing.

Charles had already been provided with a folder of information on the case so that he would have some background upon which to base his questions.

Berta and Charles began chatting, with the polygraphist asking simple, straightforward questions that had nothing to do with the case. Every now and then, Charles would make a mark on the plotter paper as it rolled out of the machine.

Charles had spent some time with Berta reviewing the questions he would ask him before the test began; the polygraphist wanted his subject to know exactly what would be asked so there would be no surprises to skew the results. Charles interspersed control questions — name, age, address — with relevant questions so that he could get a handle on what would be considered normal readings. He asked the first "real" question about 45 minutes into the test.

"Do you know who murdered Cathy Warner?"

"No."

Did you murder Cathy Warner?"

"No," Berta said evenly.

Charles spent the next 15 minutes asking irrelevant questions before moving on to the next target question.

"Did you have someone murder Cathy Warner?"

"No."

Charles followed up with a neutral question, "Do you live in Metuchen, New Jersey?"

"Yes."

Right now, can you take me to the gun used to kill Cathy Warner?"

"No."

"Okay, that's it!" Charles said. He made several more marks on the sheet, then circled the table and began unhooking Berta from the apparatus.

Brown asked Berta to leave the room while he spoke to Charles.

"Well, anything conclusive?" he asked.

"I've just skimmed the responses, and this is really preliminary," Charles said. "And I would still like to test him again, at least once, so that I have a basis for comparison."

"Well, from what I can see," Charles said, "it looks like there are definite indications that your client is telling the truth when he said he did not kill Cathy Warner."

August 23, 1983

Smerecki concluded the last of the tests he had been conducting on Cathy Warner's watch.

The watch had stopped on August 21 at 6:15 p.m. with a time of 3:53 p.m. showing on its face and a date of "11". The detective calculated that the timepiece had run 31 hours and 13 minutes from when he had partially wound it on August 20.

He loosely rewound the watch a second time on August 21, setting it to 6:17 p.m. with a date of "12".

At 10:53 a.m. on August 23, Smerecki noticed that the watch had stopped with a time reading of 10:31 a.m. and a date of "14"; 40 hours and 14 minutes after he had last set it.

"So what you're telling me is that the watch runs an average of two days when it is fully wound?" Thomas Kapsak asked Smerecki. The detective brought the test results to the assistant prosecutor in the latter's office.

"That's right. And the nurses told us that she had to have wound that thing every day, so that she could use it on the patients."

"And you're sure that the time on the watch when it was found on her body was morning?"

"That's what my tests show. She last wound that watch around 5:30 a.m. on July 8, 1983. That was the last time she was alive to do it."

"Okay, Cas, that's great. Now what we've got to do is firmly establish that the watch is in good working order. Let's try to find a Timex headquarters and see if there's someone there who can test it for us."

"We'll get right on it."

August 24, 1983

Thomas Kapsak was seated behind his desk, addressing the
investigating team, which he had summoned to his office.

"I think we're already at the point of being able to prove that Cathy
Warner was killed on July 8," he began. "We've got statements by friends
that she was last seen on the eighth, in addition to the calendars and, now,
the watch. We've also got Berta's admission that he saw her on the night
of the eighth, making him the last one to see Cathy Warner alive. But the
problem is that we have two unconnected facts: one, that Cathy Warner did
not live past July 8, and, two, that Gene Berta was the last one to see her on
that day. What we've got to do is find something that I can use to tie the two
together in the minds of the jury. There has to be some link, something that
will show he killed her."

"What about all that money, and the fact that he treated her like dirt?"
Dennis Watson asked.

"That's fine for motive, Denny, but we need more than that. We need
something tangible, at least as tangible as we can get. Now, we know she
was killed in the basement, I'm sure we can prove that with what we have.
And I'm not too concerned about Dr. Schuster's autopsy; he even told me

he wasn't sure of it himself. I think with the corroborative testimony of the friends, plus the maggots and the stuff I talked about before, I can convince a jury that July 8 was Cathy Warner's last living day."

"But that still leaves a hole," Smerecki said. "What if we had something that would show she was killed early in the day, when Berta said he was there?"

"That would be perfect," Kapsak said. "But what do we have?"

"Well, Berta said he picked her up from work, right? So maybe he killed her when she was still in her uniform?"

"That would mean there would have to be a bloody uniform somewhere." Zimmerman said. "We haven't been able to find one, either in her house or in Berta's house."

"We've found other uniforms, though," Haley said. "And we've got a shoe that has a drop of blood on it."

"Yeah, but there wasn't enough in the sample to type it, and she was a nurse," Watson reminded the group. "That blood could have been from any one of her patients."

"What if we could show, by the process of elimination, that one of her uniforms is gone?" Smerecki asked. "If he shot her when she was still dressed in her whites, he probably undressed her and threw anything incriminating away."

"That's right," Zimmerman said. "He did tell us that he took out the garbage."

"That seems like a long shot, Cas," Kapsak said. "How do we know how many uniforms she had?"

"Let me work on it," Smerecki answered. "Maybe I can come up with something. We've got a bunch of receipts and some other papers that I could look into."

"Anything is welcome at this point," Kapsak said. "Good luck."

Armed with several receipts for nurses' uniforms — purchases made by Cathy Warner — found in Warner's house, Sgt. Smerecki paid a visit to the Kent Uniform Center, formerly known as the Gilson Uniform Center, in Woodbridge Mall. He spoke with Philippa Brown, who helped the detective decipher some of the codes on the sales receipts. The detective handed

Brown the paperwork he had brought with him, a pink sales slip, a yellow charge slip and four white clothing tags.

"She bought expensive uniforms," Brown noted while looking over the paperwork. "Okay, let's see what we've got.

This first thing here, on the pink slip for $22, is the same as this clothing tag," she began. "It's a Bargo sweater, navy blue; it's just like this one over here, except this one is a newer model." Brown walked over to a rack of sweaters, picking one out and displaying it for Smerecki. On his note pad, Smerecki wrote the information he had been given followed with the notation, "Not Found".

"This second item on the slip is also the same as *this* clothing tag," Brown said. "It's a white, two-piece suit with three-quarter length sleeves."

Brown returned the tag to Smerecki; a notation on the tag's back side told the detective that this garment had been found in Cathy Warner's bedroom closet.

The next two tags were from two-piece uniforms, short sleeved blouses with pants. Smerecki noted that each of them had been recovered from Cathy Warner's house.

"Now, each of these were paid for half by cash and half going on a VISA card, which accounts for this charge slip," Brown told the detective. "She bought good uniforms."

Smerecki showed Brown the final tag.

"This is an old one, it only cost $11," Brown said. "It was for a white nurse's dress. I guess it would match up with this sales receipt; God, it's dated May 27, 1976. She really did keep records, didn't she?"

"Yes ma'am, she did," Smerecki said, as he wrote down the information he was given, followed by, "Dress not found".

Smerecki had one more sales slip to follow up on, this one from J.C. Penney. After introducing himself to several people and explaining his task, he was lead into the office of Barbara Frazzetti, the store's personnel manager. Smerecki explained what he was looking for, then showed her the sales receipt.

"This is quite old," Frazzetti said. "May 27, 1976. This is probably from our old store. We've only been here about two years. The only thing

I can tell you is that it was probably from our uniform shop, since it has "uniform" written on it, but that's really it. There's no more information to get from this."

August 25, 1983

Smerecki continued his investigation, speaking with representatives of several different uniform manufacturers. Through these and prior conversations, Smerecki was able to determine that Cathy Warner owned nine uniforms, four of which had been accounted for — three found in her closet and one in a laundry basket. The remaining five were missing, although investigators did find their receipts.

Smerecki later found out that Det. John Haley had found a navy blue sweater in Warner's house, but there were no identifying labels in it, which meant it could have been the sweater for which Semerecki had the tag.

Smerecki's next step was to take the four uniforms — along with a handbag, a number of keys, Warner's watch and sundry other garments — to Middlesex General and display them for nurses Rhonda Lane, Janina Stevens and Mary Bacorn to see if any of the garments had been what Warner may have worn on July 8.

The clothing lineup was set up in the nurse's lounge; the items were placed upon several tables that were set side by side. They were identified as "Uniform A" and "Uniform B", two pants suits, both of which were found in Cathy Warner's closet; "Uniform C", a pants suit, which was found in her laundry basket, and "Uniform D", a pants suit, which was also found in her closet. Also exhibited for the nurses' inspection was the blue sweater, assorted bras, a number of keys, a pocketbook and the watch found on Cathy Warner's remains.

Rhonda Lane was the first nurse escorted in.

"Well, Cathy always liked to wear things that were more, form fitting, you know? I would have to say that Uniform B looks like something she wore a lot. But that wouldn't be the uniform she wore Saturday, it would have had to be a different one."

"What makes you so sure of that?" Smerecki asked.

"Because it doesn't have her nursing pin on it, see? Like this." Lane pointed to a small gold and blue pin that was attached to the front of her uniform. "Cathy's was from Middlesex County College, so it would have that name on the front," the nurse explained. "And it would have her year of graduation and her initials engraved on the back. We get them when we graduate from nursing school. We always wear them on our uniforms, it's a requirement. So whichever uniform Cathy wore that day would have to have the pin on it."

"Did she ever wear dresses?" Smerecki asked, his interest piqued.

"Oh no, Cathy always wore pants suits."

"Well, we haven't found a pin like that yet, but it will probably turn up. Okay, what about the rest of these things?"

"Well, I know she always wore a bra to work; if she didn't I would have noticed." Lane picked up the Timex watch. "Yeah, that's Cathy's. I recognize that. I've never seen her keys, so I can't help you there, and I've never seen her with a sweater. I don't ever remember seeing that purse."

"Is there anything else that she would have carried with her at work?"

"She would have carried pens, patient notes and her Kelly Clamp," Lane said.

"What's a Kelly Clamp?"

"It's a scissor-like device with locking teeth. Most nurses carry them. She also would have been carrying her cigarettes."

"Do you know what brand?"

"No, I never really noticed."

Janina Stevens took several minutes to look over everything displayed on the tables before she rendered her opinion.

"I think Uniform C looks most like what she wore that day," Stevens said.

"Okay, what about the rest, did she wear a bra, how about the watch?"

"I always thought Cathy wore a bra," Stevens told him, "and like I said before, I don't recognize the watch, and this sweater doesn't look familiar to me, either."

"Did Cathy ever wear a dress?"

"No, I don't remember Cathy ever wearing a dress to work. She always wore pants suits."

"What about a Kelly Clamp, did you ever see her carrying one of those?"

"I know that a lot of nurses do, but I don't ever remember seeing Cathy with one."

"Do you know what brand of cigarettes she smoked?"

"I'm not even sure Cathy smoked," Stevens answered. "I mean, I don't really remember ever seeing her do it."

Mary Bacorn was to be next to view the lineup, but she was called away to a patient. Smerecki left word that he would reschedule her viewing, possibly for the next day.

Joy Niemiera was preparing dinner when the phone rang.

"Hello? Hello? Who is this?"

A cold chill shot down her spine; Niemiera dreaded the words she knew she was about to hear.

"I'm gonna get you."

Joy slammed the receiver down, cursing the phone.

"You son of a *bitch* leave me *alone!*" She knew it was Berta; the fact that he could make the call must mean he was out on bail.

"That *bastard!*" she cried. Then, to the air, she pleaded, "Cathy, you've got to help us, you've got to help us *get* him!"

August 26, 1983

Mary Bacorn appeared in Smerecki's office at about 9:40 a.m.

"Thanks for coming by, Mrs. Bacorn," Smerecki said. "There are a few things I'd like you to look at. We're trying to see if we can piece together what Cathy Warner wore to work on July 8."

Bacorn looked over the assortment of uniforms and other apparel Smerecki had displayed on several tables. She took her time, carefully considering each piece before she spoke.

"Well, it could be either uniform B or D," she began, "I can't really be sure about either one. Now, I know I've seen Cathy wear a blue sweater to work on occasion, bit I don't think she wore one that day."

"Would she have worn a dress that day?" Smerecki asked, already knowing the answer.

"Oh, no, Cathy never wore dresses to work."

"What about this," Smerecki continued, holding up a Kelly Clamp found in Warner's bedroom by Haley. "Does this look like something she carried on July 8?"

"Yeah, that looks like Cathy's clamp. She always carried that with her."

"Do you recall if Cathy ever smoked?"

"I think she did; in fact, I think I remember her giving a cigarette to somebody at the hospital, a doctor. I don't know what her brand was, though."

"Okay, Mrs. Bacorn, just one more thing." Smerecki picked up a ring of keys. "Do these look familiar to you?"

"No, I don't remember ever seeing Cathy with those. But you know, who notices keys?"

"So none of the nurses could make a positive I.D. on any of the uniforms, huh?" Thomas Kapsak was leaning back in his chair, his hands clasped behind his head. Casimir Smerecki sat upright in the chair in front of the assistant prosecutors large, wooden desk.

"Nope, nothing positive. But they *did* identify individual things, like the sweater and the Kelly Clamp. Now, Mary Bacorn said something interesting this morning; she said she saw Cathy walking toward a pay phone at about 1:30 that afternoon."

"Is she sure?"

"Yeah," Smerecki said. "She told me that she and Cathy had lunch that day late, and that she distinctly remembers Cathy getting a phone call after. A few minutes later, Bacorn was coming out of a patient's room when she saw Cathy walking out of the nurse's station. She said Cathy told her that she had to make a phone call, and then she walked in the direction of the pay phones."

"And that was at 1:30?" Kapsak asked.

"That's what she said."

"I don't see how that could be, when the nurses had that party for Rosemary Cascella at noon," Kapsak said. "Why would she eat two lunches? And why, when the other nurses who saw her said she was upset at 1:30, after she took a phone call, wouldn't Mary Bacorn notice that? She must be mistaken about the dates, Cas. It just doesn't add up."

"Well, I agree. I just wanted to let you know what she told me," Smerecki said. "I'm going to go back to the house, Rhonda Lane told me yesterday that the uniform Cathy Warner wore on the eighth would have her nurse's pin on it; that's a small pin they get from their school when they graduate. I haven't found it yet, but it must be somewhere in the house."

"Or," Kapsak noted, "it could be in a landfill, attached to a bloody uniform."

The Metuchen Police Department pressed on with its end of the investigation. On the afternoon of Friday, August 26, Lt. Studnicki and Sgt. Salamone interviewed Kevin Carroll of Metuchen, a past member of Edison Rescue Squad.

"I'd heard that Gene got arrested," Carroll said. "Geez, him shooting somebody; it kind of figures."

"Why do you say that?" Studnicki asked.

"Well, Gene was always fooling around with a gun. I heard that he pointed a rifle at two squad members once; it was right outside the squad building, and he was sitting in his van. He just pulled that sucker out and pointed it at the window at them!"

"Do you know who he pointed it at?"

"Yeah, it was Bob Vala and Richard Schreck," Carroll answered.

"You know how we can reach them?"

"I know where Rich is, but I don't know what happened to Bob."

"Okay, did you ever see Gene with a gun?"

"Once, I seen a twenty-two behind the driver's seat of his van, but I never seen him use it."

"How else did he 'fool around' with his gun?" Studnicki asked.

"Oh, you know, stupid stuff. Once Gene told me he liked to shoot cats. We were standing outside the squad building one time, and this big bird landed in front of us. Gene looks at me and says, 'Geez, I wish I had my gun now!' Stupid things like that."

"Okay, Kevin, that's all we need. Could you do me a favor and get a hold of Mr. Schreck and tell him that we'd like to talk to him later today? Ask him to come down to the station and ask for me."

Carroll's motivation in disparaging Berta's reputation may not have been completely altruistic. Berta later noted that he "kicked" Carroll off the first aid squad because he had had a lot of problems with him.

Schreck appeared at Metuchen headquarters about an hour later.

"I was only a member of the squad for about a year," Schreck said. "I quit about two months ago."

"I understand Mr. Berta once pointed a gun at you and a friend," Studnicki said. "Can you tell me about that?"

"Me and Bob Vala and Gene were just BSing one day last summer," Schreck began, "just cracking jokes, you know? All of a sudden, Gene gets out of his van, and he's carrying this rifle. He says something like, 'I always keep this loaded,' and then he points it right at Bob! Bob doesn't waste a second, he runs right back into the squad building."

"Did Bob say something that got Gene mad?"

"I don't know," Schreck answered. "I couldn't tell if Gene was mad or not.

"Can you tell us of any other times you've seen Gene with a gun?"

"I heard a rumor once that Gene said he was going to shoot this cat that was hanging around the squad building," Schreck said. "Another member tried to chase the cat off so Gene wouldn't get it, but, according to the rumor, he shot it anyway."

After his short meeting with Kapsak, Smerecki returned to Warner's house, where he began his search for the nursing pin and any unaccounted-for uniform.

The detective was looking through the top right drawer of Cathy Warner's bedroom bureau when he found the ornament. As Lane had said, it was blue and gold, with Middlesex County College markings. On the back was engraved "1976 — CT."

"Cathy Tingley," Smerecki muttered to himself. While he was pleased that he found the pin, he was disappointed as well. The fact that the pin was separate, in the drawer, meant that his task of finding the uniform Cathy Warner wore on the day she was killed would be even more difficult.

Smerecki's persistence paid off again when, in a spare bedroom, he found a fifth pants suit uniform in another laundry basket. The suit, along with the two pair of jeans found with it, looked as though it had been recently laundered.

August 30, 1983

Smerecki did not have an opportunity to examine the fifth uniform until the following Tuesday. The uniform's label identified it to be a product of Formark, Inc., a nurse's uniform manufacturer based in Charlotte, N.C. Smerecki called the North Carolina-based company and learned that that particular style was manufactured only during the 1979 season.

Janice Warner Walsh, sister of Cathy Warner's late husband, John Warner, was next on the list of persons to be interviewed by county detectives Zimmerman and Watson. The pair caught up with her at her home at about 4 p.m.

Walsh said she knew Warner and Berta since about 1973, and the last time she spoke with Cathy Warner was around Christmas, 1981. The last time she saw Berta, Walsh added, was at Cathy Warner's memorial service.

"Did you ever know your brother to own a gun, Mrs. Walsh," Zimmerman asked.

"No, I don't think I've ever seen John with a gun," she replied.

"Did you know that Mrs. Warner and Mr. Berta were having a . . . relationship?"

"I knew that Cathy was seeing him," she said. "I suspect they were seeing each other while she was still married to my brother."

"Do you think your brother believed that?"

"I don't think John suspected anything," Walsh said. "You know, Cathy always had a thing about Gene Berta. She couldn't get him out of her system. And something else I'll tell you; I know that she gave him more than the $10,000 the papers talk about."

"Is that so?" Zimmerman said, his eyebrows arched. "Tell me, how did your brother and Mr. Berta get along?"

"They were best friends at one time," she said.

"You said you last saw Mr. Berta at Cathy Warner's memorial service; did you have any conversation with him?"

"Well, as much conversation as I've ever had with him. I told him that even though Cathy wasn't one of my favorite people, because I didn't think she was good enough for my brother, she didn't deserve what happened to her. I told him they should hang whoever killed her."

"And what did Mr. Berta say?"

"Nothing," she replied. "He just gave me a blank look and didn't say anything."

September 1, 1983

Smerecki was tireless in his investigation of Cathy Warner's uniforms. In an effort to get more information on another uniform — this one manufactured by the Whittenton Corp. of Taunton, Mass. — the detective asked one of the secretaries in the prosecutor's office to model it while he took photographs. The six pictures were then sent to the Whittenton Corp.'s Paul Levine for him to research his records and ascertain the approximate date of manufacture and, therefore, possibly cross-check it against one of the unaccounted-for receipts held by the investigators.

Smerecki also sent a pants uniform with an unreadable tag to the F.B.I. lab in Washington, D.C., hoping the F.B.I. could use ultraviolet light to determine what the label read. Along with the uniforms, the detective sent some soil scrapings from Cathy Warner's car tires, on the outside chance of chemists being able to determine where her car may have recently been driven.

One of Thomas Kapsak's rules of thumb was that when you're running with a circumstantial case, you might as well pursue every avenue that is opened to you. Thus far, detectives had been able to gather some pretty convincing evidence that Cathy Warner was killed in her basement on July 8, 1983, then, at some point, carried up to her first floor bathroom and immersed in a tub filled with water. The next questions were how long had she been in the basement, and how long had she been in the tub?

Kapsak had a partial answer with the report he had been given by the Rutgers University entomologist, Dr. Louis Vasvary. The entomologist's finding that the maggots taken from Cathy Warner's body were approximately six or seven days old was a help, but it could not prove conclusively when she was placed in the tub.

Kapsak was in his office, puzzling out the problem with Watson, Zimmerman, Smerecki and Haley when the latter detective had a brainstorm.

"There was a ring around the tub, right?" he asked Watson and Zimmerman. They nodded their agreement. "That means there was water in there at some time. The drain was closed, so that water had to go somewhere, right?"

"It evaporated," Zimmerman said. "It was like a sauna in that house."

"Right," Haley said. "So there's got to be somebody around who can give us an idea how fast water would evaporate in those kinds of conditions."

"That would probably be, what, a meteorologist?" Kapsak offered.

"That would be my guess," Zimmerman agreed. "Rutgers has a weather station, doesn't it? Maybe somebody there could help us out."

"Let me make a few calls," Smerecki volunteered. "I'll see what I can find out."

"If you come up with somebody, Cas, try to set up an appointment for us next week. We'll both go down and talk," Zimmerman said.

Smerecki found exactly the expert for which he was looking in Dr. Mark Schulman, head of the Rutgers University Meteorology Department. The detective called Schulman later that afternoon and explained the case and the kind of information he was seeking.

"Well, detective, based on what you've told me, there are several variables that would influence the rate of evaporation; temperature, the humidity level, whether there's any foreign matter mixed in with the water, the type of environment the water is in and whether there's any seepage in the drain."

"About foreign matter," Smerecki asked, "what would something like blood do to the evaporation rate?"

"It would slow it down. So would a closed environment, like a closed bathroom."

"Okay, so based on the fact of the high temperature, the closed bathroom and blood in the water, can you give me a ballpark figure of how fast the water would evaporate?"

"Oh, I'd say between one-quarter to one-half an inch per day."

Rosemary Ann Cascella appeared in Dennis Watson's office at 4:15 that afternoon. Watson had asked the nurse to stop by after work so that he could take a formal statement from her. Cascella was Cathy Warner's best friend at Middlesex General Hospital. Watson called in stenographer John Mumber to record the statement.

Cascella said the last time she really talked to Cathy Warner was about 6 p.m. on June 24, 1983 — the day before Cascella's wedding — when Warner stopped off at her house to drop off an outfit Cascella was borrowing for her honeymoon trip. Warner, Cascella added, was accompanied by Gene Berta.

Cascella repeated what she originally told the detective, that she tried to call her friend at 5 p.m. and 7 p.m. on July 8, when she returned from her honeymoon, but got no answer.

"Did you try to call her subsequent to that?" Watson asked.

"Yes. I then called her that entire week from the 8th till the following Saturday morning," Cascella said. "Approximately twice each night in the late evening — well, between 5 and 9 on those days. And there was never an answer."

"Okay. You describe Gene Berta as being Cathy's boyfriend, I believe," Watson continued. "Could you tell me anything more that you might know about their relationship?"

"Just that she was planning on marrying him, and perhaps he gave her the impression that he was going to marry her. You know, she seemed to think so, anyway."

"Do you know anything about Gene Berta's marital status?"

"I know that he was . . . is married presently and has five children."

"And Mrs. Warner still thought . . ."

"That he was going to leave his wife and marry her." Cascella's tone of voice indicated she realized how ridiculous a notion that was.

"Did Cathy ever discuss any arguments that she might have had with Gene Berta?" Watson asked.

Cascella nodded her head.

"Apparently, there were times when he promised her that he was going to go with her, and at the last minute broke the plans," she replied. "Or would promise to be some place with her or go some place with her or call her at a certain time and wouldn't, and just get her really upset. But one particular time, I can't remember what happened actually that one time, just that I remember her telling me she was so livid that she started beating him up. And he hit her back in return, I don't know how hard or whatever."

"Do you know when this particular argument occurred?"

"I'll say approximately three months ago. That's an approximation."

"Is there anything else that you'd like to add to this statement that you think might be helpful to us?"

"Yeah." For the first time, Cascella looked straight at Watson. The hatred he saw reflected in her eyes chilled him. "I think he killed her. I do. That's the only thing I can tell you."

September 2, 1983

Pat Bauer showed up at the Parsonage Diner wearing a smile and her arm cast. She had agreed to meet Watson and Zimmerman at 8 p.m.

"How's the arm doing?" Zimmerman asked, after they said hello.

"Oh, well, it's getting there," Bauer said. "I felt like *such* a fool; here I was on a rescue squad call, and *I* end up needing the squad!"

"You haven't had any more problems with that Edison policeman, have you?" Zimmerman asked.

"No, I haven't heard anything from him lately. But my husband told me what happened."

"The important thing is that we took care of it," Zimmerman told her. "That guy won't say anything anymore and he won't bother you."

"Well, I appreciate that."

"Now, it's payback time. There are some things we need you to tell us." Bauer blanched. "Like what?"

"Well, first off, we need to see the route you took when you met Gene at MetroPark on the eighth. I want you to take us to MetroPark and show us exactly where you picked him up and exactly what he was doing."

"Okay, that sounds easy."

The three piled into Bauer's car; she made sure Zimmerman sat in the front seat, next to her. Bauer drove the two blocks from the diner to her house, then began her narrative.

"I started here," she told the detectives, "then I went up to 27, and drove over to the Dunkin Donuts at the corner of 27 and Parsonage Road. That's it, over there," she pointed to the right, as the donut shop came in view.

Bauer pulled into the Dunkin' Donuts lot and stopped.

"Okay, I got out here and bought two containers of coffee to go," she continued. "Then I got back onto 27, I guess this would be north."

Bauer drove to the Wood Avenue intersection at Route 27, where she made a right turn. She continued through the residential area one block to the Middlesex-Essex Turnpike and turned left, and then made the first left into the MetroPark train station lot.

"That's where I saw Gene when I pulled in," Bauer said. She was pointing off to the left, at a concrete island situated at the end of a row of parking spaces in the lot's daily section.

"He was just standing there?" Zimmerman asked.

"Yeah. He had a suitcase with him. Just one."

"Did you see his car? Did you know how he got here?" Watson asked her, from the back seat.

"No, I didn't know how he got here," she replied.

"Okay, now exactly what did he do when you pulled up to where he was waiting," Zimmerman asked.

"Well, he put his suitcase in the trunk, and then I got out and kissed him hello, and then I sat in the passenger seat and he sat in the driver's seat. And then he drove us to the Howard Johnson's in Newark."

"Who rented the room?"

"He did."

"And then you went to dinner, right?" Bauer nodded her head. "What did you do afterwords?"

"We went back to our room," Bauer told Zimmerman. "Gene gave me a present."

"A present!" Zimmerman smiled. "What did he give you?"

"Oh, it was a nightgown," Bauer answered shyly. "One of those slinky black fishnet ones."

Zimmerman quickly changed the subject.

"What did you do the next morning?"

Bauer shrugged her shoulders.

"We woke up and left for Minnesota."

"Okay. Now, tell me exactly what happened after you got your car at Newark airport when you got back from the trip."

"Well, Gene drove us back here and stopped near where I picked him up on Friday. He got his suitcase out of the trunk, we said goodbye and I just drove away."

"And did you see how he left the lot?"

"No; he was still standing there when I drove away."

"Okay, Pat, that's all we need for now. But if there anything you want to add, you just call us."

September 9, 1983

Joe Zimmerman walked into Thomas Kapsak's office carrying a manila folder, inside of which were the results of a survey conducted by Casimir Smerecki.

"You've gotta admit, he's thorough," Zimmerman said, as he handed the file over to Kapsak.

"That's why he's good," Kapsak smiled as he opened to the first page of Smerecki's report.

The investigators were beginning to realize that they would never be able to get a definitive answer to the question of how many uniforms Cathy Warner owned. Although the answer would have been helpful in proving to a jury that Warner was actually killed in her basement after returning from work on July 8, it was not considered a key point of the case against Gene Berta. Having determined that Cathy Warner probably owned five uniforms, Smerecki decided to find out how that total compared to the average nurse in the area; in that way, he reasoned, he would be able to better judge the probability of Cathy Warner owning more uniforms.

Smerecki began this phase of his investigation around the middle of August. He developed a questionnaire, then sent it to the heads of nursing departments at Perth Amboy General Hospital, John F. Kennedy Hospital in Edison, and Middlesex General and St. Peter's hospitals in New Brunswick. Smerecki explained to the supervisors what he was doing and asked that they survey all their nurses who fit certain criteria, then send the information back to him as soon as possible. Smerecki set two guidelines to keep the survey relevant to his purposes: to be interviewed, all nurses must be full-time R.N.s or L.P.N.s. and dresses as well as pants suits would be considered uniforms. In addition to asking each nurse the number of uniforms they owned, Smerecki requested the supervisors to note the respondents' years of tenure in the profession.

"So the average number of uniforms owned by these nurses is eight, huh?" Kapsak muttered, as he scanned Smerecki's report. "And Cathy Warner had five that we know about. That could or could not mean that she had more, and that she was wearing one on the day she was killed."

"But at Middlesex, most nurses have either six, eight or 10 uniforms," Zimmerman noted. "I would bet Cathy Warner had six."

"You're probably right, Joe, but I don't think this is going to be very helpful to me when I bring this thing to court. I think Cas has gotten a little carried away with this," Kapsak said, closing the folder. "But it was a good thought; he was going in the right direction. But we need more tangible evidence."

September 20, 1983

"Hey Ralph, how's it going?" Dennis Watson greeted Sgt. Ralph Salamone from the lobby of the Metuchen Police headquarters. Watson had called the Metuchen policeman and arranged to meet him at the station.

"Can't complain," Salamone answered, "but I usually do anyway. What's on the agenda?"

"We're gonna take a little drive," Watson told him. "There are a few people we need to talk to."

Their first stop was at the home of Vincent Nuzzo of Edison, Gail Berta's father. Nuzzo invited the two men in after they had identified themselves.

"Figured you'd be coming to see me sooner or later," Nuzzo said. "You want a beer?" Both detectives declined. Nuzzo ushered the pair into the living room and gestured to chairs. The three sat down.

"We're here to talk about your son-in-law, Gene Berta," Watson began. "What can you tell me about him?"

"I don't like him," Nuzzo said. "I think he's a bum. He hardly ever works; he should be out working to provide for my daughter and their children. Who knows what he does with his time?"

"Do you see him a lot?"

"Gene? Nah. He's never around here. And that's fine with me. Hey, I got something for you." Nuzzo rose from his chair, disappearing into another room. He returned several minutes later carrying a stuffed horse.

"My other daughter, Ursula, bought this last month and gave it to the kids," he said, handing the toy to Watson. "We don't hear nothing from them, and then, after Gene got arrested, I walked out one morning and there it is, sitting on my porch!"

"Do you know who left it?" Watson asked.

"I guess it was Gene," Nuzzo answered. "He never really wanted his kids to have anything from us anyway."

"Do you mind if we take this?"

"Nah, go ahead. What do I need it for?"

"Mr. Nuzzo, do you know Gene to own a handgun?"

"No, I knew he owned some rifles, but I never saw him with a pistol or anything like that."

"You don't suppose he hid the gun in this stuffed animal, do you?" Salamone asked Watson when they were back in the county detective's car.

"I don't know," Watson replied. "But I'm going to let our ID man have a go at it when I get back to the office. He can open it up, or run it under an x-ray or something. But I don't think even Gene Berta would be so stupid as to put a murder weapon in such an obvious place."

"Yeah, well, you never know what goes through a guy's head."

"Hey, remember how some people have been telling us that Gene bragged about shooting his neighbor's dog?" Watson asked. "Why don't we stop and talk to whoever's around and see if he's full of shit, like I think he is?"

"Sounds good to me," Salamone said.

The first of Berta's dog-owning neighbors that the detectives could find was Steven Marcinko, whose property abutted the Bertas' along their backyards.

Watson introduced himself and Salamone and explained why they wanted to talk to Marcinko.

"What can you tell me about your neighbor?" the detective asked.

"Nothing really," Marcinko said. "I just know him to see him; we don't really talk. Although I have talked to his kids a few times, though."

"I notice you have a dog, have you ever had any trouble with Mr. Berta over your dog?"

"No . . . well, once he asked me to keep my dog in my yard, on account of he kept jumping over the fence and messing around in his back yard. But other than that, there's really been nothing."

"He's never harmed your dog?"

"No, nothing like that's ever happened."

"Okay. Do you know if you next door neighbors own a dog?"

"The Kunz'? No they don't. But Tim Edwers does. He lives a couple doors down."

"Nope," Edwers said when he was asked the same question about his pet. "In the six years we've had Rusty, we've never had any trouble with Gene Berta."

"And he's never been hurt, never been shot or anything like that?"

"Nope, nothing."

"You know, the more I find out about this guy, the more I see what a Class A bullshitter he is," Watson said. He and Salamone were in the detective's car, on their way back to Metuchen headquarters.

"I know what you mean," Salamone said. "He's one of these guys who's always telling stories about himself. Wants to make people scared of him, make them think he's a badass."

"Yeah, but the guy's a slob! He's fat, he's not tough. He's dirty; I don't understand."

"Maybe that's why he has to do all that talking," Salamone suggested. "Make up for how he looks by what he says."

"He's got a line, all right. He has to, to get all those women."

September 21, 1983

Dennis Watson had no strong desire to drive all the way down to Deptford, N.J., so he decided to try his luck and telephone Michael Amaniera, Gail Berta's first husband. Remembering what P.M. had told him about Berta bragging to her that he had arranged for Amaniera to stop visiting his children, Watson wanted to speak with the man to validate the story.

"Threaten me? Never!" Amaniera said. "He always left me alone. I never had any problem with him. In fact, when he and Gail were together, she always did all the talking. He pretty much kept his mouth shut."

"Now, you were married to Gail in 1972?" Watson asked.

"Yeah, October 28, 1972," Amaniera said. "We got divorced in August of 1975. We had twin girls."

"And you were ordered to make child support payments?"

"Yeah. But I was in college at the time, you know, a poor college student. I could barely buy food, I had a lot of trouble making those payments. Gail took me into court, God, it was probably at least 10 times over three years."

"And when Gene wanted to adopt the girls, you consented to that willingly?"

"Oh yeah; I agreed to that so I wouldn't get thrown in jail for non-support.

"And did you see your children often before that?"

"No, not really," Amaniera said. "I had visitation rights between 1975 and 1978, but it seemed like the kids were never available to me. Gail always seemed to have some excuse why I couldn't see them; either they were sick, or I was too late, or something like that."

"Did you speak to Mr. Berta often when you visited the house?"

"No, we only spoke about two times. Like I said, he pretty much stayed away from me; he let Gail do all the talking."

"When was the last time you saw Mr. Berta?"

"Geez, it musta been about 1976; that was one of the times Gail dragged me into court for non-support."

September 30, 1983

"Mr. Kapsak? This is Barry Albin, I represent Gene Berta? I'm calling to discuss the court order we received demanding handwriting samples from our client."

Kapsak was expecting the call. "When do you think you and your client will be able to come to New Brunswick?" he asked.

"Well, before we set a time and date, I'd like some information," Albin said. He was used to dealing with hard-nosed prosecutors. You just had to show that you weren't intimidated. "What exactly are you going to be requiring?"

"Well, we have a number of items here, and we need to determine whether they were written by your client, or the woman he killed," Kapsak said.

"*Allegedly* killed, Mr. Kapsak," Albin interrupted. "We're still innocent until proven guilty in this country."

The assistant prosecutor ignored the barb. "They're things like greeting cards, notes, we've got a hold mail notice, things like that."

"Okay, I guess we would have no real problem with that. But while I have you on the line, let me ask you about something else. Back in

August, after our client was arrested, we issued to your office a demand for discovery which included the demand that all handwritten notes of participating investigators and police officers be preserved. We've gotten a number of pages of discovery since then, including investigation reports, but there were no notes. Do you know anything about this?"

"Well, I never saw the order you are referring to," Kapsak said. "And to tell you the truth, I'm not certain whether they have already destroyed their notes. But I will assure you that I will direct the investigators that from here on in, they are to preserve any notes they may take."

"I certainly hope no one willfully disregarded that court order, Mr. Kapsak," Albin said.

"We play by the rules, counsellor," Kapsak shot back. "Now, when do you think you and your client can come to New Brunswick to provide those handwriting samples?"

Satisfied that he had made his point, Albin decided to be cooperative. "How about Thursday, October the fourth, say 2 o'clock? Will that be okay?"

"That will be fine, Mr. Albin. We'll be expecting you then." Kapsak hung up the phone before Albin could say goodbye.

In the file memo he later dictated, Albin recounted the discussion he had with Kapsak regarding the handwriting examples and the discovery order, then added a recommendation:

"In the event that any handwritten notes were destroyed after receipt of our request for discovery, it would be appropriate to file a motion for dismissal of the indictment, or in the alternative a motion to bar the testimony of the police officer who destroyed the notes and the testimony of any witness interviewed by an investigator who destroyed his notes pertaining to the interview."

October 5, 1983

Thomas Kapsak appeared at the door of Casimir Smerecki's office with Dennis Watson in tow.

"Cas, why don't you and Denny go on down to the conference room, I'm expecting Gene Berta and his attorney to be there any minute."

Albin had called Kapsak the day before to postpone their 2 p.m. meeting; Albin explained that he would be held up in court all day. The two agreed on a new time of 9 a.m. this day.

Barry Albin and Gene Berta showed up at the prosecutors' suite at nine o'clock sharp.

Kapsak ushered Albin and Berta into the conference room, where Smerecki and Watson awaited them. On the long wooden table were a number of pieces of paper, arranged in small piles, as well as several pens and pencils.

"Have a seat, Mr. Berta," Kapsak offered. "This may take a while."

The first item pushed in front of Berta was a pre-printed form, divided into two columns. In the left column were a number of questions asking personal information of the test-taker, such as name and address, date and place of birth, height, weight, eye color, whether the person is right or left handed and occupation. Below that, the testee was asked to reproduce the alphabet, upper and lower case, as well as the cardinal numbers.

In the right column were a number of names and addresses which the testee was asked to reproduce. Smerecki asked Berta to write out the last four addresses in longhand.

Berta was next asked to reproduce—five times, in ink and pencil—the writing on a number of items police had found at the murder scene: the "Things To Do" list which enunciated trip-related tasks; the "Mother to hospital" note police found in Cathy Warner's purse; an envelope upon which was written, "Merry Christmas to my beloved"; the beginning—"Dec. 82, Catherine"—and end—"Gene xoxo"—of a letter, and, finally, a "hold mail" card recovered from the Metuchen Post Office. As Berta finished each sample, they were marked K-1 through K-5, then initialled by Casimir Smerecki and Dennis Watson.

The test was completed by about 9:55 a.m.

"I'd like a copy of all the originals, please," Albin asked Kapsak. "As well as copies of all the samples."

"That will be no problem," Kapsak replied. "Denny, would you make Mr. Albin some copies, please?"

Later, Smerecki turned over all the samples and originals, plus some other items, to John Haley. Haley was going to transport the material to the State Police laboratory in West Trenton.

Included in the material were 44 of Catherine Warner's cancelled checks and a blank, lined note pad upon which seemed to be indentations caused by writing. Smerecki wanted the State Police analysts to determine what, if anything, had been written on the pad.

Sunday, October 9, 1983

Pat Bauer normally looked forward to visiting her mother, Lillian Moore, but on this day she felt nothing but trepidation. Resting on the car seat next to her was a transcript of everything she had told Zimmerman and Watson about she and Gene and their trip to Moose Lake; the detectives asked her to review the document and sign it if she felt it represented an accurate record of their conversations. Before she did that, however, Pat Bauer wanted to have it looked over by a legal eye, one that she could trust. She chose her brother, who she knew was also going to be visiting her mother today.

Her younger brother Paul was a district attorney in Manhattan. Pat and Paul had had their share of brother-sister fights, but she hoped that he would be in her corner for this battle.

Pat and her mother had barely exchanged hellos when Paul walked into the living room.

"Well, Patty," he said, his hands on his hips, "what have you gotten yourself into this time?"

Pat Bauer's hope for brotherly understanding was short-lived.

"I can't believe you would do something like that, Patty!" Paul cried, rising from his seat at the kitchen table, after she had recounted her story and shown him her statement. "I can't believe you would disgrace the family like this!"

"Oh, Paul, knock it off," his mother admonished him. "We've been through worse things before, we'll get through this. The important thing now is for you to help your sister."

Pat Bauer was near tears. She'd half expected this kind of response from her brother, but it still hurt.

"Paul, I'm sure he didn't do it," she said, hoping he would believe her, and half wondering if she really believed it herself. "This is all just some mix-up. He was with me the whole weekend, he couldn't have killed anybody!"

"But you're *married* Patty! Doesn't that mean anything to you?" Paul had strode to the other end of the kitchen; he stood with his back to the sink, glaring at his sister, his upper body framed by the oak cabinetry.

"Of *course* it does," she cried. "It just doesn't seem to mean anything to my *husband*!"

"So to get back at him for whatever you think he's doing, you go and run off with some guy to Minnesota? To *Minnesota*? I don't understand you!"

"Paul, she didn't come here to talk about her marital problems," his mother scolded. "She came to you, as her brother, looking for some legal advice. Now, are you going to give to her or not?" She posed the question with a look that dictated to Paul what his answer would be.

"Sure, sure I'll help her," he said, his voice softer. Sighing heavily, he walked back to the table and sat down opposite his sister, picking up her statement once again. "It doesn't look like you're anything but an alibi witness, Patty. I don't think you have anything to worry about, from what you told me, it doesn't look like they suspect you of anything."

"Why would they suspect me?"

"Because you were with him, because you were the 'other woman'," her brother answered. "Anyway, it doesn't look like much, but I think you'd better get a lawyer anyway."

Pat's eyes grew wide. "A lawyer? If all I am is an alibi witness, why do I need a lawyer?"

"Just in case," Paul said. "Just to protect yourself. You never know what he could say when the reality of what he's charged with sets in. I've seen it happen before."

"You mean, he could blame *me*?" Pat thought the idea that Berta could implicate her was ridiculous.

"I'm just saying that I've seen stranger things happen, Patty. Now I think you'd better get yourself a lawyer."

"Well, the only lawyer I know is my divorce lawyer, Ira Rosen. Maybe I could talk to him tomorrow; maybe he knows somebody."

"I think that's a good idea, sis."

Lillian Moore was pleased by what she saw.

"Now that you two have settled your business, how about some dinner?" she asked, pasting a cheerful smile on her face.

Monday, October 10, 1983

Pat Bauer managed to busy herself around her house until 10:30 a.m., when it was time for her to leave for her appointment with her attorney, Ira Rosen. She hurriedly gathered the items she wanted to show Ira, taking a last, quick glance at her statement to refresh her memory. Bauer left her house thinking that perhaps this nightmare was close to ending.

Ira Rosen sat stone faced while Pat Bauer recounted her story. He interrupted her occasionally to ask a question or clarify a point, but, for the most part, he let her ramble on. After he had read her statement, Rosen took off his glasses, leaned back in his rocker and folded his hands over his belly. After several minutes he spoke.

"I'm not a criminal lawyer, Patty, but from what you told me, it sounds like your brother was right; you're nothing but an alibi witness. I really wouldn't worry about it."

"My brother said I should retain an attorney, what do you think?" Pat was cheered by his assessment, but still nervous about not protecting herself.

"I'll tell you what. I know a guy, he's a good friend of mine, he used to be a prosecutor, now he's a criminal attorney over in New Brunswick. His name is Steve Altman; let me give him a call."

Bauer listened, hopeful that Rosen's friend would be her savior: "Hello Steve? Ira Rosen here, how ya' doing? Good. Listen, I got a girl here, she needs some advice. I can't help her, but I told her you probably could. Can I send her over to you today? That would be great. Her name's Pat Bauer. Yeah. Thanks, Steve. See you soon."

"Can he see me?" she asked.

"Yeah, no problem. He's free until this afternoon. You go over there and tell him the whole story, he'll help you out." Rosen pulled out a piece of paper and scribbled something on it. "This is his address. Go over there now, and, Patty, don't worry, this will all work out."

"Thanks, Ira, I really appreciate this," Bauer said as she picked up the paper, folded it and slipped it into her purse. She gave him a quick smile as she walked out of his office.

"So Ira says you've got a problem? What can I do for you?" Steve Altman was in his mid-thirties, on the short side and balding. But there was a warmness in his smile that Pat Bauer found comforting.

Bauer sat down in the chair Altman offered and took a deep breath. She didn't know where to begin.

"Well, the gist of it is that I went away with this guy and now he's accused of murder," she said, as she reached into her purse for the statement. "This is what I've told the detectives so far. They wanted me to sign this and give it back to them, but I wanted to talk to a lawyer first."

"That's probably the prudent thing to do," Altman said as he took the statement from Bauer and began reading it.

"Do you think he did it?" Altman asked, after he had gone through the document.

"No! Of course not!" Pat replied, her voice rising. "He was with *me* all weekend! When would he have had time to do anything like that?"

"Well, I don't think there's anything to this, but let me give Dennis Watson a call and see what I can find out. Why don't you take a seat in the reception area, and I'll be with you in a minute."

"Finally," Bauer thought as she left his office proper, "someone with some connections to the inside!"

Pat was mindlessly leafing through a magazine when she caught bits and pieces of Altman's conversation with Watson. She did not like what she heard.

"Ohh!" she heard, followed by "Oh! OHH!"

"Oh God," Bauer thought, "*what* is he telling him?" Her question was answered several minutes later when Altman appeared at his door, motioning for her to come inside.

"Maybe you better start from the beginning and give me the whole story," he said as a terrified Pat Bauer walked through the doorway. Altman quietly closed his door and returned to his desk chair. "And I mean *everything*."

Bauer began with the problems she had been having with her husband, then progressed to how she met Berta. She told Altman about how Berta first brought up the idea of going to Minnesota, concluding with a detailed description of the actual trip. She also told him about how Berta acted toward her after they returned, and about the strange telephone call she received shortly after he was arrested.

"So then I went to talk to Morris Brown, and he had this tape recorder, and I told him everything," Pat said, wringing her hands in her lap. "I mean, I told him things that I didn't even tell Zimmerman or Watson. And there were things that I told him that I didn't say in the Grand Jury!"

"And he took it all down on tape?" Altman asked, his brow knitted. Bauer nodded her head.

"Why didn't you tell those things to the detectives?"

"Because they didn't ask me. I mean, they asked all the wrong questions. And I guess, I don't know, I guess I didn't want to say anything that would get Gene in trouble."

"Okay, listen Pat. If I can clear it with the prosecutor's office, will you go down there with me and tell them the things that you told Morris Brown but didn't tell them?"

"Will I get in trouble?"

"I don't think so. We'll just say you forgot. But if you don't tell them, and they found out you held back, Tom Kapsak may just go after you."

The thought of being prosecuted sent a chill through Pat Bauer.

"Okay, I'll do it. But I just want to get this over with. Let's just do this as soon as possible."

Bauer gave Altman her home number, then rose to leave. He opened the door for her; Bauer's eyes opened wide as she looked into the waiting room.

"Joey? Joey Spicuzzo! How *are* you?" Pat hadn't seen Spicuzzo, the Middlesex County Sheriff, in years. The two embraced warmly.

"You know each other?" Altman asked.

"He was one of my very first boyfriends," she said.

"Patty, what are you doing here?" Spicuzzo asked. Bauer didn't answer, she just turned her flushed face toward Altman.

"She's the alibi witness in the Berta thing," he said, with a slight smile.

Spicuzzo made a face as though he had bitten into a sour lemon.

"Oh Patty," he said, shaking his head. Bauer didn't want to hear another lecture, so she quickly said goodby and rushed out of Altman's office. She was beginning to rue the day she joined Edison Rescue Squad No. 1.

Tuesday, October 11, 1983

"You're not going to believe this, Tom." Joe Zimmerman walked into Thomas Kapsak's office with a light step and sat down in one of the two green naugahyde chairs in front of the second assistant prosecutor's desk. "I just got a call from Steve Altman. It seems *he's* representing Pat Bauer!"

"Geez, everybody's getting a lawyer," Kapsak remarked. "What did he say?"

"Well, his client just happened to 'remember' a few things that she neglected to tell us, and he wanted to schedule an appointment as soon as possible so she could give us that information."

"Looks like her Grand Jury appearance shook her up a bit," Kapsak said. "If you're free, set something up for first thing tomorrow. I can't wait to hear what she has to say."

Kapsak had only spoken to Bauer once or twice up to this point, but each time he did, he never neglected to tell her the punishment for perjury, as well as his proclivity to prosecute witnesses who lie. "And rest assured," he had told her before she testified at the Grand Jury, "if I find out that you lied on the stand, I *will* come after you."

Dennis Watson and John Mumber, a county investigator who is
also a certified shorthand reporter, left early that morning on a flight to
Bloomington, Minnesota, to take formal statements from everyone who had
contact with Berta, Bauer and Cathy Warner. Their initial appointment was
with employees at the Thunderbird Motel; it was there that Gene Berta and
Cathy Warner had been scheduled to stay during the weekend of July 8.

The first person with whom they spoke was Rodney Wallace Sr., the
motel's president and general manager. Watson wanted information from
him about the reservation that was made on June 22, 1983, in the name of C.
Warner.

"Okay, Mr. Wallace," Watson began, after he had formally introduced
himself and Mumber, "can you tell me in more detail about a reservation
made in the name of C. Warner on June 22, 1983?"

"When you called me, I checked our records and found that a
reservation had been made by American Airlines on June 22, 1983, through
the Menlo Park Travel Agency, and they, in turn, through the Best Western
Reservation Center, for arrival on the night of Friday, July 8th, for two
people."

"Is there any other notation on the card under the special information
section?"

"Yes," Wallace answered, "it was made by a Mrs. C. Warner. And the
reservation was to be held on a guaranteed basis based upon the use of Mrs.
Warner's Master Charge card.'

"Do you know how many people were supposed to stay and any of
their names?"

"There was no other name listed, but I believe it was for a double
occupancy or two people."

"Okay, did anyone ever come and take the room . . . did Miss Warner
come?" Watson asked.

"Not as far as I know," Wallace replied, "nobody ever was registered by
that name. And the reservation was cancelled by a person who identified
themselves as being Ms. Warner at 7:32 p.m. Central Standard Time on July
8th."

The person who took the cancellation, Colleen Maki, had since left the
motel and moved to Paris, France, Wallace said.

"Since she was the one who had taken the cancellation and it was marked cancelled by self, after the detective called me, I questioned her as to what was the meaning of the word self. Could it have been, have possibly been a man? And she said no, that she had realized the reservation had been made by a woman and it was cancelled by a woman."

"Is there anything else that you'd like to add?" Watson asked.

"Well, you also asked if we had any record of a gentleman by the name of Berta. I'm not even sure if you mentioned some aliases."

"Yes," Watson said, "we gave you that name, Berta."

"Right. We checked our records for that entire month and could find no indication of he having stayed here or his having stayed here."

Watson and Mumber next travelled to the Hertz car rental office at the Minneapolis/St. Paul Airport to speak with Susan Dee Rostkoski about the car Berta rented while he and Pat Bauer were in Moose Lake.

Rostkoski told Watson that the car was booked at 5:21 p.m. on June 21 under the name C. Warner, through a travel agency, and was to be picked up on July 8.

"Was the car picked up by C. Warner on July 8th?" Watson asked.

"No," the woman replied. "This particular document that was listed under the name of C. Warner was picked up by a G. Berta on July 9th."

"If a car was not picked up, a car that was *reserved*, not picked up on the date in question, would someone have to contact you or would the car be held indefinitely for them?" Watson asked.

"Normally what occurs, is that we'll hold the reservations for a given day; for example, July 8th, until midnight," she said. "Our midnight shift person then takes all of the reservations for July 8th and marks them as no-shows, anything that's left over.

"If, however, someone contacts us and says please hold the car that was booked for July 8th until the 9th or whatever date, then we hold the actual reservation and simply mark the reservation with the change of date."

"Just so I understand, Mrs. Rostkoski, since the car was not actually picked up on July the 8th, and it was in fact picked up by a G. Berta on July 9th, would it be safe to assume that some contact, someone had to contact your people and hold the car?" Watson probed.

"Yes, because we have pretty strict paper processing standards. And for a reservation to be left over to the 9th from the 8th without a contact, would be almost impossible."

"And from what you said," the detective continued, "this contact would have to have been made before midnight on July the 8th, is that correct?"

"That's right, and it would have to have been made here locally."

"Now, when someone calls, is there any type of documentation, anything written down and kept permanently that such a call was made?"

"No. The rental representative would simply pull the reservation from the places where we keep them on the dates that the person is picking up, mark the outside of the reservation envelope which is not attached, get an envelope that the contract is put in, and the date would be changed then on the outside."

Rostkoski said the fact that none of the clerks on duty July 8th remembered taking such a call from either a Berta or Warner did not mean much because those types of calls are very common.

"But," Watson continued, "we would have to assume that one of them did take such a call?"

"Yes," she replied.

"Because the car was held."

"Oh, yes."

"When the car was picked up by G. Berta on the ninth, can you tell me more about that transaction?"

"It was picked up at 10:10 in the morning. A $75 cash deposit was taken from the customer at the time that he rented. And otherwise it was a pretty standard transaction."

"Can you tell me the address used by Mr. Berta?"

"Yes, the one we show is 635 Grove Avenue, Edison, New Jersey."

October 12, 1983

It was 9:45 a.m.; the hot, summer-like morning sun made the air feel sticky, promising a steamy afternoon. Pat Bauer thought about how she would much rather be at the shore than standing on the front steps of the Middlesex County administration building, waiting for her lawyer.

Steve Altman joined her several minutes later. "You okay?" he asked, giving her arm a reassuring squeeze. Looking at her expression, he already knew the answer to his question.

"I'll be okay when this is all over and I can put it all behind me," Bauer answered. "I couldn't sleep at all last night."

"You've got nothing to worry about," Altman told his client as they entered the austere county building and made their way down the main hallway to the bank of elevators. "Just tell the truth. If they get rough, I'll be there for you. Just relax, this will be over before you know it.

The pair was greeted at the prosecutor's eighth floor suite by Joe Zimmerman; they exchanged pleasantries, then Zimmerman ushered them into the prosecutor's conference room. The group was soon joined by a dour-faced Tom Kapsak.

The second assistant prosecutor nodded hellos all around, then looked Bauer squarely in the eyes.

"I understand you have something to tell us?" he said.

"Just a few words before we begin," Altman said, hoping to break the tension. "My client is coming forward, on her own volition, because there are several details that she had forgotten in previous conversations with your office. She's coming here with nothing to hide, and in full cooperation with your office."

"And we appreciate that," Zimmerman said, trying to play peacemaker.

"He's playing 'good cop' today," Altman thought.

Kapsak maintained a stony silence, standing at the head of the table with his arms crossed in front of his chest, waiting for Bauer to begin.

Pat Bauer looked at Joe Zimmerman. She felt she could trust him more so than Kapsak. "Do you mind if I smoke?" she asked.

"No, go right ahead Pat," Zimmerman told her.

Bauer reached into her purse and pulled out a pack of cigarettes, then nervously placed one between her lips. Adding to her sense of frustration, she had to strike a match several times on the matchbook's flint before the sulfur ignited. She took a long, deep drag on the cigarette, exhaled slowly, with her eyes closed, then plunged into her story.

"Well," she began, looking directly at Zimmerman, "the last times I spoke with you, I forgot to tell you about one particular call I got from Gene on Friday . . ."

"That would be Friday, July 8th?" Zimmerman interrupted.

"Yes, I guess so," Bauer answered, her train of thought momentarily derailed. "Whatever the date was that we were supposed to leave. Anyway, Gene called me at home at about twenty after three in the afternoon. He was whispering, and he asked me to pick him up in the Durham Cafe parking lot."

"He was whispering?" Kapsak asked.

"Yeah, I could barely hear him," Bauer answered, still looking at Zimmerman. She decided she would be much calmer if she did not acknowledge Kapsak's presence. "He asked me to pick him up at the Durham Cafe, that's at the corner of Central Avenue and Durham Avenue. He asked me to be there at 4:00 p.m."

"Did you know why he wanted you to meet him there, at that time?" Zimmerman asked.

"I thought we were going to leave for our Minnesota trip," she answered, brushing ashes off the table top, onto the floor. "I mean, I knew that our flight out of Newark was sometime before 5 o'clock."

"Okay," Zimmerman continued, "did Mr. Berta meet you there at four?"

"No, I stayed in the parking lot at the Durham Cafe until about 4:40 p.m. By that time, I thought that I'd been stood up, so I left."

"Did you go home?" the detective asked.

"No, I didn't go home," Bauer answered, after she took another long drag on the cigarette. "I was fuming. I just rode around for awhile and then called a friend of mine, George Taylor — he's on the squad, too — and asked him to meet me at the squad."

"So, you called this George Taylor, and he met you at the rescue squad, right?" Kapsak asked. Bauer nodded yes, her eyes downcast. "And what time was this?"

"I don't know exactly," she replied. "We met sometime between 5 and 7 o'clock. Anyway, I told him the whole story; I told him about my plans to take the trip with Gene, and that he had made arrangements with me to pick him up in the Durham Cafe parking lot and then stood me up. George told me that Gene already told him he was going away from July 7 to the 14th or 15th. And *then* he told me that Gene's girlfriend, Cathy Warner, lived right across the street from the Durham Cafe." Bauer felt herself flushing with anger at the memory.

"And what did you do after you spoke with your friend, Pat?" Zimmerman asked.

"I went home. I guess it was about 10 after 7. The phone was ringing when I walked in; it was Gene. We had a really abrupt conversation — I was still mad at him — and he said he'd call me back at about 7:30 to see if I felt better and to talk with me more about our trip to Minnesota."

"Was he whispering during this particular conversation?" Zimmerman asked.

"No, in fact he was talking in a normal tone," she said. "He called me back at about 7:30, and I said I'd still go with him to Minnesota."

"Okay, Patty, is there anything else you may have thought of since the last time I spoke with you?" Zimmerman asked. His use of Bauer's nickname did not go unnoticed by Kapsak.

Bauer turned to her attorney, a pensive expression on her face. Altman closed his eyes halfway and nodded slightly, urging her on.

"Well, I remember that when we went to Minnesota, Gene was carrying one large suitcase and a shopping bag with plastic handles," she said. "As far as I knew there were two cameras in the bag; I remember either carrying it onto the plane in Newark or Minnesota, I'm not sure exactly. But the bag was heavy. Gene told me he could use the bag to get a gun through airport security, because the bag was a special bag for film and a gun wouldn't set off an alarm at the airport security post."

Tom Kapsak was sitting by now, gazing intently at Pat Bauer as she related her story, but, for the most part, purposely not interrupting. But the mention of the bag and of Berta talking about getting a gun through airport security set off the normally placid prosecutor.

Kapsak jumped out of his chair and , with a sharp "crack!" slammed both his hands palms down on the table.

"You didn't *just* remember this!" he bellowed, pointing an accusatory finger in Pat Bauer's horrified face. " You *lied*! You were under oath and you *lied*! I *told* you what would happen if you lied! I'll have you arrested, and I'll have you thrown in jail for perjury and contempt of court!"

"Oh no you *don't*!" Bauer screamed, wondering where she found the strength to even speak. "I told you the absolute truth to *every* question you asked me!"

"Then why didn't you tell us about the bag before?" Kapsak yelled.

"Because you didn't ask me!" Bauer yelled back, half rising out of her chair.

"Okay, okay, let's simmer down here," Altman said, putting his hand on Bauer's shoulder. Kapsak paced the front of the room slowly, like a giant cat ready to spring on its prey.

Zimmerman decided to continue with the interview while Kapsak cooled down. "Is there anything else you want to tell us, Pat?"

"Yeah," she said, smoothing out her blouse as she regained her composure. She took another deep breath, cast a glance at Kapsak, who by now had his back toward her, and continued. "I remember that when we got to Newark Airport on July 9, we were running a little late, so Gene dropped me off at the front door of the airline terminal and then went to park my car. I had all the tickets, and I remember handing them either to the ticket agent at the front counter or the boarding area. I think the ticket agent asked me if my name was Bauer. A few minutes later, Gene came running up to the counter and the same ticket agent asked him if his name was *Warner*. I got mad, but I didn't say anything."

"Now," Zimmerman interrupted, "this was only the second time you'd heard the name Warner connected with Gene?"

"Yeah," Bauer replied. "Like I said, I got mad because of what George told me. But I figured I'd better not say anything because I didn't want to ruin the whole weekend.

"So then, when we got to Minneapolis, we went to the Hertz rental car counter, and Gene asked for the car reserved in his name. And the clerk had trouble finding a rental under his name; and then Gene said, 'Look under the name Gail Berta'. I saw that he was having trouble, and I knew that the airline ticket was under the name Warner, so I just walked away from the counter so Gene could use another name . . ."

"Like Warner?" Kapsak asked, his back still facing Bauer.

"Probably," she replied, staring straight at Zimmerman. "A few minutes later, he walked over to me and said that he had straightened everything out."

"Was there any other time that you heard another name used in regard to reservations?" Zimmerman asked.

"At one point, I had an opportunity to go through the rental car's glove compartment," Bauer said. "I fingered through the paperwork that Gene put there and saw that the car rental reservation was in the name of Warner."

Kapsak spun around, once again glaring at Bauer.

"And all this time, we asked you if you knew the name 'Warner', and you told us no!" he said accusingly. Then, turning to Altman, he said, "Counsellor, I suggest you inform your client that if she's holding anything else back, she'd better come forward with it now. And I suggest you educate her as to the penalties for perjury!"

Pat Bauer stiffened in her chair as she turned to face Steve Altman. "Counsellor," she said, her voice not quavering in the least, "please tell this jerk that I *know* the penalty for perjury. And that I have *nothing* else to say!"

Meanwhile, in Minnesota, Watson and Mumbers' first stop this morning was the United Farm Agency real estate office. They walked into the office at about 11:30 a.m. and asked for Gary M. Neumann, the agency's Moose Lake area representative, with whom they had made an appointment. The two Middlesex County detectives were accompanied by Mary Bergen, a local Notary Public, who performed the swearing-in required for a formal statement.

Neumann had earlier written a letter to the Prosecutor's office, relating all the information he had regarding Berta's transaction and asking that his office be exempt from any further involvement in the matter. Watson and Mumber's presence in Moose Lake was proof that his request had not been honored, a fact about which Neumann was not happy.

"Can you tell me when's the first time you had any contact with Eugene Berta?" Watson asked.

"I can't remember the exact time for when I had the first conversation with him," Neumann snapped. "I couldn't give you that. All I got is when he was to arrive, which was the eighth."

"Okay," Watson continued, trying to remain calm so as to not alienate Neumann. "Do you recall that you previously spoke to me on the telephone, is that correct?"

"Yeah."

"At that time, I believe you told me that on June 24, 1983, Mr. Berta called your agency. Does that refresh your memory?"

"Yeah."

"And he told you that he would be here . . ."

"He would be flying in around the eighth," Neumann interrupted.

"The eighth of what?" Watson asked.

"Of July."

"Okay. Did he ever actually appear here?"

"Yes, he did."

"Okay. In between the time that he called you in June and when he actually arrived, did he call you over the phone?"

"Yes," Neumann said. "He called me on the eighth and told me he would be in the next day instead."

"Do you recall about what time it was he called?"

"I couldn't give you a time."

"Now, can you be more specific as to what he said during that phone call on the eighth?"

"He just called me and told me that he would be coming out to look at the farm that was in the brochure. It was 3175, which is the number of the listing that he wanted to look at."

"Am I to understand that originally he was scheduled to come out on July eighth?"

"He was due in here July eighth, but he come in the next day."

"And that's why he called you on the eighth?" Watson wanted to be sure he had the facts down on paper as clearly as possible.

"Yeah," Neumann said, "just to let me know that he would be about 24 hours later."

"Did he give a reason at that time why he would be late?"

"Not that I can remember, something about his flight or change of plans or something, but I couldn't remember exactly."

Watson felt a slight panic. *This isn't what you told me before, asshole,* he thought.

"I believe you stated earlier in our earlier conversations that he had told you that he could not make connections on his flight?" Watson asked, trying to jog the man's memory.

"Something to that effect," Neumann replied, "but exactly I couldn't ...."

"Can you tell me how you came to have contact with him?" Watson interrupted; he didn't want Neumann to blow the credibility of his statement. "I mean, how did he come to you to buy ...."

"Through the advertising in the United Farm Office in Kansas City, in them mailing brochures out, and he contacted us back."

"Okay," Watson continued, believing he had regained control of the interview. "Did he actually come here on July 9, 1983?"

"Yes, he did."

"Can you tell me if he was with anyone?"

"Yeah, he was with a young lady, blonde lady. I don't know what her name is 'cause I don't remember."

"Do you remember about what time he came?"

"About three o'clock."

"Did you show him the property?"

"Yeah, we showed him the property that he had called on," Neumann said. "And when he got into my office, he had seen one other one that he wanted to look at. And so we looked at that that same day. And then I was — when we got back in, he asked if I would be in on Sunday and I told him I had to be out for a while but he could stop back in Sunday afternoon."

"When you were looking at the properties, was this woman with you?"

"Yeah."

"Did he ever refer to her by any name or anything?"

"Just as honey or . . . that's all I ever remember."

Neumann told Watson that he made reservations for the couple at the Northwoods Motel in nearby Barnum that night.

The next day, Neumann continued, Berta and the woman dropped by his office and, "at that time, he asked me if I would draw up a contract on the 3175, and that he would be back in Monday morning to sign the contract."

According to a copy of the contract, which Neumann handed to Watson, the parcel's total price was $29,500, on which Berta left a $3,000 deposit.

"What was the arrangement supposed to be for paying of the balance, which was $26,500?"

"The balance was to be paid in full with a cashier's check on the 15th day of October, 1983," Neumann answered.

"That was the day of the scheduled day of the closing?"

"Yes."

"Did you ever have any conversation with Mr. Berta as to whether he would be able to fulfill his end of it financially?" Watson asked.

"I called — he called me and asked if the papers were in order, and I said yes, they were," Neumann explained. "And well, at first, I'd wrote him a letter about July 15th, and told him that we had the papers for him to have a title opinion of. And then he called me and told me that I should have a lawyer in town handle the transaction. And we had two lawyers offices in town, and one of them was the attorney that was . . . had the power of attorney on contract, so we used the other attorney and that's the last conversation I had with him."

Neumann also said that Berta asked him to remove the hay in the yard, and also asked him if it would be feasible to add a bathroom and two rooms on one side of the house.

"At any time when you were showing Mr. Berta and this woman the property," Watson continued, "did you ever pass any hospitals?"

"Yeah, we passed the Moose Lake Hospital," Neuman answered. "And they asked if, if there was a rescue squad because they had . . . that was what they was doing for a living at the time."

"Okay, Mr. Neumann, that's it," Watson said, as Mumber closed his steno pad. "Do you think you could take us out to the property?"

"I don't see why not," Neumann said. "We'll go in my car."

"Jesus," Watson thought, as Neumann pulled to a stop in front of an empty farmhouse, *"this place is really out in the middle of nowhere."*

Neumann and the two detectives exited the car and walked up to the house.

"Do you want to go inside?" the real estate agent asked.

"No," Watson answered. "That won't be necessary." Looking to his right, he asked, "What's this over here?" The detective was pointing to an old, dilapidated wooden shed, set off a little from the main house.

"That's a tool shed," Neumann answered, walking the men over to the structure.

Watson walked inside and looked around; *"Just a bunch of junk and rusty old farming tools,"* he thought. *"Nothing useful in here."*

"Okay, we might as we get back to town," Watson told Mumber as he exited the shed. "There's nothing out here."

Their tasks completed, Watson and Mumber drove back to the Minneapolis airport — stopping along the way for dinner — where they caught an early evening flight back to Newark, New Jersey.

October 19, 1983

Joe Zimmerman popped his head into Dennis Watson's office around noon.

"Hey! Back from your whirlwind trip to Minnesota I see. How do you like the fast life?"

"Watson laughed. "I *love* watching grass grow!"

"I'll read your report for the details, but for now, were you able to get in touch with those two gals that moved into Mary Beth Neal's apartment?"

"Yeah," Watson answered, "I was." He shuffled some papers on his desk until he found the one for which he was looking.

"Now, Mary Beth already told us that Cathy had never called her before or during the weekend of July 8 to tell her she was coming down for a visit, but there's always the possibility that Mary never received the message. The two women I spoke to are Tracey Friday and Annette Lange. They both said they were in and out of the apartment all day on July 7 and 8, and that neither had taken any phone calls from a Cathy Warner. Now, the Lange woman did say that she took a message for Mary Beth from a 'Cathy' on June 24, but she didn't know that the 'Cathy' was Mary Beth's sister until Mary Beth came home after that weekend and told her roommate that she had been at the Jersey Shore with her sister, Cathy. And they both said that they had never met Cathy, so they wouldn't know what she looked like."

"So it looks like Cathy Warner didn't call her sister that day, or the day before, to tell her she was coming down for a visit, right?" Zimmerman asked.

"That's the way it looks, Sarge. And Mary Beth said Cathy never came down without at least calling, and she would definitely have called at that period of time because she knew Mary Beth was moving, and could be in either Pennsylvania or Virginia."

"So Mr. Berta is telling us another tale, hmm?"

Watson nodded his head.

October 20, 1983

Joe Zimmerman and Dennis Watson spent the morning huddled in the former's office, bringing each other up-to-date on the information they had uncovered during the past week. Zimmerman clearly had the more interesting tale.

"She said he was whispering?" Watson asked, after Zimmerman had apprised him of the things Pat Bauer "suddenly" remembered. "He was probably calling from Cathy Warner's house and didn't want her to hear."

"Yeah, well, he told Pat to meet him at the Durham Cafe, which is right across the street from the Warner house, so that's not too far-fetched," Zimmerman agreed. "He probably thought he could do it quick and easy and be out of the house in time to make their flight."

"So who's this George Taylor?"

"A friend of Pat's. I think we met him that first night, when we first went to talk to Pat Bauer at the rescue squad. In any case, we're going to meet him again. He'll be waiting for us at the squad headquarters by the time we get there."

"Hey," Watson said, as he grabbed his jacket and followed Zimmerman out his office door, "any friend of Pat's is a friend of mine."

The two Middlesex County detectives found George Taylor in the rescue squad's recreation room. Taylor, who had been a paid fireman for seven years and a member of the rescue squad for 12 and was named acting captain after Berta's arrest, was sitting at a card table, staring idly into space.

Taylor shook the detective's hands, then gestured for them to join him at the table. Watson and Zimmerman could tell by the gruff welcome they received that Taylor was not happy about being questioned.

Zimmerman briefly explained the reason for the visit, then dispensed with the chit-chat. He knew it wouldn't soften up Taylor anyway.

"How long have you known Gene Berta, Mr. Taylor?" Zimmerman asked. He liked to start potentially difficult interviews with easy questions.

"I guess since I joined the squad," Taylor replied.

"Uh huh. And were you good friends, I mean, did you go out together, things like that?"

"No we never really socialized," Taylor answered, shaking his head. "About the only time I deliberately saw him outside of the squad was when I had him do some electrical work at my house."

"So you never really got to know him socially, then? What about professionally?"

Taylor's eyebrows arched. "Professionally, he's one of the best first-aid people I know. One of the best."

"I understand you witnessed a scene that occurred at John F. Kennedy Hospital on May 10, when Mr. Berta was involved in an accident," Zimmerman continued. "What can you tell us about that?"

"Oh that," Taylor laughed, again shaking his head. "What a mess that was. Well, I was in the emergency room at Kennedy, bringing in a patient with the squad. While I was there, I found out that Gene was in the emergency ward as a patient, because of the accident he had with his truck. So I went over to see him, to see how he was doing, and he asked me to call Cathy Warner and tell her about his accident, and to tell her to not come to the hospital because he thought Gail might show up. So I called Cathy and gave her Gene's message."

"So you knew Cathy Warner?"

"Yeah, I knew her from the squad."

"Did you know Cathy Warner socially?"

Taylor nodded yes. "I think it was back in '73 or '74, we had a few dates. It was only three or four times."

"And were you intimate?" Zimmerman asked.

"Yeah, we had sex after we went out. But then I found out that she was sleeping with other guys, including Gene, so I broke it off."

Zimmerman let a conspiratorial smile creep onto his face. "From what we've been told, this Mr. Berta is quite a hit with the ladies."

Taylor laughed. "Yeah, Gene's a ladies' man all right. That's Gene."

"I understand Cathy and Gene had set a date to get married, did you know anything about that?"

"No I hadn't heard that," Taylor said, with a genuinely surprised look. "I didn't think Gene was interested in marrying Cathy, although I know Cathy wanted to marry him."

"What about his temper, did you ever see or hear him threaten anyone?"

"I never saw anything, but another squad member, Teresa Mota, once told me that Gene pointed a .22 calibre rifle at her. But I know Gene, I'm sure he was just fooling around."

"Uh huh." Zimmerman stroked his chin. "Did you ever know Gene to drink or use drugs?"

"Well, I don't think he's much of a drinker," Taylor said, clearly uncomfortable with the question, "but it's possible that he still smokes marijuana."

"Still? You've seen him smoking pot in the past?"

"Well, yeah. I've seen him smoking in the squad parking lot."

Zimmerman and Watson glanced at each other. Watson recalled the bag of green leafy matter that was found in Berta's house when he executed the search warrant.

"Okay, Mr . Taylor, I want to take you back to the the end of June, the beginning of July. Can you tell us what Mr. Berta did during the several days before he went on his trip in July?"

"Yeah, I guess so. But I don't really remember the date he went away, you know?"

"That's fine, just tell us what you can remember."

"Okay," Taylor agreed, folding his hands on top of the card table. "I guess it was the Thursday before he went away, he left a note for me in the log book that he was going away on vacation from the next day until the following Thursday, and that I was going to be in charge of the squad."

"Did he say who he was going away with?"

"No, but I thought he was going away with Gail."

"Do you have the note?" Watson asked.

"Nah, I threw it away after I read it. There was no reason for me to hang on to that. Anyway, the next day I got a call from Pat Bauer at about 5 o'clock; she asked me if I would meet her at the squad. So we met there, but it was too crowded so we went over to Roosevelt Park to talk. She told me that she was supposed to go away with Gene for the weekend, and that she was supposed to meet him at the Durham Cafe, but he stood her up. She asked me what she should do."

"Okay," Zimmerman interrupted. "Did you know that Pat Bauer and Gene Berta were seeing each other before you met in the park?"

"No, I had no idea! I was shocked when she told me; I told her that I thought she had more class than to go away with Gene Berta. And when she told me about the Durham Cafe, I told her that it sounded like Gene was probably at Cathy Warner's house, which was right across the street from the Cafe. I thought she was a fool for going away with him, so tried to talk her out of going."

"What happened after you two concluded your conversation?"

"Well, we drove back to the squad, then I went home. I was only there a little while, and I got another call from Patty. She told me that she and Gene were still going away together."

"And did you see either Pat or Gene at all that weekend?"

"No, neither one of them. I think it wasn't until the following Monday night or Tuesday morning that I saw Gene at the squad. I asked him if he was back from his vacation. He said that he had been looking at a farm in Minnesota over the weekend, and that he was now leaving with Gail to spend a couple of days at Seaside Heights. He said he would be back on Thursday."

"When was the next time you spoke with Mr. Berta?"

"It was that Thursday, when he got back. I don't know why, but I told him that Pat had called me the Friday before and told me about the trip that she and he were supposed to go on."

Zimmerman perked up. "Oh? And how did he react to that?"

"Well, he didn't really say anything, but I think he resented the fact that Pat had called me."

"And you say that before you had that conversation in Roosevelt Park with Pat Bauer, you never suspected that Gene was seeing her?" Zimmerman asked.

"Well, no. I mean, I figured he was seeing *someone*, In January, Gene and Gail separated for awhile, and Gene slept at the squad. Whenever Gene was on duty, he would leave and say he would be on the walkie-talkie. I figured he was going out to meet someone."

"Do you ever recall hearing Gene and Pat discuss this case?"

"Well, I remember in July, that night you two talked to Pat, Gene came to the squad and spoke to her after you left, but I didn't hear what they said."

"Uh-huh. Has Mr. Berta ever said anything to you about Catherine Warner's death?"

"No," Taylor said, slowly shaking his head. "He never said anything to me about her death or about his arrest."

Pat Bauer's life was once again in a state of flux.

After not hearing from him for nearly two months, Pat received a telephone call the previous week from Gene Berta. He had called her at work and typically, he treated the his arrest and indictment as a joke. The main reason he called, Berta told Bauer, was that he wanted to see her again.

"Why do you want to see me?" Bauer had asked in what she hoped was a casual voice.

"It's been so long, I just want to talk, you know, like we used to," Berta told her. "It doesn't have to be for very long, but I just want to see you."

Pat Bauer's intellect was screaming NO! but she agreed to the meeting anyway. Bauer asked the accused murderer where he wanted to meet, anticipating he would say a diner or the MetroPark station.

"How about the Greenwood Manor, do you know where that is?" he asked.

Pat Bauer felt the blood drain from her face when she heard Berta mention the name of the restaurant where the mystery caller had wanted to meet with her back in August. The fingers on the hand in which she held the telephone receiver gripped it until they, too, turned white.

"Yeah, I know where it is, Gene," Bauer said, again, trying to sound calm. "Why would you want to go all the way out there?"

"I'm doing it for you, babe," he told her. "You don't want to be seen with a guy like me in a place we could be recognized, do you?"

Bauer could almost swear that Gene was enjoying this notoriety.

"Well, I guess that's all right," she said, hesitantly. "What time and when?"

"How about tomorrow, about 6:30? Is that okay?"

"That sounds fine, Gene, I'll see you then."

Bauer replaced the receiver without saying goodbye. She stared at the instrument for several minutes, wondering what she should do. On the one hand, she thought, he could be sincere in his desire to see her. On the other hand, he may be angry about something she told the police, and he may want to exact his revenge in Woodbridge.

"It's no coincidence that he and that jerk who called me wanted to meet at the Greenwood," Bauer told herself. "Something is up."

After reflecting on her options, Pat Bauer decided to take out some insurance of her own. Feeding a piece of company stationery into her typewriter, she began to compose a letter addressed to Sgt. Joe Zimmerman, Middlesex County Detectives.

"Dear Joe," she began, "There is a possibility that I may have erred in my judgment of Gene Berta . . ."

Finishing half an hour later, Pat Bauer folded the letter, placed it in a plain white envelope, and wrote "Lt. Joseph Joe Zimmerman, Middlesex County Prosecutor's Office" on its front. She then put the envelope in her desk drawer, where it would be easily seen by anyone searching for — she shuddered at the thought — clues to her murder.

"This way," she thought, "if I don't come back from that meeting, at least they'll know who to go after."

November 27, 1983

Dennis Watson was clearing up some paperwork at about 3 p.m. when his phone rang. It was Bill Kallio, a member of the Edison Rescue Squad to whom Watson had spoken several days earlier. At that first interview, Kallio, who had been a squad member for five years, called Gene Berta a "snake in the grass, someone who was not to be trusted." In seeking out information on Berta's character, Watson had been told that the accused killer was fond of shooting cats, and had once done so from the front of the rescue squad property. Watson was told that Kallio was a witness to the incident, but Kallio could not remember ever seeing Berta shoot a cat, although he did say he recalled seeing a .22 calibre rifle in Berta's van.

Kallio called this day to tell Watson that he had been thinking about the incident for the past few days and that he vaguely remembered it.

"Yeah, me and Gene and Theresa Mota were standing outside the squad one day," Kallio explained, "and there was this cat walking across the tops of some cars at the Getty station across the street. So Gene says, 'Man, I wish I had my gun,' and he makes like he's going to his van to get it. Well, Teresa, she loves cats, so she figures she'd run across the street and save it. I just ran after her, grabbed her and carried her back into the squad building."

"Did Gene shoot the cat?" Watson asked.

"You know, I don't really remember seeing Gene with a gun, to tell you the truth."

"Well, why did you grab her? Did you think she was going to get shot?"

"Nah, like I said, I didn't see a gun. I was more scared of her getting hit by a car."

November 22, 1983

Smerecki received the F.B.I. analysis on the fingerprints lifted from Cathy Warner's house, but they were not very helpful. About the most interesting finding was that prints on the underside of the downstairs toilet lid were Berta's as were prints on three dishes. The prints found on the newspaper proved to be of the investigating officers, and several other prints could not be identified.

Kapsak mentally filed the report with other information he felt was the least helpful. The fact that Berta's fingerprints showed up on the plates and toilet lid was not extraordinary because Berta had admitted that he spent a great deal of time in Cathy Warner's house.

Of far more importance was a report he received earlier in the month concerning the results of Berta's handwriting test. An analysis showed that Berta had indeed filled out and signed Cathy Warner's name to the "mail hold" card recovered from the Metuchen post office. Berta had also signed a Christmas card detectives found among Warner's papers. The other documents — several notes and a newspaper payment envelope — were written by Cathy Warner, according to the State Police handwriting expert.

A test on indented writing on a blank pad found on Warner's kitchen table revealed that Cathy had written down her sister's Blue Ridge, Pennsylvania address and phone number, along with some other incidental notes.

While Kapsak understood that the knowledge that Berta filled out the mail request card was not intrinsically damning, along with the other evidence of Berta's deceptions and manipulations of Cathy Warner, it helped to paint the picture of Berta the State wanted the jury to see, that of the consummate con man, devoid of the burden of a conscience, who preyed upon the emotions of vulnerable women.

Voices — Pat Bauer

"I reconciled with my husband right after Thanksgiving of 1983. He had filed for divorce, he was suing for custody of Andrew, and the court ordered that we go for a psychiatric evaluation. They wanted Andrew to see a child psychologist and talk to him. And we did. And I think John believed they were going to say that she's an unfit mother and you'll get custody, and when they didn't, he came back to me and said I can't see putting Andrew through this. Then again, they had asked Andrew who would he prefer to go with, and Andrew said me. And I think that John realized at that point that he was going to lose. So one time he was bringing Andrew back and he just said, what are we doing this to the kid for? And I said, well, this was your idea. He said, I just can't stand the thought of you being with that guy. And I said, well, what about you? What's good for the goose is good for the gander. And he said it's different, and I said it's not.

"Andrew went to a counsellor, John or I took him. I don't even know what we did about bills, I think he just listed them down and he gave me half, because that was what his lawyer told him to pay. Then, when we got the report from one of the psychologists, who said he couldn't find any kind of character deficiencies, he found me to be sensitive and something else.

He said in his opinion, either parent is capable of taking care of Andrew without any harmful effects, but that the child had a closer relationship with his mother than his father. And he didn't see how any kind of ill effects could come about by being with me.

January 17, 1984

By the end of 1983, Gene Berta was out of money. The $10,000 he had obtained from Cathy Warner that summer did not last to the fall: his bank statement of July 18, 1983, showed a beginning balance of $5.92 and an ending balance of $4,051.66, that figure having been bolstered in the preceding month by the two deposits of $5,000 each, against which he incurred debits of $5,954.26. Included in the debit column was a $3,000 check to the United Farm Agency of Moose Lake, Minn.

But now that Cathy Warner was gone, so was the flow of her money into Berta's bank account, a fact enunciated in Berta's bank statement dated August 18, 1983. He had managed to deposit only $1,768.68 during the intervening 30 days, but had withdrawn $5,759.22 – including more than $3,500 that went to repairs on his East Walnut Street home – leaving him with a balance of $61.12.

After he was arrested, Berta turned to his parents for financial aid so that he could afford to retain Morris Brown of the firm of Wilentz, Goldman and Spitzer, an attorney he had used in the past. But by the end of the year, the Berta family could no longer afford the pricey representation of the Woodbridge firm. In fact, they could afford no lawyer, so Berta applied for and was assigned a public defender. On January 17, 1984, the final order authorizing the change in attorneys was signed, and Berta's defense was taken over by Middlesex County Deputy Public Defender Bradley J. Ferencz.

A native of Queens, New York and raised in Randolph, New Jersey, Brad Ferencz was in the third year of his second stint with the State Department of the Public Advocate — of which the Public Defender's Office is a division — when the Berta case landed on his desk. Ferencz had graduated from Ohio State University with degrees in economics, political science and history, then decided to move back to his adopted home state and study law at Rutgers University Law School in Camden, New Jersey.

Ferencz remembered law school as being "the first time that I had to work. Getting my undergraduate degree was a breeze. When I went to law school, I really wasn't sure what I wanted to do, but I thought it was fun."

In 1973, a year after attaining his juris doctor degree, Ferencz found himself working for the Middlesex County Legal Services office, for which he was a staff attorney for about one year. He became a Public Defender, a position he maintained until 1977, when he went into private practice.

"I really had no desire to go into private practice when I was in law school," he noted. "I always wanted to work in the public sector."

It was that desire to be a "public servant," as Ferencz phrases it, that led the attorney to maintain his relationship with the Public Defender's office even while he was in private practice. Finally, in 1980, Ferencz was offered an administrative position in the office, which he readily accepted.

While they are always on opposite sides of the courtroom, Brad Ferencz and Tom Kapsak do share one common trait, a firm belief that the law must be upheld.

"I have a deep, abiding respect for authority and I believe in the law," Ferencz said. "It seemed to me at the time I was deciding on a career path that the best way to ensure that the law was being upheld was to ensure that the law was being followed. I look at my job as the policeman's policeman; the day they can strip away one segment of the population's ability to be fully represented is the day the next layer is in jeopardy."

"Sometimes people come up to me and say, how could you get that person off? I don't look at it as getting someone off, I look at it as ensuring that that person is fully and completely represented, and that the facts are truthfully presented to a jury. If I can do that, then I consider myself successful, no matter what the outcome of the trial."

Ferencz had tried more than 100 cases when he took up Gene Berta's defense, although only a handful of them involved murder.

The Wilentz firm had turned over all the case materials to Ferencz, including a number of interviews conducted by the firm's contracted private investigator. Not willing to base his case on the work habits of someone he did not know, Ferencz directed his team of investigators, Anthony Cataldi, Al Goldstein and Claude DeRogatis, to reinterview everyone that the Wilentz firm had contacted, and then to pick up the case where Berta's former attorney had left off.

On February 17, Kapsak and Ferencz were informed by Superior Court Judge Barnett Hoffman, who would be trying the case, that the trial would commence on April 16. On February 24, Ferencz wrote to Hoffman, arguing that the trial date should be postponed because he had only been given the case six weeks earlier and had not had sufficient time to prepare a suitable defense. As of early March, Hoffman had not responded to Ferencz's request.

March 2, 1984

Regardless of what television shows and feature films would have one believe, much of a detective's time is spent filling out reports; it's not very glamorous, but is nonetheless a vital component of a detective's agenda during an investigation.

So it was on this day that Dennis Watson found himself completing yet another series of reports; information that he hoped would further seal the fate of Gene Berta. Watson, as well as the other members of the investigating team, were all too aware of the fact that the trial was scheduled to begin in just six weeks.

The two reports Dennis Watson had just written were based on interviews he had conducted over the past two weeks. On February 22, Gloria Neal called to pass on some information that she thought would aid the detective in his investigation into her daughter's murder. Actually, Mrs. Neal had two things to tell him: First, she had heard that Berta and his wife had recently bought wedding bands at a Woodbridge jewelry store, Fords Jewelers, "probably with the money he stole from my daughter," she added. Second, while Cathy was taking tractor-trailer driving lessons, she had become friendly with another student, Lee Cole of Ramsey. Watson promised Mrs. Neal that he would follow up on what she had told him.

The detective had called Mrs. Cole at her home earlier on this brisk March day. Cole told Watson that she and Cathy attended the Action Tractor Trailer Academy together and became friends. As other of Cathy Warner's friends had told the detectives earlier in the investigation, Cole said that Cathy constantly talked of her boyfriend, who she called her "Huggy Bear".

"She was head over heels in love with him," Cole said.

"Did she ever tell you what their plans were?" Watson asked.

"Oh yeah," Cole replied. "She said that she was going to marry him after he divorced his current wife. She said that she had bought a house for them to live in after he got his divorce, and that he was helping her fix it up. She even said that the reason she was learning to drive a tractor-trailer was so that she and her boyfriend could buy a truck and be over-the-road drivers together."

"Did you and Cathy keep in touch after you completed the training, Mrs. Cole?"

"Well, we called each other, up until last summer," Cole said. "All I really remember is that she used to complain that she was mad at her boyfriend because he wasn't keeping his promise that he would leave his wife and marry her. One day she'd call me and tell me that she broke up with him, and then another day she'd call and say she took him back. Like I said, she was head over heels for him."

Cole's information closely matched that given to Watson late in November by Thomas DiMesa of Howell, the former director and instructor at the now-defunct tractor trailer driving school. DiMesa told the detective that Cathy would often talk about her "Teddy Bear" and told him that she was going to marry her boyfriend after he divorced his wife.

"She even said she was going to invite me to the wedding!" DiMesa added, laughing.

"Did you ever meet her boyfriend?" Watson asked.

"Yeah, I think he came here once," DiMesa said. "He told me he was a truck driver, but that now he was working as an electrician. And we traded stories about tractor trailer accidents that we'd been in."

"Did you ever see Mrs. Warner after she graduated?"

"She came back to visit," DiMesa said.

"And did she ever tell you about any problems she was having with her boyfriend?"

"Well, I remember one time, she said that she had given her boyfriend an ultimatum about leaving his wife. I don't know what came of it, though."

On February 27, Watson interviewed Barry Berman, the owner of Ford's Jewelers. Berman, after checking his files, confirmed that Gene Berta and his wife ordered matching wedding bands on July 25, 1983. They picked them up, Berman said, about two months later. Berman also told the detective that Berta was still paying off the rings.

Voices — Donna Tokar

"Cathy's whole life was based around Gene Berta. For some reason she just had this mad desire to have him. The feelings she had for him were just intense. It was like she had to change him. Who knows, maybe if she got him, she wouldn't want him. She just felt like she could help him some way. She was the type who always wanted to help people. Even with me, she always wanted to do something for me. But I didn't need anything from her.

"And another thing; she always had to drive everywhere. She always had to be the person who drove. Like when we went out somewhere; she knew she didn't drink, and she had to get me home safe. She drank a little. She would drink whiskey sours, one whisky sour. She would have that same drink the entire night.

"Most of their relationship revolved around sex. She wanted to look sexy, wear sexy things, and she would do anything he wanted. And she would feel apt to tell me about these things. She didn't tell me about him, she didn't tell me about her life, but she would tell me about these things they used to do. It just struck me odd. That was their main thing, that they had sex together. Or that he stayed over. He was always there, he stayed there overnight. I was beginning to think he left his wife, too. I could see why she would believe it.

"He was really living at the house, he used to go to the apartment, too. That's why she bought that house. I could never understand why she bought that house in that terrible area. That was a terrible house when she bought it. It didn't have cabinets. She had to get a new stove, refrigerator, counter tops, everything was new. She had to get the whole bathroom done, then she got new flooring, new railing, new steps. I remember whenever I used to go over there, I used to have to walk on newspapers. It was like, 'You can't walk on there, you can't walk on there!' She was real fanatical about this house, too. I mean, you don't buy a house near a bar, that's the worst area. And then she had all that money. I can't believe she had all that money, I couldn't understand why she didn't spend it on herself.

"She always said they were going to buy a truck, that's why she took those truck lessons."

April 11, 1984

In a joint letter to the two lawyers, Judge Hoffman informed Kapsak and Ferencz that he had acceded to the defense attorney's wish and had set a new "firm" trial date of June 4, 1984.

> "It is extremely important that this case is tried on the 4th," Hoffman wrote. "It is anticipated that this trial will take three weeks. If the trial is not started on June 4th, severe problems with regard to witness availability will arise. Likewise, summer vacations will also interfere with scheduling. If the trial is not started on June 4th, it will not be able to be moved until well into fall . . . I am satisfied that both sides have had ample time to prepare for trial."

But that did not satisfy Ferencz.

In a letter dated April 23, Ferencz said he "can not emphasize more how strongly I feel that I will be unprepared to proceed at that time.

> "I received from your honor the strong indication that your honor wanted to move the case only relatively recently. And while

your honor believes that three to four months is a sufficient amount of time to prepare a case of this import, I cannot disagree more. I indicate unequivocally that while I am attempting to get this case ready to move, discovery appears to be many hundreds of pages and the witnesses are significant both in number and import. I request again that your honor reconsider attempting to move this case in June and set this matter down as one of the first cases in September."

Hoffman did not accept Ferencz's argument. In his response, dated April 25, the judge noted that by the June 4 date, Ferencz would have had half a year to prepare his case, and, "Second, the case was investigated by the firm of Wilentz, Goldman & Spitzer, your predecessors. Whatever they did is that much less 'leg work' your office has to do."

But Ferencz would not take no for an answer. In yet another missive, this one dated April 24, the attorney wrote:

> "I have been attempting as best I can over the last several days to put together some understanding of exactly what will be necessary to prepare the Berta matter. I want to advise you as soon as possible that in my opinion the amount of time that you have given me to prepare Berta does not give me a reasonable opportunity to meet the charges and prepare a defense for my defendant.
>
> "It is my opinion that to force me to proceed on the 4th day of June will violate the defendant's due process and will result in the defendant's proceeding to trial in violation of his sixth amendment rights. . . . setting a date on April 11th of June 4th for trial with this case, is in my opinion unfairly burdensome and I believe that your honor is bending to the will of the State in setting priorities. I see no reason other than the State's desire to move this case in a particular order that this case must be tried as quickly as your honor wishes it to be tried. I hope I have not in any way offended the court in my previous sentence, however, I feel that it is incumbent that I make said representation to the Court, so

that the Court may at least consider what I am saying fairly and
objectively."

Hoffman was offended. In his response, Hoffman told Ferencz that he
could appeal to the judge's superiors if he felt "aggrieved" by his decision
to schedule the trial on June 4th.

"As to your statement that I [am] bending to the will of the State
in setting priorities,' " Hoffman continued, "I find this statement to be
totally irresponsible, unfounded and unprofessional. In the interest
of moving this matter forward, I will attribute such an intemperate
remark to be the pressure of getting the case ready rather then (sic)
an intentional attack on my credibility."

Ferencz followed that up by asking Hoffman to postpone the trial date
from June 4, backing up his request with a demand for additional pieces
of evidence he claimed were crucial to his case. Once he had received the
additional discovery, Ferencz noted, he would need more time to review
it. Ferencz also told the judge that he had not been able to meet with his
forensic expert, and had not had time to interview an entomologist. The
attorney's goal was to push the trial date up as far as he could, possibly to
the fall.

Judge Hoffman eventually relented and did postpone the trial start date,
but he did not immediately set a new one.

May 8-9, 1984

As fate would have it, the postponements won by Ferencz worked in favor of Kapsak and the county detectives. With an extra several weeks on his hands, Kapsak found he had more time to try and tie up the several loose ends that were plaguing the case.

One of those loose ends that could now be addressed was the issue of the hot dogs, ground beef and hamburger and hot dog rolls that were found scattered around Cathy Warner's car on July 16th. The detectives believed the food was placed there as a diversionary tactic by Berta, but they could not determine the store from which the items had been purchased. Noticing from the bags' labels that the rolls had been baked by Arnold Bakery, Tom Kapsak and Detective John Haley traveled to the firm's headquarters in Clifton, New Jersey.

Kapsak and Haley met with Don Wells, Arnold Bakers' New Jersey district sales manager.

"All we need is if you can tell us when these rolls were baked, Mr. Wells," Kapsak said. "If you have any other information, that would be a help, too. But we're mainly interested in when these things were made."

"This shouldn't be too hard," Wells told the assistant prosecutor. "The freshness tags are still on the bags."

Wells led Kapsak and Haley to his office and motioned for them to take a seat in front of his desk. "Let me just check our files."

Haley handed Wells the four packages: two packages contained hamburger rolls which had "sell by" dates of July 20, one package contained hot dog rolls with a "sell by" date of July 19, and the fourth package contained hot dog rolls with a "sell by" date of July 22.

"Okay," Wells said, placing an opened three-ring binder on his desk. "I've got what you were looking for. All the rolls were baked at Nissen Bakery in Portland, Maine. The hamburger rolls that are stamped July 20 and the hot dog rolls that are stamped July 19 were transported to our Greenwich, Connecticut bakery on Monday, July 11 and were shipped to our distribution center in Middlesex, New Jersey early in the morning of July 12. They were sent out to stores that same day. The rolls that are stamped July 22 were shipped to Greenwich on July 13 and then to Middlesex early in the morning of the 14th, and delivered to stores later that day."

"Can you tell me how long these things usually stay on the shelves?" Haley asked.

"Generally, our rolls stay on the shelves about four days, then we take them back."

"So that means the hamburger rolls and one package of the hot dog rolls were on the shelves from July 12 to the 16th, and the other package of hot dog rolls was on the shelf from July 14 to the 18th, right?" Kapsak asked.

"Yes," Wells said, nodding, "that would be our procedure."

"So, if he bought both packages at the same time, he had to have gotten them on the 14th, right?" Watson asked. He and the Second Assistant Prosecutor were in the latter's car, on their way back to New Brunswick.

"He couldn't have bought them earlier, because he was in Seaside Heights from the eleventh to the fourteenth," Kapsak agreed. "Obviously, when he came back from his 'second honeymoon', he panicked when he found out that Cathy Warner's body hadn't been discovered yet. He knew that if it wasn't in the next few days, his alibi was shot."

"So he goes to the store and picks up some bread, then to a butcher to get the meat, and spreads it all over the driveway to make it look like she got jumped!" Watson added. "Man, this guy thought he had it all covered."

"That's usually where they make their first mistake, Denny."

Although Kapsak was convinced that the tests Sgt. Smerecki conducted on Cathy Warner's watch proved that she last wound it on July 8, the assistant prosecutor felt that such an important piece of evidence warranted extra corroboration. Kapsak decided in early April that he wanted an expert to bolster Smerecki's findings on the watch's run-down time and also to assure the jury that the timepiece was not damaged.

As he would do more than once in this case, Kapsak started his search at the top. On April 8, he contacted the Timex Corp. at its Waterbury, Connecticut headquarters and spoke to Paul Wuthrich, the company's manager of product engineering. Wuthrich agreed to take a look at the watch.

On April 9, Det. John Haley found himself face to face with the man who designed the watch that had become such a vital piece of evidence. He handed the timepiece over to the engineer, who recognized it on sight.

"This is one of mine," Wuthrich told the detective. "It was designed with nurses and children in mind. You can tell because it has a sweep second hand and it's so small."

After inscribing his initials on the watch's back plate, Haley was assured that only Wuthrich and his assistant, Edward Kaulins, would have access to the watch while it was at Timex.

The report Kapsak received on May 9 supported Smerecki's findings. The Timex engineers tested the watch four times, finding its run down time to be between 47 hours and 49 hours, validating Zimmerman's findings.

"To duplicate critical run down condition," the report continued, "watch was fully wound, set at 6 AM date 8. Run down occurred at 5 AM date 10."

June 27, 1991

Tom Kapsak and County Investigator Kenneth Mazza interviewed Alan Demcoe on two occasions, June 21 and June 27. It was Demcoe, who knew Berta and John and Cathy Warner, who called the Metuchen police station on the afternoon of July 16, 1983, and, after divulging his knowledge of Cathy Warner's murder to Lt. Studnicki, told him that he'd heard Warner's former husband, John Tingley, had recently tried to reconcile with her.

Demcoe, a sergeant with the Middlesex County Park Police, told Kapsak that he had known Cathy Warner for nine or 10 years and knew John Warner and Gene Berta for a few years longer than that.

"What was your relationship with Mrs. Warner?" Kapsak asked.

"Well, before she married John and I married Janet, we dated a few times," Demcoe said.

"Were you just friends, or were you romantically involved . . .?

"Well, I mean, we had sex, but like I said, that was before we both got married."

"Why did you stop seeing her?"

"Well, she got involved with John, and he's I guy I really liked and respected, and when they started seeing each other, I just backed off."

"And after you got married . . . uh, when was that?"

"That was in 1978," Demcoe said.

"Okay, after you got married and Cathy and John Warner got married, did you continue to have contact with them?"

"Oh, sure," Demcoe said. "Me and my wife were friendly with them. And we stayed friendly with Cathy after John died."

"Did you ever go to Mrs. Warner's home at 125 Durham Avenue?"

"Sure. I finished up some electrical work in her house that Gene never bothered to finish, and Janet helped her with a lot of odd jobs, like stripping and staining her bannister."

"Did you always visit the house with your wife?"

"No, sometimes I went by myself, you know, to see how Cathy was doing and have a cup of coffee."

"Okay, sergeant, do you remember the last time you saw Cathy Warner alive?"

"Yeah, it was about, I'd say, two or three weeks before she was killed. I don't remember the circumstances exactly, but I think I saw her outside her house while I was on my way to work."

"Do you recall if you said anything?"

"No," Demcoe said, shaking his head, "I really don't remember."

"Do you recall ever seeing Cathy Warner with a gun, or ever hear her talking about a gun?" Kapsak asked.

"Yeah, it was sometime during the summer of 1982. I met Janet over at Cathy's house; I had just come from the shooting range and I was carrying some targets. I had a pretty good day, so I showed the targets to the girls. Janet said that she had gone shooting, too, and had done pretty well. I remember that Cathy was surprised when she heard that Janet had gone shooting, she said that she had a gun and wanted to go target shooting, too."

"She said she bought a gun?"

"No, she said it was John's gun. Anyway, I promised I would take them both shooting one day. I never did. And I can remember talking to Cathy about the different grips on our guns, but I don't remember if it was that day or another."

"In the time you knew John Warner, did he ever talk about having a gun?"

"Big John? Yeah. I remember, we both worked at a gas station about 12 or 15 years ago, and he talked about buying a gun."

July 13, 1984

One of the first real skirmishes between the prosecution and defense was slated for this day. Colleen Duffy, a neighbor of Cathy Warner's, told defense investigators that she had seen Warner outside her house on July 11th, and that she had also seen a light on in the house on the nights of July 11th and 12th. Ferencz was elated; proving that Cathy Warner was alive on July 11, while Gene Berta was in Seaside Heights, would blow the State's case out of the water. But, on May 21, 1984, when Tom Kapsak and County Detective Joseph L. Smith interviewed Duffy at Metuchen Police Headquarters, the woman changed her story.

According to the report filed by Smith, Duffy said the last time she saw Cathy Warner alive was when Duffy returned from a July 4 weekend trip to the shore. "After thinking about it a little longer," Smith wrote, "Colleen said she wasn't at all sure when she saw Cathy Warner for the last time."

Two of the defense investigators, DeRogatis and Goldstein, then went to speak with Duffy to find out why she changed her story. Upon arriving at her house, they were told that not only could they not speak with her, but that she no longer wished to cooperate with the defense.

Ferencz immediately filed a motion to determine who besides Kapsak and Smith were at that interview and what, if anything, had been said to Duffy to get her to change her story. He also questioned why she was interviewed in the police station, rather than her home.

The motion was filed with no hearing date, as is sometimes the procedure.

As Ferencz' luck would have it, the motion was heard on July 13; Brad Ferencz had married and was off on his honeymoon during that time, and two of Ferencz' associates stood in for him. Following is a transcript of that hearing:

THE COURT:	State versus Berta. Ready, Prosecutor? Mr. Kapsak, are you ready?
MR. KAPSAK:	Yes, I'm ready on a limited basis, Judge.
THE COURT:	Did you get served with the papers?
MR. KAPSAK:	No.
THE COURT:	Is Mr. Ferencz here?
MR. MIGNELLA:	He's on vacation.
THE COURT:	He made a motion returnable when he's on vacation?
AN ATTORNEY:	Your honor, he got married last weekend, and I believe he went on a honeymoon.
THE COURT:	That would account for his cloudy mental process. That motion is dismissed. First of all, he should have served the Prosecutor – Let me put this on the record so several Public Defenders can take it back to him. First of all, he should, in a case, a murder case, when we have a specific Prosecutor, serve the papers on the specific Prosecutor rather than sending it to the Prosecutor's office. That's been done too many times. The other is that if you're going to be away, at least have the courtesy to call the Court to say you are going to be away and that you want an adjournment. "Third of all, the motion is not worth a hill of beans anyway. Okay, thank you."

Upon returning from his wedding trip, Ferencz was angered to learn that he had been insulted by the judge, and that Hoffman had summarily dismissed his motions. In a terse letter to Hoffman, Ferencz wrote,

"In terms of your honor dismissing my motions, I am somewhat perturbed as I file the motions pursuant to your honor's direction without date. I did this so your honor could set them and schedule them at your honor's convenience. I would respectfully request that your honor reinstate my motions without my filing a formal request as your honor is aware that I was on my honeymoon and requested that your honor set these matters down at your convenience subject to my return."

July 31 – August 10, 1984

A pre-trial conference — at which the prosecution, defense and judge settle the issues that will be brought up during the trial — was finally held on July 31. It was during this hearing that the two attorneys argued their reasons for wanting to introduce certain pieces of evidence and prohibit others; for example, Kapsak wanted to show color photos of Cathy Warner's remains, which Ferencz wanted the judge to disallow. For his part, Ferencz wanted to introduce testimony relating to Cathy Warner's relationships prior to Berta, but Kapsak maintained that that had no bearing on the case.

In a letter to the attorneys dated August 3, Judge Hoffman declared that hearings on these and other points of contention would be held during the week of September 4, and – again acceding to Ferencz's wishes – that the trial would start on Monday, September 10. Also to be heard before the trial was a new motion filed by Ferencz, this one asking the judge to recuse himself.

During one meeting in Hoffman's chambers, Ferencz noticed hanging on the wall a photo of the judge when he was a prosecutor. In his brief supporting the motion, Ferencz claimed that he felt the judge, given his background, holds an "innate bias . . . in favor of the Prosecutor or against the defendant or defense counsel."

Kapsak, naturally, objected to the motion, pointing out that Hoffman had spent more time as a defense attorney than he had a prosecutor.

Ferencz was actively seeking an entomologist who could refute Vasvary's findings and a forensic pathologist who could support Shuster's. Additionally, another expert who Ferencz hoped to hire was Dr. Robert Buckhout of Brooklyn (NY) College's Center for Responsive Psychology. Ferencz knew that Kapsak would attempt to introduce as evidence color slides and photographs of the crime scene, including some showing the victim's remains as they were found. Buckhout had been doing research on the effect on juries of just that type of evidence. In a letter dated August 2, 1984, Buckhout explained his research:

> "In a recently published dissertation, my colleague and I found that the mere showing of an autopsy slide had the effect of reducing the accuracy of the observer's memory for details," Buckhout wrote. "We also found that observers rated the slides as extremely upsetting, remembering mainly the shock they experienced. Observers frequently missed essential details on the slides themselves. We concluded that exposure to gruesome slides creates a momentary stress reaction which in turn leads to a disruption of the memory process referred to as anterograde amnesia."

Ferencz thought he could build an argument that his client's right to a fair and impartial jury of his peers would be abridged by such a display.

Tom Kapsak caught himself laughing. He held in his hand notice of Brad Ferencz's intention to petition the court to dismiss the indictment against Eugene Berta.

"Based on the failure to state with specificity the time of death of the victim," Kapsak read aloud. The second assistant prosecutor shook his head as he walked into his office. "He must really be desperate to be grasping at straws like this."

The trial was scheduled to start in exactly one month. A number of legal maneuverings by both Kapsak and Ferencz had punctuated an otherwise quiet spring and summer.

In May, Ferencz had unsuccessfully appealed Judge Hoffman's motion to suppress the evidence gathered in the searches of Berta's house and van. Also in May, Kapsak, through Dennis Watson, won a court order requiring Berta to submit a sample of his hair, which would then be matched with some hairs found by the detectives on Cathy Warner basement steps.

Once obtained, the sample was sent with the control to the state police laboratory, but no match was made. Kapsak and the detectives consoled themselves by reasoning that the presence of Berta's hair on the steps really didn't prove anything, other than that he was in the house, much as the fingerprints identified earlier in the investigation did.

On June 29 and August 9, Donna Tokar and Mary Neal, respectively, met with John Haley at his North Brunswick office to identify several items that were found in Cathy Warner's house. Among the things displayed by Haley were several calendars, bank books and check registers. Both women identified the handwriting on the various items as being that of Cathy Warner.

Tom Kapsak was a cautious man who liked to be prepared for any eventuality. And he especially disliked surprises with a trial start date looming closer and closer.

But surprised he was in early August when he received a copy of a letter from Dr. Lewis Roh, the medical examiner of Westchester County, New York, to Ferencz. In it, Roh basically backed up the findings of Dr. Marvin Shuster, the Middlesex County M.E., relating to Cathy Warner's estimated time of death.

Kapsak showed the letter to Joe Zimmerman. The two were sitting in the second assistant prosecutor's office, discussing the case.

"I could have lived with Shuster because he admitted that it's very difficult to be exact about the time of death, especially when weather becomes a significant factor because then it's not a natural progression of decomposition," Kapsak told the detective. "He's already admitted that if the weather is extreme, either cold or hot, it makes it very difficult to estimate the time of death. And he also told me that he didn't take into account the entomologist's report, because he obviously didn't have it by the time he did the autopsy.

"But I can't live with this," he added, pointing with disgust to the letter Zimmerman had read and placed on Kapsak's desk. "Now, we know that her body was left in that basement for awhile before it was put in the bathtub, right? That's what the stain on the floor tells us. What we don't know, and what we really need to find out, is whether the stain was just caused by blood from the head leaking out over the course of a few hours, or whether it was from body fluids that escaped while the body began decomposing. If it was from body fluids, that has to mean that she was there for a few days before he carried her upstairs and put her in the tub.

"How do you think we can prove that?" Zimmerman asked.

"I've got to find someone who can tell us that, someone who's so credentialed in forensics that a jury won't question his findings."

Staring off into space, Kapsak's eyes came to rest on his bookcase, in which he kept a number of reference materials. One in particular caught his eye, "Medicolegal Investigation of Death – Guidelines for the Application of Pathology to Crime Investigation". Rising from his chair without lifting his gaze, Kapsak retrieved the book and returned to his desk.

"This is the guy," he told Zimmerman, smiling again. "This is our spoiler." Kapsak was pointing to the book's editor: Werner U. Spitz, M.D.

The book Kapsak held in his hand was the primary textbook used by forensic pathologists in the United States. Its editor, Dr. Werner Spitz, was the chief medical examiner for Wayne County, Michigan, a post he had held since 1972. Wayne County includes the city of Detroit, ranked fourth among American cities in the number of yearly homicides. Spitz is generally regarded as the father of modern forensic pathology. Among his many accomplishments is the fact that he was the only forensic pathologist on the 1975 committee charged by Vice President Nelson Rockefeller to investigate the assassination of President John F. Kennedy. At the time, Spitz was in the process of working on an atlas of forensic pathology entitled "Atlas of Criminal Pathology – A Study of Patterns and Mechanisms of Injury."

Kapsak soon had Spitz's phone number. In a short conversation, the assistant prosecutor outlined the case's details and asked for Spitz's assistance. The doctor told Kapsak to send him the crime scene photos and other information as soon as possible.

Kapsak collected the photos, as well as Roh's letter, the autopsy, detective reports and Dr. Vasvary's report and sent them to Spitz that day, via Federal Express.

Spitz called Kapsak several days later to tell him of his finding: namely, that Catherine Warner was killed approximately eight days before her body was found. The medical examiner summarized his opinion in a letter sent to the assistant prosecutor on August 21. In it, Spitz wrote, ". . . it is my opinion that the death of Ms. Warner occurred at least eight days before the body was discovered. This opinion is based on the degree of decomposition of the body, including but not limited to the partial skeletonization of the head, mummification of the hands, and the age of maggots on the body."

During the conversation, Spitz agreed to serve as an expert witness for the State.

"If you have any more material, I would like to take a look at it," Spitz said.

"Well, why don't I bring it to you myself?" Kapsak asked.

"Fine," Spitz replied. "We can continue our discussion then."

Kapsak made a tentative appointment with Spitz for the following week, then secured airline reservations to Detroit.

At last, Kapsak had what he had been looking for since the beginning of the investigation: an expert who would unequivocally state that Cathy Warner was killed on July the eighth. And, as he had said many times to the detectives and Prosecutor Rockoff, if it was the eighth, it had to be Gene Berta. Like all the other pieces of evidence Kapsak planned to introduce during the trial, Spitz's report wouldn't convict Gene Berta all by itself. But, taken in conjunction with everything else, it helped to paint the portrait of a man who used Cathy Warner primarily for her money and secondarily for sex, then, when he was certain she could be of no more use to him, killed her in cold blood.

August 24, 1984

Pat Bauer was at her desk, trying to concentrate on her work, when she was startled by the shrill ring of her telephone.

"Hi Patty, it's John."

"John! This is a surprise! How are you feeling, is everything all right?" Her husband had been in the hospital since July 18, undergoing treatment for leukemia.

"I'm okay, same as usual I guess."

"Is there anything you want me to bring tonight? Anything from home?"

"No, no, that's not why I called." He paused; Pat knew he was trying to say something, but was having trouble with it. "Listen, Patty, I have to tell you something, but before I do, I want you to know that I'm not mad at you, I'm just telling you what happened, okay?"

"John, what's the matter? What are you talking about?" Pat was frightened and confused, she couldn't fathom what he was getting at.

"Well, last night, these two guys came to the nurses' station, and they said that they were from the prosecutor's office and they wanted to talk to me."

"You mean Joe Zimmerman and Dennis Watson?"

"Wait a minute, let me finish. So the nurses asked me how I felt about it, and I said hell, they're on the right side of the law, I had no problem with it. So these two guys come in, and they flash their badges real quick, and they start talking. And then it occurred to me that I didn't recognize them, And I said, 'you guys aren't from the prosecutor's office!' And they stopped and looked at me and they said, 'no, we're from the public defender's office. But we have the same right to interview people as they do.' So he looks at me and he says, 'you have anything you want to get off your chest before you die?' "

"I don't believe this," Pat said, "Of all the low . . . "

"Oh, Patty, it gets better. So this one guy says to me, 'listen, we're talking about a murder trial here, our guy could get life! Why should he get life when he's not guilty?' And I said he is too guilty! And I started talking about all the circumstantial evidence and all that, but they didn't want to hear that. So the guy says, 'why don't you take the rap for him? You're going to die anyway?' And I said, 'I'm not going to die! I'm not taking the rap for anybody!' They must have said that two or three times. So finally I just told them they had a hell of a nerve coming up here and bothering me like this when I'm fighting for my life, and this guy says, 'Well, Gene Berta is fighting for his life, too.' I just told them to get lost, and they did."

"This has to be Gene's idea," Pat said, fuming. "He was the only one who knew that you were in the hospital. I can't believe he would do something like this!"

"Patty, I just want you to know that I'm not mad at you."

"Well, I'm not taking this. I'm calling the prosecutor's office, there's got to be something they can do about this!"

"No, you don't have to do that," John Bauer said. "I didn't call you to tell you to do that, I just thought you should know what they said."

"Well, I'm sorry they put you through that. But don't worry, I'll take care of it."

"And I'll take care of Gene Berta, too" Pat Bauer thought, as she hung up the phone.

Pat Bauer didn't call Kapsak, but she did phone her attorney, Steve Altman, and tell him what her husband had just related.

"I want to meet with the prosecutor again, Steve. I want to tell him everything that I told Morris Brown. I don't give a damn if it is damaging, I want them to know it."

"That kind of conversation is privileged, Patty," Altman said. "You don't have to divulge any of it if you don't want to."

"I know, but Gene's lawyers already know about it. And it will only be a matter of time before Kapsak finds out, and then he'll hang me. You heard what he said the last time we talked."

"Patty, listen, take my advice. You're hot now. Take a few days and cool off, and then we'll discuss this. If you still want to meet with them, I'll set up an appointment and go down there with you. Okay?"

"Okay," Bauer said. "But I don't think my answer will change."

September 5, 1984

Thomas Kapsak was told that Samuel Harris, Cathy Warner's next door neighbor, had asked to see him and was in the waiting area. Kapsak had been trying to reach Harris for some time.

Harris, an affable man, appeared nervous in as he took a seat in Kapsak's office.

"Sorry I didn't get in touch with before," he said, "but my father just died, and I've been going back and forth to Virginia."

"That's no problem," Kapsak said. "Thanks for coming by. I just wanted to get a statement from you about Cathy Warner; did you know her well?"

"I didn't know her real well, I helped her once in awhile with odd jobs around her house."

"Do you remember the last time you saw her?"

"Yeah, I think it was June 25, 1983."

"What kind of person was she?"

Harris smiled. "She was good people; she was friendly. She always treated me well."

"Had you ever met her boyfriend, Gene Berta?"

"Yeah I talked to him a coupla times."

"Did she ever talk about her future with him?"

"Yeah, she said she was going to marry him. In fact, he told me that a couple times, too. Once in 1982, and I think once last year."

"Mr. Harris, do you remember about how many times Gene Berta visited Cathy Warner at her house?" Kapsak asked.

Harris sat back and thought. "Well, I'd guess it was about two or three times a week, up until about May of last year," he said. "He stopped coming around in June, but then started up again in July. Except in July, he didn't park his van in front of the house like he used to."

"Do you recall any other men visiting her during that time?"

"Yeah, there was this county park policeman, he came by twice. I think it was April and May last year. Then one day I saw this Edison police car stop by. That was last summer sometime. And there was one weekend, I saw this Jaguar with MD plates parked in front of her house. It was kinda blocking her driveway. I remember it was a Jag, because I was fooling around, slap fighting, with my friend, and he backed me up against it, and he said, 'Sam, you getting your ass kicked against your favorite car!' And then there were the workmen, they were always coming and going."

"Okay, that's very helpful. One more thing, did you ever notice where Cathy Warner parked her car?"

"Yeah. She always parked it at the front of the driveway, and she always went into her house through the front door."

"I want you to think about the weekend of July 9 through the eleventh. Do you recall seeing her car in the driveway any of those days?"

Harris again paused several moments while he thought. "No," he said, slowly shaking his head. "It was definitely not in the driveway any of those days. But I know that on the 12th, I saw it parked in the back of her driveway, and I thought that was strange 'cause she never parked there before."

September 6, 1984

Patricia Bauer and Steve Altman showed up at the prosecutor's office promptly for their 2:30 p.m. appointment. They were ushered into a conference room, where they were soon joined by Lt. Joe Zimmerman and Det. Dennis Watson. Bauer was relieved to see that Kapsak was not in attendance.

Steve Altman had set up the appointment the day before with his old friend, Watson.

"As I told you yesterday, Denny," the attorney began, "my client has remembered a few things that are relevant to this case that she had forgotten to tell you in past interviews."

'Well, we welcome all the help we can get," Watson said. Neither he nor Zimmerman believed Bauer had "forgotten" anything, they were just grateful that she had decided to tell everything that she knew.

As was the custom, Zimmerman took over the interview.

"Okay, Patty," he said, after offering her a cigarette and lighting it, "why don't you tell us what you ... remembered?"

"Well," Bauer began, taking a quick drag and blowing it noisily through pursed lips, "first of all, the day after Gene was arrested, I was contacted by his attorney, Morris Brown. I went to his office that night and told him everything I told you before and everything I'm about to tell you."

Bauer repeated what she had already told the detectives about Berta "standing her up" at the Durham Cafe parking lot, then subsequently meeting with George Taylor and, later, receiving a call from Berta at her home. Zimmerman and Watson did not want to break her concentration, so they let her continue.

"Gene called me back at 7:30," she said, "and that's when I agreed to go on the trip with him. But he said something funny before we hung up, he said, 'I have to clean up, I'll call you later.' "

"What do you think he meant by that?" Zimmerman asked.

"I just figured that he had to take a shower," Bauer said. "That was how I interpreted it.

"Anyway, Gene called me again at 8:30 that night. He told me that he had changed our reservations, but he said that we were still going. And then he asked me if I still loved him and still wanted to go with him. And then he said he had to get off the phone because he had to finish cleaning up."

"Did you know where he was calling from?" Zimmerman asked.

"Well, I figured that he was calling from Cathy Warner's house. I mean, George Taylor had just told me that he was still seeing her, and that the Durham Cafe was right across the street from her house, so that's where I figured he was.

"Gene called me one more time, at 9 o'clock. He talked about the trip again, and asked me if I was still going with him and he asked me again if I still loved him. Then he said he'd call me back and tell me what time to pick him up. And, again, right before we hung up, he said he still had to finish cleaning up."

"Sounds like he was pretty dirty," Watson mused aloud.

"He called me back at about 9:20," Bauer continued, ignoring the remark. "We had the same kind of conversation, about the trip. Then he asked me if I was ready to go, and I said yes. And he said his watch read 9:30 p.m., and told me to set my watch to 9:30 and to meet him in 10 minutes at the MetroPark parking lot. So I got in my car, and on the way to MetroPark I stopped in a Dunkin' Donuts on Route 27 and then drove to the train station and met Gene.

"We were on our way to Newark . . ."

"Just a minute, Patty," Zimmerman interrupted. "Do you remember how you went there? What route you took?"

"Oh, I don't know, it was either Route 1 or the Turnpike," she answered. "Anyway, we up near Elizabeth, I think, when Gene asked me to rub the back of his neck."

"Did he tell you why he wanted you to do that?" Zimmerman asked.

"He said he was very tense," Bauer replied. "So I was rubbing his neck, and he said, 'Do you love me?' And I said yes. And then he said, 'Do you believe that I love you?' And I said no. And then he said to me, 'you'd better, because I just killed three people and I'll blow your goddamn brains out.'"

That comment momentarily stunned the two detectives.

"What did you say to that?" Zimmerman asked.

"I didn't say anything, I didn't know what to make of that."

"Okay, Patty," Zimmerman said. "Go on."

"Well, it was near the end of our trip, and we were returning the rental car to the airport in Minneapolis . . ."

"This would be July 11?" Zimmerman asked.

"Whatever the date was, I'm not good with dates. So I opened the glove compartment to clean it out, and then I saw the car rental agreement was made out in the name of Warner. That got me so angry, I just pulled it out and left it on the seat, so that Gene would see it when he got back in the car. Then Gene asked me if I wanted him to get all the souvenirs from our trip, and I told him to just junk them."

"Did he see the rental agreement?"

"Yeah, he saw it, but he didn't say anything. In fact, we didn't talk at all while we were waiting to board the plane. I was so mad! He just kept asking me, 'What's the matter, what's the matter? And he kept saying that we should talk about things.

"He kept that up on the flight back to Newark, saying that we should talk about things," Bauer continued. "So I told him that I didn't want to live like that, sneaking around with him while he was seeing other women. And then he said that he loved me and I said, 'How could you? I saw the car rental agreement!' And then he said to me, 'You don't have to worry about her, she's completely out of the picture.'"

Pat Bauer was oblivious to the impact her information was making in Watson and Zimmerman. The comment about Warner being "completely out of the picture," coupled with Berta's statement that he had just "killed three people," had Watson's mind racing. He cast a glance at Zimmerman; the detective's brows were knit and he was slowly scratching the side of his face, deep in thought.

Bauer paused to replace the cigarette that she had smoked to its filter. After it was lit, she took several calming, deep drags and resumed her narration.

"Okay; one day last October, Gene called me and asked me to meet him at a place called the Greenwood Manor. I think that's on Green Street, in Iselin. He wanted me to meet him there at a quarter to six that night. That really scared me."

"Why?" Zimmerman asked.

"Because I didn't know why he wanted to meet with me! So before I went, I wrote a letter to you, Joe, and addressed it 'Lieutenant Joseph Zimmerman/Middlesex County Prosecutor's Office'. I left the letter in my desk at work; I figured if anything happened to me, someone would find the letter and get it to you."

"And what did you say in the letter?"

"Just that I was going to meet with Gene that night and, in case I didn't come back, I wanted you to know that there was a possibility that I had erred in my judgment of Gene."

"Obviously, he didn't do you in at this meeting," Zimmerman said, good-naturedly. "What did happen?"

"Gene just told me that he still loved me and he asked me if I was going to be on his side at the trial. I told him that I would be a character witness for him."

"And have you spoken with him since?"

"Well, since that meeting, Gene called me at my job almost every day, up until June. And we met several times, I guess about seven or eight."

"Where did you meet?" the lieutenant asked.

"Different places; the parking lot at Piscataway High School, the Sears parking lot, place like that."

"And what did you do there?"

"We talked. Gene kept saying that he loved me, and we mainly talked about my testimony and whether or not I would be on his side."

"Okay, Patty," Zimmerman said when it looked as though Bauer was finished, "is there anything else you can think of to tell us?"

"No, just that two public defender investigators came to me recently and wanted to talk to me about all this. They started saying things that I had told Morris Brown, and that really bothered me because I didn't know how they had found out about it."

Bauer also told the detectives the story she had been told by her husband, about the two public defender investigators posing as county detectives to get him to talk. Zimmerman promised that he would look into it, and that he would mention it to Mr. Kapsak.

"Patty," Zimmerman added, "we've spoken several times over the past year, why are you telling us all this now, with the trial starting next week?"

"Well, like I said, I told all this to Morris Brown, and when the public defender investigators confronted me with it, I figured everybody knew and I just wanted to make sure that I discussed it with you."

"Also," she said, grinning sheepishly, "I didn't tell you this stuff because I loved Gene. But lately, my conscience has been bothering me about keeping it from you. I just couldn't do it anymore."

September 11, 1984

A total of 569 incidents of domestic violence were reported in Middlesex County during 1983, but on this day, Second Middlesex County Assistant Prosecutor Thomas Kapsak could concern himself with only one: the murder of Catherine Neal Warner.

After two days of jury selection, Kapsak would begin presenting his case to a jury at 9 a.m. the next day; on his shoulders would fall the arduous task of explaining the State's highly circumstantial and somewhat complex case against Eugene Thomas Berta, and then convincing the panel of seven men and five women that the evidence gathered by the State indeed proved beyond a reasonable doubt that Eugene Berta deliberately and in cold blood murdered Catherine Warner.

Sitting at his desk piled high with reports, photographs and amid pieces of evidence, Kapsak patiently outlined his presentation on a yellow legal pad. Points of importance were inscribed in red ink, everything else was jotted down in blue.

For Kapsak and the county investigators, it had been a long 14 months since Cathy Warner's body was discovered in her bathtub; 14 months characterized by the disappointment of false leads and the euphoria of bonafide breakthroughs. And for Tom Kapsak, the last several months was a time of false starts and frustration generated by two trial postponements at the behest of Gene Berta's defense counsel, Bradley Ferencz.

But opening statements would start the next morning, when Kapsak would tell the jury why the State believed Eugene Thomas Berta, the Man of The Year, father of five, murdered Catherine Neal Warner.

Brad Ferencz also had his opening statement on his mind. For him, it had been a hectic nine months, but he thought he had finally been able to mount an effective defense. He kept reminding himself that he did not have to prove Berta's innocence, he merely had to plant the seeds of doubt in the jurors' minds.

His premise would be that Cathy Warner's affections were not necessarily exclusive to Gene Berta, and that she had in fact seen other men in the months preceding her death, including, possibly, several policemen. Any one of those men, Ferencz would argue, could have been her killer.

In addition, Ferencz thought he could get the jury to believe that the police were lackadaisical in their investigation, quickly focusing in on Berta and neglecting to thoroughly search for the facts.

Beyond that, he had a witness who swore she saw Cathy Warner alive on July 11th, as well as a neighbor who said she saw lights on in an upstairs room of Warner's house on July 12th and 13th.

Ferencz was somewhat confident that his forensic expert's report, buttressed by the findings of the county medical examiner, would suffice to overcome whatever effect Dr. Werner Spitz, the State's "hired gun", would have on the jury.

Ferencz' real concern at this point was Pat Bauer. He would have to convince the jury that she played fast and loose with the facts and could not be trusted.

Ferencz felt he could do that by comparing what she had told his investigators, and the county detectives, in the beginning of the investigation, with what she had said lately. The defense attorney thought he could introduce enough contradictions in her testimony to discredit Bauer in the eyes of the jury.

Strategy-wise, Ferencz had been somewhat effective up until now. He had managed to win two trial date postponements, and had been granted most of the discovery he had demanded from the prosecution. He was a little concerned, however, about the abuse he had suffered at the hands of Judge Hoffman. His effort to have the judge recuse himself failed, as he had expected, so Ferencz felt he had to tread carefully, lest he once again incur the wrath of Hoffman. A routine last minute motion to dismiss the indictment against Berta was also denied.

Ferencz leaned back in his chair and let his eyes wander over one wall in his office. His gaze settled on a wooden plaque hanging there. Softly, he read aloud its inscription, "Reasonable Doubt for a Reasonable Price."

Judgment

September 12, 1984

Second Assistant Prosecutor Thomas Kapsak rose from his chair at the prosecution table in Superior Court Judge Barnett Hoffman's courtroom. Slowly approaching the lectern which faced the seated jurors, holding his yellow legal pad of notes in both hands before him like an offering, Kapsak did not smile as he surveyed the jury of 10 men and six women, which included four alternates. He spent several seconds flipping through and arranging his notes, then introduced himself to the jury.

The murder of Catherine Neal Warner, Kapsak began, speaking slowly and clearly, "is a classic murder mystery. It had to be solved step-by-step by police, and it was. In a sense, each of you will be solving it yourselves and reaching your own conclusions in your deliberations."

Greed, Kapsak said, was one of the prime motivators behind the killing of Catherine Neal Warner by Eugene T. Berta. The second assistant prosecutor then noted that Warner had received $100,000 from her late husband's insurance policy, and that she was receiving $1,000 a month from the sale of his gas station.

"Gene Berta lived in a squalid, dilapidated house," Kapsak pointed out, by way of comparison, adding that the defendant was in debt and on welfare.

Kapsak then recounted the pertinent events of the past year, beginning with the discovery of Cathy Warner's body by her father and brother.

As soon as the county medical examiner determined that Warner had died of a gunshot wound to the head, Kapsak said, police had to "determine how she was killed, when she was killed, where she was killed and by whom."

The second assistant prosecutor then briefly summarized the major pieces of circumstantial evidence that led to the arrest of Gene Berta: mainly Warner's day/date watch and her habits of crossing off the prior day on her calendar and of speaking to some of her friends almost daily.

Although Middlesex County Medical Examiner Dr. Marvin Shuster estimated that Cathy Warner was killed on July 14th, Kapsak said, Dr. Shuster did admit that he could not be totally accurate because of the condition of the body and because of the fact that the entomologist's report had not yet been completed. As an alternative, Kapsak said, he turned to Dr. Werner Spitz, who, Kapsak told the jury, was the "best medical examiner in the country."

Kapsak recounted how the investigators talked to Warner's family and friends — including the defendant — finally determining that Gene Berta was the last one to see her, and that he had the motive, means and opportunity to kill her, Kapsak theorized, following an argument begun when she found out that not only was he taking another woman on a trip to Minnesota that Cathy Warner had arranged and had financed, but also that all her dreams of marrying him were based on nothing but his lies.

"When he picked her up at work that Friday and drove her home, Cathy found out that she was not going to Minnesota with Berta and that she was not going to marry him," the prosecutor said. "There was an emotional explosion that resulted in her murder."

The assistant prosecutor told the jury that the witnesses he would bring before them would, in more detail, prove beyond a reasonable doubt that Eugene Berta did murder Catherine Warner.

Thirty minutes after he had introduced himself, Thomas Kapsak collected his notes and silently walked back to his seat at the prosecution table.

"Mr. Berta is innocent until he is proven guilty. And the State won't do that," Deputy Public Defender Bradley Ferencz declared at the beginning of his remarks.

During his statement, Ferencz showed himself to be more exuberant and animated than his adversary. "I would just like you all to understand that Mr. Berta is coming here, saying, 'Wait a minute, what the prosecutor is saying is not totally true.' "

Ferencz suggested that the jury listen for "lapses and gaps" in the State's case against Berta.

"As you listen to the testimony, try to figure out why he would kill her, then take her check and deposit it in his account," the defense attorney said. "The prosecution says that Mr. Berta told her at some point they would go to Minnesota. Cathy Warner's friend, Donna Tokar, told us that on the night of the 7th, Cathy called her and said she was going to visit her sister."

Ferencz also took aim at Kapsak's use of Werner Spitz.

"Why would the State want to use another medical examiner?" he asked. "What's wrong with the one that had been used for case after case after case? I'll tell you. Because before the State decided that the murderer was Berta, the county medical examiner said that the date of Mrs. Warner's death was the 14th. Mr. Berta was down the shore on that day, so the State said, 'Let's find someone else'.

"The State also said that Mrs. Warner was last seen on July 8. We have a witness who said that she saw her on Monday, the 11th," Ferencz continued. "The testimony of one woman states that she saw lights on in the Warner home on the evenings of the 12th and 13th."

Ferencz walked over to his client and motioned for him to stand. The Gene Berta the jury saw was quite different from the one who had been arrested 13 months before. This day, he wore his hair short and neat, his beard trimmed. Replacing his coveralls was a pale blue leisure suit.

Looking back toward the jury and pointing to his client, Ferencz said, "You have to know about him, you have to understand him and you can't hold against him the fact that he was having a relationship with more than one woman. Please consider things you didn't hear, gaps, things that don't add up. Don't compound the tragedy of Mrs. Warner's death with the tragedy of convicting an innocent man."

His attorney's remarks completed, Gene Berta eased back into his seat, his eyes on the jurors, his face betraying no emotion.

Kapsak's called his first three witnesses — Cathy's father, Richard Neal; Metuchen Police Sergeant Pasquale Sardone and Middlesex County Detective John Haley — to paint for the jury a picture of the events of July 16, 1983.

In general, Kapsak used representatives from various law enforcement agencies – including the county Prosecutor's Office, Metuchen Police, New Jersey State Police, and the Federal Bureau of Investigation – to set the scene of the murder for the jury, and to introduce and identify the various pieces of evidence taken during the month-long investigation.

Kapsak would use a number of Cathy Warner's friends and co-workers to demonstrate the depth of Warner's largely unrequited love for Gene Berta.

Richard Neal's difficulty in speaking cast some doubt as to whether he could be heard by the jury and the court stenographer. In a discussion among Kapsak, Ferencz and Hoffman prior to the start of Neal's testimony, two solutions were posed, the first being that Neal would be provided with a microphone to amplify his voice, and the second that a "translator" – a certified interpreter for the deaf, skilled in signing and lip reading – would be brought in to interpret what he said. After a short test with a microphone, during which Neal answered some general questions from Kapsak, Judge Hoffman decided that the microphone should be sufficient. He did ask, however, that the translator secured by the State, Maryanna Jacobsen, remain in the courtroom in case she was needed.

Neal, his testimony made more dramatic by his emotion and difficulty in speaking, related to the jury the telephone call that had alarmed his wife, and how he and his son, Gary, had driven to his daughter Cathy Warner's house and tried to get in through the front, side and back doors. He testified about telling the policeman who responded that something was wrong and they had to get in the house. The policeman hesitated, Neal recalled, after which Neal suggested that they break in through a cellar door.

Kapsak asked Neal what happened after his son Gary opened the kitchen door.

"He opened the back door. The police officer followed him. I followed the police officer and they headed for upstairs. I started to follow them, but then I heard the back neighbor, Mr. Jones, I believe, he followed in the back door, too ... I started to go (upstairs), but then I heard Mr. Jones go into the downstairs bathroom. I had forgotten all about that, that the bathroom was off the kitchen, so I turned around and Mr. Jones had opened the bathroom door and was standing there. So, I went over and he passed me and went outside. I continued into the bathroom and I pulled back the shower curtain ..."

But the memory was too painful for the frail man. His voice broke, and he choked back the tears, closing his eyes tightly, as he struggled to retain his composure.

"Just take your time, Mr. Neal," Judge Hoffman said softly.

"... and there was Cathy." A year had passed, but the pain Richard Neal felt on July 16, 1983 was as fresh as the day he first suffered it.

"After you saw Cathy in the bathtub, what did you do?" Kapsak asked, after Neal had once again composed himself.

"I couldn't call, so I banged on the wall so the officer would come down. And he come down and took over from there."

During his cross-examination, Brad Ferencz asked when Neal first remembered speaking to Jones on July 16. Neal answered that Jones approached them while they were outside and said Cathy was on vacation, but Neal disregarded him and told the officer he wanted to go in.

"Did he say anything else to you?" Ferencz asked.

"Not that I recall."

"Did he say that he was talking to her on Thursday to you?"

Neal admitted that it was possible, but added that he did not recall it. Ferencz then gave him a copy of the statement made to Zimmerman to refresh his memory, after which Neal said that yes, Jones had made that statement to him.

Ferencz asked if Jones was drunk on the 16th. Neal replied that he couldn't remember.

"Mr. Neal," Ferencz asked at one point, "do you remember the day your daughter had a car accident shortly before her death?"

"Yes, I remember it," Neal answered.

"Do you remember her telling you (that the officer who investigated the accident) used to frequent her house on a friendly basis?"

"I heard her say he was over there, that's all."

"You remember telling the prosecutor that, because you thought ... the officer would necessarily have a gun?"

"I was asked if I knew of anybody that carried firearms."

"Who knew your daughter?"

"Correct."

Metuchen Police Sergeant Pasquale Sardone was next to take the stand, describing, through answers to Kapsak's questions, the events of July 16, 1983.

Sardone recounted how he told the Neal's to leave the house, then called the death in to headquarters and requested that the Prosecutor's Office be called. He also said he went into the back yard and dispersed a group of neighbors who had gathered there.

Jones, Sardone testified, was known to the police as the town drunk. He had been in and out of the municipal lockup a number of times for being drunk and disorderly, Sardone said.

"Can you describe (Mr. Jones') physical size, if you will?" Kapsak asked. He wanted to show the jury that it would have been physically impossible for Jones to carry Cathy Warner's dead body up a flight of stairs.

"He's about 5'4", maybe 150 pounds, grayish hair ... about 52, 54," Sardone answered.

Kapsak's next witness was Detective John Haley, an identifications officer with the prosecutor's office. Haley, who came on late in the afternoon, and would be called upon again later in the trial, was used to identify a number of items that were found in Cathy Warner's house on July 16, 1983.

Included in Haley's presentation were the chair, wooden door and plywood that were found in Warner's basement. Haley pointed out the nick in the chair and the hole in the wood; all caused, he said, by a bullet.

September 13, 1984

Kapsak wasted no time in confronting the jury and courtroom spectators with the horror of Cathy Warner's murder. With Detective John Haley once again on the stand, and first ensuring that the Neals had left the courtroom, Kapsak asked that the lights be dimmed. He then proceeded to show gruesome color slides of the victim and the crime scene, asking Haley to identify what was represented in each slide. From time to time, Kapsak would interrupt Haley's narrative by introducing into evidence something recovered from Warner's home and ask the detective to identify it.

The slides — wide angle and close-up views of Cathy Warner's body as it appeared on July 16, 1983 — violently assaulted the sensibilities of nearly everyone in the courtroom. Up to this point, a decomposing body had been just an abstract notion to the jury and courtroom spectators; but now, confronted by large color images of a body literally being eaten away by insects, there was no escaping the demoralizing reality of the depths to which humans can sink.

Most of those in attendance managed to stoically fix their gazes on the brutality on that screen, as though they felt that by confronting the horror, they could overcome it; but there were some who had to escape it, although the means to that escape consisted of tightly shutting one's eyes.

In stark contrast were the reactions of the courtroom "professionals", to whom scenes like what was being shown had long since ceased to stir any extreme reactions. Haley and Kapsak, in particular, approached the photos from a clinical standpoint, Kapsak asking questions matter-of-factly, and Haley answering in kind.

These slides, and others like them, would be shown several more times during the course of the trial. And although their impact was lessened with each viewing, there were still some in the courtroom who could not bring themselves to look.

Before Kapsak began showing the slides, Judge Hoffman told Ferencz and Berta that they could move to a better position if they could not see the screen, which was set up across the courtroom from the jury box.

Ferencz emphatically shook his head. "I've seen them, your Honor, thank you."

The defense attorney had initially objected to the slides, calling them "disgusting" and "really gross." Earlier in the summer, during pre-trial motions, he had even hired the services of a behavioral psychologist in an unsuccessful attempt to persuade Judge Hoffman to not allow Kapsak to use the photos. It was the psychologist's theory that a jury exposed to such horrifying scenes would forget what they had heard immediately before and after the showing, and instead focus on the victim.

The impact on the jury of Kapsak's slide show was immediately apparent; the courtroom was stone silent when the lights were brightened, but a petite brunette juror was seen wiping tears from her eyes.

After the showing of the slides was concluded, Kapsak asked Haley to identify several more pieces of evidence taken from the Warner house. Included were her bank records, pieces of flooring, several years' worth of calendars which showed every day marked off, up through and including July 7, 1983, and Cathy Warner's Timex watch.

Kapsak also had Haley identify the various guns that were found in Berta's home, as well as all the ammunition that went with them. It was Kapsak's intention to show that Gene Berta was not unfamiliar with guns.

Also introduced at this time were a slew of photographs taken outside and within the Warner house by Haley, showing 125 Durham Avenue as it appeared on the day Cathy Warner's body was discovered, as well as photos taken of Gene Berta's Metuchen home.

It was one of Ferencz's intentions to show that Cathy Warner did, indeed visit her sister Mary Beth on July 8th. To prove that, he handed Haley an Amtrak schedule found in Cathy Warner's purse on July 16.

In describing it, Haley said the schedule was outdated, in that it had expired in April of 1983.

Asking Haley to open the schedule, Ferencz requested that he "tell the jury from where to where that train schedule runs; that is, ... where the farthest point north is and where the farthest point south is?"

"It appears that it runs from Boston-Providence to Washington," Haley answered.

"Now, officer, do you see any marks on that first page?"

"I see a small mark right over here," he replied, pointing to the top middle of the page.

"And what is it next to?"

"Right next to it it says, '406, 254 Metro Park, New Jersey, Iselin'."

"And if you follow that along, could you turn to the next page? See another mark?"

"Yes sir ... it's just to the left of Metro Park, New Jersey, Iselin."

Through questioning, Ferencz had Haley point out two more marks on two subsequent pages, each of which was next to "Metro Park, New Jersey, Iselin."

Dwelling on the second page, Ferencz asked, "Are there any other marks on that page?"

"It's under column 187, 'The Independence'," Haley answered.

"And what is 'The Independence', if you know?"

"Well, according to the schedule, that's the name of the train. And then when I follow that down, it says, 'R 6:56 p'."

Turning to the next page, Ferencz drew Haley's attention to another mark made next to a notation for "Metro Park, New Jersey, Iselin".

"To the right of that column, it says '9:12 p'," Haley said, in response to a question from the defense attorney.

"Nine-twelve p.m.," Ferencz corrected. "What else?"

"Three columns to the right of that, it says 10:58 p."

"If you go straight up is there a name of a train?"

"Yes. Around the first mark, that 9:12 p., the 'Merchant's Limited'."

"And around the next one?"

"The next one is the 'Benjamin Franklin'."

"If you look very quickly there, just to complete it, tell the jury if you see any other marks."

"I see a small dot here next to 'Springfield, Maryland', just to the left of it."

Ferencz then went on to confirm that Haley had found the Amtrak schedule in Cathy Warner's purse, "And this schedule has circled, Metro Park, or has a line by Metro Park and has circled the times or the numbers to 2:12 p.m., to 12 p and 10:58 p, is that correct?"

"Yes, sir."

Ferencz next turned his attention to the other pieces of evidence to which Haley had earlier testified, especially the guns found in Berta's home. Through questioning, he had Haley admit that none of the rifles or shotguns were thought to be the murder weapon, and, in fact, that there was no direct evidence that the firearms even belonged to Gene Berta, other than that they were found in his house.

The second assistant prosecutor's first new witness this day was Dr. Marvin Shuster, the Middlesex County Medical Examiner. It was Kapsak's intention to introduce Shuster's findings — that Catherine Warner had been killed an estimated two to four days before her body was found — then have the medical examiner admit that he could have been mistaken.

After having Shuster admitted as an expert witness, Kapsak set about asking him questions about the autopsy of Cathy Warner. As he would for the majority of his witnesses, Kapsak remained seated during his questioning of the doctor.

"Can you tell us in more detail about your external examination of the body, please?" Kapsak asked.

"Yes, the body looked to my eye well nourished and well developed," Shuster began. "An adult white woman, and her age wasn't too easy to estimate; I figured by the configuration of the body more than anything else that she was between 20 and 30 years of age. She had an advanced state of decomposition generally on the body, and there was quite a foul odor because of that decomposition. Rigor mortis was absent at the time I saw her and we looked for what is called a line of lividity, that is a line of settling of the blood and because the color changes due to the decomposition, that wasn't readily ascertained. I couldn't tell a line of lividity."

"What would be the value of determining a line of lividity?"

"A number of things; it helps one in determining the time interval between death time and the time you see the body and also tells you the position the body was in for a given time following death."

"And also you mentioned, what was your testimony, a lack of rigidity?"

"Lack of rigor mortis, rigidity, yes."

"What is the significance of that?"

"Again, it's an adjunctive help in determining the interval, postmortem interval."

"Well, if you would have discovered rigor mortis, what would that have told you?"

"That we were probably dealing with a death within 36 hours, given some other help with that in terms of body build, temperature, environment, condition of the body."

"Did (the lack of rigor mortis) tell you any more than that with regard to time of death?"

"Well, let me go back over that. I said that given normal circumstances in terms of temperature and body build and things like that, 36 hours would have been a reasonable outside limit. Given changes in the atmosphere, for instance, rigor mortis can come and pass off in a considerably shorter period of time, so that we are saying that, I listed 72 hours as being a good estimate of outside time ... the shortest period of time that rigidity would have disappeared totally given a normal temperature, that is ambient temperature of around 70 degrees.

"In addition to the fact that I couldn't find a line of lividity, and I did notice that she had what is called bloating, that is swelling of the tissues, and on touching various parts of the body, there was a spongy feel to it that is usually due to the fact that the decomposition that is occurring occurs because of bacterial action and as this happens, gas is produced by bacterial action within the tissue, and we get what's called subcutaneous emphysema, that's the medical term, and she had this rather extensively.

"In addition to the body, generally there were discolorations that we call marbleization, and that is a discoloration due to the breakdown of blood in the blood vessels underneath the skin's surface, and as the tissue absorbs the broken down blood pigment, it gets a streaky or marbleized sort of appearance and a generalized greenish-gray discoloration variously depending on how much decomposition has occurred ... You can see it well established at 48 hours."

"Does it disappear?"

"No, it stays and gets worse."

"So, what would your conclusion be as to what that told you about the time of death?"

"That she was dead probably more than the 48 hours.

"In addition to the changes of the body that I've already noted, there was what we call skin slippage, another part of deterioration or decomposition of the body. The tissues get infiltrated by fluid that seeps out of the blood vessels and the top surface of the skin starts to peel, and as you touch the body in this condition, it slips away and actually you are left with the under or deeper surface of the skin. That is also about 48 hours. It gets worse with time and as decomposition proceeds and becomes more generalized and more established more of the body gets affected by the skin slippage, so you may see it primarily on areas where the skin is rather delicate and thin, for instance on the forearms or on the chest, and where the skin is tougher, on the face, on the elbows, on the knee area, on the feet, it takes longer for this to happen.

"She also had some drying change of the fingers, they looked rather hard and dry and almost, I said mummified in the report. In addition to that, she had a lot of animal activity about the body and that was in the form of many, many maggots, fly embryos or caterpillar kinds of things, and these were literally all over the body, but especially close to the body openings, body orifices, and she also had newly deposited fly eggs on various parts of the body, most particularly on the hands.

"At that point, I made collections of these maggots and eggs trying to get representative numbers. There were different size maggots, small ones, medium and large ones, and I tried to select a representative sampling of the maggots and also of the egg cases for analysis in terms of assisting with establishing time of death."

"And what did you do with those items?"

"Put them in fixatives so that it killed them and preserved them and then gave them to an entomologist, that's a scientist who deals with insects, in order to identify the bug or the insect that was the source of both the eggs and the maggots, and also to help in determining the age of them and find out when the eggs were laid."

At that point, Kapsak introduced into evidence two glass vials, each of which were filled with maggots of various sizes. Shuster identified the vials as the ones he had prepared during the Warner autopsy.

"In addition to those findings," Shuster continued, "we noted that there was a large hole on the front of the face below the left eye or where the eye would have been — actually both eyeballs had been digested away or were not present probably as a result of maggot activity in the area — but there was a hole about one inch in diameter beneath the left eye, and this could easily be probed with a finger and encountered a number of fragments of bone. On the back of the head, beneath the left ear canal, there was a hole in the scalp which was about a quarter of an inch in diameter, and below this, after we dissected the area, we found a lot of hemorrhage or bleeding into the scalp tissue for a three-inch diameter zone around that hole, and immediately below the hole in the scalp, the skull had a generally round hole about three-eighths of an inch in diameter which looked like a bullet hole of entry. The wound on the front of the face, under the left eye, had the characterization of an exit wound of a bullet-type."

After noting the watch and other jewelry Cathy Warner was wearing, Shuster said, "The breasts were bloated out, and, again, there was erosion of the nipples; again, that was maggot activity eating away the flesh. On the back of the body, there was some peculiar marks that I didn't know the source of, but they looked like small, blue circles and some of them had additionally smaller circles on either side, so there were round circles and then there were round circles with two dots on either side. These seemed to be almost a stain of some sort within the body, but they were very irregular.

They seemed to be on the skin surface, but they could not be wiped away."

Kapsak then asked Shuster for his estimation on the time of Cathy Warner's death.

"I had estimated that she had died on the fourteenth of July, three days before."

"Did you take into consideration, in reaching that conclusion, the results ..."

"Objection," Ferencz bellowed, half rising out of his chair. "I ask the question be, what did you take into consideration."

"I don't think that the particular question as it's phrased, so much as I've heard, necessarily suggests an answer, and that would be the guise of a leading question," Judge Hoffman said. "The objection is overruled."

Thus vindicated, Kapsak repeated his question.

"Did you take into consideration the results of the entomological examination which you had initiated?"

"No," Shuster answered, "I did not, because the eggs and the larvae were not submitted to the entomologist for some days after the autopsy and after I had prepared the death certificate."

"If you had gotten the results of the entomological examination and it differed with your conclusion, would you have changed it or would you have stayed with the same conclusion, or what would your reaction have been?"

"I would have changed it to a longer time."

Satisfied that he had made the impression he sought, Kapsak turned his witness over to Ferencz.

After having Shuster reaffirm that he was the head of the county Medical Examiner's office, and had been for 13 years, Ferencz introduced into evidence Shuster's autopsy report.

"Now in writing a report, an autopsy report, doctor, I would assume that you want to include in it all of those items which in the future may be important in determining the time of death?"

"Well, yes and no," Shuster answered. "We frequently do not."

"Well, I would assume, and correct me if I'm wrong, that it's your responsibility to fill out an autopsy report as clearly as possible?"

"That's correct."

"So, I would assume that you want to be as clear as possible and put as many of your findings down as you can recall because you may be called to testify a year or two years later?"

"That's correct . . ."

After having Shuster identify several photographs taken from Dr. Werner Spitz' book, "Medicolegal Investigation of Death", Ferencz asked, "You had no idea what this case was about when you had the body sitting in front of you, is that correct?"

"I don't know what you mean by 'no idea'."

"You had no idea of what the State's theory of the case was?"

"No, I did not."

"You had no idea of any statements it may have collected?"

"I did not."

"And you actually had, if you will, the body in front of you?"

"That's correct."

"And you estimated the time of death as the fourteenth?"

"That's correct."

Having made his point, Ferencz relinquished the witness.

Kapsak was not finished, however, He wanted, through redirect questioning, to emphasize that estimating a time of death is no easy matter.

"Is it a relatively easy part of your job to estimate time of death?" he asked.

"It's probably one of the hardest," Shuster admitted.

"Have you ever been wrong before in estimating time of death?"

"I certainly have, yes."

That was too much for Ferencz.

"Objection, your honor. Assumes in there, admits he's wrong."

"Objection is sustained," Hoffman ruled.

Kapsak rephrased the question.

"Have you ever been wrong in estimating the time of death?"

"Yes."

Kapsak's next witness was Dr. Louis Vasvary, the Rutgers University entomologist who studied the flies, fly eggs and maggots found on and around Cathy Warner's body. Now that Kapsak had gotten Shuster to admit that he had been wrong about estimating the time of death in other cases, and that he would have changed his estimation had he seen the entomologist's report, the second assistant prosecutor would use Vasvary's testimony to help prove the State's contention that Cathy Warner was killed about eight days before her body was found, not the four days that Shuster had estimated.

After having Vasvary accepted as an expert witness, Kapsak first asked him to identify the two vials he had earlier introduced.

"Can you tell us how long it takes the fly to get to the decomposing flesh after the human or animal dies, if you can?"

"Well, generally they are attracted to fluids originally, perhaps around the eye or within the nose or mouth, those would be the areas that would be first involved, and, of course, the fly ultimately would have to seek out this particular location. They are also very common in wounds and things or areas where flesh had started to become necrotic or dead."

"Assuming that there is an open wound, how long, if you can tell us, does it take the flies to get to that wound?"

"Well, it depends on the specific location of the site. Outdoors, generally during spring and summer and fall months, it's a matter of a very short period of time, generally within minutes or perhaps hours, but the flies have the ability to seek out this particular type of site and the interval of its exposure to when the flies deposit their eggs is generally not too long. Under other conditions, however, it could be longer."

"Well, for instance, in a closed and locked house ... well, let me ask you this, do these flies infest houses when there is no rotting flesh; are they in everybody's house?"

"Only purely by chance, if one would leave the door open or if there happened to be a window open, of course, they could fly in, but generally they are a cumbersome-type flying insect, so they are very easy to swat or to control, but generally they are not commonly found in homes."

"All right, assuming then they are not in the home and a home is locked up tight, windows and doors, how long does it take them to get into that house?"

"Until they could find an opening that would be large enough to accommodate their bodies, I guess I really couldn't give you anything from my experience or from my reading that would indicate a time factor."

"When the fly reaches rotting flesh, what does it do?"

"Deposits eggs."

"The fly itself does not eat at the flesh?"

"It may imbibe in, I guess, what would be any mucous or liquids that would be present, but does not nibble or bite into flesh, their mouths are not so constructed that they would consume flesh."

"How then does the fly eventually consume the flesh?"

"The adult fly does not consume the flesh, it's the immature state or maggot, and the fly deposits its egg or group of eggs on the area that ultimately will become attacked by the maggots."

"Do they lay their eggs under water?"

"No, to my knowledge, they do not go under water to deposit their eggs."

At that point, noting that the hour was drawing late, Hoffman asked Dr. Vasvary to return the following day, then recessed the court.

September 14, 1984

Thomas Kapsak resumed with Dr. Louis Vasvary, allowing the entomologist to continue with his lesson on the life cycle of the maggot.

"Once the flies do get to the body," Kapsak asked, "what happens?"

"Generally, they go seek a location where there is some fluid, body fluid or in the event there happens to be some necrotic area (where the tissue has already started to break down) or blood, they will deposit eggs in or adjacent to that site."

"Well, does that happen immediately when a living organism dies? I mean, within minutes or hours?"

"It could be, depending upon the conditions under which the body is found, temperature is important. It could be at least a matter of hours."

After the fly lays the eggs, which could number anywhere from 75 to 150, Vasvary testified, the eggs go through an incubation period where they hatch into the larval stage, "that feeds on this fluid or decomposing matter."

"How long does it take for the egg to hatch into the first larval stage?"

"The hatching time is dependent on temperature. There have been studies done to indicate that in an optimum temperature of 99 degrees Fahrenheit, that it would take approximately 8.1 or 8.13 hours or so."

"Well, can you give us some idea of how the time would vary with temperature?"

"From 99 degrees, if the temperature were above 99, there has been studies done, and I can get it more accurately if I can just look here, I believe it was a hundred and three degrees ..." Vasvary paused several moments while he checked notes that he had brought along as an aid to his testimony. "Researcher Melvin found that at a constant temperature of 59 degrees Fahrenheit, it required nearly 52 hours for eggs of this species to hatch, while at a hundred and four degrees Fahrenheit, only 8.7 hours were required. He also found that none of the eggs hatched at a hundred and nine degrees Fahrenheit.

"The optimum temperature for the incubation of eggs appears to be approximately 99 degrees Fahrenheit. With the temperature 8.13 hours are required to complete the incubation."

"So do I understand correctly, then, that the period of time that it could have been would be anywhere from 8.13 hours to 52 hours, depending on the temperature?"

"Yes."

With the help of diagrams he had created for the prosecutor's office, Vasvary further explained that after the egg passes into the first larval stage, it feeds for a period of time — depending on the environmental temperature — then passes on to a second and finally a third, immobile stage before transforming into the common blowfly. Vasvary said the larval stages could take as many as four days to complete, again depending on temperature.

The background completed, Kapsak handed the two vials to Vasvary and asked him to identify them as containing the maggots he was given to study.

"Will you tell us what stages (the maggots) were in in terms of the explanation you just gave us?" Kapsak asked.

"Well, since there were two vials, I labelled them vial one and vial two, and within vial one I found third-stage larvae as well as second-stage larvae, and I believe those were the two that I had, first-, second- and third-stage larvae were found in the first vial.

"The second vial contained the eggs of the blowfly, and the second instar larvae. They did not contain any third-stage larvae."

"And at some point, did you become interested to know whether there were any pupa stage at the scene from which those, excuse me, at the scene from which the body was removed and those larvae taken from the vial?"

"The pupa stage would be the next stage in the life cycle of this particular insect, and of course that would be helpful in determining just the length of time that had transpired. I visited the site with two detectives and I did find some pupa stages, yes."

"Now, after studying the specimens in the vials and in view of your background and training, did you, at our request, attempt to estimate the period of time those specimens had been on the body for us?"

"Taking into account the stage of development that was the oldest and in this particular case the vial one contained third instar or third-stage larvae, and knowing that it takes at least four days of larval activity to reach that point, I did try to make some type of determination as to the length of time that these larvae were associated with the body, yes."

"And did you assume any temperature in trying to make that estimate?"

"I assumed optimum conditions because that had been the only ones that I had been familiar with, yes."

"And would that be a constant 99 degrees?"

"Yes."

"And what was your conclusion?"

"From the standpoint of longevity of the eggs' stage and also the length of time for the larval development, being that we did have final stages of larval development, I judged that these larvae were between four to six days old."

"Based on optimum temperature?"

"Yes, and this, if we were to add the egg stage which, under optimum condition is 8.13, there is some variation, I included another eight hours to 16 hours. From that, I determined that the body became infested at 4.3 or 4.6 days to another period which would be the other extreme, 6.3 or 6.6 days prior to the time that the samples were collected."

At this point, Kapsak asked an associate to hand him a chart depicting low, high and average temperatures for each day of July, 1983.

"And if the temperature during the period of time after the eggs were laid until the specimens were taken and preserved had in fact been or averaged between 75 and 80, would that have affected your estimate?"

"Well, during a lower temperature period, the length of time of egg hatch and larval development would be increased."

"Well, were the samples that you looked at consistent or inconsistent with a period of, say, seven, eight or nine days, assuming, again, 75 or 80 degrees?"

"It could fall within that range, yes."

Satisfied, Kapsak invited Ferencz to cross-examine.

Ferencz knew that this was the weakest part of his case. For all his attempts, the attorney could not find another entomologist to dispute Vasvary's findings.

After asking Vasvary how much of his time is taken up with identifying insects — to which the doctor answered 75 percent — Ferencz honed in on specifics within the entomologist's report.

The report he submitted to the prosecutor, Ferencz asked Vasvary, "indicates 4.3 or 4.6 days to 6.3 or 6.6 days from the time the samples were collected, is that correct?"

"That's my estimate, yes."

"Now, in terms of this optimum temperature, of 99 degrees, hatching occurs after 8.3 hours, is that correct?"

"Yes."

"You do not state anything in the remainder of the report about temperature? You don't indicate what optimum temperature is in the report?"

"No, I don't; no I did not include specifically the optimum temperature."

"How long does it take before a dead body or flesh that's beginning to decay will attract flies; let's put it outside so we don't have the problem with the house."

"Okay, it would be a matter of hours, would be as short as minutes, it depends upon the time of the year, certainly it would be . . ."

"Let's talk summertime?"

"Summertime, it would be a matter of, say, with an hour."

"And by the way, what is it that exactly attracts the fly, if you know?"

"To my knowledge, they are attracted as a result of subtle odors that may be emanating from the particular egg-laying site."

"And if in fact there had been a significant amount of blood that had been spilled in a basement, for example, would that be an attractive scent?"

"Yes, it would."

"And if there was a matter of hours to clean that up, would that be an attractive scent, if it was there for a period of hours?"

"I really don't know, it depends upon how well it was cleaned up, I would imagine, because these insects are very sensitive even to micro amounts of odors, and I would suspect even if there was just a suggestion, that would have flies attracted to it."

Ferencz's strategy was to remove, as best he could, the concept of varying temperatures from the minds of the jury members. His last few questions focused on Vasvary's use of the phrase, "optimum conditions."

"Just judging from the last stage, that is the oldest larvae that you found that was given to you in the sample ... given the best possible temperatures, 8.13 hours for the eggs to hatch, is that what you based your final conclusion on?" he asked.

"Well, there was a temperature, right," Vasvary answered. "That was the optimum conditions, it was 8.13 hours for the eggs to hatch and then from the eggs, you get into your larval stage."

"And how long is that larval stage?"

"As far as from the passing through the three stages, it would take approximately four days."

Ferencz let the jury consider the scientist's answer for several moments before he decided to end his questioning.

Kapsak's next four witnesses — Sgt. Casimir Smerecki and, once again, Det. John Haley from the county detective staff, and medical personnel Ellen Bump from John F. Kennedy Memorial Hospital and Vivian Heany from Muhlenberg Regional Medical Center — were called to the stand to identify evidence.

Smerecki provided more details on some of the physical evidence that was taken from Cathy Warner's house. The sergeant, who was John Haley's supervisor, testified about the several tests he had conducted on the watch found on Cathy Warner's wrist July 16, and the fact they showed it ran for about 48 hours when fully wound, and also went into more detail about the chair and wooden door found in the basement.

Ferencz began his cross-examination by quizzing Smerecki on the value of finding a bullet at a crime scene.

"If (the bullet) is in good shape, you can trace it to a weapon if you can find a weapon, is that correct?" he asked.

"Well, you can identify the bullet as to calibre, the manufacturer of the bullet itself, the lines and grooves that it demonstrates, the twist of the bullet; these are called its rifling characteristics."

"And based on that, a bullet fired from the same gun would have the same grooves?"

"It could be, yes."

"And that is, if you will, pretty common police knowledge, isn't it? That bullets can be traced if they are not too badly destroyed?"

"Yes."

Ferencz moved on to gun ownership. In answering several questions, Smerecki said that after 1968, anyone buying a handgun in New Jersey would have to register it and would also have their fingerprints on file with the State Police.

In his re-direct examination, Kapsak attacked Ferencz's last line of questioning, asking Smerecki if the same rules applied to someone who inherits a handgun. This question must have puzzled the jury, because even though some of Cathy Warner's friends told police that she had inherited a handgun from her late husband John, the jury wouldn't hear anything about it because Kapsak had been prohibited by Judge Hoffman from bringing out that testimony.

"I would think not," Smerecki replied. "I'm not sure, but I don't think it's required."

Haley was recalled to the stand to testify about two rolls of film he had developed, both of which were found on a coffee table in the living room. One roll was in a camera, the other was right next to it.

When developed, the pictures turned out to be of two different weddings. But, Haley noted, there was also a picture of a nude woman. She was not identified.

Ferencz questioned Haley about the brands of cigarettes that were taken from an ashtray in Cathy Warner's living room on the 16th. He noted that while Cathy Warner smoked Merits, there was also another unnamed brand found in the debris.

Through his redirect, Kapsak brought out that during the course of the investigation's first day, several officers were seen by Haley to be smoking in the living room.

Ferencz was incredulous.

"I take it that's normal police procedure, to allow officers to smoke in the house and put their cigarettes out in any available receptacle?" he asked.

"We try not to allow that, no," Haley replied.

"And if you were responsible for securing that crime scene, you would be responsible to make sure that people don't add items that could be mistaken as evidence or take items that are already at the scene and move them or in any way alter the scene, is that correct?"

"Yes."

Ferencz had earlier brought out that during the course of the investigation, and while the crime scene photos were being taken, certain items in the house had been moved around.

Bump and Heany were called to testify about Cathy Warner's blood type, using blood donor cards from their respective hospitals as a reference.

Through Haley and Smerecki's testimony, the jurors learned that several pieces of the house, including part of the basement floor, stairs and part of a wall alongside the basement stairs, held what appeared to be blood stains and droplets of blood. Upon chemical examination, the blood was found to be A-Positive, which, Heany and Bump testified, was Cathy Warner's blood type.

Gloria Neal was next on the stand. Kapsak called her to identify several samples of Cathy Warner's handwriting, as well as to describe a habit she had unwittingly passed on to her daughter.

From the moment she took the stand, Mrs. Neal, a round-faced, soft spoken woman, did not move her eyes from Gene Berta. She made no attempt to disguise the hate in her gaze.

The jury got its first inkling of Gloria Neal's attitude toward Gene Berta when Kapsak asked her if she and her husband went to Cathy Warner's house every time they were invited.

"No," she said. "We were invited and Mr. Berta was there and we didn't care to go."

Gloria Neal said she and her husband weren't even aware their daughter had bought a house until about a year after she had. She said Cathy invited them over to see the work she was doing on it.

"In 1983, and before that time, were you aware of any particular habit she had with regard to calendars?" Kapsak asked.

"Evidently, she did the same thing that I did, which was to cross off the days."

"Well, were you specifically aware yourself, did you have personal knowledge while she was doing that?"

"No."

"What was your habit or custom with regard to calendars?"

"In the morning, after I'd fix our juice and coffee, I'd cross off the day before," she said.

"For how long have you been doing that?"

"Thirty years."

"Did Catherine ever say anything to indicate to you that she was aware that you were keeping the calendar in the way that you suggested?"

"Yeah. She used to kid me about it." The memory brought a smile to Mrs. Neal's lips. "She would say things to me like, 'Well, when do you expect to get out?' Meaning that you've seen it in the movies that prisoners do it, crossing off the days."

Mrs. Neal made a point of looking at Gene Berta as she made that last statement, as if telling him that she expected him to soon be doing the same thing.

After having Gloria Neal identify two notes as having been written by her daughter, Kapsak read them to the jury: they were the "To Do" list and the preparatory notes she made on the flight to Minnesota, both of which were found on her kitchen table.

In his cross-examination, Ferencz concentrated on Gloria Neal's knowledge of Cathy's calendar habit.

"Up until the prosecutor showed you the calendars," he asked, "you had never seen your daughter cross off dates, is that correct?"

"Not to my recollection," she replied.

Ferencz called Mrs. Neal's attention to the statement she had given Zimmerman, in which she mentioned that she had had a conversation with Cathy about the man who lived behind her, specifically, about how he used to follow her into her house, uninvited.

"He used to follow her, but I understand he did that with the woman who owned the house before," she said. "He was in, like, a habit."

"And you indicated that you did not go over to the house in Metuchen very much because you didn't like Mr. Berta, is that correct?" Ferencz asked.

"We didn't know when he would be there, and we didn't want to cause any problems. It was a bone of contention."

"Basically, your daughter wanted to continue seeing Mr. Berta, and you didn't want her to see him?"

"Basically we argued about it, and in order not to have the arguments and have a peaceful time, we did not mention him."

"And this goes back for quite some time ... back into the 70s, as a matter of fact, right?"

"The first time I met him was at least 10 years ago, yes."

September 17, 1984

Kapsak's first witness this day was Donald Wells, the New Jersey regional manager from Arnold Bakery, who testified to the earliest possible purchase date of the hamburger and hot dog rolls found scattered around Cathy Warner's car the day her body was discovered.

Wells repeated what he had told Kapsak earlier in the year, that based upon the date stamped on the bags' "quick-lock" tags, those rolls would not have been on store shelves until July 15th.

Ferencz pointed out that, according to the report filed by Det. Watson, Wells said the rolls would have been available on the 14th. Wells replied that he could not have said that, based upon the tags he was shown.

The second assistant prosecutor followed Wells' testimony with Thomas Moorefield, a fingerprint specialist from the FBI, and three New Jersey State Police lab technicians.

Moorefield, the technician who tested the fingerprint samples sent to him by Det. Haley, recounted his findings, including that prints found on dinner plates and the downstairs toilet bowl lid were matched with samples provided of Gene Berta. Moorefield also testified that about 15 prints were not identified, including some lifted from the downstairs bathroom wall, the washing machine and the downstairs sink.

So that the jury would not miss anything, Ferencz spent some time reviewing all of the FBI technician's findings, pausing only to confirm that Moorefield had been supplied with all of Gene Berta's fingerprints.

The three State Police Laboratory technicians — Phillip Beasly, Christine Pringle and Stephen Andrews — testified to the procedures used in testing the blood and hair samples submitted by the Prosecutor's Office.

Kapsak's main witness for the day, Dr. Werner Spitz, was scheduled to take the stand later in the afternoon. Spitz's testimony would be used to cast further doubt on the findings of Dr. Marvin Shuster, the Middlesex County Medical Examiner.

Before Spitz was called, however, Kapsak recalled Det. John Haley to introduce and identify more photographs that were taken at the scene on the day Cathy Warner's body was found.

It was now time for Kapsak to cross his first major hurdle to winning a conviction from this jury. The bailiff called Dr. Werner Spitz, and several minutes later a bespeckled, white-haired gentleman entered the courtroom and confidently made his way to the witness box.

Kapsak spent some time reviewing Spitz's credentials, partly as a matter of procedure, but mainly for the benefit of the jury. Dr. Werner Spitz had been Chief Medical Examiner for Wayne County, Michigan — which includes Detroit and its suburbs — since 1972. He claimed to have personally conducted an estimated 50,000 autopsies during his career, the majority of which were on homicide victims. Spitz served on the 1975 and 1978 Vice-Presidential committees which investigated the assassination of President John F. Kennedy, had authored 73 forensic journal articles, and was also the chief editor of "Medicolegal Investigation of Death," considered the foremost textbook in forensic pathology.

Spitz's authority on the subject established, Kapsak began his direct questioning.

"After studying the photographs, the autopsy report and the entomology report in particular (which Kapsak had sent to Spitz earlier in the summer), did you reach a conclusion concerning the time of death of the victim shown in the photographs?" the second assistant prosecutor asked.

"My conclusion was that this deceased, in the bathtub, was dead approximately eight days," Spitz answered, in a slight German accent. "It was my opinion that this individual was in the basement in a certain place where there is a big stain depicting the outline of the body for a certain length of time, until such time as there was staining on the floor in that area, and that subsequently the body was taken upstairs into the bathtub where the body was in the water for the rest of the time. Taking into consideration the degree of decomposition, the changes in the body at the time of autopsy, the infestation with insects, it was my opinion that this body was dead for about eight days."

Kapsak then walked to the evidence table and removed several blown up photographs of the body and crime scene that had been testified to earlier. These were also enlargements of the photos Kapsak had originally sent to Spitz.

A large chalkboard on a wooden frame was then brought out placed in front of the evidence table. It was on that board that Kapsak would display the pictures.

"All right, Dr. Spitz," he resumed. "I'm going to place these photographs on the board one at a time and ask you to explain to the jury how each of them helped you to reach your conclusion, if you will please."

Kapsak displayed the first picture, that of Cathy Warner's body in her bathtub. Spitz, after asking permission to do so, left his seat and walked over to the board, removing a pen from his jacket pocket with which to point.

"This is, this is the body in the bathtub," Spitz began. "The water has seeped out of the bathtub a little bit, as is noted by the ring around, some of it may also have been due to evaporation.

"There is a lot of gas formation in the whiteish parts of the body but it is evident that they too are already decomposing to a significant extent as noted by areas of discoloration on these areas and in particular in the area of the face.

"The hands are dark brown and the hands are dark brown because they are what is known as mummified. That means they have never been under water, the water level has never passed the hands and they were able to dry. If you look at the hands you can see that there's a very significant amount of drying because the fingers look like spindles. Flies don't like dry environments, they don't lay eggs where it's dry and cool. They like where it's warm and moist, therefore the amount of eggs in this whiteish material are fly eggs. There's only really one area where the flies are more abundant on the hands and that is under the ring which is where, where humidity will be preserved; between the fingers when they are closed because that is where the humidity will be preserved, and right under this or next to the ... this little Christmas tree type plastic binding which is often used to bind trash bags which was applied, not for the purpose of tying the body but for the purpose of keeping the arms together so they don't flop after death."

Kapsak removed that photograph, then replaced it with one showing a close-up of Cathy Warner's decomposed face and upper torso.

"First of all," Spitz began, "the entire mouth and the entire face and the nose, mouth, eyes, are entirely filled with maggots. The eyes were described in the autopsy report as nonexistent, substituted by maggots and although you don't see the eyes here, you can see this big chunk of maggots crawling all over each other, that's what maggots do. And, these are blowfly maggots, and they are of a length which is such that, ah, putting that together with the degree of decomposition would be suggestive of a certain number of days. You can also see here where the water level has gone down in the, in the bathtub."

Stepping up to the board, Kapsak again removed the photo and replaced it with a third, this one being a longer body shot taken during Cathy Warner's autopsy.

"Of course, here's one breast, here's one arm," Spitz said, pointing out the body parts as he spoke. "The nipple has been chewed away by the maggots and here's the head. There's some teeth noted. The degree of decomposition of this head is such that tissue and skin and the underlying fat and muscle has melted down. That means it has exposed the bone underneath. This area that you can see here, this whiteish pearly area, is around the left eye. The entire head is much more decomposed that the rest down here, and for a very good reason; that is that the head has eyes and a nose and a mouth, which are humid and moist and warm, and which will attract the flies to settle and multiply. I don't think that at any time the head was under water and if it was, it probably floated to provide access for the maggots. The additional factor is that there's a wound in the head, there's a gunshot in the left cheek and that, being moist and warm, will attract flies. The same as raw meat will attract flies."

Kapsak took down that picture and replaced it with the final one, a photo of the basement floor, near the washing machine and dryer, on which was a large, dark stain.

"This is the floor of the basement ... there is an outline on the floor which is that of a human being and it is not an outline only in blood, it is an outline in fluids. A sample taken from anywhere here and tested for blood will give a positive test for blood, although it is not all blood. It is when the body is left to purge ... to decompose, to develop an odor, and to make blisters on the body because that's part of the decomposition process, blisters which fill with foul brown fluid ... these blisters break and stain the floor. There's no way of getting this washed up, this is going to stay there and it is my opinion that this body was in the basement for a certain length of time, maybe a couple of days, maybe three days, and then was put in the bathtub. It is not my opinion that the body was in the bathtub all the time."

Spitz's statement raised several eyebrows in the courtroom; Kapsak had not even hinted in his opening remarks that part of the State's theory was that Cathy Warner had been killed in the basement, left there for several days, and then taken to the bathtub.

"Why do you say that, doctor? Can you explain that any further?" Kapsak asked.

"Well, this is primarily because there is absolutely no question in my mind what this is, I've seen that many times before, this kind of configuration. That's what that is, and also this coupled with the degree of decomposition. You see, the temperature down here in the basement, I never measured it, I don't know what the temperature was in the basement, but it's bound to have been less than in the house because basements are normally cooler and dryer, so, this stain in the basement coupled with the number of days in the bathtub, leave no doubt in my mind as to be responsible for the degree of decomposition that is evident here and with the bottom line of or equal sign of approximately eight days."

"But why do you say that that stain was not made entirely by blood?"

"Because when a body lies on the floor (and) when it is bleeding ... there will be no blood under the body, there will only be blood around the body. This outlines the body. When blood is lost it congeals, there'll be a big cake of blood maybe around the head but there won't be blood down here by the feet. This is a, a picture of a body decomposing on the basement floor because that fluid, anybody who has ever seen it knows it is like water. It is not fluid that will congeal, it will never congeal, it will be soaked into the porous cement, unlike blood, which will stay on the top."

Kapsak then invited Spitz to return to his seat, and turned the witness over to Ferencz. But Judge Hoffman, seeing that the time was 11:40 a.m., decided this was a proper time to break for lunch. He recessed the court, telling everyone to be back in one hour.

Ferencz, knowing he had to somehow discredit Spitz, came out swinging.

Reviewing the doctor's earlier statement that he had testified as an outside expert on forensic pathology in many states and countries, Ferencz asked, "Correct me if I'm wrong; excepting Detroit where you're the medical examiner – the person who actually performs the autopsy – that's always been done before they call you in?"

"Mostly, yes," Spitz replied.

"And you've indicated that in determining the time of death, one of the important factors is the circumstances surrounding the death, is that correct ... such as whether newspapers stop coming ... when the last time the person was seen. ... and those are all things that you consider in coming to your decision?"

"Yes."

"And in this case I assume you also considered those items, like when was the last time the person was seen, that type of thing?"

"In the final rendering of an opinion, that's correct."

"So when the prosecutor came and spoke to you he laid out all the facts to you, right? He told you about Doctor Schuster's report, is that correct?"

"No," Spitz corrected him, "he had sent me the autopsy report of Doctor Schuster."

"He sent you Doctor Roh's report? And Doctor Roh is the Medical

Examiner of Westchester County, is that correct?"

"Yes."

"And that (Roh's report) gives the time of death two to four days prior to discovery of the body, is that correct?"

"Yes."

"Doctor Schuster's report also gives the time of death as three days, the 16th. You had that report, didn't you?"

"Yes."

His foundation laid, Ferencz moved in for the kill.

"Now in reviewing a situation such as you have here, I take it you rely on the autopsy report, photographs and the attendant circumstances as the State lets you know what they are, is that correct?"

"Yes."

"Now, it is better, is it not, to have the body in front of you than to have a photograph, wouldn't that be true?"

But Spitz, an accomplished witness, would not bite the bait.

"I think that also depends on the number of factors. I think certainly it is advantageous to have the body. I don't want to say that it is just as advantageous to have the pictures of the body and a good description of what was observed at the time of the autopsy."

"Did you have a good description of what was observed at the time of the autopsy?"

"Yes, I think I did."

"From Doctor Schuster?"

"Yes."

"So he was the first doctor, if you will, and the only doctor, who was able to take a look at the actual body?"

"Yes."

"Now, are you going to tell us, doctor, that it is not better, not more advantageous, to see the body than to just see the photographs?"

"No, I'm not saying that; only, I'm saying that seeing the body is a very good way to assess the time of death but it's not the only way . . ."

"Well, is it better to see photographs doctor?" Ferencz asked, interrupting the pathologist.

"Can he finish his answer?" Kapsak interjected, coming to the aid of his witness.

"Yes," Hoffman ruled, turning to the doctor. "Finish your answer."

"There are a number of other factors which have to be considered," he said, "not only the body."

"Uh-hum," Ferencz muttered.

"All these factors have to be put together."

"Could you go through the factors again?"

"Well, the factors I considered were the body, the description of the body, the appearance of the body, the location of the body, and the fact — and I attribute a fair amount of significance to that — where the body had been before it reached the bathtub and the infestation of the body with insects. All these things together, plus the fact of when this person was, was last seen, although I do not make my opinion to fit that."

"I'm sure you don't," Ferencz said, sarcastically.

"I base my opinion on what I found on the body and on the description of the body and on the scene."

"By the way doctor, you indicated that maggots are a factor, is that right?"

"Maggots are a factor, yes."

"And did you say that looking at them, some of them were relatively large and they were all over the body?"

"Yes."

"And, some of them, I think you said, were about an inch?"

"Close to, yes."

"And that's based upon your knowledge and training and expertise that that size is significant, an inch."

"Some are ... what I'm testifying, they look like they might be an inch on the photograph. Some are large and some are very small."

"Well, if they weren't an inch, if they were a quarter of an inch or a half an inch, would that change your opinion?"

"It would not make a lot of sense to have a quarter of an inch maggot because flies don't just lay eggs at a certain time and not at others; flies keep laying eggs and therefore you have maggots of a certain size that date back to the first . . ." Spitz stumbled for the correct word, but Ferencz tried to help him out.

"Infestation?"

" ... episode of, for example, laying and subsequently there were additional eggs laid which matured at a later time and therefore, you have larger maggots and smaller maggots."

"Now, the question was, doctor, that if the maggots, the largest maggots were not an inch, but a half inch, substantially smaller, would that make a difference to you; obviously, they wouldn't have grown as much as your estimate, isn't that true?"

"That's correct."

"That's correct. So, if they don't have inch maggots, that makes a difference in your perception of how long those maggots have been on the body?"

"No, all it would tell you is that the chances are that the first eggs were laid a bit later."

"Well, according to your report, the three items that you used are, including but not limited to, the partial skeletonization of the head, mummification of the hands and the age of the maggots?"

"Yes."

"So if the maggots are substantially smaller than you say, an inch, if they're smaller than an inch, that's one of the three considerations you listed as inaccurate?"

"Well, firstly, I've never stated that they are an inch. I've stated that they look like they could be an inch, there's no way I know how to measure the size of the maggots on the picture, because there is no scale. They look like they could be approximately an inch. They could be less than an inch. I'm not saying that. And, therefore, if you read my letter, if you did, where it says, 'My opinion of the degree of ... This opinion is based on the degree of decomposition of the body including but not limited to partial skeletonization of the head, the mummification of the hands and the age of the maggots on the body.' All factors combined allow me to make this observation. I should have perhaps also added to that, although I think this is indirectly implied here, that the body had been moved."

"Can we take one factor at a time, doctor? You said that by the photographs the maggots look like they could be about an inch? Okay? Now I had been asking you before if it's better to have the actual body there, right? Remember I asked earlier?"

"Yes."

"And what is your answer to that? Is it better to have the actual body there?"

"My answer to that is, to have the body there and consider the body alone, wouldn't make all that much difference. You'd have to still consider all other factors together with the body."

Spitz did not want to give a direct answer to the question, but Ferencz was relentless.

"Considering all of the factors, okay? Is it better to have the body or not have the body?"

"For me, to have the body there, yes, I would have preferred to have the body there but I cannot speak for somebody else seeing the body."

"Then you'd be able to tell if the maggots are an inch, or substantially smaller?"

"Maybe I could, yes."

"Well, you'd have the body, I mean you could look at the maggots, right?"

"Yes. Although on the other hand, what I would probably still do if I knew it was important to determine the absolute age, I'd probably collect some maggots and send them to an entomologist."

Ferencz next turned his attention to Spitz's observation of Cathy Warner's hands. He showed the witness a close-up photograph of Warner's hands taken by the investigating officers when her body was found.

"In 90-degree temperature, how long would it take hands to become mummified?"

"You'd probably get beginning mummification in a day or two. But we're not talking about beginning mummification here."

"Would you call that early mummification or full; could we characterize it that way?"

"What you would get in a day or two? Yes."

"Okay, and clearly, according to what you see, you don't consider that early mummification?"

"No, this is not early mummification."

"But you didn't have the body in front of you, you're looking at photographs, right?"

"That reminds me, you know; what you're trying to say suggests when you look at a heap of beans of about two inches, is it a lot of beans or a few beans? That depends who looks at them. This degree of mummification that is shown in the picture is without a doubt an advanced stage of mummification and I realize full well that Doctor Shuster in his report describes it as an early degree of mummification. What Doctor Shuster considers early and what he considers late I don't know, but I can assure you that these hands were parchment-like hands, which does under no circumstances occur in just a few days."

Ferencz referred Spitz to Shuster's autopsy report once again.

"In the one, two three, four, five ... the 10th or 11th line down, 'drying out . . .' 'facts of early mummification affects the fingers of each hand', and what you're saying is Doctor Shuster, the medical examiner for Middlesex County, chief immediate examiner since 1972, is inaccurately describing what he saw?"

"No, I'm not saying that, I'm saying that's how he described it. I would have described it as an advanced stage of drying or an advanced stage of mummification."

"Now, doctor, is it accurate to say that the temperature is a very important factor in the decomposition of a body?"

"Yes."

"The warmer the temperature, the more likely it is that the body will decompose faster?"

"Yes."

Ferencz walked back to his table, picked up a book, and then reapproached Spitz, handing him the book.

"I just put in front of you an item," the attorney said, "could you tell the jury what that is?"

"That is the book called 'Medicolegal Investigation of Death', which is edited by myself and Doctor Fisher."

"Okay, doctor, on page 20 of your book, you state, do you not, on the bottom of the page on the left-hand side that, 'Environmental temperature is the most important single factor.' "

"Yes."

"Did you go on to say that, 'It is not uncommon to see advanced decomposition within 12 to 18 hours to the point that the facial features are no longer recognizable.' "

"That's correct."

" 'Most of the hair slips away from the scalp and the entire body becomes swollen to two to three times normal size.' Is that true?"

"Yes."

"There's a photograph on the same page, is there not? And that photograph is of two bodies ... one body being, well, could you describe it to the jury?"

"One body is, looks very fresh and is taken from the basement. And the other body is of a man who was killed approximately at the same time or for all intents and purposes within five minutes, but whose body was on the first floor of the same house and is showing quite advanced decomposition, although the facial features are very well recognizable."

"Now, when you say advanced state of decomposition, could you describe the coloration?"

"Well, it's not only coloration, but the coloration of course is, since you're asking about coloration, the body becomes a darkish color and the skin has a brownish, purple type of fluid underneath it."

"And that's over the entire body, or as you see it in that photograph?"

"In this case it's over the entire body. That depends on the position of the body."

Ferencz then handed Spitz a photograph of Cathy Warner's body as it was found.

"What's the coloration of the skin; not the hands, but the skin? Pale?"

"Well, it's pale; it's not dark, it's not the normal color of fresh, fresh skin."

"But it's much paler than that photograph shows?" Ferencz asked, referring to the picture from Spitz's book.

"Correct, yes."

Returning his attention to the photos in Spitz's textbook, Ferencz asked, "Now in this particular case, doctor, the outside temperature was 90 degrees, is that correct?"

"Yes."

"And that gentleman was dead for 48 hours?"

"Yes."

Ferencz next retrieved the temperature chart he had prepared.

"Doctor, when your made you conclusions, did you have a temperature chart with you?"

"No, but I was aware of the temperature. I had the temperature ... yes I did have a temperature chart."

"You are aware that the outside temperature reached a high of 98 degrees? And that the average temperature was 89?"

"Yes."

"And the previous day, to make a complete 48-hour cycle, you are aware that the maximum temperature was 98 and that the average temperature was 86?"

"Yes."

"And the day before that, the high was 94 and the average temperature 82?"

"Yes."

"The photograph that you have there shows a gentleman who was dead for 48 hours with the outside temperature at some point 90 degrees Fahrenheit?"

"That's correct."

"Did you say that flies would be at the body within 24 hours?"

"They can be there before."

"In fact, if you turn to page 21 of your book, don't you say they can be there almost immediately, within minutes?"

"Yes, or even before death."

"Am I correct doctor that within the first few hours of death the fingers and the toes, if it's a dry area, will in fact begin to shrink?"

"Yes."

"And that, I guess, would lead eventually to the mummification that we spoke about, would that be right?"

"Yes."

"This body was partially under water, is that correct?"

"Yes."

"In reviewing the report of Doctor Shuster, you read that the feet demonstrated a washerwoman type of wrinkling? And there's nothing in the report to indicate any slippage insofar as the actual skin of the foot coming off, is that right?"

"Well, somebody has to ... there wouldn't be because in order for this to be mentioned, somebody has to try and take it off, it doesn't come off by itself."

"Doctor, if you turn to page 356 of your book, it is true, is it not, that the skin would come off like a glove, depending on the temperature, perhaps within several hours?"

"Yes, that depends on the temperature of the water. There's a picture in my book here where somebody's skin of the hand came off in eight hours, that water was about 120 or 130 degrees, that was a hot water that came out of the tap." Then expressing some displeasure with Ferencz's tactics, Spitz added, "I'm fully aware of what this book says, you don't have to read it to me, I wrote it." The doctor's comment was met with a chuckle from the audience.

"I understand that doctor," Ferencz said. "So that you indicate that in cold water, several days could be harmless?"

"Right."

"While in warm water, several hours could create a condition where you don't just have washer woman skin, but you could actually peel the skin off?"

"That's correct."

"And Doctor Shuster's report doesn't indicate anything about being able to peel the skin off, right?"

"No, it does not."

"Now, you've indicated it's your position that the body was down in the basement for a period of time, is that correct?"

"Yes."

"Doctor, if the body was down the basement for a couple of days as you indicate and the body was then brought upstairs, wouldn't that hasten or make quicker the decomposition?"

"Well, I said the body was in the basement somewheres between two and three days, until such time as some degree of purging occurred in the basement and then the body was put in the bathtub upstairs. I don't see why this should hasten the decomposition. It would slow it down because the temperature in the basement is a lot less than what it is upstairs."

"I mean, once the body is removed from the basement and put upstairs, according to your theory, wouldn't that hasten decomposition?"

"No. What would happen is there's one rate of decomposition that's applicable to the basement just like in this picture on page 20, and there's one rate of decomposition applicable to the upstairs in the bathtub. In fact, if I may, there is a third rate of decomposition applicable to this case, because we are dealing about a body in water and not in the dry upstairs. That also plays a factor."

"Does the fact that a body was in a downstairs cellar, if you will, or in a cool area or even under water for several days, and then brought upstairs to a warm environment, does that have any effect on the speed with which the body would decompose?"

"Of course."

"What is that effect?"

"That the decomposition went on at a much slower rate while the body was in the basement."

"And how about once the body was put upstairs?"

"That is when the decomposition advanced faster, probably not as fast as it would have had it been in the dry, that is without being in a bathtub or in a dry bathtub."

"Now, doctor, is it true that in a hot environment, a body will, actually can swell to two or three times its size within a matter of a day or two?"

"Well, I don't know about a day or two, but, eventually it can swell to two or three times its size, yes."

"In 90 degree weather, can you give us an estimation as to how long it would take?"

"I find that difficult to answer, you know; you're making me guess, and I don't like to do that. It, it's, it's really so variable ... some bodies swell a lot faster than others, depending on the bacterial flora that's in the intestine at the time. It depends on the amount of fat on the body, it depends on so many factors."

"Well, the report from Doctor Shuster, who had the body in front of him, said slight bloating is present."

Spitz began nodding his head as Ferencz finished his question.

"Yes, I realize that he said that, and he also described the inner organ full of air bubbles or gas bubbles, so, I don't think you can make a time of death based on the amount of bloating of the body; I don't think that's neither fair nor accurate."

Ferencz tried another tack.

"Well, can you tell us where (Dr. Shuster) talks about blistering on the back?"

"I don't recall that he specifically says on the back of the body, but, he talks about slippage of the skin which is the same as blistering."

"Uh hum. And he doesn't indicate anything about actual slippage on the back. What he does say is, slippage is prominent in the medial aspect on the arms and both thighs, is that correct? And the vagina?"

"Well, if you look at this diagram," Spitz said, pointing to the autopsy sketch, "he's got slippage in the back of the head, he's got slippage in the back of the legs, and he's got slippage in the front all over the place."

"And on the back?"

"On the back itself, he didn't mark it or at least I can't read it, scattered blue marks he has here."

"But nothing about slippage on the back, per se?"

"On the back, no."

"This is the same back that would be under water?"

"Yes. That wouldn't, that does not surprise me that there is no slippage mentioned in the back because that's what the body is lying on in the bathtub."

"You testified that the most important thing in evaluating the time of death is the body surface?"

"No, what I testified is that the body surface in forensic pathology, in the type of work that I'm doing in general, the body surface is of utmost importance. It is the body surface that enables me to tell you when a bullet wound is an entrance wound, when a bullet wound is an exit wound. It enables me to tell you so much information only based on the body surface like what type of knife was used when a stab wound happens and these are factors which would be difficult to evaluate on the interior aspect of the body. Time of death is only one of these situations."

Ferencz then pointed out once again the picture in Spitz's book of a woman whose body had been immersed in water for eight hours, taking note of the caption, which read, "Peeling of the skin after eight hours immersion in warm water."

"Doctor Shuster's report doesn't say anything about skin peeling on the feet, does it? It just says, 'washer woman type wrinkling?' "

"Well, I don't know if he tried to take it off; you have to try and take it off, it doesn't come off by itself."

Ferencz pushed the point.

"Anything in his report about peeling?"

"No."

Ferencz next attached to the board the photo showing the basement floor, and the large splotch Spitz had described as being formed by Cathy Warner's body fluids and blood. This was the part of Spitz's testimony that Ferencz believed the least, and he wanted to make sure the jury disbelieved it, also.

"Doctor, I put on the board S-169, could you tell the jury once again what that is?"

"That is the outline of the body in fluids surging from the body or exuding from the body."

Ferencz did not try to keep the sarcasm from his voice.

"Through the pores; how are the fluids getting out of the body, doc?"

"Through beginning skin slippage, and through the decomposition process."

"And you're positive it's not a blood spill?"

"Yes."

"And how big is that area?"

"About the area of the body."

"Well, did you have a chance to go take a look at it down the cellar where this incident allegedly occurred?"

"I don't need to do that, you can see approximately how big it is by the other things that are in the picture."

"The size of the body?"

"Approximately."

"About how long?"

"Well, about the size of a body. I don't profess to know whether it is this many inches or that many inches, but it is obvious to be about the size and about the shape of a body, and having seen these kinds of configurations before — it is not like this is a novelty to me — I recognize it."

"Did you testify to this in California and Texas and Europe and South America, doc?"

"No, this wasn't an issue in the California cases; in the California cases they were all fresh bodies."

"Well, if you would doctor, you don't know how wide a washing machine is, do you?"

"A washing machine?"

"I'll withdraw that question. Doctor, that's the outline of a body, from the head down to the feet?"

"Yes."

"And the body is laying on the floor in the basement?"

"On the side."

"On its side, fully extended? You don't see any marks where the knees are bent, do you?"

"I don't know that I'm able to tell you that accurately."

"Do you know whether or not this particular cellar is level, or if it floods?"

"No."

"Do you know whether or not water from the outside seeps in and causes a dirt mark down that cellar?"

"No, I don't, but that is no dirt mark."

"Do you know from where the chips were taken in terms of ... I take it you're aware that they did some testing down the cellar and tested positive for blood?"

"Yes, they would be positive for blood, I don't know that I know chips were taken but this would be positive for blood."

"And your testimony is that does not look to you as though there was a head injury, blood spilled in the middle there, and it was wiped up towards the ends?"

"No, this is not a wiping, this is the entire body oozed out fluids here, not just the head, and I can explain that, I can give you the exact reasoning for that."

Pointing to the opposite ends of the splotch, Ferencz asked, "Well doctor, if you could, is this the head area over here, or is this the head area over here?"

"No, the head area would have been toward the bottom of the picture."

Ferencz then put up another picture, showing the same mark from a different angle.

"By the way, doc, do you see how there's a pale area that goes here?" the attorney asked, pointing to the middle of the blotch. "Can you give us a reason for that?"

"That is where the body is lying. The fluids come out, and where the weight of the body is, at that point there should be a little less of intensity of staining."

With that, Ferencz concluded his cross-examination and resumed his chair next to his client, who had been passively watching and doodling on a note pad. Kapsak had been silently making notes during Ferencz's questioning, and had several follow-ups prepared. He again delivered them from his seated position.

"Doctor, Mr. Ferencz has read to you various temperatures during the time period in question here. Do any of those temperatures change your opinion in any way?"

"No, my opinion is not changed at all."

"And in fact, do any of the questions you were asked or any of the information you were given change your opinion at all?"

"No."

"When you were looking at the picture on page 20 of your book ... did you remark about the condition of the head of the person who was upstairs? What is the significance of that?"

"In picture 20 there is some bloating of the body, there is some discoloration of the body, but, the features of the body are intact, you can look at that body and recognize the person." Pointing to the pictures of Cathy Warner, Spitz continued, "Here, there's no way you can recognize that person, part of the face is skeletonized, you can see the bone. There's no way in this body that you can make an identification of that person, because the facial features are gone, obliterated. That doesn't happen in a day or two or three or four. If you look at that picture that you have in the magnified picture, there, of the face, there is a black face with a heap of maggots on it and then the other picture, there's another picture, too. The way this picture is oriented, what you see is a chin but up above there is a heap of maggots, there must be billions of maggots in that area, crawling maggots, and among them you can see big ones and you can see a whole lot of small ones. The big ones are of course first generation, the small ones subsequent generations."

"Well, looking at the picture of the victim in this case and looking at the picture in your book which talks about advanced decomposition within 48 hours, is there a distinction between the two studies?"

"Here you have a beginning stage of somewhere near two or three days of low grade decomposition, similar to what happened to the woman on figure 20. Then the body was removed and put in a hot environment upstairs in a bathtub in a great temperature, in a higher temperature, and now you're talking about what the man shows, except in an exaggerated form. The man, yes, the man here on this picture was only there for two days but he's not halfway decomposed as much as this person (Cathy Warner) is."

"Now, I believe you wanted to explain further about the stain in the basement. I think you started to give your exact reasoning for your conclusion."

Spitz sat back in his chair as he began his dissertation.

"The decomposition process causes the uppermost layer of the skin, with fingernails, with hair, to come off," the doctor explained. "That is called skin slippage. And fluids ... let me back off a minute. The uppermost layer of the skin holds back the fluids that are in the body. Just like if you sustain a second degree burn, you get a blister; the blister ruptures, fluid comes out. Only this is not a burn, this is a postmortem occurrence, where the uppermost layer of the skin retaining the fluid becomes wrinkled, but finally bursts. That fluid finally comes out and stains the floor. Where the body is laying there is no pressure and therefore in those places there can be no ... first of all, there is not as much slippage, if any, and Doctor Shuster didn't describe any slippage on the back because in the bathtub she was lying on the back. So, where she's lying it's pale, of course it isn't as pale as I'd like to see it, because the fluids subsequently merge, especially under the body. Blood, when it comes out of the body, it ... stays in one place. I've never in 30 years of this kind of work seen blood from one area of the body outline the whole body, that doesn't exist. Even if it's cleaned up afterwords, or wiped it doesn't correspond to this picture, which is a picture of the body . . .

"As far as the decomposition process upstairs in the bathtub is concerned, two factors are important here: those parts of the body that were above the water decomposed violently as the face did and the hands dried because they were never under water. Flies don't lay eggs under water, that's why the flies are all on the face, none are in other places.

"Of course, these are all compounding issues. Therefore I emphasize that there are three situations here, three locations; the basement, the upstairs underwater and the upstairs above water. All these are taken into consideration, and there's no doubt in my mind this person was dead eight days."

Ferencz, in his re-cross, again attacked Spitz on his theory about the basement stain.

"Doctor, in your report dated August 17th, do you mention anything about this downstairs fluid, other than to say, by the way, that all factors were considered, with particular consideration of the circumstances and location under which the body was found and the cause of death, other than that?"

"No, I didn't. This report was meant to satisfy Mr. Kapsak's desire to receive a report and it was intended to be as brief as possible, but yet include the bottom line and my reasoning why I arrived at that bottom line ... "

"By the way, when you testify around the country, do you do that gratis?"

Kapsak was waiting for this. He just smirked and shook his head.

"No, I don't do anything gratis," Spitz answered. "I have a commitment to myself that I get paid for what I do."

"And are you getting paid for this?"

"I would hope that eventually I would be paid, yes."

"Have you agreed upon a particular amount of money from the

Prosecutor's Office?"

"No, I have not."

"So, it remains to be seen after your testimony, for you to discuss it with whomever?"

"It remains to be seen whether I'll be paid, yes, that is correct."

"Now, lastly doctor, you've indicated that this seepage of fluids from the body is a normal postmortem occurrence? And, you testimony is this would occur in any situation where a body was laying on a concrete floor or any floor for a period of several days?"

"Wait a minute," Spitz was again leaning forward in his chair. "A period of several days, with the provision that the environmental temperature would permit that to happen."

"So that this would be an occurrence that in your opinion any medical examiner who's had experience would have come across. That is, somebody that's been in contact with a variety of autopsies?"

"I find it difficult to testify what another medical examiner would testify based on this information. I think they should. I can vouch to you that this is my experience."

"And it's a common experience, it happens every time a body is laying on the ground, as you testified you believe this body was?"

"For a certain length of time, yes."

Seeing he could go no further with the witness, Ferencz ended his questioning.

Kapsak concluded the day by calling to the stand Paul Wuthrich, the Timex engineer based in the company's Waterbury, Connecticut headquarters.

Before Wuthrich was called, however, Ferencz objected, arguing that one of his investigators had called Timex in Connecticut and was told by an Edward Collins that he, Collins, had performed the tests and not Wuthrich. Collins said he had then submitted the results to Wuthrich, who wrote the final report.

"Paul Wuthrich was assisted by Collins," Kapsak responded, "but Paul Wuthrich is the man who supervised and directed the testing of the watch."

Ferencz offered to withdraw his objection if Collins were also called to testify. Hoffman decided to preview Wuthrich's testimony, holding a hearing outside the presence of the jury. After hearing what Wuthrich had to say, Ferencz withdrew his objection.

Wuthrich, who testified that he held 25 patents in watch engineering, told the jury that the watch found on Cathy Warner's body would run for about 48 hours when fully wound, then described the results of the test he had conducted on it. He also confirmed that the timepiece was in good working condition.

"This watch performs better than average for that model," he said. "This is exceptionally good."

In his cross-examination, Ferencz asked Wuthrich if the dater on the watch could be set back.

Wuthrich said it could, simply by pulling out the stem and turning it back, "just like any other wristwatch."

Several months of therapy designed to help her through this period of her life notwithstanding, Pat Bauer was more nervous than usual when she and her attorney, Steven Altman, called on Tom Kapsak later that evening. Kapsak had arranged the meeting with Bauer, as he did with every witness, to review her testimony and prepare her for the ordeal she would have to endure the following day in court.

After the three exchanged pleasantries and had walked into Kapsak's office, Altman excused himself, saying that he had another appointment to keep.

"Don't worry," Kapsak said, "she'll be fine."

Kapsak handed Bauer copies of reports filed by Zimmerman and Watson following the several interviews they had had with her, and asked the woman to sit down and review them. Pat Bauer took a seat directly in front of Kapsak's desk as she devoted her full attention to the paperwork, re-reading what she had said to the detectives. She was seated beneath a wall-mounted corkboard Kapsak had turned into something of a rogue's gallery, decorated by a montage of mug shots of convicted murderers Kapsak had sent away.

After Bauer had read all the statements, Kapsak asked, "Does that all seem complete to you?"

"Well, kind of," Bauer answered, leafing through the reports. "It looks like you have everything here but the gun."

Kapsak swore his heart stopped beating.

"The gun?" he asked, staring directly at Bauer. "What gun?"

'The gun," she repeated, nonchalantly. "The gun Gene had in Minnesota."

"He had a gun in Minnesota?!" Kapsak was beside himself. He didn't know whether to kiss Bauer or throw her in jail for obstruction. "Why didn't you tell me this before?"

"I told you, or maybe it was Joe, but I know I told somebody!" Bauer said, her panic growing as she opened her purse, looking for copies of other reports she had been given.

Kapsak couldn't believe his ears. After more than a year, he finally had Berta with a gun! "Denny!" he yelled to Watson, who was working in another office in the suite, "Denny! Get in here quick!"

Watson, thinking something was wrong, came running into Kapsak's office. "What's wrong? What's the matter!"

"Have a seat Dennis," Kapsak said, motioning to the chair next to Bauer. "Now Pat," the second assistant prosecutor said, trying as best he could to keep his voice level, "I want you to tell Dennis exactly what you just told me."

Bauer couldn't understand Kapsak's reaction; she was sure she had told him about the gun before!

"I just said that when I was looking through the reports, it looked like you had everything except the part about the gun," she told Watson.

Watson nearly jumped out of his chair. "What gun!? Who had a gun?"

"Gene did, in Minnesota! Look, we were unpacking in the Northwood Motel that first night we were there, and all of a sudden he had a gun."

"Where did it come from?" Watson asked.

"I don't know, I guess he had it in his suitcase. I just know that he had it. I asked him what he was doing with it, and he said he always carried it with him. So I just told him to put it away, that I didn't ever want to see it again, because I don't want to have anything to do with guns."

"Did he show you the gun again?" Kapsak asked.

"No, he put it away and I never saw it again."

"I don't believe this!" Watson exclaimed. "Why didn't you tell us this before?"

"But I did!" Bauer protested, resuming her search through her purse. "I know I told you about this, there's a report somewhere, ah, here it is, see!" Triumphantly, Bauer whipped a multi-paged document out of her purse and proffered it to Kapsak. The first thing to which his eyes were drawn was the letterhead: it was that of the law firm of Wilentz, Goldman and Spitzer, Berta's first lawyers.

Bauer saw it at the same time, her victorious smirk rapidly disappearing from her face.

"Well, I knew I told it to somebody," she said, sheepishly.

"Denny," Kapsak said, after Bauer had left, "I'll need a report on this first thing in the morning. I've got to show this to Ferencz and the judge before we go to court."

"Okay," Watson agreed. "It'll be on your desk when you get here. Do you think the story will stick? I mean, coming this late in the game?"

"I don't see why not," Kapsak told him. "I don't think a jury will have a hard time believing Pat Bauer forgot to tell us something, do you?"

September 18, 1984

Brad Ferencz was beside himself.

"Your Honor, I have to object to this. I mean, the trial has been going on for a week now, and all of a sudden the prosecutor comes up with this? This is incredible! And Pat Bauer says she forgot?"

Ferencz, Kapsak and Judge Hoffman were in the judge's chambers, where the jurist was hearing the pros and cons of admitting Pat Bauer's late statement. The trial had been delayed pending the outcome.

"Judge, I know it's late, but I just found out about this last night," Kapsak said. "I got it to you and Mr. Ferencz as fast as I could."

"How do we even know she's telling the truth?" Ferencz asked. "It's obvious from reading the reports that she's lied before. How do we know she's not lying now?"

"There's no reason for her to lie," Kapsak countered. "She has absolutely nothing to gain by fabricating this story. She's not on trial."

"I'm going to allow the statement," Hoffman said. "I believe Mr. Kapsak did everything in his power to quickly bring this information forward as soon as he received it."

Hoffman overruled Ferencz's objections, then directed the two attorneys to return to the courtroom.

Kapsak saw Bauer outside the courtroom. He walked up to her and drew her aside.

"The judge is allowing the statement you gave me last night," he said.

"I can't, I can't do this," Bauer said. She was pale and, Kapsak thought, shaking.

"What do you mean you can't do this?" he asked.

"I can't do this; I'm gonna get up there, and I'm gonna throw up!"

"You don't understand, Pat, you have no choice," Kapsak said. "You're going to be fine. If you can get through your husband's illness, you can get through this."

Knowing the bombshell that was going to be dropped later in the day, Kapsak did his best to focus on the three witnesses he was calling to the stand before Pat Bauer — Lt. Joe Zimmerman, Mary Neal and Shirley Jones, the daughter-in-law of Ed Jones, the man who rented the bungalow at the rear of Cathy Warner's property.

Zimmerman, a veteran of more than 200 homicide cases, recounted in his testimony in general terms the early stages of the Warner murder investigation, but focused on the three interviews he held with Gene Berta. Hoffman had declared that the fourth interview, conducted after Berta had already contacted a lawyer, was not admissible.

It was in the third interview, Zimmerman said, that he wanted to "learn all about" Gene Berta. By this time, he said, police had started focusing their investigation on him, so he was given his Miranda rights.

Zimmerman told the jury about Berta's version of what happened July 8th, and how the defendant said the last time he saw Cathy Warner was that day, as she was walking toward the Metro Park train station. Berta admitted that they had quarreled over the fact that she was not going on the trip, Zimmerman said, and also that Berta had borrowed $10,000 from the victim.

"And did you ask him to describe (Cathy Warner) particularly?" Kapsak asked.

"Yes, ... I asked him if he would describe for me Catherine Warner and his answer to me was that she was a good piece." Zimmerman shook his head in disbelief as he spoke. "It really wasn't the answer I was looking for. I was looking for pedigree."

Ferencz did his best to poke holes in Zimmerman's testimony.

Through his questioning of the witness, the defense attorney pointed out that Zimmerman did not review his report with Berta to check for accuracy. Zimmerman also admitted that although he had access to a small tape recorder, he chose to not use it.

Turning his attention to the subject of Edison Police Sergeant John Bauer, Pat Bauer's husband, Ferencz asked, "Do you know whether Patricia Bauer's husband's service revolver is a .38 calibre?"

"I don't know," Zimmerman replied.

"But he would, as a police officer, be issued a weapon, would he not?"

"That's correct."

"A weapon that Mrs. Bauer may have access to if they were living together?"

But Zimmerman wouldn't fall into the trap Ferencz was setting. "I don't know," was all he would answer.

Drawing Zimmerman's attention to a report that a neighbor of Cathy Warner's said she saw upstairs lights on when Cathy Warner was supposed to be dead, Ferencz asked, "In a homicide investigation, isn't it important to investigate all of the incidents surrounding that death?"

"Surrounding the death, yes."

"And it would be important, would it not, if somebody saw lights on on July 12th and 13th, in the upstairs right rear area of the victim's house?"

"It would be questioned."

"And you'd go back to that person's house, and you'd speak to that person, and you'd write a report on it, wouldn't you?"

"If I was doing it, yes."

"Did Detective Watson work for you?"

"Yes."

"So he'd report to you?"

"Yeah. He would report to me, sure."

"Did Detective Watson report to you that a Mrs. Gierlich stated that on Tuesday night, July 12th, 1983, at night she observed a light on in the upstairs right rear area of the victim's home?"

"I would say yes," Zimmerman answered, nodding his head.

"And that would be something you would go back and check normally, wouldn't it?"

"That's what we were doing, yes."

"Are you aware of any written reports indicating that that was checked out?"

"I'm not aware of written reports," Zimmerman replied, "but I'm aware of reports."

Before he ceased questioning, Ferencz had Zimmerman point out that Berta always talked to the police when asked and gave Zimmerman some information in specific detail, even after he was Mirandized.

Mary Neal, Cathy Warner's sister, was Kapsak's next witness. Neal repeated the information she had given the detectives in her statement the year before, testifying that although her sister had visited her in Virginia a number of times since John Warner died, Cathy would always call first to make sure Mary would be home. Mary Neal also said that although Cathy had once mused about "throwing her stuff in the car and just showing up," she had never travelled to Virginia by car.

"She always came by either train or plane and called me in advance so that I could pick her up at the station or the airport," Neal testified.

Kapsak asked Neal what she knew about her sister's involvement with Gene Berta.

"We talked about their relationship quite a bit," Neal said. "She was ... she was in love with him and intent on moving in with him after he was supposedly to separate from his wife."

"Did she tell you whether she had any idea when that was going to happen?" Kapsak asked.

"There was different projected times. Every time something was supposed to happen, something would come up to prevent his actually starting the process of separation. She had set different dates where if he didn't do something by this certain time she would call it off and the dates always came and went without anything happening."

Cathy also planned to buy Berta a truck, Neal testified. "I know she had also taken lessons to drive an 18-wheeler and they had gone out pricing cabs a couple of times."

Neal said the last time she saw her sister was over a weekend in June. Cathy, Gene and Mary spent the weekend in Seaside Heights. Cathy and Gene had gone down on a Friday, then were joined by Mary on a Saturday. Cathy and Gene had left that afternoon to attend a wedding, after which Cathy returned alone, and the two sisters finished the weekend together.

"During the course of that weekend, did you have an opportunity to speak to Mr. Berta about his relationship with your sister?" Kapsak asked.

"We talked some while Cathy was in the shower," Neal answered. "There was always this problem; he couldn't understand why our family was so opposed to their relationship and he expressed again his love for Cathy and his intent of one day being together with her on a permanent basis."

"Did you see your sister again after that weekend?"

"No. We drove back to South Plainfield and had a barbecue and that was the last time I saw her."

Neal testified that Cathy Warner was aware of Neal's plans to move from Virginia to Pennsylvania and, in fact, Berta had even offered to help her move.

"She wanted to come up and assist in the move or at least in getting settled, but the particular weekend that I moved, which was around the 8th, well, prior to that time she said she couldn't make it. I believe she was working that weekend or had said she was working," Neal said.

"You discussed at different times with your sister that she was in fact seeing other men, did you not, other than Mr. Berta?" Brad Ferencz asked Mary Neal during his cross-examination.

"Seeing them, yes."

"Okay. In fact, I think you gave a statement to the Prosecutor's Office on July 19th, if you remember, in which you said that she saw a man named Richard a lot, is that true."

"She saw him a couple of times," Neal said. "A lot was my choice of words."

"And the question was, do you know Richard's name. You said, no, I don't. I just know he's an optometrist or something like that. They go to New York."

Ferencz next took aim at Neal's assertion that Cathy would always call before she visited.

"It is true, though, that you had discussed the possibility of her just popping by?" he asked.

"Yeah. But I know that as far as popping by, she was very hesitant about driving down by herself."

"Well, back again on July 19th when you gave the statement, under oath, by the way, if you recall, to the Prosecutor's Office, did you say to them she did talk sometimes about wanting to just put her stuff in the car and pop up at the door one day but she knew, you know, she wouldn't really know where to catch me?"

"That sounds correct."

Ferencz also had Mary Neal admit that she did not like the men who lived next door to and behind her sister, because she felt that they both, in their own ways, were getting too "nosy".

During his redirect examination, Kapsak asked Mary Neal if her sister ever called to tell her she was coming to visit during the weekend of July the 8th.

"No, she did not," Mary answered.

Shirley Jones, daughter-in-law of Edward Jones, Cathy Warner's backyard tenant, was called to buttress Mr. Jones' coming testimony that he last spoke to Cathy Warner a few days after July 4th. The elder Jones had originally said he saw her on July 12th, but he was mistaken, according to his daughter-in-law.

She said that on either July 5th, 6th or 7th, she and her husband were visiting Mr. Jones when, at about 2 p.m., Cathy Warner knocked on the door. She said she was going on vacation in a couple of days, Shirley Jones testified, and she asked Ed Jones if he would take care of the yard and watch the house for her.

"Did she say when she expected to return from vacation?" Kapsak asked.

"Around the 14th of July."

"Why do you remember that?"

"My father-in-law had been suspended from his welfare for awhile and he wasn't going to get paid 'til the 11th, which was the second Monday of July, and we were talking, we were laughing with him, he wouldn't spend the money before she came back from her vacation, you know. Because he was happy, you know, because he was going to pay the rent and everything, you know."

Ferencz wasted no time in pointing up the discrepancy in Shirley and Edward Jones' statement to police.

"Are you aware that (Ed Jones) told Detective Watson that the conversation that you believed to have taken place on the 5th or 6th took place on the 12th of July?" he asked.

"He had made a mistake in the date because everyone was upset at the time, you know," Jones responded. "And then we had looked back on the calendar and we remembered the conversation that we had with her."

Ferencz also asked Jones if she was sure the conversation had taken place at around 2 p.m., which Jones affirmed. He did not bring up the fact that Cathy Warner was working at that time, preferring to save that information for his summation.

Pat Bauer was sitting nervously in the hallway outside Judge Hoffman's courtroom, waiting to be called in, her eyes riveted on the courtroom's big wooden double doors that were kept closed during the trial. Her heart skipped a beat when she saw one of the doors open, but resumed its normal rhythm when she saw Tom Kapsak walk out and come toward her.

"Well, you don't have to testify today, we ran out of time," Kapsak told her.

"Oh, thank God," Bauer sighed. "Thank God."

"What do you mean, thank God? You could have gotten this over with today. Now you have to wait until tomorrow."

"No," she shook her head. "I don't think I could have done this today. I don't think I was ready. I probably would have started crying or something."

"Well, I hope you're ready tomorrow, because you're the first witness. Why don't you just go home, relax, go to bed early so you get a lot of sleep.

Then you'll be refreshed for tomorrow."

"Sleep?" Bauer said, laughing. "You really think I'm going to sleep tonight?"

September 19, 1984

"Patricia Bauer!"

Pat Bauer woke up that morning confident that she could get through
this ordeal. But hearing her name called out by the Sheriff's deputy renewed
the doubt she had felt the day before.

Bauer was oblivious to the fact that the courtroom was packed, or to
the audience's stares as she walked through the courtroom door and stride
down the aisle. This, they all knew, was the femme fatale who had lured
Gene Berta away from Cathy Warner. Bauer's full attention was fixed on her
destination, the witness box that sat to the left of Judge Barnett Hoffman.

Pat Bauer had been seeing a therapist to help her cope not only with
the upcoming trial, but also the difficulties she was experiencing with her
husband. Now, as she walked down that aisle, she could hear her therapist's
advice: "Now Patty," she had begun, holding her hands palm down at two
different levels, "when you're up on that stand, pretend that you're way
up here, and everyone else is down there, and they're trying to climb this
ladder to get information from you. If you just keep looking down, you'll
get through it; remember, they've got to come to you." Bauer chuckled
to herself as she drew closer to the stand and noticed that it was, in fact,

slightly elevated.

Acceding to Kapsak's suggestions, Bauer was conservatively dressed in a business outfit, a dark jacket and skirt and white blouse, highlighted by a wide, polka-dotted bow tied at her throat.

After being sworn in and seating herself, Bauer took advantage of the few moments Kapsak needed to arrange his notes to steal a look at Gene Berta. She tried to will her thoughts to him. *"What are you thinking, Gene? Let me know, did you do it, or didn't you?"* Bauer thought she could divine the guilt or innocence of her former paramour by looking in his eyes, but the results of her exercise startled her. *"It's as if I'm not even here,"* she thought. *"He's looking right through me. Gene Berta, you are cold, you are callous. You don't care who you hurt."* It was then that Pat Bauer knew she would have no trouble doing what she had to do.

Kapsak began slowly with Bauer, having her recount the details of how her relationship with Gene Berta started. She testified about him giving her the Valentine, of his offer to talk, and of how the relationship turned sexual about a month later.

"What did he tell you about his relationship with him?" Kapsak asked at one point.

"That he cared for me, that he loved me," Bauer answered.

"Did he tell you anything about his relationship with his wife?"

"He said it wasn't very good, that they had been separated, that they were back at the present time, but that they were going to get a divorce."

The second assistant prosecutor then led Bauer through the events leading up to July 8th, and had her go through, in detail, each of the 11 phone calls Berta had made to her from 7 o'clock that morning to 9:20 that evening.

"What was your feeling toward him on that day?" Kapsak asked.

"I loved him," Bauer said.

The jury and courtroom audience listened with rapt attention as Bauer told of how Berta was whispering during a call he made at about 3:20 p.m. and also of her anger when he "stood her up" for 45 minutes after he'd told her to meet him at the Durham Cafe at 4 p.m.

Bauer recounted how she drove to the rescue squad headquarters and later spoke with George Taylor, who told her that the Durham Cafe was right across the street from the house owned by Gene Berta's girlfriend, Cathy Warner.

Bauer also testified that Berta called her at her home later in the evening, and said that he had to "finish cleaning up" before they could leave on their trip.

Then it was the time for which Kapsak had been waiting. After leading Bauer's narrative through to the point where she had picked up Berta at the Metro Park train station and they were finally on their way to the Newark Howard Johnson, Kapsak asked, "Was there any conversation on your way to the airport?"

"Well, initially we didn't say very much and we were maybe towards Elizabeth and he said to me, aren't you going to talk to me? I was really worked up. And he said, do you love me? I said, yes, I do. He said, do you believe that I love you? I said no. He said, do you believe that I love you. I said no. He said, I just killed three people and you better believe I love you or I'll blow your goddamn brains out!"

Kapsak remained silent for several moments, letting that sink in to the stunned jury.

"How did you react to that?" he finally asked.

"I was surprised, but I did not take it as a physical threat."

"Was there any further conversation along those lines?"

"Along those lines? No. He rubbed the back of my neck because it was very tense, and just that quickly it was over."

Damaging as that statement was, Kapsak knew he had more ammunition yet to unload.

The second assistant prosecutor led Bauer through the entire weekend, asking her questions about the properties she and Berta viewed and the one Berta eventually bought, and also about their discussion of his infidelity toward her on the flight back to Newark.

Backtracking, Kapsak asked the pivotal question, the answer to which he most wanted the jury to hear.

"During the course of your stay in Minnesota, did Mr. Berta show you an object?"

"Yes, he did."

"Do you recall what day or night that occurred?"

"It was Saturday when we first got into the motel."

"What did he show you?"

Bauer did not hesitate in giving her answer.

"He showed me a gun," she said, matter-of-factly. Her statement was met with a spate of hushed exclamations from the spectators, causing Hoffman to bang his gavel several times to restore order.

"How did that come up?" Kapsak asked.

"He just had it; he said, this is my gun."

"Did you ask him about it?"

"No, I didn't. I just said, get it out of here, get it away from me."

"Can you describe it in any way?"

"It was a big gun, it looked like a cowboy gun."

"Well, are you talking about a rifle or a handgun?"

"It was a handgun."

"Did you see that gun again on the trip?"

"No, I didn't."

Having made his point, Kapsak returned to questioning Bauer about what happened on the return trip on the plane. He didn't want to belabor the point about the gun; he would later tie in Bauer's description of the weapon with the findings by Dr. Shuster that Cathy Warner was probably killed with a large-calibre gun.

The rest of Kapsak's questioning proceeded quickly. He asked her to recount, generally, what happened in the weeks and months following the couple's return from Minnesota, particularly stressing the fact that when they met after he was arrested, the majority of their conversation revolved around the upcoming trial.

Brad Ferencz had declared at the trial's onset that "Pat Bauer is a liar, and I will prove it in court." Now came his opportunity to do that.

Pat Bauer stiffened when Judge Hoffman told Ferencz to begin his questioning. She again tried to picture herself high above Ferencz, with him having to climb a ladder to reach her, but somehow the image didn't settle her nerves. But she was determined not to let her nervousness show through. She would not let Gene Berta have that satisfaction.

"Mrs. Bauer," Ferencz began, slowly strolling up to the witness box, "everything you're telling the jury today is true, is that correct?"

"That's right."

"And you're not exaggerating, you're not lying, if you will, you're not making anything up today, is that correct?"

"No, I'm not."

"At some point, did you retain your own lawyer?"

"Yes, I did."

"And, of course, everything you're telling us today you've told him, right?"

"I'm pretty sure."

"Okay, all the important things anyway, is that correct?"

"Yeah."

"All the things about the telephone calls, right?"

"Yeah."

"All the things, for example, the weapon, that kind of stuff?"

"That was brought up the other day, he does . . ."

"For the first time?" Ferencz interrupted.

"For the first time," Bauer nodded. "He does not remember whether I told him or not."

"So basically, what you're saying to us Mrs. Bauer, that for the first time since — by the way, when did you retain Mr. Altman?"

"Sometime in October, '83."

"All right, you felt for some reason you needed representation?"

"My divorce lawyer advised it."

"Okay ... and from that time until September the 17th, the day before you were to come in and testify, you never said to him or he has no recollection of anything about a weapon, is that correct?"

"That's correct."

"Okay. Now, given the information you've told us today under oath and the information you've told your lawyer, in between those conversations that you've had, you've had numerous conversations with policemen, is that correct? ... You've had a conversation with the prosecutor, with investigators, is that correct?"

"Yes, it is."

"And in amongst those two — as you called them — 'truthful' conversations, there are a variety of out-and-out untruths or lies that you've stated, isn't that correct?"

Bauer felt a flash of anger, but she quickly cooled down; Kapsak had prepared her for this.

"No," she said levelly, "that's not correct."

This was just the opening for which Ferencz was waiting.

"Well," he said, as he busied himself looking through some documents, "you testified in front of the Grand Jury, didn't you?"

"Yes, I did."

"Under oath?" he asked, looking up at her over his glasses.

"Yes, I did."

"You didn't mention anything about Mr. Taylor, did you?"

"No."

"But you don't consider the fact that you admitted that to be a lie?"

"I was not asked that question in the Grand Jury testimony."

"Okay," Ferencz said, nodding his head thoughtfully. "You remember the first time that you spoke to the police?"

"Yes, I do."

"When was that?"

"After we had returned from Minnesota ... the middle of July."

"Well, when was that?"

"It was a Saturday night, I'm not sure of the date."

Ferencz shook his head and let forth a sarcastic laugh.

"Well, Mrs. Bauer, you have the times (of Berta's calls on July 8) down to seven o'clock, nine o'clock, nine-thirty, three-twenty, three-thirty, six-twenty, seven-thirty, in terms of the calls that were made, but you're not sure of the day?"

"That's right. They were important to me."

"By the way," Ferencz said, shifting gears, "when you came back to New Jersey after going to Minnesota you had an argument with your husband, is that correct?"

"Yes, it is." Bauer was visibly annoyed at being asked anything about her married life.

"Your husband is also a police officer, is that not also correct?"

"That's correct." Pat Bauer did not like where she thought this was heading.

"A police officer with what police department?"

"Edison Township," she said tersely.

"And he has a service revolver, is that not correct?"

"Yes, he does."

"And, if you will, are you aware that he spoke to the Prosecutor's Office?"

"Yes, I am."

"Were you aware that he told the Prosecutor's Office that on July the 11th he checked out where you were by going to the Menlo Park Travel Agency?"

"I was not aware of what he told the prosecutor. He has never told me himself exactly what he told the prosecutor. He told me a lot of things. He said he tracked me down."

"And you were unaware at the time that he had . . ."

Kapsak had had enough of this line of questioning, also.

"Objection, Judge," he said, drowning out the remainder of Ferencz's question. "She said she was unaware of what he said to the Prosecutor's Office except . . ."

"Well, he said various things," Ferencz argued. "I'm going to ask her if this is one of the things she was aware of."

"Well," Judge Hoffman said, "you can ask her what he told her."

Well, I think this is cross-examination," Ferencz said. "Can I ask her specific, 'Did he tell you X?' "

"Well, why don't you ask your question?" Hoffman told the defense attorney.

"All right," he said. "Did he tell you while at the Menlo Park Travel Agency the agent came across the name Catherine Warner and mentioned to him that this was the woman who was killed in Metuchen?"

Ferencz hoped to get an answer to the question, because he knew that with John Bauer in the hospital, this would be the only way he could get the statement in front of the jury. But Kapsak objected once again.

"Yes, that's objectionable," Hoffman agreed. "The reason it's objectionable is basically you're getting into the statement of John Bauer, which is at this point a hearsay statement," he told Ferencz.

"He indicated that he was going to get even with you, is that correct, when he came back?" Ferencz continued.

Pat Bauer thought she could head off further questions along this line.

"He told me that he tracked me down and went to Menlo Park Travel Agency and found the tickets. He did not tell me they were in the name of Berta. He did not tell me they were in the name of Warner. He told me that he was going to take my child away."

Ferencz decided to change the direction of his questioning, and return to the theme of Pat Bauer, the Liar.

"The first time you spoke to the police department or the Prosecutor's Office, do you remember just saying to them that on July the 8th at approximately 10 p.m., you picked up Gene Berta at the railroad station in Edison, you drove to the Howard Johnson in Newark, stayed there, and the next morning you flew to Minnesota?"

"Yes. That's what I told them."

"And you told them no more than that."

"That's right."

"You didn't indicate anything about telephone calls at that time?"

"No."

"You didn't indicate anything about anything other than the fact that you picked him up at 10 o'clock?"

"That's right."

"And the next conversation (with the Prosecutor's Office) took place in early July, is that not correct, or mid-July?"

"The following Tuesday."

"Now, do you remember the ... conversation that you had with prosecutor's detectives going back to July in which you basically said to them — and this is with officer Watson and Zimmerman — said to them that you received a call at seven and nine and 10? You recall that? Seven o'clock in the morning you received a call, nine o'clock in the morning you received a call and 10 a.m. in the morning you received a call, is that correct?"

"I guess so."

"Okay. And you then indicated that at approximately seven p.m. Mr. Berta called again? You remember telling him that?"

Pat Bauer nodded her head.

"Now, during this conversation, you didn't mention anything, did you, about those calls that were made allegedly in the afternoon?"

"No."

"So you withheld information?"

"Yes, I did."

"You didn't tell them the full truth, right?"

"I agree," Bauer said, matter-of-factly.

"You agree?" Ferencz was surprised by her answer. "Do you think there's a significant difference, Mrs. Bauer, between withholding all the evidence and lying about evidence, being untruthful about evidence?"

"Yeah."

"So it's okay . . ."

"I'm not saying it's okay," she interrupted. "I think there's a difference."

"It's not as bad to withhold the truth, right?"

"It's not as bad."

"But it is bad to lie intentionally, with malice, right?"

Bauer did not respond.

Ferencz then introduced into evidence a report filed by Zimmerman of his July 21st interview with Bauer.

"On July 21st, you recall having a two-hour or so conversation with Detective Zimmerman?"

"Yes."

"At that time, did you tell Detective Zimmerman that you knew the time you'd be leaving on the eighth of July?"

"I don't remember."

"Well, he did ask you questions concerning the trip, didn't he?"

"Yes, he did."

"And you wanted to be truthful with him, didn't you?"

"To a point."

"So you wanted to hide things from him?"

"Yes, I did."

"Okay. Mrs. Bauer, do you remember testifying a couple minutes ago that you stated to Detective Zimmerman that you did not know Cathy Warner nor did you ever meet her and that statement was made on July

21st, right?"

"That's right."

"I take it you knew who Cathy Warner was by July 21st?"

"Yes, I did."

"That's because Mr. Taylor told you . . ."

"Yes, it is."

"You didn't say anything about that whole thing with George Taylor that day?"

"I left out that whole period of time."

"But that is not in your opinion to be lying, that's just leaving things out?"

"That's right."

"Okay. Now, remember testifying at the Grand Jury? Did you tell the whole truth there and nothing but the truth?"

"I answered the questions that were asked."

"So you didn't once again say anything about a weapon in the Grand Jury?"

"No."

"Didn't say anything about those other telephone calls and the whisper, none of that stuff?"

"I only answered the questions that I was asked and I did it as briefly as I could."

"And you were asked what his general mood was during the trip, is that correct?"

"Yes, yes it is."

"You said he was in a good mood, you did a lot of laughing and a lot of talking?"

"That's correct."

"There's nothing about anybody being tense on the ride up?"

"They asked me the general mood and the general mood of the entire weekend was good."

"Now, did you deliberately not tell the Grand Jurors this stuff and deliberately not tell Detective Zimmerman and Watson or was it a matter of forgetting?"

"I deliberately didn't tell them."

"So on October 11th when you spoke to Lieutenant Zimmerman, when he wrote down Mrs. Bauer stated in my previous conversation that she forgot to inform me, that's a lie or a mistake?"

"I didn't forget to inform him. I didn't inform him."

"Now, also in this statement of October the 11th, you didn't say anything about cleaning up, is that correct?"

"That's correct."

"And that's because you weren't asked?"

"No."

"That's because you chose not to tell?"

"I chose not to tell."

"You remember speaking to people from my office?"

"Yes, I do."

"Do you remember speaking to them on April 4, 1984, a Mr. Goldstein and Mr. DeRogatis? You remember saying to them that you had a great deal of respect for Mr. Berta?"

"Yes, I do."

"You remember saying to them that you've never seen him violent, even when provoked?"

"That's true."

"You remember saying to them that Mr. Berta is a man who likes and respects women and would not harm them?"

"Yes, I do."

"Okay, and you also made the statement that you were not jealous of Gail Berta but you were jealous of Catherine Warner?"

"No, I don't remember saying that."

"So that if Mr. DeRogatis and Mr. Goldstein came in and testified that you made that statement, that would not be correct on their part?"

"I don't know whether it would be correct. I don't remember saying that. I don't remember them asking that."

"During that conversation, you never indicated to those gentlemen anything about cleaning up, is that correct?"

"They never got that far. They started to ask me questions and I got very upset."

"And when you spoke to the prosecutors back on September the 7th, you still had mentioned nothing about a weapon to them, is that correct?"

"I thought it had been brought up."

"But you spoke to Mr. Altman, didn't you, and Mr. Altman said he didn't remember any conversation about a weapon?"

"I thought it had been brought up when I originally talked to Joe Zimmerman. I was reviewing the testimony the other night and I was trying to go over and make sure they had everything and it just came up."

"The statement that's on the 7th of September is the first one in which you ever tell the Prosecutor's Office anything about having to clean up, correct?"

"Okay."

"And still nothing about a weapon, and that's because you thought you had told them already, correct?"

"I did."

"By the way, remember when the prosecutor was talking to you and asking you questions, just earlier today when you were under oath?"

"Yes."

"It is true, is it not, that on direct examination you didn't mention anything about the gun until Mr. Kapsak said, 'and did he show you anything?' correct?"

"Correct."

"So then Mr. Kapsak actually had to — pardon the word — suggest did he show you anything?"

That assertion brought Kapsak to his feet.

"Judge, I object to that!"

"That objection is sustained," Hoffman ruled. "The jury will disregard that remark."

"Okay, fine. Mrs. Bauer, what were you doing on the day after you got back from Minnesota?"

"I took my son and nephew to Great Adventure."

"And do you know where your husband was on that day?"

"Yes, I do. He was in court in New Brunswick."

"Okay. And your husband did say to you that he would get even, is that correct?"

"He told me he was going to take my child away."

"Did he tell you he was going to get even?"

"I don't remember."

"Okay," Ferencz said, turning on his heel and walking back to his chair at the defense table. "I have no further questions."

Kapsak did not believe that Ferencz had done much damage to his witnesses' credibility, but he thought he should do some minor repair work anyway.

"Mrs. Bauer, during our first conversations with you in July when you did not tell us ... that you were stood up, why didn't you tell us that the first time around?"

Bauer looked at Berta as she gave her answer. "I did everything in my power to protect him. I felt it was damaging. I didn't want to be the one to say it."

"Well, why did you decide to say it?"

"There was a number of things that I knew I hadn't said. When I told my own attorney, he suggested I go to a criminal attorney and discuss it with him and I went to Steve Altman and I explained the whole situation to Steve; one of my main concerns was the fact that I had already spoken to another attorney and gone through the entire story with him and I was afraid that the other attorney was going to turn around and use it on me in court for not telling the truth. So Steve Altman told me to talk to you guys and to get it all out there. He said there were certain things that I didn't have to say because it was private conversation. He thought I should say it but he wasn't going to force me to tell it to you. So he took me down here and I met with you for the first time for a meeting and I told you as much as I felt at that time I could possibly say."

"Was that the first time you had met me?"

"I had met you at the Grand Jury."

"Which time was it that you decided I was a bad guy?" Kapsak's question drew laughter from the audience.

"All the times," Bauer answered, which drew even louder laughter. "You kept saying to me, you have to tell the whole truth, you have to tell me the whole truth, and you said if you're withholding information I'll prosecute you to the fullest extent of the law and I was scared and it was at that point that I had just gotten Steve Altman and I was scared."

"When you spoke to us in October, did you tell us the entire truth at that point?"

"No."

"When did you tell us the additional information?"

"When I came back and talked to Joe Zimmerman and Dennis, about two weeks ago."

"What caused you to come forward at that time?"

"I was afraid that I was going to get hung here in court. I felt pretty rotten about it. I knew that one side knew and I knew the other side didn't."

"How did you reach that conclusion?"

"When the investigators came into my attorney's office, they started questioning me about things that I had said to Gene's first attorney. The day after Gene was arrested I went to his attorney and went through the entire story with his attorney and I thought that was the end of it. I told this attorney how he stood me up, I told him what he said on the plane, I told him everything that I could possibly think of in hopes that he would be able to use it to defend Gene. When I went to my own attorney, he told me I had to say certain things but I didn't have to say the conversation, but he felt I should, that I may get hung up in court for it later.

"When they came to my attorney's office to interview me, in April, March, they brought up Morris Brown and they said you made some very damaging statements in Morris Brown's office and I was really upset. They said that you said Gene said he just killed three people and I went crazy. I said why are you guys looking at that stuff, that's privy conversation, that's between me and the attorney, he's not supposed to tell you that. They said, well, the point is, we have it in the notes. And I said don't let the Prosecutor's Office get ahold of them, I never told them. They said, oh, you never told the Prosecutor's Office. I said no. Oh, that's nice. And I started crying and said I just can't talk anymore. They said okay, we'll make an appointment, come back when your lawyer is here."

Kapsak then asked what Bauer's motivation was for requesting a meeting with the prosecutor's detectives several weeks before; she related the story of the public defender's investigators bracing her husband on his death bed and asking him if he had anything he wanted to get off his chest.

"I was furious that they could go up there," she said. "The only way that they could have found out that John was in the hospital was if Gene had mentioned something. And I ranted and raved and I called you and I asked you if you could do something. You said only if this hospital would give a statement. And it was like the hospital refused to give a statement. I was just furious.

"And then maybe two days later on a Friday morning, a girlfriend of mine called me, she said how is John and I said he's hanging in there and she said, Patty, Gene has to talk to you. I said, oh no you don't, tell him to leave me the hell alone, I've got nothing to say to him. She said Patty, he's been trying to get in touch with you, he said your line at work is busy and he's afraid to call you at home. And I said first of all, I have three private lines at work, there's no way he couldn't get me, second of all, if he did try to get me at home there would be no reason to be afraid because I am there with just my son and I said I don't understand how he could think that I would be so rotten, his wife is supporting him throughout his trials, the least he can expect me to do is support my own husband. That was it."

"Well, were the incidents you just described part of your reason for coming forward a couple of weeks ago?"

"I don't think it was — I think it contributed. I knew I would have to say something sooner or later."

"And when you came in and spoke to us a few weeks ago, was there anything at all that you had told us that wasn't true?"

"No."

"And when you spoke to me and Denny Watson just a couple nights ago and told us about the gun, was there anything about that that wasn't true?"

"No."

"That's all I have, Judge."

Finally , it was over. Judge Hoffman told Bauer that she could step down; Pat Bauer felt as though she glided rather than walked down the several steps. Bauer made a point of not looking at Berta as she passed him on her way out. She felt woozy, and wanted nothing more than to get out of that courtroom and into the fresh air. As she started down the aisle, she vaguely heard a man's voice say, "grab her!"

"*Oh, no,*" she thought, instantly terrified, "*they're going to arrest me!*"

Pat let herself be gently led the rest of the way by a Sheriff's deputy down the aisle and through the large double doors at the head of the courtroom. Once outside of the courtroom, she turned to the officer and said, "Are you going to arrest me?"

"Arrest you?" he said, a bemused look on his face. "I'm not going to arrest you, I just wanted to catch you because you looked like you were going to pass out!"

Edward Jones was the next witness called by Thomas Kapsak. Jones, a smallish, weatherbeaten man who repeatedly asked to hear questions again, had been living in the little shack behind Warner's house for the past four years, he told the jury.

Jones testified that on July 16th, he had been at a friend's, drinking, then returned to his home to find Cathy Warner's family and a policeman at her house.

"I came down there and I was wondering what the cops was doing there," he said. "Everybody was there. Because she told me she was going on vacation and to keep an eye on the place."

Jones told Kapsak that the request to watch Cathy Warner's house came from her on the 7th or 8th of July.

"I was talking to her about the rent because she said she'd be gone," he explained. "So I said I wouldn't get the money 'till the 11th, which is that Monday. That's when I get the check. And she said I won't be home. She said I'm going on vacation, I won't be back 'till, I think it was Thursday, the 14th, something like that."

Jones said that in looking around the house on the 16th, he saw flies on the windows and thought they were drawn to the house because Cathy Warner had left some meat out before she went on vacation.

Asked to recount what happened when he went into the house, Edward Jones testified that he had followed a "tall man" into the bathroom, saw him push aside the shower curtain and then saw Cathy Warner's knees sticking out of the tub. He said after that, he just turned around and went back to his house.

As he had with Shirley Jones, Ferencz brought out with Edward Jones the discrepancy between what he told police on July 16th and what he was now saying, about the last day he saw Cathy Warner alive.

Jones said he had made a mistake and that he didn't remember seeing Warner after his son and daughter-in-law were with him.

A nervous Sam Harris took the stand next. Harris lived next door to Cathy Warner, in a house owned by his godfather.

Harris testified that he noticed renovation work starting on Cathy Warner's house around March of 1982. He described Cathy Warner as a "beautiful" person, saying that he would talk to her outside, and that he sometimes helped her with yard work and once assisted her in moving some furniture around.

Harris also testified about the numerous friends who visited at Cathy Warner's house. He said among the autos he saw parked in front of her house were a Jaguar with M.D. license plates and a Middlesex Park Police car.

He met Gene Berta, Harris continued, when the defendant began electrical work at Cathy Warner's house. Harris said he didn't know "the man in the blue van" was doing work until he asked Cathy about him.

"She said he was a contractor," he explained. "He was the one doing the wiring. I said oh. And then she started talking about him. I looked at her, I smiled. I said, Cathy, why you smiling? She said, I don't know. She said he just make me mad sometime, he tell me he going to do one thing, he never show up. She would look at me ... I noticed whenever she be cheerful and happy, her eyes would, like, bright up. I said, Cathy, you in love! She said, uh-huh, and I smiled. That was it."

Harris' nervousness came to the fore when he was asked by Kapsak to tell the jury exactly when he saw Cathy Warner's car parked at her house during the week of July 8th. Avoiding looking at the second assistant prosecutor, Harris testified that he had seen it on July 16th. When Kapsak reminded him that he had earlier said he saw it on the 12th, Harris asked that he be allowed to talk to Kapsak and the judge.

A hearing among Harris, Hoffman, Kapsak and Ferencz was then held in Hoffman's chambers. The hearing's record was ordered sealed by the judge, but an unsubstantiated rumor floating among the press afterword was that Harris said he was scared because, he said, he had run into Berta on his street several days before, and that Berta had threatened him. There was no other proof of the allegation, so it went no further.

Upon returning to the courtroom, Harris was excused for the day and the court was recessed until the next morning.

September 20, 1984

Sam Harris, looking more confident than he had the day before, was recalled to the witness stand. Kapsak had allowed Harris to review a letter, written by Kapsak and sent to Ferencz, which recounted what Harris had told the second assistant prosecutor earlier in the summer. After reading the letter, Harris said the first day he saw Cathy Warner's car parked in her driveway during the week of July 8th through July 16th was July 12th, adding that it was parked further back in the driveway than normal.

"How do you know that, Mr. Harris?" Kapsak asked.

"My godfather asked me, did I see my friend there, our neighbor? I said no. I said, she home? He said, her car in the driveway. When I walk out the door and look and saw the car, I smiled. I figured she was home. I told my godfather, I said, what is her car doing parked way back there? He said, she parked there. I said, no, Dad, she don't park her car right there, she always park her car right in the front just as she come in the driveway."

Harris also testified that Berta would park his van right in front of Cathy Warner's house while he was doing work to it. That practice stopped, he said, when Berta completed his work, although the defendant would still visit Cathy Warner, he would park his van in different places on the street and sometimes on the next block.

Ferencz knew that he had a good chance to discredit Harris' testimony in the jury's eyes.

Did Mr. Harris remember, Ferencz asked, that he had testified the day before that Cathy Warner's car was parked there Saturday and Sunday, and the reason that he remembers that is because he saw it when he was returning home from a party?"

"I made that statement because, to be honest with you, I was scared to say anything," Harris said.

Ferencz quickly dropped that line, turning his attention to Harris' testimony about the workmen he saw entering and leaving Cathy Warner's house — including Gene Berta — as well as the different police cars he saw there.

Ferencz asked Harris several times if he remembered seeing Berta's blue van parked near Cathy Warner's house in May and June, to which Harris answered yes. Ferencz didn't tell Harris that he was mistaken, since Berta's van was totaled in the May auto accident. This was another piece of information he would save for his summation.

Kapsak's next 10 witnesses, called on September 20 and 21, were comprised mainly of some of Cathy Warner's nurse friends from John F. Kennedy Hospital and Middlesex General-University Hospital, namely Joy Niemiera, Donna Tokar, Mary Ann Burns, Merelyn Daniel, Rhonda Lane, Janina Stevens, Rosemary Cascella and Dawn Farnell.

Also called were Eric Greenwood and Lee Cole, whom Cathy Warner met while taking tractor-trailer driving lessons.

Before Kapsak called the first in this group of witness, Hoffman reminded the prosecutor that he would not allow any testimony by her friends of her saying she had a gun in the house, nor would he allow Joy Niemiera to testify that Cathy had once told her that Gene Berta hit her.

As had their statements when they were first interviewed by police, the testimony offered by Cathy Warner's friends painted the same picture; one of a trusting, vulnerable woman — who wanted nothing more than to settle down and raise a family — being continually lied to and victimized by a cruel, cold calculating man, one who was more interested in her money than her love, and one who would say anything to her to get what he wanted.

Joy Niemiera testified that she had tried to get Cathy to date other men, but Cathy just was not interested.

In his cross-examination, Ferencz tried to build a similarity between Niemiera and Gene Berta by noting that Cathy Warner had loaned Joy and her husband money for their house.

"Cathy was a good person," Niemiera said.

"And of course, you did pay her back, right?" Ferencz asked.

"No. We made payments to her but I was not able to get the amount of money back to her."

"Okay, okay, in any event, she was good-hearted and there was no problem, you asked, you were her friend, and ..."

"No," Niemiera interrupted, "I didn't even ask. My husband had just lost his job and we had just purchased the home and I was crying to her and she says, how much do you need?"

Dropping the subject when he saw it wasn't going in the direction he wished, Ferencz just reviewed the rest of Niemiera's testimony.

Donna Tokar told the jury that Cathy Warner and Gene Berta attended her wedding and also that, after Cathy Warner had discovered in May that Gene was living with his wife, Warner called Tokar and asked her to return to the defendant a charm Berta had given Warner. Tokar said Warner had placed the charm in an envelope, along with a note.

"She called me to find out what happened after I gave him that envelope and I said, you know, don't you, that he went back with his wife?" Tokar testified. "She said, yes, she found out and she said that all her plans were ruined. No!" Tokar said, quickly correcting herself. "Everything that she ever wanted was ruined, and that all she wanted was to get married, settle down and have a baby, and that she'd never be able to do that now because she only wanted Gene. She said that she would never have what she wanted, never be happy and she was really depressed."

Tokar also testified about calling Warner on July 5th to invite her to the shore on the weekend of the 8th, but Cathy said she had plans. Tokar testified that she told Cathy Warner that if she were going away with

Berta, to "make up something else" because Tokar "didn't want to hear it." Warner, Tokar continued, said she was going to see her sister.

On Thursday, the 7th, Tokar said she called Cathy back and told her that if she changed her mind, Tokar would be home until 5 p.m. or 6 p.m the next day.

When Kapsak asked Tokar if she called Cathy's house after Warner was supposed to have returned from her vacation, Tokar said that she and Cathy had made a pact that Cathy would call her as soon as she got home from any vacation. Tokar testified that she called her friend from Monday the 11th to Friday the 15th and, when she did not receive an answer, figured that Cathy had just decided to extend her vacation.

Tokar's last statement concerned Ferencz. Beginning his cross-examination, he asked Tokar why her assertion that she called Cathy Warner the week of the 11th was not included in the police report. He handed her a copy of her statement, asked her to read it, then said, "That statement doesn't say anything about anything for the rest of the week, does it?"

"I did call her all week!" Tokar insisted.

"The question was, did you tell Mr. Kapsak this, or is this new?"

"I did. Yes. I told him that."

"And that's just not in the statement?"

"I guess not. I did say that! I said specifically that because I felt that was important."

"You're not just, you know, exaggerating a little bit, by any chance?"

"No way!" Tokar shot back, visibly annoyed at the question.

Ferencz also asked Tokar about her statement that the only other man Cathy had been seeing was an optometrist. Tokar dismissed that, saying it was only a "casual" relationship.

Before he sat down, Ferencz had Tokar reiterate that on July 5th and July 7th, Cathy Warner told her that she was going to visit her sister.

Lee Cole, a classmate of Cathy Warner's at the Action tractor trailer driving school, testified that Cathy was "head over heels" for Gene Berta.

"She'd come in some mornings, she said they'd argued all night and that they'd try to straighten things out. Then she'd be happy for awhile. Then she'd say, I'm not going to see him anymore, but the next day she was seeing him," Cole said. "Her favorite thing was to give him ultimatums,"

Cole continued. "(There were at least two) during the period of truck school."

Mary Ann Burns testified that Cathy and Gene appeared together in November of 1982 at her son's christening.

In response to Ferencz's question about the optometrist, Burns said that it was not a "recent" relationship, adding that Warner had seen the optometrist shortly after her husband John died in 1980.

Some legal posturing occurred during Merelyn Daniel's testimony, when Kapsak attempted to enter into evidence a photograph of the Daniels, Cathy Warner and Gene Berta, taken at Rosemary Cascella's wedding. In a sidebar conference, out of earshot of the jury, Ferencz explained his objections.

"Judge, I want to enter an objection, first of all, to the prosecutor attempting to move it into evidence in front of the jury because even if I have to object for a valid reason, if it's kept out, it gives the impression I'm trying to hide things from the jury. I ask that things that he requests to be moved into evidence be done outside the presence of the jury.

"In terms of this particular photograph, if your Honor will notice it, Mr. Berta's, you know, beard is ... rather ... long ... "

"Rather what?" Hoffman asked, arching his eyebrows.

"Rather long and he looks relatively scruffy and I think it is being introduced only for those purposes because nobody denies he was at the wedding."

Kapsak shook his head. "It shows only that they were at the wedding, your Honor," he countered, "but it shows that on June 25th Cathy Warner was very happy to be with Mr. Berta and this witness testified that's exactly how they looked on this date. If Mr. Berta looks scruffy, well, I didn't stage the photograph. I can't help that. This is the photograph I have and it's the only one I have of them together happy. I think their relationship is certainly relevant and I want the jury to see it."

"I don't think he looks scruffy," Hoffman said, studying the picture. "I think it's just a matter of opinion, but I think his beard is just ... bushier, that's all. I would not even have thought that if you hadn't said it," he added, turning to Ferencz. "Seriously."

"Well, I did and I do," Ferencz maintained. "I think that's the reason it's being entered and nobody's denying they were together ... I think it's prejudicial."

Hoffman allowed the picture, ruling that it was "all part of the mosaic of what was going on between these two people."

Daniel testified that she and Cathy Warner had been "buddied up" during Cathy's orientation period at Middlesex General, and that they had become good friends. In time, Daniel continued, Cathy started talking about the man in her life.

"This man named Gene," she testified. "I don't remember his last name, but his name was Gene and she used to call him her Teddy Bear because she said he was built big and had a beard."

"How often did she talk about Gene?" Kapsak asked.

"Every day."

Daniel also recounted the day in May when Cathy found out that Gene had moved back with his wife, and afterword had gathered all his things at her house and dumped them on his front porch.

"All right," Kapsak continued. "After that incident ... did she talk about Gene anymore?"

"No, because they weren't seeing each other at that time. Then a while went by and she said Gene had called her and he was going to come over that night and talk, and I tried to discourage her from seeing him again, but she said, no, she was going to see him and talk to him... And when she came back to work she said that she had talked to him and they had ironed things out. She wasn't specific but she said that things were going to be on her terms now, that she had given him a time limit to get everything straightened out, and that's all she said about it."

Daniel also identified Cathy's Timex watch, and said that that was the one she wore to work every day.

September 21, 1984

Dawn Farnell, the last of Cathy Warner's friends to testify, was the first witness called by Kapsak on this day.

Farnell, who lived with Cathy for about six weeks in 1980, testified that each morning, Cathy Warner would cross off the preceding day on a calendar she kept next to the phone. Farnell said Warner would do this prior to leaving for work.

The second assistant prosecutor rounded off his case with testimony from Lt. Frank Kraft, from the Port Authority of New York and New Jersey police department, and Det. Dennis Watson.

Kraft testified that any piece of baggage carried on board an airplane would be passed through an x-ray machine and, if the pieces' contents could not be seen this way, the passenger would be asked to open the parcel for inspection before being allowed to board. Baggage that is sent to the plane's baggage compartment is not checked, Kraft said.

"And if there were a weapon in that baggage, would it be discovered by any security measure that you're aware of?" Kapsak asked.

"No," Kraft replied.

Watson was recalled to the stand a final time to testify about everyone he and the other detectives had interviewed. Kapsak's questions were of a general nature, but Brad Ferencz had some specific issues he wanted addressed.

Ferencz wanted to know why, if Watson was present when Gary Neal gave his statement, the investigator did not look into Neal's assertion that a Metuchen policeman named "Jim" — who had investigated Cathy Warner's automobile accident — came over and "impressed" Cathy with his gun. Watson testified that the Metuchen policeman told him he was never at Cathy Warner's house.

Watson said the officer told him he investigated the accident and, when Warner gave him her address, he realized that hers was the property with a small shack at its rear. The officer was looking for a place for his stepson, so he asked Warner to contact him if the shack ever became available. Watson said he did not investigate the matter any further.

Ferencz then asked Watson if Dorothy Gierlich had told him that she saw an upstairs light on in Cathy Warner's house on July 12th and 13th. Watson said yes, she had, but he did not investigate that any further, either.

After Watson had been dismissed, Kapsak picked up a large white envelope and removed from it a Christmas card, which he had entered into evidence. He then read the contents of both to the jury.

From the envelope, he recited, "Merry Christmas to my beloved."

Opening the card, Kapsak read in a slow, solemn tone, "Catherine, I love you with all my heart. With all my heart this comes to say I love you for all the thoughtful things you always do. It comes to say how very much I need you and how you make my every dream come true. With all my heart this comes to say I love you and although I've said it many times before, with every hour of every day that passes, I hope you know I mean it ever more. With love at Christmas and always, Gene."

Slowly closing the card and placing it on his desk, Kapsak looked up at Judge Hoffman and said, "Your Honor, subject to offering various items into evidence, the State rests."

"Reasonable Doubt at a Reasonable Price"

Bradley Ferencz was not happy with the defense he was about to present. Judge Hoffman's prohibition on bringing in testimony about Cathy Warner's sexual activity prior to 1980, Ferencz felt, left him with only half a case. His mood was characterized by a short conversation he'd had with Detective John Haley during a break when Pat Bauer was still on the stand. Ferencz had walked past Haley, who was standing near the courtroom doors, when the officer waved him over.

"Hey counselor," Haley had said, wearing a slight smirk, "when's your client gonna look scared?"

"I don't know," Ferencz had replied, "but he better start to soon."

The last-minute revelation by Bauer of the gun in Minnesota had hurt his case, but Ferencz was somewhat certain that he had cast enough of a cloud over Bauer's character through his cross-examination. He was more positive that, through the testimony of Dr. Louis Roh, the deputy medical examiner for Westchester county, New York, he could throw sufficient doubt into the minds of the jury members as to just how long Cathy Warner was dead.

Ferencz's first witness was Gail Berta. He needed her to dispel any notion the jury might hold that she was jealous of her husband's relationship with Cathy Warner, so jealous that Gene Berta would be pressured into murdering Warner to keep her from telling Gail of the affair.

It was a defiant-looking Gail Berta who took the stand that afternoon. Wearing a blue pant suit and with her black hair tied behind her head, Mrs. Berta looked like she could hold her own in a brawl if need be.

Ferencz took Gail Berta through her history with Gene Berta, starting with the fact that he was her family's paperboy in Edison when she was 9 nine years old, then how they met when she was living at home, following her separation from her first husband, and into their early relationship. Berta testified that she and Gene lived together for six months in 1975, broke up and then resumed their romance, with the understanding that they would have an "open relationship."

"Can you define for the jury what it was you meant by an open relationship?" Ferencz asked.

"Okay. We would live together. We would also be able to go out and see other people when we wanted, go out for the weekends, go out for a whole week at a time, but come back to each other and be a family."

"Now, did you go around town telling people about this?"

"Absolutely not," Berta answered, her voice rising. "That's my private life and it's nobody else's business but mine." Berta said she did not even tell her parents about the arrangement.

Ferencz then had Berta recount her marriage to Gene, the fact that he adopted her twin girls — thereby forfeiting welfare payments which the girls had been receiving — her miscarriage in 1976, and then spent some time talking about M.S., the woman with whom Gene Berta had had a baby. Gail Berta said M.S. was thrown out of her house, then came to live with the Bertas until she had the baby, even though Gail knew that Gene was the father. She said they also had unsuccessfully attempted to adopt the baby.

Ferencz wanted to probe how Gail Berta felt about Gene fathering another child. "You didn't throw Mr. Berta out of the house?" he asked.

"No."

"Did you become furious or angry with him?"

"No."

"Did you in any way act hostile to him?"

"No."

"What was your feeling about the fact he had made another woman pregnant at that time?"

"I was sorry it happened, but it wasn't the baby's fault. I don't think it was anybody's fault. It just happened."

Gail Berta testified that Gene would go out nearly every night of the week and come home when he pleased, sometimes staying away for as long as two weeks. She said she never asked him where he was going.

"Why not?" Ferencz asked.

"Because I knew what he was doing, and it was none of my business, you know? He didn't ask me where I was going when I was out."

In 1979, Gail Berta's natural father died, leaving her $10,000, she said. She testified that the money was used as a down payment on the 7 East Walnut Street house, which she described as a handyman's special.

"Mrs. Berta, by the way, when you married your husband, did you love him?" Ferencz asked.

"Very much. I still do," she replied.

Gail Berta also said that she had been over to Cathy Warner's house. She recalled one day when Gene was working at Warner's house, and Gail drove over there to deliver some messages for his business. She said she and Cathy exchanged pleasantries, and then Cathy gave her a tour of her house.

"What did you feel about her yourself?" Ferencz asked.

"I didn't like her," Gail Berta answered.

Moving off the subject of Gail's feelings about Cathy Warner, Ferencz questioned Berta about their separation in January of 1983.

"Gene requested that he would like to leave the marriage for awhile and get his thoughts together, which I agreed to," she explained.

"Did you perceive anything wrong in the relationship at that time?"

"Not at all."

"And, had he still been spending time away?"

"Oh, sure."

"When somebody would ask you where he was or something, what would you answer?"

"He was either truck driving or he'd go down to the Carolinas with his buddies."

"Why didn't you tell them he was out with other women?"

"Because that's none of their business."

The separation was in name only, Gail testified, noting that she had seen her husband more during their short period apart than she had in the previous three months.

Ferencz' next subject was the May 10, 1983 accident in which Gene suffered eight broken ribs and a fractured wrist. Gail said she was in the back room, visiting Gene, when Cathy Warner walked in. The story she told of that incident was different from that recounted by Cathy Warner's friends.

"And she said hi to me, walked over to my husband, started asking him how he was, how he was feeling, if anything hurt. And that lasted maybe three to five minutes. And as she was walking out she looked at me and said, 'And have fun with your monsters' and left the room," Berta testified.

Berta said when she went home that day, she found on her front porch a grocery bag containing two t-shirts, a hankie and a bandana, as well as Gene's personal and business checkbooks and some letters addressed to him at Cathy Warner's address.

Gail assumed that the items had been left by Cathy Warner, so she called a friend at Kennedy Hospital and asked her if Warner was still employed there. Her friend said no, "but we had a problem with her out in the waiting room (that day); ... she demanded to see Gene, she was a nurse, she used to work at Kennedy and she was going to go see him and nobody would stop her. And they informed Cathy that his wife was with him and she wasn't a relative so she could not go in the back room to see him," Berta testified.

"I called (Cathy) up on the phone. I asked her if she placed all these things on the porch. She said yes, she did. And I said, well, you know, are you seeing Gene, and she says yes, we're dating. I said do you realize he's still married. She says, no, I thought he was still separated. I said, no, Cathy, he's been separated three weeks in January, but he's been home ever since. So she said, well, since I found out now that he's married, I will leave him alone, leave you alone and I won't bother you anymore."

Gail said when she next visited Gene in the hospital, she told him about her conversation with Cathy Warner, then asked him to stop seeing her.

"Did you tell him not to see her?" Ferencz asked.

"No ... I have no right to tell him who to see and who not to see," she answered.

"Did you expect him to stop seeing her?"

"No."

"Why not?"

"She was available."

"And that's basically the way you looked at Gene's relationships with other women?"

"Yes," Gail Berta answered, nodding her head. "Men, I feel, will go after any woman if she's available."

"Did you know that Mr. Berta, your husband, was lying to other women?"

"Not at the time, no."

"You know it now?"

"Sure I do ... it was a tactic to use to get into their bedroom."

"Look over there, Mrs. Berta, and tell the jury how it affected your relationship, if at all."

Gail Berta faced the jury with a blank look and, in a mechanical tone, said, "It did not affect our relationship at all because I was doing the same thing he was doing, and I cannot condemn something that we were both doing. We both agreed on it and this was our lifestyle. This is the way we chose to live."

Gail Berta said she knew Gene was still seeing Cathy Warner because one day, when they were in the middle of preparing to make love, Warner's keys fell out of Berta's pants pocket. Gene denied they were Warner's, Gail said, but she knew they were.

Gail said she returned Gene's set of Cathy Warner's keys to Warner after the latter had called Gene at the hospital and asked for them. Once at Warner's house, Berta said, the two women had a discussion about Gene.

"The conversation was that she should find herself another man, that Gene does not want to settle down to have a traditional marriage, and that I won again and she would always lose because she could not give him what he needed, and that was an open marriage.

"She tried a couple of times to break us up," Berta continued. "I felt sorry for her, but I also felt resentful towards her."

Ferencz' next group of questions concerned the trip to Minnesota.

The trip, Gail Berta testified, was something they had talked about for months. Berta said that she had sent away for brochures from real estate companies which handled farms, through which she and Gene looked and settled on properties they would like to visit. In mid-June of 1983, Berta continued, Gene told her he was going to borrow $10,000 from a friend– which would be paid back with 20 percent interest – so they could repair their house and move. Gail said she suspected Gene was getting the money from Cathy Warner.

On June 24, 1983, Gail said she came across a receipt for the Aztec Motel in their personal checkbook. She questioned Gene about it, she said, and he told her that he was taking her to the shore for a holiday, but that he wanted it to be a surprise.

On July 7th, 1983, Gene didn't tell Gail where he was going for the weekend, she testified, but, "that was normal."

"And this has been your relationship since 1975?" Ferencz asked.

"Yes."

"And you haven't complained about it?"

"No, I haven't."

On July 11th, she continued, Gene returned home at about 10:30 p.m. He unpacked part of his suitcase, making room for some of her clothing, they "got things ready for the babysitter," and they left, not returning until the 14th.

Finally, Gail Berta testified that everyone in their house used the guns that were kept there.

Kapsak, who never bought the defense's assertion that the Berta's had an open marriage, asked Gail Berta how many other relationships her husband had had with other women.

"Oh geez, maybe, that I know of? Maybe seven."

"How did you find out about them?"

"Well, a couple I knew of beforehand and, since your investigation, I found out who the other ones were."

"What do you think was his basic approach? Did he lie to all these women, or did he tell them about your 'classic' open relationship?" Kapsak did not hide the sarcasm in his voice when he said the last three words of his question.

"I don't think he told them about our relationship because it was nobody's business but our own," she answered.

Kapsak also brought out that Gail Berta knew about an additional $5,400 that Gene had received from Cathy Warner; money that was used to buy his van, and also to bail him out of jail when he was arrested for non-support. She also said that he had never paid that money back to Warner.

On re-direct examination, Ferencz asked simply, "Did you care what he was doing with other women?"

"No," Gail Berta answered.

Colleen Duffy was the defense's next witness. Early in the investigation, she had told defense investigators that she saw Cathy Warner on July 11, removing some groceries from her car, a statement she recanted after meeting with county detectives in the Metuchen police headquarters. That resulted in Ferencz requesting a hearing during which he wanted to ask the detectives what they had said to Duffy to get her to change her recollection. The motion was denied.

Ferencz asked Duffy to tell the jury what she saw on July 11th, 1983.

"I was leaving my house going up the street, and (Cathy Warner) was taking things out of her car."

"And she was standing in her driveway at 125 Durham Avenue . . .?"

"And putting her bags on top of the steps."

"And you're certain that was the Monday before the 16th?"

Duffy nodded her head yes.

"Is there any question in your mind at this time?"

"No."

Ferencz showed Duffy a copy of a prosecutor's office report which contained her interview.

"It says Colleen stated she remembers seeing Cathy the last time after she returned from the Shore," Ferencz read. "Did you tell anybody that?"

"I left for the Shore on the weekend for the 4th of July, but then I left again to the Shore on the 17th."

"And it was that time on the previous Monday from the 16th that you remember seeing Cathy Warner?"

"Yes."

Ferencz asked Duffy to read out loud the last line from the Prosecutor's office report relating to her: "After thinking about it for a little longer, Colleen said she wasn't at all sure when she saw Cathy for the last time."

"Do you remember ever saying that to anyone?" Ferencz asked.

"No," she replied.

During his cross examination, Kapsak asked Duffy if she ever told him or anyone from his office that she saw Cathy Warner after she returned from the Shore on July 4th weekend. Duffy answered that she did not. During her testimony, Duffy seemed nervous and confused on the stand, contradicting herself several times. Kapsak didn't attempt to refute her testimony, nor did he bother to cross-examine Ferencz next two witnesses, Kenneth Schreck and Ann Marie Regan, both of whom testified that Colleen Duffy was with them at the Shore the weekend of July 17th. The assistant prosecutor was certain that he could diminish the importance of Duffy's testimony during his summation.

September 24, 1984

Dr. Louis Roh, the Deputy Medical Examiner for Westchester County, New York since 1973, was Bradley Ferencz's only real hope of winning his client an acquittal. While he didn't have as impressive a background as did Kapsak's hired gun, Dr. Spitz, Roh did garner some notoriety during his career; he was the sole forensic expert for the prosecution in the so-called Scarsdale Diet Doctor murder trial. Roh's office gets more than 2,000 autopsy subjects per year, with Roh personally involved in between 200 and 250 cases, he said.

Earlier in the summer, Ferencz had sent Roh the autopsy photos, autopsy report and other investigative documents, and, as Kapsak had done with his expert, asked Roh to make a determination as to the amount of time Cathy Warner was dead before her body was found.

"According to my review of the records, autopsy photos and other documents," Roh answered when he was asked the pertinent question, "it is my opinion that the decedent died two to four days prior to discovery of the body."

"How did you find Dr. Shuster's report?" Ferencz asked.

"Well, I found Dr. Shuster's report is a very accurate and precise description and I think it was done professionally."

Ferencz then produced six photographs, one of the outside of Cathy Warner's house, three of the basement floor, and two of Cathy Warner's body, and introduced them into evidence.

Ferencz wasted no time in attacking Spitz's findings.

"Can you tell the jury what lividity is?" Ferencz asked.

"Lividity is one of the findings occurring after death in the body," Roh answered. "It is a dark reddish discoloration of the skin by settling of the blood to the lowest portion of the body. Initially it shows up as a dark reddish color. As time goes on, the color changes.

"This type of lividity usually starts occurring right away after death. It becomes what we call fixed lividity after 12 hours. For example, if the person is found dead face up, the lividity will show up in the back of the body, except where the portion of the body is in contact with the under surface ... Once lividity is fixed, after 12 hours or so, even if the body is turned over, it will remain on the same side."

Walking over to the evidence table, Ferencz picked up several of the oversized color crime scene and autopsy photos. Returning to his post at Roh's side, the defense attorney handed the pathologist one of the autopsy photos, depicting the back of Cathy Warner.

"Could you indicate where the lines or where the apparent lividity is and where, if you will, it isn't? What does it show?"

"Well, this shows the lividity as the dark reddish purple color, showing over the shoulder blade and the back of the waist area, as well as the side of the buttock region."

"What does that indicate?"

"This indicates that the person died and stayed in a face-up position immediately after or within six hours after death and thereafter the person was in a face-up position until the discovery of the body."

"If the body had been on its side for any period of time, would that photograph look like that?"

"No," Roh answered, "it would be different."

"How would it look if it was on its side for any period of time, doctor?"

"If the person was on one side more than 12 hours, then this type of lividity should show on the side where the person is lying on."

Ferencz picked another photo, this one of Cathy Warner's back and one side, then handed it to Roh.

"Tell us about any lividity signs you see in that particular photograph."

"Again, this photograph shows the lividity on the back."

Ferencz then had the two photos circulated among the jury. While the jurors were viewing them, the defense attorney next turned his attention to the board on which Thomas Kapsak had displayed pictures during the testimony of Werner Spitz.

When the jurors had finished viewing the photos, Ferencz asked Roh to step over to the board, and, pinning up the returned pictures, asked him to point out on the blow-ups exactly what he had just testified to, and how that related to the autopsy report filed by Dr. Shuster.

"Doctor," Ferencz continued, "if you would refer to the report, Dr. Shuster says there is no obvious line of lividity. What does that mean to you when he says that?"

"It's not very clear to me," the doctor answered, "but it's my opinion when he says no obvious line, it means when the lividity is fresh, the demarcation is quite clear. Whereas in this case, because of the breakdown in blood cells, the delineation is not that clear as the first day."

Borrowing one of the judge's pens and handing it to Roh for use as a pointer, Ferencz asked the doctor to explain, using the pictures, exactly what he meant by a line of lividity.

"Well, first of all, the body is placed in this metal type of container, face down right now . . .You can see this border of the container on the right-hand side. There are the two feet and the left-hand side, and part of the back of the head is showing," Roh explained, pointing to the relevant body parts as he progressed.

"The lividity which I mentioned here is this dark reddish discoloration in the back. The lividity is not apparent where the shoulders are and where the buttocks are. Because this surface is in contact with a certain surface, the blood will not settle in that particular area ... Say you turn the body over face down, it will remain this color. As time progresses, the blood components and the blood vessels will hemolyze; it leaks out blood vessels and spreads to the tissue."

His dissertation completed, Ferencz asked Roh to take his seat.

"Do you see anything in these photographs to indicate the body was on the right side for a period of days?" Ferencz asked.

"I do not exactly know whether it shows the left side or the right side, but if this photograph shows the right side, then there should be a pressure point," Roh answered. "If the person is lying on the right side, then the lack of lividity should show on the side of the buttocks and the chest area."

Handing Roh a vial containing maggots taken from Cathy Warner's body and a ruler, Ferencz asked the medical examiner to measure the largest maggot he could see.

"What is the largest one you see there?" he asked.

"The largest one I see I see here, it measures approximately half an inch long."

"Have you anything in there approximating an inch?"

"No."

"Have you had the occasion to see that size maggot develop in a period of two to four days?"

"Yes."

Switching gears once again, Ferencz asked Roh, "Could you tell the jury what would happen to a body if it was in a closed room for a period of five, six, seven days, when the temperatures outside are ranging in the 90s?"

"Well, after death, the body goes through certain stages of changes. For example, there are usually three important observations we make. There are the hardening of the body, called rigor mortis, and after that, what we call decomposition occurs in the body. This is commonly known as decay or rottening of the body. And as the decomposition progresses, the body usually swells up, because the gas under the skin and the blood components in the blood vessels, hemolyze or autolyze and it seeps throughout the body and the discoloration of the body or the skin surface occurs.

"At the beginning it usually starts as a greenish coloration of the skin and then as time goes on, it becomes purplish and finally turns black ... At the same time, the skin becomes very loose and the body fluid seeps out from the body and accumulates under the skin, forms sort of a blister type of skin slippage. Sometimes this blister contains body fluid, usually dark brownish in color. Oftentimes this ruptures and leaks out."

"Stopping right there," Ferencz said, "by the time the body gets to that condition where you have the blistering, could you describe the odor of the body and the condition of the body?"

"By the time when the blistering occurs and the body swells up, there should be a tremendous odor, an unbearable odor for lay people."

"Would that odor permeate a house?"

"Oh yes. Quite often the neighbors smell this type of odor and report it to the police, and that's the way we find the body."

"At the time that this process would begin, sufficiently to seep through the blisters, would a person be able to move that body easily?"

"Well, by the time the blisters occur in the body, this is the stage we call the early decomposition stage. The body usually swells up to two or three times the normal size, with a strong odor. And because of the sloughing of the skin surface, (it would be) very slippery and very difficult for a person to move this type of decomposed body."

"What would happen to a person if she or he could move it, what would happen if they walked outside?"

"The person who handled this kind of body should have this odor coming from its body."

Ferencz let the jury mull the answer while he walked back to the evidence table and shuffled through several more pictures. Convinced the jury had had ample time to grasp his point, he turned back to the witness and continued.

"If the body was in that condition on the eleventh, what would the condition of the body be on the sixteenth, five days later?"

"Five days later, the body should be in the condition of far advanced decomposition," Roh said. "Which means the entire body should be blackened and the area of the skull should show the exposure of the skull bone, because of the soft tissue being removed by the maggot infestation, and areas like hands and fingers – which are exposed to the air – should completely dry out; what we call mummification."

Handing the doctor another of the crime scene photos, this one showing Cathy Warner lying in the bathtub as she was discovered, Ferencz asked, "Could you describe the coloration of the body as you see it, along with the condition in terms of the mummification of the hands?"

"As I described before, the discoloration of the body is seen on this neck area and part of the chest area. This is called marbling, it looks like a marble pattern."

"Is that early or late signs of decomposition?"

"This is an early sign of decomposition. As time goes on, the black discoloration should spread throughout the body ... (T)he hands and fingers ... (were) dry before decomposition occurs, that is why mummification occurred."

"Doctor, could you tell us whether that is early or late on, the mummification?"

"(This) shows early signs of mummification. If it is far advanced, this whole thing becomes a dark brownish black. It is so rigid, it is hard to bend."

"Now, if you will, Doctor, that stage of mummification, how long does that take in 90-degree weather?"

"I've seen this occur after two days."

"How about the coloration of the skin, particularly the abdomen?"

"That is another thing; due to the early signs of the decomposition, you can see this abdomen is sort of swelled up and the abdomen looks very tense because there is a lot of gas inside. This marbling ... shows a small portion of the body. This is one of the clues to let me know or determine that this is early sign of decomposition. Had it been a late sign of decomposition, the entire body should be black, like seen in the neck area."

"If that body had been on the eleventh in the state that Dr. Spitz ... testified it would be in, is that condition, the condition of the body that it would be in five days later, as you see it there?"

"No."

"Is there any question in your mind about that?"

"No."

Ferencz next took aim at Spitz's assertion that the dark stain on the basement floor was caused by fluids leaking out of Cathy Warner's dead body.

"Doctor, did you have occasion to read the testimony of Dr. Spitz, as it referred to the staining in the basement?"

"Yes."

"Could you tell us about that; what your opinion is about that item?"

"Well, my opinion is that is a blood stain. The blood stain usually shows the red color in a fresher state. As the time goes on, the component of the blood is iron, as we know, as time progresses ... iron oxidizes and becomes a rusty color. That is why if the blood stain has a certain period of time, then you will have this sort of brownish discoloration, because of the denaturalization of the blood component. That is all I can say."

"Do you know whether the fluid, if it did not contain blood, would test positive for blood?"

"The fluids that come up out of the decomposed body should not show positive for blood, especially decomposed fluid."

Wanting to leave his opponent as few openings for his cross-examination as possible, Ferencz asked the doctor, "But the way, you are getting paid for this, are you not?"

Roh smiled. "I think so."

"Did we settle upon a fee before you testified?"

"Yes. I'm supposed to get paid for my time."

"Does what you testify make any difference in terms of the amount of fee or was that already decided?"

"Depends on how much time I spend."

"Your witness," Ferencz said to Kapsak, as the defense attorney walked back to his seat.

Kapsak's first line of attack was to show the jury that Roh's credentials were not as impressive as those of Spitz, which he attempted by going through Spitz' list of accreditations, professional affiliations and journal articles and books, and asking Roh if he had similar a background.

"Now, Dr. Roh, have you considered the possibility that perhaps Dr. Spitz has had more experience with this type of matter?" Kapsak asked.

"He may have," Roh admitted. "He may have more experience than I do."

After rereading Roh's finding that Cathy Warner was killed two to four days before her body was found, Kapsak had Roh admit that even though he was supplied with reports on her watch and the calendars, the doctor did not take this so-called associative evidence into account when reaching his final conclusion.

"In fact, in this report you make no reference whatsoever to an entomology report," kapsak said.

"It wasn't my report. I can't use it."

"If the maggots found on the body were seven to nine days old, than the person could not have been dead two to four days, is that correct?"

"If that's correct, yes," Roh said.

On re-direct, Ferencz asked Roh if he had looked at all the "associative evidence" prior to writing his final report. Roh said he had, but he did not give those reports as much weight as he did the photographs and Dr. Shuster's autopsy report.

Joy Niemiera returned home that evening experiencing a sadness she had not felt since learning of her friend Cathy's death a year before. Today, during Roh's testimony, was the first time she had seen the photos of Cathy's body; a mental picture of what Mr. Neal must have gone through when he found his daughter in that state sent a chill through her body. Not wanting to remember her best friend as she had seen her in the courtroom, Joy collected all the pictures of Cathy she could find and set them up at different places in her house. Then, exhausted, she sat down and cried.

September 25, 1984

Ferencz' first witness this day was Joan Rupchis, a personnel secretary at John F. Kennedy Memorial Hospital in Edison. Rupchis testified that personnel records show that during the period of May 17 1980 through December 31, 1980, Cathy Warner worked only weekends. Her testimony directly contradicted that of Dawn Farnell, who stated that during the six weeks the two women lived together in 1980, Cathy was assigned to shift work at the hospital.

Kapsak chose to not stringently cross-examine Rupchis or Ferencz' next witness, Mary Bacorn. Bacorn, also a nurse at Middlesex General's Four-Tower, testified that she saw Cathy Warner make a phone call from a pay phone early in the afternoon of July 8, 1983, after she had received a call. Bacorn said Cathy returned five or 10 minutes later, got her purse, and then left.

Gary Neal, called as a defense witness, testified about his sister Cathy being "impressed" by the gun of a Metuchen police officer who had investigated her accident in the summer of 1983. The policeman, Neal said, had come to Cathy Warner's house for dinner.

Wanting to get the attention off any other man, Kapsak asked Neal what his sister said about Gene Berta. Mainly, Neal answered, about her intention of marrying him.

Ferencz' next witness, Carol Taylor, said she knew Gene Berta since 1972 and Gail Berta since 1974, and knew them to have an open relationship.

"They had an open marriage and she went and did her own thing and he went and did his own thing," she explained.

Taylor said Gail Berta would sometimes tell her, in general terms, about a man she was dating and that once Gail let it be known at the rescue squad that if she was needed, she could be found at the apartment of a male squad member.

These outside relationships, Taylor said, had no affect on the Bertas' marriage.

On cross-examination, Taylor told Kapsak that she also knew Gene to have affairs. She said she knew of at least three women from the rescue squad with whom he had dallied.

On re-direct, Ferencz asked Taylor if she had ever seen Berta lose his temper.

"No," she replied, "I never seen him get mad, outrageous mad."

Kapsak, on re-cross, then asked Taylor, "Is Mr. Berta cool under pressure?"

"He handles himself well," she answered.

Charles Favorite told the jury that he had known Gene Berta for about eight or nine years, meeting the defendant when he was a customer at the electrical supply store where Favorite was employed.

Favorite testified that Gene and Gail "let it be known" that they had an open marriage, and that he would sometimes go out with Gene and a woman he was dating at the time.

Favorite also said that when he was separated from his wife, he knew that Gene would go over to his wife's apartment occasionally to "render help."

That last statement was something Kapsak had to explore.

"After you left your wife, (Berta) went over to talk and 'render help'?" he asked, a bit incredulous.

"Not basically to talk," Favorite said. "A couple times she ran out of oil.

He went in the middle of the night and got oil."

"Did he ever send her any greeting cards?" Kapsak asked.

"No," Favorite replied, missing the sarcasm in the question.

The final witness Ferencz would call this day would be Antonio Cataldi, an investigator with the Public Defender's Office. Cataldi was one of the men who was accused by Pat Bauer of attempting to force a deathbed confession to the murder from John Bauer, her policeman husband.

Ferencz sought to address that issue directly, asking Cataldi why he went to see Bauer.

"Well, I had over a period of time, reviewed a report prepared by one of the prosecutor investigators, and this report indicated to me that conversation took place on the 11th of July about a person who had been dead. And so that created a conflict in my mind. I wanted to pursue it further ... The conversation, according to a report, went on between John Bauer and a person in the Menlo Park Travel Agency."

"And what exactly did you believe that report to indicate?"

"Well, here is a conversation taking place on the 11th of July, stating that a woman from Metuchen was found dead, and I know from other reports that I had reviewed up to then that the body wasn't discovered until the 16th."

"So did you want to find out if there was an error in the report?"

"I wanted to pursue the conversation that took place between Mr. Bauer ..."

Thomas Kapsak rose at this point, objecting to the generalized nature of the questioning. To satisfy his opponent, Ferencz admitted into evidence the report in question, which was co-authored by Zimmerman and Watson, and had Cataldi read the exact sentence that lead him to want to question Bauer.

"On the second page, page 2, there is a continuation of the paragraph on the first page, the one that starts with, 'On Monday, July 11, 1983,' that paragraph," Cataldi testified. "Well, the last sentence particularly says, 'While he was at the Menlo Park Travel Agency, the agent did not come across the name Catherine Warner and mentioned to him that this was the woman who was killed in Metuchen.'"

Ferencz next introduced into evidence Cataldi's identification card, which contained his name and the fact that he works with the county Public Defender's office.

Ferencz then asked Cataldi to describe what happened on the day he and another Public Defender investigator, Claude DeRogatis, visited John Bauer in John F. Kennedy Memorial Hospital.

Cataldi said that when he and DeRogatis arrived at the hospital's main information desk, "we presented our identification and we requested of the two ladies that were there to obtain the proper clearances from the hospital officials for Mr. DeRogatis and I to have a visit with Sgt. John Bauer. After displaying our cards to the two people at the desk, they held them, the girl held Mr. DeRogatis' card, gave me mine back, made telephone calls, asked us to sit down.

"We went over and sat down and probably some 15 to 20 minutes, when they motioned us to come back to the desk and told us that we had clearance, I don't know the floor and the room, to go upstairs to Mr. Bauer's room."

"What occurred when you got upstairs?"

"When we got upstairs, we went to the nurse's station, sought out the nurse. We again identified ourselves, indicated to her that we had clearance and that we were there to see Mr. Bauer."

"And what occurred at that time?"

"The nurse escorted us to the room where Mr. Bauer was."

"Without telling us specifically what Mr. Bauer said, did you see him?"

"Yes, sir."

"And could you describe the nature of the conversation, without telling us exactly what he said, and then what transpired?"

"Well, I didn't see Mr. Bauer before, that was my first day I ever saw him. Mr. DeRogatis, I think, had seen him and recognized him, and Mr. DeRogatis said, John, do you remember me . And we again displayed our credentials; it's a habit, we do it."

"Did Mr. Bauer seem to recognize Mr. DeRogatis?"

"Yes, he did. And in turn Mr. DeRogatis introduced me, we exchanged generalities. After it appeared that Mr. Bauer appeared to be upset, he was in pain, it appeared to me."

"Did you ever ask him about that statement?"

"No sir, we never got around to that."

"Why not?"

"Well, after seeing Mr. Bauer in bed, with his IV and the way he was positioned, we — Mr. DeRogatis and I — just made the decision, why?" Cataldi shrugged his shoulders with his palms facing the ceiling as he asked the rhetorical question. "So we never pushed it. We had a social visit, is what I really call it, everything that transpired after that."

"Did you ever say anything to him about wanting to get anything off his chest?"

"Absolutely not," Cataldi said, firmly.

Thomas Kapsak still believed Pat Bauer's assertion that Cataldi and DeRogatis had impersonated prosecutor's investigators to get into John Bauer's room. The jury and audience sat in stunned silence as they watched the normally staid assistant prosecutor lace into the man sitting in the witness box.

"Mr. Cataldi," Kapsak began, his voice already louder and more forceful than it had been during the entire trial, "do I understand you to say that after reading Detective Watson's report, you thought that perhaps the travel agent had murdered Catherine Warner?"

"I didn't know what to do, other than I would have liked to talk to Detective Sergeant Bauer as to the nature of this paragraph," Cataldi replied, trying to remain calm in the face of Kapsak's intensity.

"But according to that paragraph, it says that the travel agent told him that Catherine Warner was dead?"

"Sir, my interpretation of that is that's not true. This reads, the agent did not come across the name, and mentioned to him. Now, I don't know who the antecedent is in this particular case. That is what I was trying to develop."

"You didn't know if it was the travel agent or Mrs. Bauer's husband that really murdered Catherine Warner?"

"It is the realm of possibility that either one of them did murder Catherine Warner."

"Because of that possibility, you were instructed to go speak to Mr. Bauer, is that right?"

"To develop this particular paragraph," Cataldi replied, nodding his head.

"The person who asked you to do that was Mr. Ferencz, your boss?"

"Yes sir, I am working for him."

"Yes."

"But I'm an investigator and this has always bothered me."

"Well, did you go and see him before Mr. Ferencz asked you to go and see him?"

"I didn't go there to see him before that time. I was waiting for the opportune time."

"You mean when he was dying of cancer?" Kapsak shot back, "was that an opportune time?" The second assistant prosecutor was clearly losing his patience with this witness.

"I didn't know until that day that is where Mr. Bauer was. I had no knowledge of his condition or that he was ill," Cataldi replied, his own voice rising a bit.

"All right, Mr. Cataldi," Kapsak said, visibly reigning in his anger. "So on that day ... and when was that date, exactly?"

"At this particular time, I can't give you the date, I don't know," the investigator said. "I've done so much work on this, I can't give you the date."

"Well, did you prepare a report of your social visit with Mr. Bauer?"

"No sir, I did not."

"Let me understand. You thought that you had hit on who the murderer possibly was, is that correct?"

"Well, if I could have pursued it or if I would have pursued a conversation, I could have developed some intelligence and I could have done something."

"That was your suspicion?"

"Nothing materialized."

"That was your suspicion when you got that, that maybe this was going to lead you to the real murderer, is that correct?"

"All investigations are conducted as a possibility they are going to lead to something." Cataldi had by now regained his composure.

But Kapsak wouldn't let go.

"Mr. Cataldi," he said, with the tone of voice of one who has wearied of repeatedly asking the same question, "we are talking about this paragraph in this report. That is what caused you to go to the hospital, isn't it?"

"I went there to pursue something."

"The something that you went there to pursue was to find out who the real murderer was, wasn't it?"

"That sounds good, yes sir."

Kapsak smelled blood and was homing in for the kill.

"When you got there and you saw his condition, you turned it into the social visit, is that what you are telling us?"

"Well, it turned itself into that, yes." Cataldi was staring to squirm in his chair.

"It turned itself into a social visit?"

"Yes, sir."

"Is that when you saw him lying in bed dying with the IV in his arm? Is that when it turned into a social visit?" Kapsak was just about at full throttle now, his voice rising in pitch as he completed the question.

"When Mr. Bauer stated to us, and I'm going to tell you exactly what he said ..."

"Please do" Kapsak interjected, more as a dare than a request.

"You got some balls coming here to see me. But he reached out and more or less touched us to stay there and talk to him. Otherwise I would have done an about-face and bugged out. But I didn't do it, because he acted like he wanted me to stay. We didn't pursue anything, other than generalities."

"What specifically did Mr. Ferencz, your boss, direct you to do when you went to the hospital?" Kapsak had once again calmed himself, but all in the courtroom knew keeping it was an effort.

"We were to talk to John, see what happened, if this conversation did, in fact, happen and what is meant by it."

"This is a murder investigation, is that correct?"

"Yes, sir."

"This was important to your boss, Mr. Ferencz, wasn't it?"

"Of course."

"When you got there, you turned it into a social visit, is that what you're telling us?"

"Yes, sir."

"Mr. Cataldi, how long have you worked for the Public Defender's office?"

"Six years and seven months."

"How often have police officers expressed a willingness to talk to you when you wanted to interview them about a case?"

"I have been successful on an occasion. I would say I have been successful more than the average person."

It was probably Cataldi's superior attitude while answering the question that set Kapsak off. Several jurors jumped in their seats as the assistant prosecutor lashed out at the witness with a virulence none thought him capable of.

"Mr. Cataldi," he began, his voice booming, "you knew very well, if you had identified yourself as a Public Defender representative, Mr. Bauer would never had talked to you, didn't you know that?"

"That's not true, that's not true," Cataldi shot back, trying to match Kapsak's volume.

But Kapsak would not be deterred.

"There is a regulation in your office, is that correct, saying that when you identify yourself, when you want to speak with a witness, you have to identify yourself as a member of the Public Defender's office?"

"That's correct."

"And is that regulation even more specific than that? Does it tell you specifically not to identify yourself as a member of the Prosecutor's Office?"

"We have been instructed on numerous occasions not to misrepresent ourselves."

"Exactly!" Kapsak said, rising to his feet. "Okay. And you know very well that if you admit you misrepresented yourself, you could get fired from your job, don't you?"

That was more than Cataldi could take. Half rising out of his own chair, meeting Kapsak's fury, he said, "Sir, I never did run scared in my whole life. I am not running scared now. I never misrepresented myself. I produced my credentials every step of the way."

Kapsak wasn't finished.

"You also knew, Mr. Cataldi, if you impersonated a police officer, you could be prosecuted for that, don't you?"

"I never take actions that I regret, because I did not do what you are alleging that I did do!" Cataldi said, slightly banging the bannister in front of him for emphasis.

"You just had a social visit?" Kapsak asked, calming down enough to retake his chair.

"It ended up that way."

"All right," Kapsak said to the judge, not hiding the disgust in his voice. "I have no further questions."

September 26, 1984

Gene Berta told Judge Hoffman that he had decided not to testify. He made his announcement in court, but out of the presence of the jury. In explaining the decision, Ferencz repeated his desire to question Berta about Cathy Warner's sexual history prior to 1980, but Hoffman refused to allow it, as he had during the entire trial. He told Ferencz that he would not the attorney to "bring in through the back door what you could not bring in through the front door."

Ferencz' last two witnesses were Eugene Berta, Jr. and the defendant's father, Alexander. Both testified that several of the guns seized at Gene Berta's house were actually theirs, and that neither had ever seen Gene Berta with a handgun.

Sixteen witnesses and four days after beginning his attempt to show the jury that Eugene Thomas Berta did not kill Catherine Warner, Brad Ferencz rested his case.

Although it was still early in the day, Judge Hoffman decided to let the jury go home. Because the next two days were Jewish holidays, Hoffman ruled that summations would be held on Monday, October 1.

Ferencz and Kapsak agreed that two stipulations — facts that neither

attorney would refute nor felt the need for direct testimony to support —
would be entered into the record. The first stipulation was that as of June,
1983, that the total liquid assets of Gene and Gail Berta and their children
were less than $100.

The second stipulation related to the cancelled reservation at the
Thunderbird Best Western Motel in Minnesota. Colleen Maki, the former
reservations clerk, said in a written statement that on July 8, 1983, someone
identifying themselves as Warner called and cancelled her reservation for
that night. Maki, following usual procedure, stamped the reservation card
"cancelled" and wrote "self" to show that it was cancelled by the person
who made the reservation.

The stipulation was necessitated by the fact that Maki had moved to
France, and could not get her passport validated in time to personally
appear in court.

"Do Justice ..."

Monday, October 1, 1984

Bradley Ferencz carefully studied the jury of nine men and six women. The jury had been originally comprised of 10 men and six women, but one of the sitting jurors was excused during the trial because there was some concern that he had discussed the case with a relative who worked for the Prosecutor's Office, his place having been taken by an alternate. He was standing at a podium that had been set up to facilitate the attorneys' summations, arranging his notes.

During his 3 1/2-hour summation, Ferencz would, as he did in his opening statements, ask the jury to consider not only things that they heard, but things that they did not hear. He would, by examples, attempt to convince the jury that the police had not thoroughly investigated this case, and that they settled on Gene Berta as the suspect because they did not like his lifestyle. Ferencz would also propose a number of other people who could have committed the murder.

"The State has the obligation to prove to you that a man who has been captain of the first aid squad almost continually since 1975, a man who, if you will, has brought people back from the dead, has saved people's lives, has now taken a life," Ferencz began. "... a man who you've heard through the various people who has never lost his temper, who has never been angry or volatile."

The State, Ferencz continued, would have the jury believe that perhaps Gail Berta's jealousy of her husband's paramours was one of the motives for Cathy Warner's murder, but, he added, "I produced Mrs. Berta ... think about her testimony."

As far as money being a motive, he said, money never played too important a role in Gene Berta's life. He noted that when Gene Berta adopted Gail Berta's two daughters, welfare payments the girls were receiving were halted.

"Mr. Berta gave that up, he said, 'I don't need the money.' Did he? Perhaps. But the money was not something that was particularly important to him."

Ferencz pointed out that three people had taken the stand and, "uncontradicted," testified that Gene and Gail Berta had an open relationship.

"Now, you may not like their relationship. It may not be for you, it may not be for me, but they were satisfied with it," he said.

Cathy Warner's mother, sister and brother all testified that Cathy Warner did, at times, see other men, Ferencz argued, trying to cast doubt on the State's assertion that she was devoted to only Gene Berta. As he would many times during his summation, Ferencz re-read testimony, this time of Richard and Gary Neal testifying about the Metuchen policeman who they said would visit Cathy.

The policeman, Ferencz continued, denied visiting Cathy Warner's house, and said he was interested in the back shack for his stepson.

"The house in the back is one room," Ferencz said. "Is that logical? Would he want a place like that for his ... stepson?"

"Why would Mr. Neal remember a conversation with Cathy Warner concerning the officer visiting frequently?" Ferencz continued. "Why would the sister remember it? Why would the brother remember it if it didn't occur? And why would (the officer) deny it? And why would Dennis

Watson not follow up?"

And in 1983, Mary Neal told police that her sister saw an optometrist "a lot" Ferencz reminded the jury, while Sam Harris talked about the various police cars that would be parked in front of her house, as well as all the workmen who were there.

"Now, I'm not going to come here and tell you that she didn't say to a variety of nurses how much she loved Gene Berta, I'm not going to come here and tell you that those things she said are not true," Ferencz said. "But what I am going to say is, so what?"

Ferencz re-read Sam Harris' testimony where he said he saw an Edison police car in front of Cathy Warner's house, then noted that Pat Bauer's husband, John, was an Edison police, with a gun.

Edward Jones, Ferencz continued, originally told police that he spoke to Cathy Warner on July 12th, then he said he'd erred and really spoke to her on the 5th, 6th or 7th. And his daughter-in-law, Shirley, said that they spoke with Cathy early in the afternoon, but Merelyn Daniel testified that Cathy worked until 3:30 p.m. all that week, so she couldn't have been home early in the afternoon.

"If you have a chain link fence, and the State comes to and says, look at all the links we are going to put together, how strong is that chain link fence when all the links are maybes and possibilities and probabilities at most?" Ferencz asked.

Ferencz suggested that the telephone call that Cathy Warner received on July 8th, after which she said her mother had been taken to the hospital, might have been a ploy so she could get out of work early.

"We've agreed that her mother did not have a heart attack, and we also know that she told people, she lied to people, she mislead them in order to get out early," he charged. "Were her actions of saying what she did, if she did say it, of appearing upset, if she did, a result of a desire to get out early and a result, if you will, to indicate to people that there was a problem when there wasn't one? Flip the coin, ladies and gentlemen. Flip the coin. What does it mean?"

Ferencz also pointed out that all of Cathy Warner's friends said that she would continually break up with him and take him back. "If that's the case over five or 10 years," he asked, "why would he think that she wouldn't take him back one more time?"

Ferencz next turned his attention to the calendars – and the State's theory that Cathy Warner crossed off each day on a regular basis – her watch and her connections with her friends.

Dawn Farnell, Ferencz said, was "100 percent wrong" when she testified that Cathy Warner was doing shift work in 1980 when they lived together, "and she's probably also wrong on whether the calendar was crossed out every day, once a week, at the end of the month, whatever."

Cathy Warner may have crossed out the days consistently, Ferencz argued, but she didn't do it every day. She wouldn't, for example, if she was on a trip.

And as far as the phone calls from her friends during the week of July 8th through the 16th, Ferencz suggested, "isn't it possible that when Cathy Warner didn't want to answer the phone, she didn't?"

Picking up Cathy Warner's watch, Ferencz argued that the State has not provided "one shred of evidence that the (watch's) calendar part was ever used."

Ferencz restated his theory that the police settled on Berta early in the investigation, to the exclusion of investigating any other possible suspects.

"The two pieces (of evidence) that the State has produced before you that in any way connect Mr. Berta were the testimony of Bauer and the testimony of Spitz," he said. "Yet, they indicted the man a year before they had that! What does that tell you about the investigation that they did in this murder case?"

The defense attorney noted that there were 16 unidentified fingerprints found at the scene, six of which were from the kitchen sink.

"If a murder had been committed there and a man washed his hands after committing this crime, where would you find prints? How about the sink?" he asked.

Ferencz blasted the police for not broadening their control group of fingerprints when the samples were sent to the FBI.

"If those prints came up as being Mr. Bauer's or being (the Metuchen policeman's), and I'm not saying whether they are or not, I don't know, but wouldn't have that been interesting? Wouldn't that have been just fascinating? But they never bothered to compare it."

The police, he continued, didn't dust the hot dog and hamburger bun rolls for fingerprints, either. "What if they found Cathy Warner's fingerprints on those?"

Ferencz reminded the jury of the testimony that had heard concerning the police's search for a bullet. If a person with an unregistered gun had shot Cathy Warner, he argued, he could have thrown away the weapon. But, "if the person who committed the murder had a weapon and that weapon was registered and that person would not get rid of that weapon, that person was accountable for that weapon, then and only then would there be any reason to get rid of the bullet ... If Mr. Berta owned a handgun illegally, then why would he worry about the shell if he was going to throw the gun away?

"Police officers own guns, have them registered and cannot, if you will, get rid of them."

Perhaps, Ferencz suggested, John Bauer had found Cathy Warner's name and address at the travel agency, then went to her house and threatened her to get information on his wife's whereabouts. Ferencz pointed out in Bauer's testimony where she said she and her husband had had a fight, and that she called the police. The defense attorney questioned why officers would respond to a call like that unless Mrs. Bauer said her husband threatened her.

Pat Bauer, Ferencz continued, was probably telling the truth up to the time she testified before the Grand Jury.

"Why would Gene Berta tell her to tell the truth if he had something to hide?" he asked. And if Pat Bauer had nothing to hide, "why did she need a lawyer?"

Ferencz also totally discounted Bauer's testimony about the Public Defender's investigators scamming their way into John Bauer's hospital room. Maybe Pat Bauer was mad that the defense team would approach her husband and thought, "now I'll get (Gene Berta)," Ferencz speculated.

"Now, I don't say that Mr. Bauer did it," Ferencz told the jury. "I don't know. But I say that maybe Mrs. Bauer thinks he might have done it."

"And now we have the coup de grace," he continued, "the gun. That, ladies and gentlemen, is something that I just don't believe. Period. First of all, if you killed somebody, can you imagine taking a gun with you and showing it to the woman? No sense! Absolutely no sense."

Pat Bauer said nothing about the gun for more than a year and a half, and then it suddenly comes up, he added. "Nonsense. It just doesn't make sense."

Ferencz turned his attention next to the forensic evidence.

"If the body had been decomposing for three days and was decomposing sufficiently to cause the staining, that whole house would have reeked," he argued. Still, three people walked around the house and smelled nothing, and no one noticed anything until the bathroom door was opened.

Two medical examiners examined the maggot samples and said they were consistent with maggots that were from two to four days old, Ferencz said. Dr. Spitz testified that the longer maggots were several days old, while the shorter maggots were maybe two days old.

"Well, the maggots were collected on the 17th," he continued. "What's several days ago? The 16th? Fifteenth? Fourteenth? Maybe the 13th? Now we're getting pretty long. The 12th? That's not several days anymore, now you're talking almost a week."

Dr. Spitz, while he has an impressive background, may have been boosting himself a bit, Ferencz told the jury.

Zeroing in on Spitz' claim to have performed 50,000 autopsies in his 25-year career, Ferencz reminded the jury that the doctor would have had to have performed 2,500 autopsies a year to reach that number.

"This is the same doctor who travels around the world testifying," Ferencz said. "I suspect he would have had to bring a body on a plane to autopsy to be able to do what he claims to have done. I suspect he was huffing, telling you things that just aren't true, and I suspect it was deliberate."

The stain in the basement was not the outline of a body, Ferencz argued, saying that Spitz testified it was, because he wanted to believe it was.

"When you go outside and you look at the moon and you see a picture of the man in the moon, you know it's a man in the moon and you also know it isn't," Ferencz said. "You also know you can put together bits and pieces and come up with a picture of something that may not be there. When you look at these photographs, you're not going to see a place where the head was. You're not going to see a place where the knees were bent ...

You're going to see what appears to be maybe a spill. You're going to see some wiping up and you're going to see gradations as a result of probably water. But (Spitz) never bothered to go to the scene to check it out. All he based his findings on were photographs and the report."

Ferencz repeated that there was no odor in the basement, which there should have been if Spitz was right about what happened.

Showing the jury one of the autopsy photographs – Cathy Warner's back – Ferencz pointed out that the marks seen on her back show that she was lying on her back, not on her side as Spitz testified.

Ferencz' forensic expert, Dr. Roh, testified that Cathy Warner's body would not be in the condition it was if it was in a state of advanced decomposition. "It would have been much worse," Ferencz said. "This was early decomposition."

Concluding his remarks, Ferencz reminded the jury that "We tell you (Gene Berta) comes here accused of something he didn't do ... When you go back into that jury room, ... do justice. Follow the law."

As was his custom, Thomas Kapsak had not slept the previous night, instead choosing to work on his summation. In fact, he didn't actually finish it until about midway through Ferencz' closing remarks.

But now, at 2:30 p.m., Kapsak was ready. He rose from his chair, and quickly and confidently walked over to the podium, greeting the jurors.

"This case," he told the jury, "was a little bit harder to solve than most murders ... This was a planned murder by a practiced liar, by a man who was cool and calm and careful under pressure. The clues were a little harder to dig out. The facts were a little harder to analyze.

"What we did in the Prosecutor's Office was we worked a little harder and we thought a little harder and we searched a little harder to come up with answers."

"Every human tragedy has a history, has a backdrop, has a sequence of events that preceded it and help you to understand it. And Cathy Warner's murder was no different." Kapsak said. "When her husband John died in February of 1980, you heard all her friends telling you she was lonely, she was depressed, she was without a husband, she was without children, she was without a family of her own, and she was unhappy. But, more importantly for Gene Berta, she was vulnerable, and she was relatively wealthy."

Berta, Kapsak pointed out, must have thought that $100,000 was all the money in the world; he lived in a "ramshackle house that needed repairs very badly. He had all kinds of financial problems. He was virtually destitute, really, in mid-June of 1983 ... That money was very important to him. He worked infrequently. He was often on welfare. He spent most of his time at the rescue squad chasing women, and he was an opportunist and a liar. His own wife tells us that."

But Berta quickly recognized Warner's vulnerability, Kapsak said, and played into that, telling Cathy what she wanted to hear so that she would stay with him, even throughout all the breakups and ultimatums.

Toward the end of 1982, Berta and Warner began to be seen out together, Kapsak continued. "There was no longer the secret relationship in her apartment and her house ... That's what Cathy wanted and it had to make her happy, until January of 1983 when Berta finally told her that, yes, he had left his wife and now it was just a matter of time until they were to be married. And I suppose I can almost see Cathy Warner marking off the days on her calendar, waiting for that to happen."

But things changed in February of 1983, the prosecutor said. "And you have to understand this to understand what a thorough liar he was, what a cheater, a man without character. Because while he was telling Cathy Warner that he had left his wife and they were about to be married and it was just a matter of time, he started up with a third woman ... Pat Bauer."

Kapsak noted that Bauer, like Warner, was vulnerable; her marriage was going badly, and she needed someone to talk to.

In May of 1983, when Cathy Warner and Gail Berta showed up at Gene Berta's hospital bedside at the same time, things changed with Gene's relationship with Cathy. And although she broke up with him, Cathy let herself be talked into resuming the relationship.

"If Cathy Warner had resisted his next approach, I suppose she'd still be alive today, but she never acted wisely where Gene Berta was concerned," Kapsak said.

Warner agreed to go back with Berta, but on her terms this time. Kapsak surmised that two of the terms could have been Cathy giving Berta a check rather than cash on the day before they were supposed to leave for their Minnesota trip, and that she could hold the plane tickets in her purse, to ensure that she went along.

"Well, I'm not so sure she did all those things," he added. "Certainly the history of that relationship indicated she was not so wise in controlling the situation.

"But here is the important thing. Berta had to be aware that she could have done all those things. You see, when he got her $5,000 check on July 7th, he was aware that if he had gone up to Minnesota without her, she could have stopped payment on that check. He was aware that if he took her to Minnesota with him, that she could insist that her name go on the deed. He was aware that if she kept the tickets, obviously he couldn't go on the plane trip. He had no money. She made all the arrangements and paid all the expenses. He was aware that if he didn't do what she wanted him to do, that she could sue and tie up the property. He was aware of all these things on July 8, 1983, and he had to feel trapped."

Berta never had any intention of taking Cathy Warner on the trip with him, Kapsak continued, because weeks before he asked Pat Bauer to go with him.

"Pat Bauer was his new love. Things were heating up with Pat Bauer. Pat Bauer is the one he wanted to take and the one he did take. Another thing is clear. Cathy Warner thought she was going. No question about that."

"So, on the eve of July 8, 1983, Cathy Warner was sure that she was going to Minnesota. And Gene Berta was sure that she wasn't. Something had to give."

But is Gene Berta capable of murder? To answer that, Kapsak said, you have to take a look at the man. Berta, the assistant prosecutor said, has a "very strange attitude about guns," thinking nothing of taking his 3-year-old children shooting.

"We know that he's a liar and a cheater in his dealings with women," Kapsak continued. "We know he's callous and malicious enough to call Cathy Warner at work and tell her her mother had a heart attack and it wasn't true." Ferencz suggested that Warner made that story up so she could get off work early, but Kapsak doubted that. "If she wanted to get out of work at two instead of three, why didn't she just ask her supervisor . . .? I mean she would have had to answer for that sooner or later."

"What I say to you, ladies and gentlemen, is this is another thing that gives us some insight into the kind of person Gene Berta was: totally selfish, totally callous, (feeling) absolutely nothing but contempt for Cathy Warner by July 8th."

It was totally understandable that on the night of July 7th, Cathy Warner would tell her friend Donna Tokar that she was going to visit her sister the weekend of July 8th, Kapsak said, because Tokar was one of Berta's harshest critics.

Warner never had any intention of visiting her sister that weekend, Kapsak continued, because she knew that Mary Beth Neal was moving and that she'd be back and forth between Virginia and Pennsylvania.

"She never intended to visit Virginia. She only told Donna that she was going to visit her sister because Donna would not hear otherwise."

"Now this is important, and it's important for this reason: Berta was there that night. He tells us that he was there that night. And he must have overheard Cathy Warner tell Donna Tokar that she was going to Virginia to be with her sister.

"So when we questioned him later on, that's the first thing he told us ... That's where he got the idea. He heard Cathy tell it to Donna, and he figured that would be a good story to follow through on ... "

Kapsak then quickly reviewed the three interviews Zimmerman had with Berta, pointing out the inaccuracies in the defendant's stories.

"Everything she did, every step she took indicated to anyone who wanted to look and analyze that she thought on Friday morning, July 8th, 1983, that she was going to Minnesota," Kapsak said.

"When that call came in around 2 p.m., she was genuinely upset, agitated, depressed. She wasn't expecting that call. That was a call telling her her mother was sick and had been taken to the hospital.

"Now, there must have been a violent argument almost immediately when Berta picked her up. I mean, can you imagine, you're waiting to go on a trip, you're on top of the world, your mood is great, and suddenly you get a call from the man you love who is supposed to take you on that trip and he says, 'Your mother is in the hospital. She had a heart attack.' So he picked her up, and she finds out almost immediately that her mother was not in the hospital. Her mother had not had a heart attack.

"Now, how do you think she reacted to that? Well, based on Berta's prior history of lying to her and using her and manipulating her, she had to know almost immediately that he was up to something. She had to know or suspect that she wasn't going on that trip. She had to know or suspect that her whole relationship and, in Cathy Warner's mind, her whole future was going up in flames. And I'll bet that she even suspected that, just maybe, Berta was going with another woman."

Cathy Warner's reaction upon realizing that, Kapsak said, "had to be immediate, and her reaction had to be violent."

Turning again to Berta's statement of what happened July 8th, 1983, Kapsak recounted that the defendant said he and Warner had an argument about the trip, but that later they made love, "and she calmed down and she gave him the tickets that were in her name to go with someone else to Minnesota. She let him keep her money to take someone else to Minnesota. She gave him her car to drive to the train station so that he could go to Minnesota, and she had no problem with the fact that he was going to be going with another woman. Do you really believed that happened? No way."

Cathy Warner died on July 8th, Kapsak asserted, and the evidence points to that fact.

Recapping the credentials of Dr. Spitz, Kapsak then reminded the jury of his findings, that Cathy Warner was killed eight days before her body was discovered, and that her body was left for three days in the basement of her house.

"Mr. Ferencz would like you to think apparently that Dr, Spitz came here and lied to you. Well, you know, a murder in Middlesex County, New Jersey, just isn't important enough to Dr. Spitz to come in and lie, to undermine his reputation around the world," Kapsak added.

Kapsak said an important reason the jury should believe Dr. Spitz' report is that he was the only pathologist in the case who considered the entomology report, which said the oldest maggots found on Cathy Warner's body were between seven and nine days old.

Dr. Shuster, Kapsak pointed out, "said that if he had seen the entomologist's report, his conclusions would have been different. . .Dr. Rho almost said the same thing, but he didn't go quite as far."

Kapsak said the jury should also look at the association evidence, such as Cathy Warner's calendars.

"Mr. Ferencz would like you to think that maybe when she gets depressed, she doesn't (cross off the days on the calendars). Well, I'm going to ask you to look during the month of February, 1980, because that's when her husband died, and she made a note in her calendar that her husband died on that day and she crosses off the date. I don't know how much more depressed you can get than that."

Turning to the watch, Kapsak reminded the jury that an expert from Timex testified the watch was in good shape and was designed to run for 48 hours when fully wound.

"Well, if Cathy Warner is a nurse and the watch is a tool of her trade and she wound it on Friday morning, July 8th, and it stopped on Sunday morning, July 10th ... and it ran for 45 or 46 hours, what does that tell us? Well, it tells us that she wound it on Friday for the last time, and she wasn't alive to wind it on Saturday or Sunday," Kapsak said.

Another piece of association evidence, Kapsak continued, is the fact that Cathy Warner was a very social person and spoke with her friends on a daily basis.

"Donna Tokar told you that she called her every single day, day and night, even three o'clock in the morning sometimes, to try and catch her. Never an answer. She wasn't alive, ladies and gentlemen, past Friday, July 8th," he said.

"And what does the defense offer in response to that testimony?" he continued. "Well, they offer you Colleen Duffy... Let me tell you what my impression of Colleen Duffy was. I think she was a young girl who was a little bit confused. I think she probably enjoyed the importance of her moment in the sun on the witness stand. I think she had a poor memory, and I think when she was approached eight months after the incident and when for the first time she told somebody that she had seen Cathy Warner eight months after the incident, she was simply wrong. It had been the previous week.

"Now, Mr. Ferencz suggested to you it couldn't have happened because

Cathy Warner worked the entire week previously. Well, that's not true." Kapsak picked up a large photo and showed it to the jury. "This is a blow-up of the last day on her calendar, and you can see for yourself that she has marked July the 5th 'off'. She was off that day. And that's probably when Colleen Duffy saw her.

"Another way to look at Colleen Duffy's testimony is this. If in fact she's telling the truth and she's accurate when she said that Cathy Warner on July 11th was taking groceries out of her car, just think what that means. We know from Berta that he took her car to the station on Friday, July 8th and when he got back on Monday, July 11th, the car was still there where he parked it. So if Colleen Duffy saw Cathy Warner taking groceries out of her car, that means Cathy Warner had to go to Metro Park, find the car, drive it home, do her shopping, drive it back, somehow get home in time to be murdered. It couldn't have happened."

Kapsak told the jury that another conclusion he had reached was that Cathy Warner had been killed in the basement, stripped, and then placed in her first-floor tub.

"I finally decided that when I wondered why she was put in the tub, I was really asking the wrong question. The question I should have been asking was, why was she naked in the basement? ... I really think the only reason she was put in the tub was because she was naked in the basement and that wouldn't have made sense, and that would have got us thinking, why would she be naked in the basement?

"Well, how about if the murderer didn't want us to know what she was wearing when she was murdered in the basement? And how about if what she was wearing was a nurse's uniform? That would have told us, wouldn't it, that she was killed on July the 8th, and that would have led directly to Mr. Berta's door because he was the one who was with her on July the 8th."

And, Kapsak continued, if Berta took Cathy Warner's uniform off after he shot her, he would have gotten blood all over himself and he would have had to clean up. "Isn't that interesting? Doesn't that fall right into what Pat Bauer told us about cleaning up?" he asked.

Kapsak reminded the jury that Berta said he put the garbage out on July 11, which means, he added, that Berta could have thrown away the bloody nurse's uniform and whatever rags he may have used to clean up.

Kapsak next reviewed Pat Bauer's testimony, including what she said about the many phone calls from Gene Berta on July 8th, his statement that he had "just killed three people" and her assertion that he had had a gun with him in Minnesota. But, he told the jury, he believed they could convict Gene Berta even without Bauer's statements.

Concerning Colleen Maki and the notation of "self" over the cancellation on the Best Western reservation slip, Kapsak suggested that perhaps Berta himself called and disguised his voice.

"Do you really think that a man who is capable of searching for and finding a bullet that passed through the head of a murder victim, a man who is capable of carrying her body from the basement and putting it in a tub, a man who is capable of planting, and I say planting, hamburger rolls and hot dog rolls and chopped meat and hot dogs in front of her house to make it look like she had just died or she had been attacked in some way, do you think a man who is capable of doing all that is not capable of faking a woman's voice for a few moments over a long distance line? I don't think so."

Returning to Bauer's testimony, Kapsak reread part of Bauer's statement when she was asked why she did not tell the police everything she knew back in July of 1983.

"And she said, 'I did everything in my power to protect him. I felt it was damaging. I didn't want to be the one to say it.'"

"Now, I also think it's very interesting that all of a sudden the murderer should be John Bauer ... a dying man, dying from cancer, unable to defend himself ... He's now the murderer, a man who is unable to step out of his hospital bed and come into this court and tell you, 'I didn't do it. I had nothing to do with it.' It's ridiculous. So I have to do it for him, and I will and I do. John Bauer had absolutely no motive whatsoever to kill Catherine Warner ... He's a scapegoat, and he's a scapegoat because he's unable to come here and defend himself. I think it's wrong, and I resent it."

Ferencz' tactic of suggesting other men might have committed the murder was just "dust in the air," Kapsak told the jury. "That's just trying to distract you from the truth, trying to get you off the track."

"There's only one person who had a motive, one person who had a key," he added.

The murder weapon, Kapsak said, "is probably at the bottom of Mosse Lake, somewhere in Minnesota."

"Ladies and gentlemen," Kapsak said, resting both hands on the podium and staring intently at the jurors, "in my opening statement I told you this was a murder mystery. The thing you have to understand is that this is a murder mystery that was solved. It's a murder mystery in which the murderer was apprehended. The murderer was none other than the Man of the Year, Gene Berta. Gene Berta. The murderer of the year. Please, please, don't let him get away with murder."

It was now 4 p.m. Due to the lateness of the hour, Hoffman decided to let the jury go home, get a good rest, and begin their deliberations the next day. The judge turned down a request by Ferencz that the jury be sequestered, saying that it was unreasonable to ask them to call home for clothes now, and also expressing a concern over the cost to the taxpayers of putting the jury and court officers up in a hotel for the night.

Tuesday, October 2, 1984

Judge Hoffman spent a considerable amount of time during the morning instructing the jury on the law, and giving them guidelines on how to conduct their deliberations. The charges they would consider would be murder, aggravated manslaughter and reckless manslaughter, in that order.

His instructions completed, Hoffman adjourned the jury at 10:42 a.m.

Joy Niemiera had been supporting the Neals throughout the trial, sitting with them in the spectator section. As they were filing out of the courtroom, she turned to Mary Beth Neal and asked her what she thought the verdict would be.

"It doesn't matter," Mary Beth told her. "My father said if they find him not guilty, he'll kill him himself. He's dying of cancer, he's got nothing to lose."

A sheriff's officer, standing within earshot, made a mental note of the conversation.

4:05 p.m.

The jury quietly shuffled into the courtroom. Some of the members stole quick glances at Gene Berta as they took their seats. The audience section was packed, in fact, it was standing-room only. Everyone could feel the tension in the room. Behind the defendant's table sat Eugenia and Gail Berta, each of whom wore worried looks. Gene Berta, as he had for the entire three-week trial, looked calm.

The Neals and Joy Niemiera, having been told the jury had reached a verdict, walked into the courtroom in the middle of a crowd. Immediately a sheriff's officer approached Richard Neal and Niemiera, asking them to step out into the corridor.

Neal and Niemiera, having no idea what was going on, followed the officer around the corner, where they were joined by several more officers.

"If you would just raise your arms, sir, I'm going to have to check you for weapons," one officer told Neal.

"What? I don't believe this!" Niemiera cried, as a female officer searched her. "You think we're going to do something?"

Finding no weapons, the officers escorted Neal and Niemiera back to their seats.

Seeing the courtroom had settled, Judge Hoffman instructed his clerk to receive the verdict.

Turning to Agnes Nemergut, the jury's forewoman, the clerk asked, "Madame Forelady have the members of the jury reached a verdict?"

"Yes, we have," she answered.

"Is the verdict to be returned a unanimous verdict of all 12 jurors?"

"Yes."

"How do you find the defendant on the first count of purposeful or knowing murder of Catherine Warner?"

The tension in the room was overbearing. All eyes were focused on Nemergut.

"We find the defendant guilty of murder."

Although Judge Hoffman had cautioned the audience on refraining from any outbursts of emotion when the verdict was read, a murmur arose immediately as the guilty verdict was read. Gail Berta silently burst into tears; her mother-in-law simply scowled at the jury. Gene Berta didn't even blink.

Hoffman restored order in the courtroom, banging his gavel several times. He then told the clerk to continue.

"How do you find the defendant as to the second count, possession of a firearm?"

"We find him guilty."

Kapsak requested that Judge Hoffman immediately rescind Berta's bail, noting that he had purchased land in Minnesota and was a risk to the community. Ferencz objected, noting that his client had been in court on time for the entire trial.

Hoffman said he appreciated that, but he agreed with Kapsak and remanded Berta to the state workhouse in North Brunswick until he was sentenced.

Ferencz then asked if Berta could have a few minutes alone with his wife, to which the judge agreed, directing the Bertas to a side room off the courtroom. It was at this time that Berta displayed any type of reaction to his situation, and even that was minute: while standing up, his hands visibly shaking, he dropped a manila file folder on the floor. He quickly composed himself, however, retreating into his cool façade.

The attorneys' reactions to the verdict were predictable; Kapsak called it a "fair decision", while Ferencz, promising an appeal, blasted it as a "travesty. I don't see how they could have considered all the evidence in five hours."

A tearful Gloria and Mary Beth Neal were led out of the courtroom by Richard and Gary Neal.

"Maybe my daughter will rest in peace now," Mrs. Neal told a reporter.

Voices — Donna Tokar

"I think about her every once in a while. The fourth of July. I always think that I was about to go to her house the day she was found. If I saw her car there, I think I would have tried to get in.

"I'm kind of glad that he's not dead and that he's in jail being miserable.

"It figures; all the good, good people go. All she wanted him to do was to love her."

Voices — Dennis Malinosky

"He needed the structure of prison, There ain't anything he can't fix. He needed the structure, that was what was missing from his life. He was a structure-oriented person who could not stay within a life structure. If he had done some military time, he would had made out well. He would have been a lifer.

Gene, if you were here, I'd call you a stupid . . . it hurts . . . fucking asshole . . . how could? . . . frustration is not being able to choke the shit out of some asshole who really needs it. Gene, my hands are around your neck, if your ears are burning. Stupid ass."

Voices — Joy Niemiera

"Cathy's death put such a strain on me, I ended up miscarrying and lost my daughter. As I was burying my daughter, I thought, 'Cathy, I wish you were here'."

Epilogue

On December 2, 1984, Eugene Berta was sentenced to the maximum non-capital penalty for murder in the State of New Jersey, life imprisonment with no parole eligibility for 30 years. He is currently serving his time at Trenton State Prison, where he is said to be a model prisoner.

He will be eligible for parole in 2014.

Two appeals filed on his behalf were denied.

In November of 1990, Gail Berta divorced Gene Berta and subsequently moved to Florida.

Alexander Berta died on July 6, 1991. His memorial service, which, under the watchful eyes of state corrections officers, a leaner, prison-hardened Eugene Berta attended, was held at a local funeral home in Metuchen. Characteristically, any evidence of import of the funeral date to Gene Berta was not reflected on his face.

It was July 8.